MW01010167

# WHEN THE POOR BOYS DANCE

Other Novels by G. F. Borden

*Easter Day, 1941*

*Seven Six One*

# WHEN THE POOR BOYS DANCE

a novel by

G. F. Borden

LYFORD
Books

LYFORD Books
Published by Presidio Press
505 B San Marin Dr., Suite 300
Novato, CA 94945-1340



Library of Congress Cataloging-in-Publication Data

Borden, G. F.
When the poor boys dance : a novel / G. F. Borden
p. cm.
ISBN 0-89141-545-9
1 . United States. Marine Corps—History—Fiction. 2. United States—History, Military—Fiction. I. Title.
PS3552.069W44 1995
813'.54—dc20 94-38985
CIP

Typography by ProImage
Printed in the United States of America

*This book*
*is for*
*A. L. Hart*

# Acknowledgments

Colonel John Joseph Bubon (USA retired) assisted me with a difficult point of terminology and has for more than twenty-six years given me his friendship and the benefit of his experience—military and otherwise.

Captain Dale A. Dye (USMC retired)—author and actor—was kind enough to read the manuscript of this novel and to point out several errors of fact and terminology. His corrections improved this book and saved the author much embarrassment.

Al and Jo Hart of The Fox Chase Agency are aware of my regard for them and of my gratitude for their long years of effort on my behalf.

Hildegard is more aware than anyone except myself how much she contributed to the writing of this book.

I could not have written this book had I not, for thirty years and more, read many histories of the Marine Corps and many books by individuals who served with the Marines in various wars. I thank the authors of those books for their efforts to describe the history of the Marine Corps and to portray the experience of individual Marines.

# WHEN THE POOR BOYS DANCE

HE TURNED, AS THEY had trained him to turn to face the enemy, toward the first faint tint of daylight gray as dried milk at the border of the desert horizon and the night sky flecked with stars.

He licked his cracked lips with his dry, stiffening tongue and thought: three days and three nights out here and not enough food. And not enough water.

He tilted his head at the dark to the northwest. An irregular mechanical screech piercing a rumble seeped through the dark sky. Machine, he thought as he turned toward the sound. Not a tracked vehicle: a single truck traversing the desert, bumbling along, the racketing of its solitary passage expanding and waning as it drives up each stony, sandy rise and descends into the draw beyond.

He stared at the dark: to try to figure where the truck was coming from, to estimate where it was going. As the truck approached he turned degree by degree toward the east, tracking its sound; and then he saw it: three hundred yards east of his post at the edge of the dusty track, a six-by-six jounced along, silhouetted against the narrow strip of dawn above the desert horizon. The truck's bumper ploughed the stunted scrub and its tires jerked and juddered against the stony surface of the desert. Boxy, utilitarian, its mottled camouflage gray, brown and sand, the truck rocked along inside the roil of dust its cleated tires stirred up, moving left to right across his field of vision.

"Hey!" he yelled. But even as he yelled the word, he knew the sound of it would not be big enough. He took a chemical light from his pocket, twisted and bent the slick plastic tube and waved its modest green light back and forth above his head.

The truck drove on, its steady laboring mutter riven now and then by the screech of whatever it was in the engine that was breaking down.

Great, he thought as the first light breeze rustled through the scrub. Can't find the track, can't maintenance their ride. They're inattentive. No, they're *oblivious*. They should be keeping watch.

If this were a war and I were the enemy, I would kill them and take their crummy truck and drive home.

But this isn't war. And no one calls it that anyhow. The sergeants who were in Vietnam, and a couple of old men old enough to have served in Korea, have different fond names for it: a special ticket; a voyage; a chance to see the elephant; shit and perdition; a turn in the barrel; chance, guts, killing, filth and horseshit; the best and most terrifying thing you'll ever see; a vicious horror; a fuckedup mess; a thing that will bring out the worst in you, and the best.

But it's Sergeant Kline's description I remember best, he thought. Sergeant Kline said: war is when the poor boys dance. I asked him where he'd heard that and Sergeant Kline said, from a Negro Sergeant in the 24th Infantry I met in Washington, D. C. in 1942. He'd been in the first war. Name of Reardon, had orders to go to some Negro tank outfit down in Texas or Louisiana.

But this isn't dancing. I hear no music: I hear nothing but the clicking desert and a sick truck and the shift of a light rising wind through the brush. This isn't even close to war. This is a three-day exercise creeping toward dawn of the fourth day. And now the exercise is finished: they're heading home, flocking along the tan and red desert tracks, easing along far to the southeast, rolling back to base. All of them are getting out of this empty waste, returning to the Palms, each of them hoping for a pass that will let him out of the desert and into Los Angeles.

Lucky them.

And my ride? My way out of this dusty gully in the absolute middle of nothefuckwhere full of warming gray light? Where the hell is lieutenant whosis who set me down here to stand road guide and was supposed to come back and pick me up? Where are the guys who were with me in the back of the truck? Doesn't one of them remember I rode with them too?

Through the haze of dust swirling up around the truck trundling left to right across the draw in which he stood, he saw two ghostly figures up in the cab, the driver's face bent as though he were listening for the irregular noise from the engine's guts to screech again, the passenger to his right staring straight ahead from under the rim of his helmet through the windshield at the last of the night. As the truck passed on he saw men hunched forward on the bench seats along the sides of the bed. Just great, he thought. Facing inboard, rifles between their knees, helmeted heads bent beside their rifles' muzzles, forearms on their thighs, every last one of them dozing beneath the canvas stretched over the staves rattling in the sockets welded to the sides of the truck's bed. They ought to be looking out.

The light dawn wind flung grit against his face. Dust filled his nostrils and clotted the moisture in his mouth and throat, coated his pack, web-gear and utilities, powdered his face and hands and sifted into the fine interstices between the interlocked parts of the rifle slung over his shoulder.

He waved the dull green glow of the chemical light above his head as he wondered what the driver was doing off the track; and wondered who would pick him up if this truck did not—for this vehicle seemed to be the last one leaving the desert. But even as he shouted again, he knew the grinding racket of the truck would blot out the sound of his voice and the dust in which the vehicle moved would obscure the faint glow of the illume.

They don't see, he thought. And they don't hear. Not across three hundred yards of gray light full of dust swept up by their ride's tires into the breeze rising with the dawn.

"Hey, you guys! You're leaving me out here!" he shouted, explaining their dereliction to them as he waved the chemical light above his head.

Maybe, he thought, the guy will forget about his engine for a moment and look in his rearview mirror. Maybe the guys in the back will look up.

But the truck bumped on, heading southeast, jouncing as its tires ground over stones, whatever it was that was breaking down in the engine screeching now and then. Back to base, back to water and showers and food: back home.

He heard the driver shift down, listened as the engine accelerated. The bright red slits of the truck's taillights brightened as the truck topped the low rise to the southeast and flicked off as it drove down the far side.

He stopped waving the light, glanced at its faint glow and thought, worthless. As worthless as shouting into the dark and the rising wind. *More* worthless. He flicked the glowing, green plastic tube away among the stunted gray bushes.

He listened as distance and the intervening slope of dust, scrub and rocks diminished the racketing of the truck's defective engine.

Heading home, he thought. OK, then: leave me here in the desert. You've had a long night going this way and that, rolling around bored and pissed off, and now you want to get on home.

But you're leaving me here, he thought as the erratic sound of the truck's engine dwindled. You're leaving me behind.

The sound of the truck slipped away and all he heard was the sweep of the wind through the desert scrub.

Left me here, he thought. Stand out here all night on the shouting lieutenant's orders. *One* man, Goddamnit, the lieutenant had shouted at the sergeant eight hours before. The sergeant had rolled his eyes and questioned the lieutenant's order: he *knew* two men were required to be posted together. But the lieutenant had shouted again and he had jumped down from the rear of the truck with his gear and his weapon and stood in the dust at the side of the track and watched the lieutenant and the sergeant climb back up into the cab.

From the dark beneath the canopy over the bed a voice had called out, "We'll be back."

In the last two hours before dawn he had stood his post, holding up one chemical light and then another to guide Jeeps, trucks, communications vehicles, self-propelled guns and tanks along the track. Above him in the sky helicopters had droned through the night, heading southeast. An hour before dawn the stream of traffic had eased. Then, as the eastern horizon began to shift through the spectrum from black to purple to gray, no vehicle had passed his post for twenty minutes. At last the single truck with the lame engine and the lame men on board had rolled by *way* out in the desert, feeling its way southeast.

Maybe they didn't know I was here, he thought. Maybe they were lost. Maybe they didn't know anyone was still out here. Maybe this, maybe that.

He cocked his head, listened: he heard no mechanical sound anywhere in the gray gloom that filled the sky above the desert.

Whoever is supposed to pick me up better hurry, he thought as he turned his face toward the eastern horizon.

But he knew no one was coming back for him, and as he realized he was alone he shivered and looked at the horizon: a narrow band of silver light edged the bottom of the gray sky. The exercise is finished, he thought, and dawn is coming.

They *better* remember I'm out here. And they *better* come back.

But he knew the lieutenant had screwed up. He said the pickup would be before dawn. And now it's dawn. A fuckup officer. Or someone gave him orders to go somewhere else and he forgot I was here. Or he picked up the other road guides and missed me.

Whoever fucked up, whatever happened, it's dawn now. And dawn means the sun.

He stood beside the desert track, shifting his weight from foot to foot, his web gear and rifle and pack pulling his shoulders down as he watched the first, smallest arc of the sun's circumference rise above the horizon; and as the unobstructed light of the sun rushed forward toward him across the desert, he turned his dusty face away and listened while the silent desert night was replaced, piece by piece, by the array of morning sounds. Clicking insects, the wind rustling the scrub, dust sifting across rock and the weird shapes of eroded gray stone, the quick hostile flutters of lizards hunting and rats fleeing through the stark brush.

The first faint warmth of the morning sun touched his face as he scanned the horizon. To the northwest stony gray hills purple at the base lay like dilapidated, shattered gravestones. To the southeast a low dusty ridge of boulders and stone blocked the horizon: a ridge beyond which, he knew, the racketing truck full of negligent tired men still travelled, following everyone else gone before. Or almost everyone else, he thought.

At every other degree of the compass lay the gritty, sandy desert. Small worn boulders, stones, rocks. Bushes stunted by the harsh dry heat of the sun and the bitter cold of the night. The flat horizon shimmered as the air warmed. Soon, he knew, the heat would begin to draw the moisture from his body. And then, he knew, he would see silver pools of light flowing toward him from the horizon, sliding like mercury, reflecting the sky and the inventions of his mind.

Time to go, he thought. Twenty miles or so to the fence if I follow a compass bearing straight southeast across the desert from where I stand. And seven, eight miles more if I follow the track.

If you're lost, stay where you are. We'll find you.

So the survival expert said: Sergeant Kline, a craggy near sixty year old retired sergeant with a seamed, scarred face, confident he could survive—could prevail—in the desert. Conserve water, stay in the shade and put out a marker: that was his advice.

But I am not lost: I know where I am. I have little water to conserve: less than half a canteen; there is no shade anywhere in this desert; and I have nothing with which to mark my position: my clothing and gear are the pattern and color of the desert: gray, green, sand and tan.

They've gone, he thought: heading back to base, thinking about the rest of the week. No one is coming. A screw-up somewhere. Be careful, they say. Do your job, they say. And now someone's screwed up.

I wonder if that fucking lieutenant will count heads when he gets back.

I should have fired my weapon at that truck. I should have put some rounds through their useless broken-down engine. That would have slowed them up. I should have fired into the air at least: they might have heard. They might have seen the muzzle flash. But I didn't think to fire.

As more of the bright silver arc of the sun rose above the eastern horizon and the light pierced his eyes, he thought, whatever, that part's over. Someone fucked up: someone's responsible. But that's for later, when they look into who did what and who didn't. Right now I've got other things to think about.

Got to go. And now, he thought as he felt the heat of the sun against his face and felt the first drops of sweat trickle through his cropped hair. Got to get out of here now, because I can't count on anyone to come and pick me up.

He turned, looked southeast at the low ridge of dust gray rocks, boulders and scrub. The track on which he stood angled up the face of the ridge. Up there, he thought. I can get a view from up there.

Carry all this gear? Or leave it?

Take what you'll need, he told himself, and leave the rest.

He removed his helmet, laid it in the dust beside the track, unslung his rifle, leaned it against the helmet, slipped the straps of his pack from his shoulders, dropped the pack beside the helmet.

What to take? Canteen, compass in my breast pocket, the rifle, magazines, the first aid kit in the pouch on my harness. The rest stays here. If anyone counts and finds they're short a man and decides to come looking, they'll find it. If they're looking. If they're thinking at all. The rest stays here. Food? he thought. He drew a ration packet from the pack, read the label, tossed it aside. I'd need water to get the food down, and I'm not going to have the time to get hungry. Twenty miles marching is all, and I've got to do it before sundown for sure: before sundown or else. Two miles an hour, maybe. If I'm lucky. If the going's clear enough.

And if you don't make it before sundown?

You must: you'll die if you don't.

What would Sergeant Kline do? he wondered.

Remember, Sergeant Kline had said. The temperature in the Mojave can rise to one hundred twenty and more. The humidity in the summer is four percent, which means: no humidity. The heat and the lack of humidity will suck the moisture out of you. You must replenish the liquid your body loses.

Half a canteen is all I've got left, he thought.

March on the track? Or across the desert, following a compass bearing?

Seven or eight miles farther on the track. Say, four more hours. Or more than four more hours.

Going to be rough if I go across the desert, he thought. But on the track it will be four hours more under the sun. And that might be rougher than going cross-country. Easier going on the track. But shorter across the desert.

Stay in the shade, Sergeant Kline had said. If you can't find shade, make it.

Take the shelterhalf, he thought. Make shade with it. Hang it over the bushes, get under it if you must. If things get tough.

Don't think about that part of it, he thought. Twenty miles. You can do twenty miles standing on your head. No pack, no load to carry. Twenty miles is nothing. Even in the desert, twenty miles is easy.

I hope that lieutenant remembers to call the roll when he gets back. If he doesn't, I'm going to write the Commandant. Short guy, compact, likes marching, those who've seen him say he's got a bluff, straightforward manner. Known not to be a politician, thinks straight, wants everyone rough and tough. And honest, they say, decent. What would he say, if he knew they'd left me out here? What would he do? What would he order?

Immediate search: that's what he'd order. Helicopters up, vehicles moving, every man looking out. Followed by courts-martial all around. Wish he were at Twentynine Palms right now, making that fucking lieutenant do his job right.

But he isn't. He's in Washington, getting into his uniform, getting ready to go down for breakfast, wondering if everything's going all right everywhere.

Forget about the Commandant. And forget about getting any help. Think about the worst it can be: think about getting out of this alone, without assistance. Think. Consider. That's what you're supposed to do. And don't just go running out there: just running out there is for dummies. Make a plan and carry it out. You're not some fucking machine we're training, Sergeant Quinlan had shouted at him during the last week *way* back there at Parris Island. *This* is a tactical exercise, he bawled.

What the hell would you do if it were real? What would you do if the lieutenant were dead and I were dead and the generals were dead and you were in charge? Come on, think about it and tell me what you're going to do. Come on, don't just fucking stand there.

Going to march out of here, Sergeant Quinlan. Going to march across this desert like it's a meadow in Minnesota, or that swamp you loved in South Carolina. Going to take a bearing with the compass, march five hundred paces, check the bearing, march another five hundred paces. Going to wet my mouth every three thousand paces.

Put a smooth stone under your tongue, Sergeant Kline had said. Stone the size of a quarter, big enough so you won't forget and swallow it, small enough to be comfortable. Smooth and flat. It will draw moisture to your mouth. *Don't* breathe through your mouth. *Don't* work up a sweat. Move slow and easy. Rest when you need to rest. Save sweat. If you save sweat you conserve water; and conserving water is the name of the game in the desert. Got it?

Yes, Sergeant Kline. I got it.

He dumped the rest of the contents of his pack on the dusty track. Rations, chemical lights, shelterhalf, spare magazines. Not much to leave as sign, he thought. And too much to haul along with me.

They should have had every man carry more water, he thought.

The lieutenant should have picked me up.

The others in the truck should have seen I was missing.

They should have done better.

Sergeant Kline, who looked like he'd lived all his life in the desert, had said, If you have to move, leave a sign indicating the direction you're going. Got it?

I got it, Sergeant Kline.

And conserve water.

Right. Conserve water; and as he thought it he glanced at the sun risen above the horizon. The blinding silver ball was cooking the floor of the desert. Sweat evaporated as it trickled from his hairline. Better hurry.

He stuffed the folded shelterhalf into his belt, touched his first aid kit, emptied all but two magazines from the ammunition pouches on his belt and slung his rifle. He placed the helmet on the ground beyond his pack, laid the chemical lights in a straight line pointing away from the helmet toward the low ridge, placed stones at acute angles to either side of the front of the line of chemical lights to form an arrowhead.

And when I leave the track? If anyone finds this sign they'll think I'm somewhere down the track.

Make another sign at the top of the ridge, he thought. Make an arrow out of stones and hope they see it. And hope the wind doesn't drift dust and sand over the stones. Nothing else to do.

Time to go, he told himself, and set off, marching along the track toward the ridge, the wind at his back full of dust and grit, the rising, warming sun to his left front.

FROM THE LOW RIDGE above the desert he stared southeast across the waste scarred with the tracks of tanks and wheeled vehicles.

Nothing moved in the barren expanse of desert in front of him.

I guess I hoped I'd see troops, vehicles—help—coming my way. Anything: one guy with a canteen would have been enough. A Lister bag would have been better. A water buffalo would have been better still.

But there is no water here, and I see nothing but the flat, red and gray desert of stunted brush, sand, rock, stone and salt pans that reflect the sunlight.

He unbuttoned his shirt pocket—the one behind the eagle, globe and anchor—and slid the compass out. He popped it open, held it in his dirty palm. The green radium tip of the needle swung this way and that, settled on north. You can find your way anywhere with this, Sergeant Kline had said, even at night.

Sweat trickled from his scalp, evaporated before it reached his hairline. I won't need this compass tonight, he thought. It's get back today or else. It's six o'clock in the morning, and by tonight, if I'm not back at the Palms, the small ocean inside me will have evaporated and I will be rotting meat, tanned leather and dry, hollow bone.

What are you going to do about it? he asked himself. Go on. What else is there to do? You go on. You're a Marine, after all, and that's what Marines do.

Or maybe when they're alone they give up, lie down and wait to die.

I know what Sergeant Quinlan would say about that: Piss on that noise.

And I would say, Right, Sergeant. The right answer is: they don't lie down and die. They go on.

He looked along the track that descended the face of the low ridge on which he stood, followed the line of it east across the desert. Far in the distance through the haze of dust that hung above the desert, the track on which he stood crossed a broader track at right angles. The broader track led straight south to the Palms.

He knew the distance: nine miles on this track east to the junction. Then eighteen more to the south on the broader track. On the other hand the hypotenuse of the triangle is no more than twenty miles. I think. A question of plane geometry. And time, space, temperature, terrain, math, chemistry, biology. A complicated problem with two possible solutions: get there, or not.

The shorter distance, then. Across the desert, through the scrub, in and out of the gullies, stone, sand and rock underfoot. Shoot a compass bearing and follow it.

He raised the compass, sighted through the slit in the lid southeast toward the Palms, rotated the bezel until the arrow scored in the base of the compass lay beneath the needle, pointing north as the needle did. The index pointer told him the bearing to the southeast was one hundred thirty-five degrees. Then, he thought, I subtract thirteen degrees for magnetic declination because we're out here in sunny California and magnetic north is northeast of Minnesota somewhere. I think.

Make it a hundred twenty-two degrees, then.

As he rotated the compass's bezel so that the index pointer was set to one hundred twenty-two degrees, he heard the faintest gritty rasping: dust in the minuscule space between the compass's base and bezel. Even with the searing westerly wind slicing at my face and sifting dust into my left ear, I hear the desert grinding at the fine tolerances of this compass's simple works.

Ready to go, he thought as he closed the compass.

Then he thought: no. *No* allowance for declination. When taking bearings in the field without reference to a map, no adjustment for declination is required.

His guts lurched as though he had not eaten in thirty-six hours. Almost made a mistake, he thought. A big mistake.

Creepy: to march across a baking nothingness, trusting a bearing thirteen degrees off? And if I hadn't thought again?

I would have marched off into the sunset. And I *mean* the sunset: the end.

He opened the compass and turned the bezel; and as he turned it his dry, dusty finger and thumb trembled. One hundred thirty-five degrees.

This compass will get you out of anywhere if you know how to use it, Sergeant Kline had said. And you're *going* to know how to use it. One look at Sergeant Kline and you knew you were going to learn about the compass, and learn fast. Everyone knew Sergeant Kline had spent years in the Corps and hadn't wasted any time in any of those years and couldn't abide anyone else wasting time.

Years in the Corps? someone had said. I heard he was *born* in the Corps. Father was a gunnery sergeant, mother the first female drill instructor, from World War Two: the guy has *never* been off a Marine base.

Except, someone else said, to go somewhere far away to kill a lot of people he never heard of.

That's a lot of shit, someone else said. He's spent *plenty* of time off bases, out in the real world. Sergeant Kline was an embassy guard in Tehran in the early sixties.

You call an embassy the real world? someone said.

The embassy in Tehran? someone else said. No shit? What's the matter with him? Why didn't he kill all those ragheads when he had the chance and save us all a lot of trouble? I mean, I ask you, what kind of a gunnery sergeant is he, anyway?

He only kills on orders, another said. Or at least that's what he says he does. Orders or no, though, and old as he is, I wouldn't want to piss him off myself.

Holding the compass in his hand, checking the bearing once again, he stared across the desert through the blinding white light and thought, I wouldn't want to piss him off either.

The numbers were the same: one hundred thirty-five degrees.

Whatever, I'll hit the wide track somewhere out there: it goes straight south: straight home to the Palms. He looked down from the low ridge on which he stood, the wind raising dust as fine as talc. Cut across the desert going southeast, reach the wide track that leads south, and coast into the Palms. It's no more than nineteen miles and a piece to where the track leading south hits the road this side of the fence. And then? Then I'll drink six gallons of water and go looking for that fucking lieutenant. And ask him where the *fuck* he was when he was supposed to be picking me up. And then ask that fucking sergeant where the fuck *he* was when he was supposed to be holding the lieutenant's elbow and pointing the way.

Or maybe not. Maybe to hell with them if I get back. *When* I get back.

Leave a sign, Kline would say, his gruff old voice full of empty whisky bottles, cigar smoke and shouting. Gruff old loud voice: too many gunshots too close to the ear, too many roaring projectiles splitting the sky above his head. But he knew what to do, and knew how to teach me to do it.

Yes, Sergeant Kline. Of course, Sergeant Kline. Leave a sign.

Use rocks. Make an arrowhead. Someone *will* find it.

Right. An arrowhead. I admire your confidence, Sergeant Kline.

Fuck my confidence. And before you make that arrowhead, I want you to get something on your head. You're out in the sun and you better get something over your head or your brains are gonna fry. Use your issue handkerchief. And use a spare bootlace to tie it down with. You remembered to bring spare bootlaces, didn't you?

Got 'em right here, he thought. And I understand fry, Sergeant Kline. So I will use the handkerchief and become a raghead in one easy lesson.

He took the handkerchief from the right rear pocket of his trousers, unfolded it and draped it over his head, pulled a bootlace from his lefthand trousers pocket, wound the lace about his skull, tied the handkerchief down.

Regular Arab, he thought. Ought to have one of those robes they wear that don't bind and let the moisture stay on the body. Instead of the constricting shirt and trousers I wear that sop the moisture up.

He remembered Sergeant Kline explaining how the Corps didn't understand desert conditions: The Corps wouldn't agree I was right about the proper uniform for the desert, Sergeant Kline said. The Corps likes trousers and shirts. So we wear trousers and shirts. It's tough, and it ain't smart, but there it is.

And he had said, Right, Sergeant Kline.

And if he were here now, Sergeant Kline would say, Now you're all set. Right now you could walk the Sahara and come back just a little dry.

And I would say, Right, Sergeant Kline.

You keep saying 'Right, Sergeant Kline'. You some kind of college guy?

No, Sergeant Kline. Two years college is all.

Two years. That's good: that you didn't waste any *more* time. Because *this* is where you're going to learn what you need to know.

Right here in the desert, Sergeant Kline?

No, dumbfuck. In the Corps.

Right, Sergeant Kline. In the Corps.

And what would Kline say about the sergeant and the lieutenant and the captain and the major and the colonel who forgot me out here? Is that where they learned what they need to know about picking up road guides? In the Corps?

He'd say: Don't worry about those fucks right now. Sure, you're supposed to show them respect. When you speak, they want to hear the first letter of their rank capitalized. But what you think is up to you, and some of them don't deserve a capital letter. Or the rank they hold either. As for what they were supposed to learn, they learned it and then they fucked up and forgot it. And for forgetting, the Commandant's going to rip their lungs right up their throats. I know the Commandant personally and he doesn't like shit like this.

You mean 'if I get out of here', don't you, Sergeant?

No. I don't. You're going to get out of here. Or *I'm* going to rip *your* lungs up *your* throat.

Yes, Sergeant Kline. But if I don't?

You *will.* What the hell did Quinlan teach you on Parris Island, anyway?

To ignore my limitations, Sergeant. That's what I learned on P.I.

A Marine doesn't *have* any limitations, you cunt!

Uh, yes, Sergeant.

You bet your two years of college ass yes Sergeant. What did I teach you about that rag on your head?

To put it on my head, Sergeant.

And?

And to tie it down with a bootlace, Sergeant.

And?

And to, ah . . .

Tie it so a twist of the cloth hangs down your face far enough so you can suck on it. For the salt and the moisture. There won't be much, with the humidity this low. But there'll be something. You forget a thing like that and you call yourself a *Lance Corporal in the United States Marine Corps*?

I guess so, Sergeant Kline.

You *guess* so?

I know so, Sergeant Kline.

You know so what?

I know I forgot that about the twist of cloth, Sergeant Kline.

Don't forget: understand me? Don't forget anything me and Sergeant Quinlan told you. And keep watching. Look around. Keep your mind sharp. Think about what's worth thinking about and to hell with worrying about this and that. Adrenaline can carry you an extra twenty feet with both your legs blown off. But you know that.

He slid the bootlace from his head, rearranged the square of cloth until a corner of it lay to the left of his mouth, and fitted the circle of bootlace around his forehead and the back of his skull.

I know that, Sergeant? That I can go an extra twenty feet with both my legs gone?

Where the hell were you when they taught you The History. Jerking off? Asleep? It had to be one of the two.

I think I was awake, Sergeant. I remember some of the history. Some names, some places.

You remember Lieutenant Lummus on Iwo Jima? Both legs blown off, got up on his stumps and waved his men forward? You remember him? Tried to go on *on his stumps*, calling on his men to go on? 1st Lt. Jack Lummus, from Ennis, Texas? Football player. You remember him, don't you?

Something. I remember something. I don't know much about football. But sure, I remember him.

Then you know you can do whatever you have to.

Yes, Sergeant Kline.

You're all set, then. Start marching along that compass bearing. And while you're doing it, I want you to *show me you've got a pair.*

Yes, Sergeant Kline. I'll try, Sergeant Kline.

*Try*? What good is trying? Fuck trying. Give me fifty. No. Fuck fifty. Give me a hundred.

Right now, Sergeant?

Of course not right now, *Lance Corporal.* You're going to need all the strength you've got and every drop of water in your body. Later. You'll give me a hundred when you get back to the Palms.

Alone on the ridge, the searing hot wind swirling dust and grit about his face, he surveyed the desert below. He bit down on the tag of cloth hanging by the corner of his mouth, held up the compass and took a final sighting along the bearing he would march. He closed the compass, slid it into his breast pocket and buttoned the pocket.

Time to go. And time to stop repeating conversations you had with Sergeant Kline years ago.

You forgot something, numbnuts.

Forgot? Oh, yes. A marker. Sorry, Sergeant Kline.

Sorry? What good is sorry? Sorry sucks: didn't Sergeant Quinlan tell you sorry sucks? Look. I'm tired of standing here fucking with you. Get the fuck on with it, all right?

Fine, Sergeant Kline.

*Fine*? What the fuck does *fine* mean?

Whatever, Sergeant. All that's behind us right here right now. Isn't it?

But Sergeant Kline did not answer him.

I mean, he thought, I do not answer myself, because I do not want to hear what I have to say about what's behind me and what lies ahead. Not out here. Not in the middle of this waste that was a sea a million years ago, before heat drained and dried it and wind ground the stone and dirt to sand and dust.

He bent down through the wind, glanced up to confirm the direction he would march—would have to march—and arranged fist-sized rocks in the shape of an arrowhead that pointed the way: one hundred thirty-five degrees. Off the track into the brush and the stony red and gray desert.

All right, he thought as he stood up. *Now* everything's ready. I'm ready and the desert's ready. And you're ready too, aren't you, Sergeant Kline?

He heard nothing but the wind and the swift smooth flowing of dust and grit swirling along the ridge and pouring down the slope before him.

Of course, he thought. Kline isn't here: you're talking to your memory, and no one ever asked Sergeant Kline if he was ready; and so no one ever heard him answer that question; and so the answer is not in your memory.

I wonder where he is today. Still teaching young Marines about the desert? Or retired for good?

He straightened his back and thought, wherever, he's not here: most likely he's retired, old, left his post, on a pension, in a trailer park or living beside a freeway, unable to explain what he had been.

Not here is where he is. Not killing anyone, and not here to advise me.

Gone away.

HE MARCHED DOWN THE ridge and marched southeast through the scrub over the stony uneven ground for an hour, checking his watch and checking his compass now and again to be sure he stayed, near enough, on the bearing of one hundred thirty-five degrees. As he marched, the wind that had come up at dawn slowed, dodged this way and that and whispered away. The dust and sand the wind had raised settled among the ancient bushes that had, like the lizards, snakes, scorpions and rats, learned to survive in this place of desolation.

As the wind diminished, the heat that had risen out of the chill night with the gray light of dawn became intense. At the end of the first hour of his solitary march, he assessed his condition: skin dry as the dust that shrouded it, mouth sour and coated with sludgy dried spit, muscles tense and tingling, the fine tolerances of the machine working against one another as the amount of lubrication declined. And the tag of cloth in the corner of his mouth was dry: his sweat was evaporating before it could dampen the cloth.

Hot, he thought. But how hot is it going to get?

How hot? the doctor up on the low stage had said. Good question. Plenty hot. Plenty. Hot enough to make trouble.

The doctor was tall, black, thick through the chest and wide in the hips. Spindly legs supported the mass of his torso. His gestures were as quick as his mind, he seemed scientific and kindly, and when he spoke his voice carried far enough to reach the most distant of the two hundred fifty men in the auditorium.

The doctor said: Men, listen up now. The temperature out there in the Mojave is a killer. Two problems. First, the heat, which can rise up to a hundred twenty thirty degrees. And second, the lack of moisture. There's no more than four percent humidity out there in the summertime. As you know, because Sergeant Kline's already told you about it. Four percent humidity is *no* humidity. None *at all.* Normal spring day in, say, Virginia or Ohio is maybe forty, fifty percent humidity, depending on the weather. That's not excessively damp, and it's not oppressively dry. Also, in Virginia and Ohio, even when you've got midsummer heat *and* humidity, it *never* gets as hot as it does out here in the Mojave. Now, what happens is this: the heat and the lack of humidity both draw the moisture from your body. You men understand the human body's ninety-six percent or so water? Good. Note that the human body's surface area is large for its mass. And we regulate our body temperature by sweating. Trouble is, when you sweat out here, you sweat a *lot*, even though you don't notice much moisture on your skin because the sweat evaporates the instant it comes out of your pores; and pretty soon the level of that small ocean inside you is shrinking. If it shrinks too far—if you don't, or can't, drink enough water—you're in trouble. What do I mean by trouble? Trouble is this: if you lose too much water, your body's going to seize up. First sign is what you'd expect: you get thirsty and out there in the desert, where there's no shade, you get sunburned bad. You'll develop blisters, even under your clothing. You'll get a tingling in your limbs, and you may cramp up. You'll find you can't focus your thoughts the way you want to focus them. If you keep on losing water, you're going to stop sweating and your body will shut down. If that happens, you're in trouble. *Big* trouble. You men listening to what I'm saying?

I'm listening, he thought. I remember every word you said, Doc. Some of the guys may have been sleeping or jerking off. I wasn't. But what am I supposed to do right now?

What? You some recruit? Drink water. That's what you're supposed to do right now.

I've got half a canteen, Doc. Just half. You think I should drink it now? I haven't been making very good time: the ground's no good for marching. Soft sand or stony. Hard on the feet. I'd guess I'm moving two miles an hour if I'm lucky. Which means I've got near eighteen miles to go. Which means I've got nine more hours out here before I hit the fence. If I'm *real* lucky.

You come all the way out here into the damned desert and you only brought half a canteen of water? Didn't you listen to what I told you?

I didn't have a choice, Doc. They put me down last night at midnight with a canteen and a bunch of chemical lights and my weapon and my pack. I drank half the canteen last night, Doc. They said they'd come back.

Well, *son* of a bitch, the doctor said. I'm gonna generate a memo on this. *One* canteen, and left you out there alone in the desert? That's not right. That's not right *at all.* The Commandant don't want to hear about that. But he's *going* to hear about it. And when he *does* hear about it, he's going to go off like an unguided missile and land right here at the Palms. I guarantee that, Lance Corporal. I *sure* don't want to be around when he hears about this. Going to be questions all up and down the line. He's going to come out here and ream out everyone from the battalion commander right down to the last private in the kitchen.

Sure, Doc. That's great. Great about your memo and the Commandant taking an interest and all. But what do I do right now, Doc? I listened to your lecture and I know what's going to happen if I don't get water—a lot of water—and if I can't get out of the sun. But even if I had water, the heat's bad, Doc. And the light. Sometimes it seems so bright my eyesight seems to go blank.

That's part of no water and no shade in this environment. Get water and shade and you'll be all right.

Doc, I still don't think I'm making myself clear. I have half a canteen of water and I'd guess I'm losing that much every half hour.

That's a pretty good estimate, the Doc said, as though he were happy to hear someone had been listening when he lectured on the dangers of exposure in the desert environment. Still, you listened to Sergeant Kline: you got your handkerchief over your head and a stone under your tongue and you're doing all right. Besides, you still sound logical. You're coherent. Know what I mean? Even with that stone in your mouth, you sound all right. That's a good sign.

Fuck, Doc, I don't want to talk about what sounds good and what doesn't. I want to know what the hell I'm supposed to do now without water out here in the desert in this heat.

Well, son, the Doc said. I'll tell you: you got a problem and you're just going to have to try to overcome it.

Sergeant Kline, tricked out in khaki slacks and a madras shirt, nodded his gray head and glanced at the Doc through steel-rimmed glasses that glittered when the white light that poured down out of the sky struck the lenses. Then he frowned at the Doc as though whatever the Doc had to say was useless senseless nonsense. He jerked his head as though to make the Doc disappear, turned toward him and said, So you've only got half a canteen of water. What are you going to do? Lie down here and die? I told you before: I want you to show me you've got a pair.

Right, Sergeant. But you ought to know they're a little shrivelled up right now.

No shit, Sergeant Kline said. Sometimes you'll find them so shrivelled up they'll be right up under your chin. But that's all there is: to go on. Like I said, what the hell else are you going to do? Stay here?

No, he said. Can't stay here. On the other hand, going on doesn't seem to have much point to it. Staying here, going on? Not much difference.

Not much difference? Sergeant Kline said. What the hell do you mean, 'not much difference'? The Palms are less than eighteen miles straight ahead along a bearing of one three five. You're on your way. You're putting one foot in front of the other. If you do that enough times you'll get there. And while you're doing that, someone might come by.

You think? he asked, peering at Sergeant Kline.

Think? I don't know. I just don't know. Maybe, but I wouldn't count on it: you're going to have to tough this one out by yourself. Let's face it: you've got officers and sergeants who are a bunch of irresponsible cunts who don't have the faintest idea of what the fuck they were supposed to do last night when they dropped you off and don't know what the fuck to do right now. I expect they're back at base drinking beer and fucking off, don't you? So I wouldn't count on them getting here, or on them getting any help to you. In fact, I'd count on them *not* doing a fucking thing at all. They think everything is going to work out all right every time. They *believe* that. Which as you know isn't unusual here in the Marine Corps. You remember what happened when the Navy skipped a lot of shells across Betio? Said they'd destroy the Japs and we'd walk in. But those naval rifles were designed for use on other ships. No elevation to them at all. So the shells didn't have enough arc. The ships stood in to the island, fired right at it, shells skipped like stones on water right across the island into the sea beyond. What they needed was big mortars. But they didn't *have* big mortars. So the Japs were still there, ready to go when the Navy ceased fire and we went ashore. That's what happens: everyone wants to have whatever they decide to do come out like they planned it would. But it doesn't work that way. Whatever they tell you else. So you got to count on what you learned from Sergeant Quinlan and me. Most of all, you got to count on yourself: you're all you've got now. That's the way it is. I don't care how many divisions there are: in the end, you have to do it yourself. You understand me?

I understand, he said. And if it doesn't work out like it ought to?

Sergeant Kline nodded, as though he were satisfied with the question, and said, Then you will have tried. You will have done your best.

Die trying. Is that it, Sergeant?

That's what we're about. That's what we are. Everybody else is about something else: money, place, power, a regular dull life with a death at home and a coffin to admire and an organ wheezing in the background. Snuffling wife and kiddies. We aren't like that. We aren't about that. What we're about is something else. You know what we're about as well as I do: not quitting. That's all there is to it. If you die not quitting, you'll be remembered. You'll have shown what we are. What you are.

That I've got a pair.

Yeah, that you've got a pair. But you and I know that's shouting and bullshit; that there's more to it than a big cursing coming out of a sergeant's mouth, and more than some sentimental ignorant fucked-up speech from some half-educated officer who would rather be a politician. It's more complicated than that shit you hear on P.I. and more complicated than what you hear after you get out of P.I. about how it's done and how it ought to be done. None of that gives you even a taste: you have to drink the bottle to know. You have to go through it to understand. You understand me?

I don't know, Sergeant. Whether I know what you're saying or not.

You'll find out what I'm saying. Once you're in a fight, you'll understand it.

You think I'm going to have the chance to be in a fight?

You're in a fight right now. And so you're going to find out that it's more complicated than what they told you. And less complicated.

More complicated? Less?

Yes. More and less. Now take a taste of the water and hold it in your mouth. Wet your tongue. Then take another compass bearing to be sure. Then walk five hundred paces before you swallow. Got it?

I got it, Sergeant, he said as he got his canteen out.

Don't call me Sergeant. I'm retired and I don't like anyone coming up wanting to talk about old times. Fuck old times. I don't think about them, and I don't want you thinking about them. Think about right here right now.

Yes, Sergeant.

I told you, don't call me Sergeant.

Okay, sir.

*Sir*? What the hell does that mean?

You're old enough to be my father, sir. If I can't call you Sergeant I ought to call you sir.

Humph. Okay. Call me Sergeant, then. But just until this here is over. After that, you call me by my first name.

What's your first name, Sergeant?

But Sergeant Kline did not answer.

Fucking guy keeps disappearing on me, he thought. I expect it of the Doc: that he would disappear on me. But Sergeant Kline?

He stared right and left through the bright light that seemed as thick and hot as glaucous glass brick just out of the kiln. Spare, face flushed, encouraging, caustic and angry, Sergeant Kline was gone. So was the

Doc. He looked behind himself, peered through the brightness as he might peer into a dark room without windows. The desert stretched away to the low ridge from which he had taken the compass bearing. No Sergeant Kline. And no Doc. Nothing but rock, sand, grit and stunted plants as tough and prehistoric as the reptiles and insects he knew lurked in the sparse shade and hid beneath the stones shaped by the gritty wind. And, overlord of it all, the sun riding in the bluewhite sky at ten o'clock to my line of march, rising toward its zenith, its silver light burning everything that has not coped for a thousand millennia with the extremes of its implacable rule over this desert.

Go on, he told himself. As the man said, what else is there to do? He unscrewed the cap of the canteen, raised it to his sunburned lips.

And stop talking to yourself, he thought as he took the smallest sip of water and held it in his mouth. And stop talking to Sergeant Kline. And stop thinking the Doc is out here giving you useless advice. *No* one is out here. No one can give you advice. No one is going to help you out of this: there is no one here except yourself. You've got a problem, and as the Doc and Sergeant Kline both said, you're just going to have to try to deal with it by yourself.

TWO HOURS ON HE permitted himself another sip from his canteen. He held it in his mouth as he marched on five hundred paces, and then permitted himself to swallow. Three breaths and his mouth was as dry as desiccated bone.

I can't have come more than two more miles since I last drank, he thought. If that. So I've come four miles total in three hours. I'm slowing up.

A cool tingling rose up his spine, brushed the back of his neck. He closed his hands: his fingertips touched his palms. His palms were damp. Since dawn his face, scorched by the hard silver light of the sun, had burned as it had burned when as a boy he had stayed out in the sun on a Chicago beach all day. But now his cheeks and forehead and throat felt cool. Water rushing from my body, he thought.

Losing water. And something else is happening.

A cap of cool tingling spread across his skull beneath the handkerchief.

He stared southeast across the desert through the blinding light. The desert blurred.

But he knew the desert was the same as it had always been, and he thought, something's happening to my vision. And as he thought it, the cool tingling descended through his skull, trickling through the heat that suffused his brain.

Cold, he thought. I'm *cold*. He shivered, looked up at the heavens as clear as tropical water, glanced at the sun so brilliant its light had strained all color from the sky. Across the silver sky a black dot crabbed right to left, rising as it shifted; and as it rose he heard the faint insistent ticking of an engine.

Chopper? he wondered. Fixed wing? He stared at the black dot. Coming this way? Or not? The black dot hung in the sky, crawling southeast to northeast. Where the hell are you going? he thought. I'm *here*, right where you left me.

Fire encased his spine, rose up the back of his neck, poured across the soft tissue beneath his skull, rushing from the base of the weird coruscated shape of his brain up and forward. Sparks flickered behind his blinking eyes, and he thought, I'm signalling them: the guys in that aircraft, and the sun.

He shivered; and as he shivered his right calf cramped and he stumbled, tripped and fell through the knee-high scrub onto the sand. Sharp rocks slashed at his trousers, cut his knee. His left shoulder struck the ground. He worked his knees and hands beneath himself. Can't see, he thought. Light everywhere and I see nothing. His guts heaved and he tasted acid vomit at the back of his throat. He pressed his hands against the earth, and as he raised himself onto his hands and knees, sharp leaves and stiff twigs raked his face and a spiny hard stick stabbed his cheek. Something—a rat, a reptile—skittered away through the brush. He shook his head, felt sharp stones beneath his palms, and shoved himself up onto his knees.

Chest heaving, arms shaking, fingers trembling, his face damp with a sudden rush of clammy sweat, he stared at the sky; and as he stared he heard the aircraft's humming engine. A mosquito beside my ear, he thought. Beside a lake near Canada. Somewhere in Minnesota: somewhere not here.

His vision cleared and he saw the black dot easing right to left through the sky that was blue again. Heading somewhere, flying a course, gaining altitude. Gray smoke obscured his sight and he thought: I'm losing it.

Something inside him collapsed. He tasted salty sweat slick on his cool upper lip. As he watched the gray dot of the aircraft fly out of his sight he thought, you blind sonsofbitches you, you motherless sons, you third-rate bastards. Then he fell forward into the thickening gray smoke.

HIGH IN THE LAST of the cool June night above the bending tips of the poplars on either side of the road, he saw clouds rush through the windy sky, blur the stars and mask the moon rising to the left front of the company of two hundred fifty marching men. He marched on among them for ten minutes more before the wind ceased and a thin, chilly rain began to fall straight down from the dark sky. The company front that filled the width of the road marched on through the light rain without a murmur, feet falling in unison against the wet blacktop, their ranked and filed passage to the east illuminated by brilliant flashes of light rippling across the horizon, flickering blue and white, green and red against the black night sky.

As though they are signalling us not to come up there, he thought. But we will ignore these dazzling warnings, for that is where we are going: to see the elephant, as that British soldier—the one with the scar on his cheek and the staring eyes—said. We're not out here on some training exercise: for sure not. Not after three hours of hard marching, and not after marching on through the rain while detonating shells light up the eastern sky. And we're not moving from one rear area to another: rumor says that the French have broken everywhere and are fleeing west. We're out here to see the animal snort and buck. To take a ride. To go to the dance.

He shivered and glanced at the shadowed profile of the Marine marching to his left. He did not recognize him. He faced forward and looked through the thicket of flat helmets and slung rifles at the exploding artillery shells pounding the earth far to his front, flashing silver, orange and gold.

The sling of his rifle cut at his shoulder, abraded the skin beneath his tunic and shirt. Strange, he thought: the rifle seems to be the only thing out here on this dark, rainy night that's familiar. He knew each nick in the rifle's stock, each gray spot on the barrel and receiver where use had worn the bluing away. Fired no morn a thousand rounds, the sergeant who handed it to him in South Carolina had said. But he had said that about each rifle he handed each man: nicked, scratched and worn or straight out of the grease, the quartermaster sergeant spoke the same words: fired no morn a thousand rounds.

The rocking bones of the big joint of his shoulder hurt from the sawing of the sling and the long muscles in his back on either side of his spine ached from the pull of his pack's straps. The equipment could be lighter, he thought. And the packs could fit better, and be made of lighter stuff: not all this heavy canvas and leather. At least the rifle is good, a thousand rounds fired through it or not. I can shoot at and hit anything I want out to six hundred yards. Any *one* I want to shoot at and hit, that is: the time for shooting targets is finished. If, he thought, I can see them. That's a trouble in this rolling country of small fields separated by small woods. No long vistas in this part of France. Here the ground is broken, and it seems to get worse the farther east we go.

They marched on, heading east toward the place from which, rumor said, the French had fled. The word was that the French lines had disintegrated under the shock of the German attack; that the Germans were pouring through, their infantry coming on in small groups instead of company formations, dodging this way and that, using new tactics, artillery moving up behind.

When the sergeants had shouted them into formation in full gear, MacKay, a corporal enlisted before the war, asked Sergeant Murphy about the rumors. Sergeant Murphy said, "How the hell would I know, MacKay? Do I look like some kind of officer to you?"

"No, Sergeant. But what are we doing, then, getting ready like this?"

"We're going up there to fight the fucking Germans."

"Then the rumors are true, Sergeant? That the French are retreating?"

"I didn't say that. And the rumors don't matter. Whether the Germans are coming this way or not, whether the French are running or not, we're going up there to do what we came here to do: fight the sonsofbitches and push them back and kill the ones who won't be pushed back. That's what *you* came here for, isn't it, MacKay?"

"Uh, right, Sergeant," Corporal MacKay said.

"Then check to be sure you've got all your gear together and be ready. We're trucking up and then we're marching."

Now Murphy and MacKay were somewhere up ahead, marching through the dark, heading east, the rain falling on their helmets and shoulders.

As they marched on in silence, shoulders hunched, concentrating on getting on with it, he glanced at the anonymous wet faces of the men around him illuminated by the shells detonating in the distance. Farther on, he began to see bearded men in long blue coats and crested helmets coming along the verges of the road. Headed west, he thought, shoulders hunched like ours, faces turned toward the dark beyond the trees that lined the road. As though they don't see us marching east, filling the road. Or do not wish to see.

French soldiers, he thought. And none of them carrying weapons, the useless sonsofbitches. Then he thought: better not make any judgments until you've been there and seen it and decided what's right.

They marched another mile and turned off the main road: to the northeast. The footing became muddy, uncertain and slick, and wind rose and began to blow the rain against their backs. The rain and wind made the night darker and the order was passed down the marching column for every man to hold on to the left shoulder of the man in front.

He put out his left hand and gripped the shoulder of the man in front of him, felt the bones working beneath the warm skin beneath the wet harness and soaked tunic. Wonder if this guy will be as alive in four hours as he is now, he thought. Wonder whether I'll be.

Before dawn, as the rain stopped and the black sky began to lighten, they marched through a shuttered, deserted French village. As they marched out of the village, the light brightened and the artillery fire ahead and to their right hesitated and eased; and when it ceased, he heard the faint rattle of machineguns and rifles firing in the distance. Two, three miles more, he thought: not far.

A mile on, they marched into a second village.

The second village was clogged with exhausted, weaponless French soldiers standing in doorways staring at them as they marched past. In the narrow, dirty sidestreets, horses in worn wet harness shuddered and stamped their hooves. A road sign pointed the way forward: to Château-Thierry. All the shops were closed, shutters drawn down over the windows. Civilians dressed in three layers of clothing stood on the sidewalks clutching bundles, children, odd bits of their households—clocks, candlesticks, tools. Two-wheeled carts and wagons piled with furniture, clothing, suitcases, bedding and farm implements stood against the curbs on both sides of the street.

What would I take with me, he wondered, if I had to leave? An heirloom? A tool? Nothing but memory?

An old man with a fierce mustache and a shotgun on his shoulder shouted something at them as they marched past.

"He don't sound friendly *at all*," Morgan said, his soft Kentucky drawl as easy as his gait.

"He says: 'Kill the Germans. Kill them all,' a voice four marching ranks up said. He recognized Wallace's voice. Wallace was a college boy, two years of college. Somewhere near Boston: Harvard, that was it.

"I sure hope we can do what he says," Morgan said. "But I hear they's a lot of these here Germans. And I hear these here Germans been doing this four years now. *And* almost won more than once, fighting the French and the British."

"That means there will be enough of them left for every man here," a strong voice from the right front called out, "and I expect every one of you to kill your share of the sonsofbitches." Sergeant Manley, he thought. Hard man: hard, they all said, as nails. Served as a private in Peking twenty years ago, fought in the Philippines, fought in Central America, served in the Fleet. No one, they had told one another, was better prepared for what was about to happen than Sergeant Manley.

"Bet he kills *more* than his share," Morgan mumbled, as though he thought Sergeant Manley were going to eat his own dinner and part of everyone else's too.

"I heard that, Morgan," Manley called out. "And you're right. And *you're* going to do the same thing, Morgan: you, and every last one of you motherless sonsofbitches, are going to kill *more* than your share. Now shut the hell up and get on. And stop looking at those civilians. They don't know what the hell's happened to them and they don't need you gawking at them."

But the civilians along the walks screamed incomprehensible French, gabbled sentences full of anger, shook their fists as though the Kaiser's army were marching through their village. Wallace translated their furious remarks: kill the Germans, eviscerate them, break their bones.

He looked along the line of march at the French women shouting from the sidewalks, white fists clenched in front of their shouting mouths. Not a young man anywhere, he thought: not a single male between fifteen and fifty. It's been a long war for the French: I remember the papers. The Marne—the first time on the Marne—Verdun, one offensive after another. French officers staring into the camera's lens. Nivelle, Foch. British generals. U-boats. And now Petain. Hunger, disturbance, fear. Dislodgement. A population turned over and displaced, their neat fields stirred by marching men and artillery fire into muddy swales filled with slaughtered animals, the corpses of men, broken equipment and old bones. And to the north, the British, hanging on, hanging on, their soldiers slaughtered in senseless orderly attacks. What it must be like to be attacked and occupied: to have to fight them off willy-nilly, no question, no quarter, no time for preparation or a single breath. To have a hateful enemy three miles east. To be unsure: of who must fight and who must die. Of who will be killed and shoved into the mud, and who will be permitted to come home when the guns cease pounding the earth.

Lucky we are between the oceans, he thought. They keep us away from these angry people: they permit us to be what we are and to become what we wish. That was why we left Europe in the first place: to get away from these narrow countries full of narrow people, where the favored are officers and the poor are soldiers. Where the lack of democracy, opportunity and equality defeats them all. Whoever wins this war, they will all be defeated. And they will all fight again.

Still, here we are, back in the old world, fighting for one side and not the other. There must be a reason why: and I guess President Wilson knows what he's doing. Thin face, wire-rimmed glasses, a sense of certainty in his manner, a tone of offended morality in his voice. I hope he knows what's going on; but I wonder about that, just as I wonder about the rest of it. And particularly about what's going to happen next.

As the French shouted, their voices shrieking and cracking, the company marched on, treading off the cobbles of the village street onto a damp dirt road. He saw Sergeant Manley glancing back over the bent heads of his marching men, prepared to caution them not to slouch. But they had marched all night and they were young enough and tired enough to be loose and easy now the rain had passed on and mist was rising from the fields. Marching like this together, he thought, marching in step, swinging on, surging forward, we're big enough and young enough for anything.

Or maybe not anything, he thought as he recalled a photograph of a grinning corpse in a muddy uniform, the skull exposed, the lips rotted away from the long teeth. The wasted form encased in leathery muddy skin sat upright in a muddy trench, the left hand raised to ward off the triumphant earth that had buried it and from which it had been exhumed. The uniform had seemed British: high tight collar buttoned at the throat. But it was hard to tell. In life he might have been French. And the Germans wore uniforms with high, buttoned collars.

Orders were called out against the rising light of dawn. The company halted, the men downed their packs. As he shrugged out of his pack he thought, they better arrange to bring these up to us later: I carried this sonofabitch all the way up here and tonight I'm going to want what's in it.

He looked about: he stood with two hundred fifty other men in a field green with spring growth. From the east beyond a woods to their front and the field beyond it machineguns and rifles rattled, the sound distinct, monotonous and terrifying. Like a machine running, he thought, stamping out pieces. Like a sawmill.

More orders. The dense company of men who had marched in rigid order through the night extended itself into two long lines standing in the morning mist in the fresh green field, facing the dense French woods.

How did I come to this place? he wondered.

"I want every one of you," Sergeant Manley called out to his piece of the doubled line of riflemen segmented into platoons, "to make ready."

To his left and right men unslung their rifles, worked the bolts. A rippling clicking. He held his own rifle by the forepiece, worked the bolt with his right hand, glimpsed the shining brass as the rifle's mechanism carried the first cartridge from the clip and slid it into the breech. He put the rifle's safety on: just like on the range, he thought.

"Fix bayonets," Sergeant Manley shouted. Other sergeants' voices called out from along the line of platoons.

He grounded the butt of the rifle, held the muzzle in his left hand, withdrew the bayonet from its leather and canvas scabbard, fitted the haft of it over the muzzle of his rifle, clicked it home. His fingertips and the palms of his hands were scented with gun oil. His trousers and shirt and tunic were damp and smelled of wet and earth. He raised the rifle in his hands, right forefinger lying along the outside of the triggerguard.

Almost there, he thought. His heart thumped once inside his chest. He looked along the line of men that had been a marching company. Left and right in the mist men stood, bayoneted rifles angled east.

"We're going into this woods," Sergeant Manley said to his platoon. "The Germans are across the field beyond this stand of timber. I want every one of you to be ready."

Where are the officers? he thought.

To hell with it. Sergeant Manley is enough. Been every damned place, he can take us through this woods and into the field beyond and into the woods beyond that.

"We will halt just inside the far edge of the woods," Sergeant Manley said. “The front rank will lie prone, the rear rank will kneel behind the front rank. The machineguns will be sited on the flanks. The Germans will attack toward us across the next field. The machineguns will not fire until the order is given, and none of you men will fire until I order you to fire. Or the Germans are fifty yards from the muzzle of your rifle. Is that clear?”

A mutter of assent along the line.

“Where the hell are we, Sergeant?” a voice called out.

Manley glanced along the line, raised his voice and said, “Bellow Wood, the Captain said. And don’t ask me where that is. It’s in France.”

As he watched Sergeant Manley looking them over, he took his left hand from his rifle, touched the pieces of gear slung and clipped and hung about him: gas mask, grenades, cartridge belt, canteen, bandolier. Everything else left behind, in the pack. We better get those packs back. I’ve got stuff I want in there.

And Lieutenant Barkley? he wondered. Where’s Lieutenant Barkley?

Looking forward—toward the woods on the low rise in front of him: east toward the Kaiser’s troops—he saw Captain Harris and his lieutenants—Lieutenant Barkley among them—step out of the mist floating among the trees, Gunnery Sergeant Miller right behind the Captain. He saw Captain Harris gesture with his hands as though he were scooping sand toward himself. Then he pounded his right fist into his cupped left palm. The lieutenants nodded as they watched the Captain’s moving hands. Gunnery Sergeant Miller, all six feet three two hundred thirty pounds of him, stared over their heads at the two ranks of riflemen facing the woods: stared as though he were fixing the sight in memory, or counting them, or trying to estimate how many of them would be alive at sunset.

Sergeant Manley glanced toward the claque of officers, turned to his platoon and called out, “Get ready.” His rising voice seemed to waver: as though he knew what lay beyond the woods behind his back and didn’t like it or want it.

Sergeant Manley knows something we don’t, he thought. He’s seen this before. In China. And in Central America. Maybe he knows enough to be able to figure out what happens next.

Captain Harris strode ten paces down the moderate slope that rose to the edge of the woods behind him. The lieutenants fanned out left and right toward their platoons, Lieutenant Barkley striding forward to stand beside Sergeant Manley. Gunnery Sergeant Miller stood behind Captain

Harris, watching the platoons, watching the platoon sergeants, watching the lieutenants.

Captain Harris pushed his helmet back on his balding head, looked through his glittering steel-rimmed glasses at his company drawn up in two ranks in the bright green field, opened his mouth as though he were going to raise his voice and say a few words to encourage them. His mouth open, he glanced over his shoulder at Gunnery Sergeant Miller's face as still and disinterested as stone in what the Captain might have to say. Captain Harris shut his mouth, nodded at Gunnery Sergeant Miller's blank expression, turned to his company and called out, "Let's go!" He turned and walked back up the mild slope and on into the woods, the Gunnery Sergeant in front of him now, leading the way toward the mist that hung in the shadows among the trees.

The long double line of men set off, walking out of step up the slope toward the edge of the woods. He walked with them, part of the first rank. As though we're going into the woods to do a long day's work of logging, he thought. He looked to his left: the sun stood its circumference above the horizon. Six o'clock in the morning, he thought: someone said the mornings come earlier here because Europe is farther north.

He glanced at the riflemen ten feet away on either side of him. He did not recognize them: their faces were indistinct in the shadows beneath the flat projecting edges of their helmets. Wilkes and Johnson? he wondered. He looked at them again, but still he could not make them out.

The two orderly ranks of men faltered as they entered the dark woods. The random, complex character of this narrow European woods was unfamiliar. Nothing like it back home, he thought: this is eighth-growth timber, cut and cut again, the thin trees leaping upward toward the sun, the crowns high above. The trees, he thought, seem like alder, beech and oak. Yet they are unfamiliar: some subtle difference in their girth and the shape of their crowns distinguishes them from the trees of the same names in the States.

Alien place, he thought. I sure hope Mr. Wilson was right about why we came here.

"On line," Sergeant Manley shouted. "On line, damn it all."

At Sergeant Manley's order, lagging fragments of the double line strode forward among the trees to straighten the line, the men glancing right and left, bayonets cutting at the rising mist.

"What the fuck are you *doing*?" Sergeant Manley shouted at three men who had halted. They were staring at the ground in front of them, as though to try to figure what to do. "What the fuck is going *on*? Where the fuck do you think you *are*?"

They're right here, Sergeant, he thought: in this woods full of mist and a sweet, peculiar odor, walking along, going up to fight against the Germans. He almost called out, "Where the fuck do *you* think they are, Sergeant?"

But he kept his mouth shut: he knew Sergeant Manley would curse him and his impertinent question. Particularly on this misty June morning, he thought.

Still he tried to figure what the three men were staring at at their feet; but all he could see were stilted gray and stylized black shadows shaped by the sunlight falling through the thin, interlaced branches of the trees.

"Get the *fuck* away from there," Sergeant Manley shouted at the three men who had paused to stare, and were still staring. "Keep moving. On line. On line, Goddamn you! You've seen enough of that. The rest of you take a look at it. Take a look while you're going on, you sonsofbitches. This is what it is. This is what we are. This is what we will all become, this day or the next. You hear me?"

A disconnected mutter of voices: in this place of mist and shadows and wet ground and tree trunks black with damp leaning above gray and black shapes humped on the ground, they did not—could not—answer up in unison.

Not even us, he thought. And we are the hardest. The toughest. We are the most aggressive and most disdainful of any enemy. Of his ability, his cause. Of his right to exist. Dour, tough and determined: that's us. We induce fear and horror in those we fight. Or are said to do so. Soon we'll find out whether what we're said to be is what we are.

"Jesus save us," someone to his left said. "I don't think . . . "

"Shut the hell up there," Sergeant Manley shouted. "And come on. Take a look at it and get on line, Goddamnit."

Horror in his voice, the man to his right whispered, "See them?"

See what? he wondered. See who?

"There on the ground. See them?"

He looked. The gray and black shadows on the ground were corpses.

"Smell them?" the man to his right whispered. "They been here a day and more. Smell like dead animals. Worse than dead animals." He sounded as though he had smelled the dead outside the walls at Peking, and seen them rotting on Samar.

He stared down at one of the dead. The man lay on his back. His face was gray leather. His right arm was flung across his riven chest. His wasted wrinkled fingers lay against the fearsome wound. The thin, sunken face was stoic: as though he had known all along he would be killed in a dripping woods like this one. The corpse's uniform was blue-gray. French, he thought. An undamaged eight millimeter Berthier rifle lay three paces away. A crested French helmet rested close beside the withered face. Torn leather harness criss-crossed the riven chest.

I wonder who killed him.

Beyond the killed French soldier, forward of the line of advancing men, lay another killed man. This one was German: the long shrivelled rope of his rotting guts covered his thighs. His hands were buried in the long rent in the cavity that had contained his viscera.

Ah, Christ, he thought. And as he thought it Sergeant Manley's strong voice rose shouting through the gloom beneath the dripping trees: "Don't look at them, Goddamnit! You've seen enough. Get on. Get on ahead. On line! On line!"

Stepping past the dead German, watching where he put his feet, he went forward as they had trained him to: left hand beneath the forepiece of his rifle, right gripping the stock behind the triggerguard.

I thought the French ran. But those who fought here fought to the death. Only the weak among them, and the last survivors, ran: back to the villages through which we marched at dawn. The best fought here and were killed. As they killed the Germans who attacked into this woods.

He went on, the long wavering line right and left of him advancing through the gray mist beneath the dripping trees, the men's faces in shadow beneath the broad brims of their helmets, bayonets dipping and flicking like swallows, gleaming as the rising sunlight touched the steel.

Fifty feet on the woods thinned and he could see through the trees into the broad field beyond. Three hundred yards across the field lay another dripping woods.

Sprawled and foul, corpses lay in the trampled field. The early morning sunlight revealed the wounds that had killed each of them. Blood rotted to a shiny black crust disguised their faces and discolored their sky blue and gray uniforms.

"Well, Christ Almighty," the man to his right said. His voice was hearty and aggressive. "Like a fucking butcher shop around here."

He glanced at the man. Never seen him before, he thought. Must be a transfer. I thought I knew everyone in the company. Maybe not their names: but at least by sight. But not this guy: never seen him before.

"Halt," Sergeant Manley shouted. "Get on line five feet inside the woods. Hurry up, Goddamnit. They're coming."

Across the trampled field of dead French and German soldiers, in the mist and shadows inside the far woods, he saw gray uniforms, a flicker of metal, the gleam of polished leather.

German soldiers, he thought. And then Sergeant Manley's strong voice rose and shouted out the orders: "Front rank, in the prone position. Rear rank, close up behind the front rank and kneel."

A simple order, he thought as he ran forward and lay down. We've done it a hundred times. But there's always been five or seven who couldn't figure what to do.

But this time every man in the second rank jogged up behind the first rank lying down in the mulch just inside the woods and knelt behind and between each pair of prone riflemen.

"Don't shoot and keep silent," Sergeant Manley shouted.

He wondered if the Germans could hear Sergeant Manley's shouting voice. Elbows thrust into the damp decaying vegetation that matted the floor of the woods, he stared out of the gloom across the field full of sunlight and corpses. He guessed the Germans had heard nothing of Sergeant Manley's penetrating voice. They were three hundred yards away and they were busy arranging themselves: orderly files of German soldiers were slipping through the shadows in the woods beyond the field, extending into ranks. Then the ranks were coming forward, a solid front of men in gray uniforms and gray helmets with flared rims, the distant faces pale and indistinct, the weapons in their hands thin as sticks.

Far to his right—on the extreme left of the Germans' line—he saw four men siting a machinegun: tripod, gun, ammunition. Two knelt, working at the weapon. The third was coming forward, two boxes of ammunition swinging from his fists. The fourth—*another* sergeant, he guessed—stood to one side, arms folded across his chest, waiting for the other three to get on with it.

A voice along the line lying in the scrubby wet clutter of rotted leaves shouted, "Sergeant, they're setting up a machinegun to the right."

Sergeant Manley glanced toward the German machinegunners and said, "The right of the line, as the fucking Army says, will deal with it."

A jocular urban voice down the line called out, "I hope to Jesus you're right, Sergeant."

"I'm right," Manley told him. "Now shut the hell up and get ready."

He stared across the field: the last of the Germans were coming out of the woods, rifles at high port, coming forward through the trampled spring growth, an officer with a cane leading them as though he were on parade.

"Pick the man in front of you," Sergeant Manley called. "Aim at his gut as you were taught. Do not fire until they're fifty yards away, or I give the order. You hear me?"

A mutter along the line.

From the trees above cold water dripped onto his back.

The German officer wore spectacles: gold-rimmed and polished, they flashed when he turned his head. He sported a mustache. And a formal German helmet, with the spike on it. But not a dress helmet: it was not lacquered black and chased with silver, but fitted with dark green cloth. Black numbers were printed on the cloth. No numbers were stencilled on the helmets of his soldiers. An officer's pride, he thought. Like the cane he carries instead of a rifle, and the pistol in a shiny black holster on his belt: artifacts to show he is not a common soldier. His tunic was buttoned up to the collar tight about his throat. His face was thin and white, as though he had lived below ground all winter and were just coming out into the sunlight for the first time this year.

"Make ready!" Sergeant Manley shouted.

He glanced at Sergeant Manley kneeling to his right behind and between two prone riflemen, looked back into the field and slid his cheek against the stock of his rifle. He slid his left arm through the rifle's sling, wound the sling tight around his forearm and biceps.

On the range, he thought as the Germans came on through the field. Just as though we're on the range.

Elbows planted in the ruck of damp leaves, water dripping on his back and ticking as it struck his helmet, he aimed at the officer walking straight toward him: an officer, he thought, turned out as though he's going to be presented to the Kaiser. While I lie in the muck, greasy salt sweat sliding down my forehead.

The long line of German soldiers paced toward him. A man to the officer's left wiped his palm across his forehead, adjusted his helmet. The man beside him spoke and the one who had wiped his forehead nodded and grimaced.

He watched them coming on. Two hundred fifty yards. Two hundred. A hundred fifty. At a hundred yards he could hear their feet tramping against the damp June earth, crushing the new growth among the corpses.

Far to the right along the line he heard a gruff voice call, "Fire!" and as he aimed at the German officer coming at him across the field, the first machinegun began to fire at the Germans from the right flank, ripping the quiet morning apart and hammering bullets across the field. The officer paused, glanced to his left toward the machinegun killing his men, and then came on again.

He held himself steady, as he had been taught, the front sight of the rifle on the center of the German officer, six inches above his navel behind the gray cloth of his pressed uniform.

As he curled his finger about the trigger, the machinegun on the left began to fire. Bright red tracer flicked across the green field, killed the man walking to the elegant German's officer's right, lashed the elegant officer across the chest, killed the man to his left. The elegant officer staggered backward, went down on one knee. He bent his head forward as though to look at his shattered chest. He gobbled blood out of his mouth and fell forward onto his face.

Behind the officer a German soldier began to run forward as though he thought he might outrun the machineguns' fire.

"Fire," Sergeant Manley shouted.

He tightened his grip on the rifle, pressed his cheek against the stock, aimed at the center of the German soldier running forward. Target on the range, he thought. He squeezed the trigger. The German soldier dropped his rifle, slapped the right side of his chest and turned away.

As he worked the rifle's bolt he saw the man he had shot shiver as another bullet struck him, saw him look over his shoulder as though to see the man who had shot him, watched as he fell down into the trampled fresh spring green.

"Pick a target," Sergeant Manley shouted. "Pick a target and kill him." Sergeant Manley was standing up behind a prone riflemen. He held his rifle in his left hand and shouted, "Pick a target. Aim low. Squeeze them off."

All along the line rifles were firing, the racket of single shots rising to a single roar. Twenty feet beyond Sergeant Manley, Lieutenant Barkley stood erect and fired one round after another, aiming with care at this German soldier and the next as though he were shooting targets.

He turned back: toward the Germans. They were coming on, trudging forward into the heavy fire, flinching and ducking as they came, their reduced number dwindling. Beyond them a second line of men was jogging forward to fill the empty places in the line. He aimed at one of the fresh Germans, fired, missed, worked the bolt, fired again. The German flung his rifle down as though he were sick of it, shoved his elbows against his sides, stared at his hands and, as he began to fall, sat down. His mouth opened, but whatever sound he made was overwhelmed by the roar of rifles and machineguns firing.

He aimed at another German in the second line. The German's helmet had fallen off. His hair was brown, his face narrow and pale. Blood smudged his right cheek, but he seemed unwounded: he walked forward as though he were on his way to an appointment, his rifle swinging in his right hand.

He aimed with care and fired the rifle. Something—dust, bits of cloth, something—leapt from the man's chest. He dropped his rifle and fell backward onto one of the corpses—French? German?—lying in the field.

The advancing Germans wavered, halted. Here and there among them more men fell or were thrown back onto the damp earth among the wounded, the killed and the day-old corpses. Then a German voice shouted beyond the wall of crashing rifle and machinegun fire. Other voices took up the cry. He saw waving arms, strained faces. The Germans turned and began to make their way back across the field toward the distant woods. As they went, shoulders hunched, backs bent, the crashing roar of rifle and machinegun fire paused.

"Keep firing," Sergeant Manley shouted. "Goddamn you keep firing. Shoot them. Go on, Goddamnit, fire. Kill them, you sonsofbitches."

China, he thought as he raised his rifle. And Nicaragua. All those places where Sergeant Manley learned how to fight. And this is what he learned. I don't know if I like it much.

He aimed at a broad gray back, the rifle's sight framed by the man's belt and the polished leather straps of his equipment harness. As he fired the man ducked. He worked the bolt, aimed again. Before he could fire again, the traversing fire of the machineguns on the flanks slashed across the man's back and tracked on, knocking more men out of the ragged line of retreating Germans.

To come up here like that, he thought. They must have known we were here. And still they came up here, across the field full of the corpses of men killed yesterday when the French counterattacked them and the day before when they attacked the French.

"Up," Sergeant Manley shouted. "Every damned one of you on your feet. On line. On line, damn it all."

Lieutenant Barkley walked along the line of men getting to their feet, rifle in the crook of his arm. "Come on, men," he said, raising his voice, "let's go on over there and get them. Come on, get up, boys. We're going. We can't stay here."

"On line, Goddamnit," Sergeant Manley shouted. "Goddamnit, get on up out of there."

He heaved himself up before he could think, untangled his left arm from the sling of his rifle and watched as Lieutenant Barkley walked out of the woods into the field of trampled new growth, striding forward toward the woods three hundred yards away. Lieutenant Barkley stepped to his right to avoid a leathery gray corpse in a French uniform, turned and called over his shoulder, "Come on, men. We can't stay here. They'll call down artillery on this place in an instant. Let's go on."

What about the field? he wondered. Won't they call artillery down on the field, too?

But Lieutenant Barkley was out in the field, walking toward the woods into which the Germans had run. No time for questions, he thought.

"Come on," Sergeant Manley shouted. He seemed angry: that he had to be here; that he had to be here *again*. "Get the hell forward. Go on, follow the Lieutenant. And hurry. The Lieutenant told you their artillery will be firing into this wood in seconds. And the Lieutenant's right."

He jogged out of the treeline into the field. He vaulted the huddled, fearsome corpse in the French uniform. Something jagged and moving fast had torn away the corpse's left arm at the shoulder and exposed the complex of bone fitted beneath the riven flesh and torn muscle. The bearded Frenchman lay on his back. Flies clustered at the mouth, the nostrils, the eyes.

Four years of this war, he thought, and he was still fighting them. And they killed him. Good God.

He ran on: toward Lieutenant Barkley striding on across the field. The Lieutenant did not glance back: he was the kind of officer who knew his men would follow him. And he did not crouch: he was the kind of officer who thought officers should not crouch.

Behind him Sergeant Manley shouted, "*Goddamnit* stay on line there!" He glanced over his shoulder: Sergeant Manley's square flushed face was turned toward him, his right arm extended, his forefinger pointing straight at him.

Before he could speak, Lieutenant Barkley looked over his shoulder and said, "That's all right. You come up here with me. I can use the company."

Sergeant Manley grimaced at his Lieutenant's unorthodox behavior, shook his head and made a shooing movement with the fingers of his right hand.

As he came up to Lieutenant Barkley, a rising whine filled the sky. Four artillery shells struck the woods two hundred yards to his left rear. Lieutenant Barkley said, "I knew we were better off out of that woods. And they're in disarray in front of us. Right now they don't know what to do." He sounded confident. My confident Lieutenant, he thought; who's been at war no longer than I have.

"Yes, sir," he said.

"Call me Jim," Lieutenant Barkley said. "We're in the field now."

"Yes, sir."

"Jim."

"Right, Jim."

"Where are you from?" Lieutenant Barkley asked.

Before he could answer the German machinegun began to fire from the right. That gun I saw them setting up, he thought. He glanced, saw the muzzle winking, shoved the Lieutenant down and flung himself down beneath the crackling streak of tracer whipping the air two feet above the ground.

Our turn now, he thought as he pressed himself against the earth. Ah, Christ: I knew it would come to this.

"Thanks," Lieutenant Barkley said when the chattering fire of the machinegun had swept on. "That was quick of you."

"The gun's on their left flank, Lieutenant. Happened to see it earlier."

"You did?" Lieutenant Barkley looked at him. He raised his voice: the roar of the machinegun rose again as it traversed toward them from their left. "No one told me."

"Sergeant Manley," he shouted as he put his face down into the damp spring growth, "said the men on the right would take care of it."

Lieutenant Barkley shoved his own face against the earth and said, "I would have thought that. . ." But he stopped speaking as the machinegun's fire ripped the air above them and someone behind them began to scream like an animal gutted. As the machinegun fire passed to their right Lieutenant Barkley raised his head, looked over his shoulder and said, "Ah, God."

He turned his face and looked behind. A gap ten men wide had opened in the line of men Sergeant Manley had herded out of the woods. The screaming rose from a bloody jerking olive green bundle writhing in the middle of the gap ten men wide that the machinegun had cut in the line. A dog yapping with his back broken, he thought as the screaming thinned. A pig with its throat half cut.

"Too bad," Lieutenant Barkley said. As he spoke rifle and machinegun fire from behind them pounded toward the German machinegun.

The German machinegun went on hammering rounds across the field as it traversed back and forth, chopping more gaps in the line.

"Come on," Lieutenant Barkley shouted. But the sound of his voice was small, and the noise of the German machinegun firing was huge: he pressed himself against the earth.

Lieutenant Barkley got up on his knees, stood up, stood up straight, shifted his rifle to his left hand, pushed his helmet back from his high white forehead.

"Get down, Lieutenant," he said. "For Christ's sake, get down here."

Lieutenant Barkley looked down at him as though he had said something odd. A burst of machinegun bullets struck Lieutenant Barkley across the chest, ripped him open, hammered through him, tore his back apart, flung him down dead in the field strewn with French and German corpses.

God, he thought. Right out here and the Lieutenant killed. The sonsofbitches.

He looked back: at the rest of the company, their faces white, strained and distant. Behind them the woods from which they had shot Germans like partridges exploded as more artillery shells struck the earth. Uprooted trees leapt upward, branches whipped as though a hurricane wind were blowing.

To hell with it, he thought as he turned away. I can't do anything about any of it right now. He wriggled through the calf-high pale green growth. Wheat: this must be wheat. Or some other grain, he thought as he crept into a muddy depression.

Great, he thought. Hands smeared with dirt, uniform filthy, mud streaked on the stock of my rifle. Canteen, equipment belt, gas mask, grenades: all dragging in the mud and jabbing at my chest and hips. They ought to figure some way to make this stuff fit right. But to hell with that right now.

He raised his head an inch and looked out of the depression in which he lay. From the woods two hundred yards away the Germans were firing. Men lying down were aiming rifles and working the bolts and firing. An elegant officer—another elegant officer—standing behind them was firing a pistol. And from the right and far left, machineguns worked like jackhammers. He looked toward the German machinegun on the right. As he did so the gun's methodical fire swept the air above him and more artillery shells struck the woods behind. More noise, more screams. Dirt pattered on his back and helmet. Jagged, yellow lengths of wood thumped the ground around him. Lucky I'm in this low place in the ground, he thought.

He looked to his right again: toward the machinegun traversing as it fired at the line of men lying down in the field. The machinegunner was sitting behind his weapon, staring along the barrel from under the flared rim of his helmet, easing the machinegun four inches right and then four inches left. Beside him his assistant knelt, holding the jerking belt of bullets in both hands. The muzzle of the gun flickered red and silver. He put his head down, heard the machinegun fire chitter and crack above his head. He raised his face as the machinegunner traversed the weapon away from him.

You sonofabitch, he thought. He squirmed in the muddy low ground in which he lay: to face the gunner. He eased his rifle forward, gripped the forepiece with his left hand, touched the trigger as he aimed at the machinegunner. Two hundred twenty yards, he thought. The bulk of the machinegun and its barrel inside the waterjacket and its flashing muzzle blocked his view of the gunner. He raised the rifle part of an inch, aimed at the gunner's face.

The gunner began to traverse the gun left to right again: he could hear the approaching rattle and snap of the bullets cutting the air. To his left, someone screamed. He breathed in, as he had been taught, exhaled half the breath, held himself still, and fired. He watched as the round from his rifle flung the machinegunner's hands up as though he wanted to surrender and flung him from his seat. He worked the bolt, aimed at the machinegunner's assistant rocking back on his heels, the still, glittering belt of bullets in his hands. He shot him in the side of the chest, watched the man's spine flex as he toppled away from the gun.

He looked over his shoulder. Behind him the artillery fire pounding the woods was driving the last of the company out into the field. Pieces of the ragged line were still coming on, running this way and that: but coming on. He saw one man's face explode. A haze of blood tinted the sky about his head. Another man leapt sideways as though he could escape the bullets that chopped at him and killed him. A third let his bayoneted rifle slip from his right hand, went down on one knee, bent his head and toppled onto his side.

He buried his face in the muddy earth, clutching his rifle with his dirty hands.

A voice above him in the roaring sky said, "Get the hell up out of there."

He looked. Sergeant Manley, standing up in the fire, stared down at him.

The woods behind Manley erupted, crashed. Trees exploded, earth leapt upward. From the woods at the foot of the field rifle fire rattled.

"Get the fuck up out of there," Sergeant Manley shouted. Anger and intention jammed all the menace he had learned in the Philippines, China and Nicaragua down into his rough shouting voice.

He scrambled to his feet, bayoneted rifle in his left hand, tugged at his dirty uniform.

"You killed those machinegunners," Sergeant Manley shouted. He seemed angry: as though the machinegunners had been Marines. He did not seem to notice the German rifle fire, or the rattle of the other German machinegun tracking toward them from the left.

"Yes, Sergeant."

"Lieutenant Barkley's dead," Sergeant Manley shouted.

"Yes, Sergeant. I saw him shot. Killed, I mean."

"You did all right," Manley shouted as the artillery crashed in the woods behind them and the diminished line of infantry moved on across the field.

"Thank you, Sergeant."

"But right now the hell with that. Get on. Get into the woods over there and kill them. Kill every last one of them."

"Yes, Sergeant," he said.

Sergeant Manley turned and jogged away toward the woods, darting right and left as though he knew how to dodge bullets.

He ran after the Sergeant, rushed and zig-zagged as he listened for the approach of the traversing German machinegun's fire.

In front of him the woods from which the Germans fired erupted as artillery shells struck it. The explosions snapped the trunks of trees and flung German soldiers up among the whipping branches. Between one explosion and the next, he heard men screaming in the woods.

The Germans' fire diminished, the steady sweeping racket of the machinegun to the left ceased. The men advancing through the calf-high green wheat stopped dodging and weaving. The line coalesced, straightened and surged forward toward the burning woods.

Ahead of the line, Sergeant Manley turned his flushed angry face over his shoulder and, between one cracking shell burst and the next, shouted, "Come on you sonsofbitches."

He looked left along the line. Determined, neutral expressions, clamped jaws thrust out, helmets tilted forward, shoulders hunched, bayoneted rifles swinging.

The artillery fire ceased. They ran forward toward the silent smoldering woods, ran into the fog of mist and smoke that smelled of burned powder. In the shadows beneath the trees a swaying German stood, his rifle raised. Sergeant Manley shot him in the gut. The German dropped his rifle and flung his hands up. Sergeant Manley worked the bolt of his rifle, shot him in the chest. The German shouted as the round shoved him back and pitched him into a smoking shell crater.

Deeper in the woods German machineguns began to fire, cutting yellow scars in the bark of the trees.

More Germans, he thought as he darted behind a tree. Another line of them lurking in the woods. Some of them withdrew just before our artillery started. Smart. And they're shooting this way, even though some of their men are in front of their guns, and still alive. Pretty tough.

Panting, he ran on through the woods, running men on either side of him darting from one shadow to the next. A German lurched from behind a thick tree in front of him, a rifle in his left hand, a stick grenade in his right. He slashed at the German with his bayonet, slashed his throat, watched him stumble back into the mist, blood staining his gray tunic, his stricken face staring and staring as blood flowed from his savaged throat. The German flung the grenade at him as he fell backward.

He leapt behind a slim tree, leapt to the cover of the next tree on as the grenade detonated behind him. The explosion shoved at him. He smelled burned powder. Hard bits of wood and pulpy wet hunks of something else struck his back. He ran on. To either side men were falling: shot through the chest, shot through the throat, shot through the groin. Some fell and rolled over and stared up through the smoke and mist. Some fell face down, arms caught beneath them as though to hide their hands. Some extended their arms in front of them as though with a single last reach they might still win the race.

Ahead, a hammering German machinegun swivelled right to left. He halted behind a tree, heard bullets rip bark from the trunk, listened as the gun's fire traversed onward. Crouching, he slid from the tree's protection, darted forward. The gun was fifty feet away, in profile, its muzzle flashing yellow and silver. The gunner's face was bent over the receiver. Kneeling beside the gun, the assistant gunner steadied the jerky flipping progress of the belted rounds into the clattering mechanism.

Fucking machinegunners, he thought.

He slid the bolt of his rifle back, picked a clip from his ammunition belt, shoved it into the magazine with his dirty fingertips, rammed the bolt home, raised the rifle. He aimed at the machinegunner. Another pair of them, he thought as he took up pressure on the rifle's trigger. From the corner of his right eye he saw movement. He turned his face: a German soldier was aiming a rifle at him from behind a tree. The German's face was pale and his long blond hair was plastered across his forehead half-hidden by the rim of his helmet. The German squinted at him and fired the rifle.

The round struck the forepiece of his rifle, twisted it from his stinging fingers and palms. Splinters of wood slashed his right cheek and forehead. A film of blood slid into the orbits of his eyes. He glanced away from the German working the bolt of the rifle. The muzzle of the machinegun was twitching toward him, the gunner behind the weapon leaning to his right as the gun's muzzle swivelled left.

Hands stinging, his rifle jerking and swinging on its sling from his left elbow, he leapt behind a tree half as thick as himself. The rifleman fired again: the bullet slashed at his left biceps, pounded bone above the elbow, yanked at his arm as though to tear it from his shoulder, jerked him from the thin cover of the tree. Left arm flapping, he fell down through the drifting mist and smoke into the damp leaves.

Move, he told himself: *move*. He twisted on the warm floor of the forest, rolled away from the tree, grabbed his broken rifle with his good right hand. His left arm flopped, the jagged ends of the shattered bone grating against one another. Yet he felt no pain: the arm was numb. He gagged on the bitter smoke layered in the mist and began to cough; and as he coughed the machinegunner fired a vicious ripping burst above him pressed against the earth. He can't see me, he thought. I'm hidden beneath the mist and smoke.

The rifleman fired a third time. The bullet struck him in the left thigh. His leg kicked, jerked, stretched, trembled. Through the thin skein of blood in his eyes, through the haze and smoke, he saw his leg bent at mid-thigh: as though he had been granted another joint. And through the blood in his eyes he saw blood flowing from his leg, staining his trousers, dripping onto the damp earth.

Still he felt no pain; and he thought, to hell with waiting for this guy to take another shot.

Another vicious burst of machinegun fire slashed the murk above him. Ought to depress the gun's muzzle, he thought.

He let go his rifle, tore a grenade from his Mills webbing, fitted the ring on the cotter pin over his inert left thumb, gripped the grenade and pulled. Pain lanced upward from his hand through his forearm and biceps to his shoulder.

Fuck it, he thought. He opened his fist: the grenade's spoon flicked away. One of the Germans behind the machinegun shouted. Knows the tinny sound of a grenade arming itself, he thought. Fuck the rifleman. He raised himself and lobbed the grenade at the machinegun. One of the Germans shouted again: a curse, or a warning.

The grenade detonated: a bright flash of white light trailing smoke and yellow flame. One German screamed, another cursed, coughed, moaned. He raised his head: the German rifleman was aiming his rifle. He heaved himself back and down as the German fired.

Missed, he thought. *Must* have missed. He coughed, tasted salt in his mouth, felt warm blood pouring over his lower lip, sliding down his chin. Warm grease, he thought.

Didn't miss. He looked down at his chest. Blood spread across his tunic. But it did not spurt: it flowed. A good sign. I think.

A rifle fired, fired again. Through the smoke he saw the German rifleman drop his weapon and slap both hands to his throat as though he could stop the gush of blood with his hands, rebuild the intricate structure of flesh, muscle, tendon and bone with his fingertips.

A voice above him shouted, "Keep down," and Sergeant Manley leapt across him, bayoneted rifle extended, the long shining blade sliding through the thin shafts of sunlight falling down through the layers of smoke and mist among the trees. Panting, he propped himself up on his right arm. Each time he breathed the shattered bone in his thigh grated. He felt sick: going to puke, he thought. He swallowed, bit his bloody tongue in his bloody mouth to stop himself screaming.

He watched as Sergeant Manley—shoulders hunched, rifle thrust forward, bayonet glittering—rushed toward the machinegun he had grenaded. The machinegun's muzzle pointed at the canopy of branches high above. He could not see the gunner or his assistant. But a German officer stood twenty feet behind the gun, shooting at Sergeant Manley with his pistol. As he ran forward Sergeant Manley fired his rifle twice. His second shot chopped the officer's left leg from under him. The officer fell, got up on his right knee and began to raise his pistol just as Sergeant Manley slid the bayonet beneath the officer's collarbone and shoved, leaning his weight on the rifle as though he were levering a shovel jammed into hard, baked ground. The officer screamed as Manley lifted him. The officer threw the pistol away and gripped the muzzle of Sergeant Manley's rifle. Sergeant Manley shot the officer through the chest, jerked the bayonet out of him, looked right and left, turned and jogged back toward him.

All around him the company slid and strode and darted forward through the woods, bayoneted rifles extended in front of them. Threatening the east, he thought. Infantry attacking, he thought: ready for anything. Or almost anything.

Sergeant Manley stood above him. "We'll be back," Sergeant Manley shouted. He held his rifle across his heaving chest. "Don't worry. We'll come back for you." But his face was full of stolid doubt. Still he said, "You're all right," as though he were a doctor and had checked each of his wounds and assessed the damage and were handing over his informed opinion.

Sure, he thought. Sure. He nodded and tried to speak. But he could not: his mouth was full of warm salt blood. "Don't worry," Sergeant Manley told him. "I know your name." Then he turned and jogged away through the shadows and shafts of sunlight, advancing east with the rest of the company: toward the next field on.

He turned his cheek against the damp floor of the woods, spat blood onto the mucky leaves. More blood seeped up his throat. He coughed: pain slid through his chest, clawed upward to his shoulder, ran like fire along his left arm, seared his wrist and hand and fingers. He recalled marching through the black night, three four hours before, his hand on the strong, rocking left shoulder of the man in front of him.

He looked along the ground. An insect was approaching: claws like a lobster, a curled, serrated tail raised behind. Scorpion, he thought. Didn't know they had scorpions in France.

He spat blood at the scorpion, spat again. The scorpion paused, scuttled left and right, came on again.

Bastard thing, he thought. I hate the vicious mechanical look of it.

He reached with his right hand, gripped his rifle behind the shattered forepiece. Pain flowed up his arm. More pain pierced his chest and made his leg tremble. Shot three times, he thought. Arm, chest, leg. Great.

He dragged the rifle across himself, raised it, gauged the distance, and pounded the butt down on the scorpion. He heard the segmented carapace crack and crack again, thought he heard the devilish insect screech as it dragged its disjointed claws right and left and whipped its sectioned tail across its back. He raised the rifle and pounded the butt down on the scorpion a second time, crushing the frenzy out of it.

He dropped his useless rifle and rolled onto his back. His useless broken arm and useless broken leg anchored him to the earth. His chest heaved and he coughed blood into his mouth and spat it onto his chest. Through the thickening mist he watched men in flat helmets carrying bayoneted rifles slipping among the trees, heading east through the shadowed woods toward the sunlight that filled the next field: toward the diminishing mechanical clatter of machineguns firing and the fading crack and roar of artillery rounds ploughing the earth.

TINY, DELICATE FEET MARCHED across his dirty cheek, paused, scrabbled at his skin. The scorpion? I thought I killed it.

Grit and a dry pebble filled his sticky mouth. His left arm was caught beneath him. A sharp stone thrust against his left thigh, another against his chest.

The tiny feet marched on. Evil small lobster, he thought. But didn't I kill it?

He put out his right hand, reached for his rifle. His fingers touched stone, sand, a rock.

But I was in a woods. Damp leaves, mist, the bitter smell of burned powder, my mouth full of blood, the sky full of noise and smoke.

His swollen tongue touched abrasive mucous, the pebble, his cracked lips. No blood, he thought. A memory slid away: of a dripping misty woods, shattered trees, gunfire, a German officer standing up firing a pistol across killed German machinegunners.

I was somewhere else, he thought. And now I'm not. The last of the memory—men advancing through a woods, bayoneted rifles in their hands—dissolved, sliding like smoke over the edge at the farthest corner of his mind.

And now I'm here: back in the fucking desert where they left me, an insect crawling across my cheek.

He flicked his fingers at his face. A plump beetle fluttered to the sand, interleaved the plates of its carapace and set off marching across the sand.

Harmless, he thought. He spat Sergeant Kline's pebble from his mouth. And the scorpion?

He raised his head from the stony sand, tugged his left arm from beneath himself, pressed his hands against the ground—give me fifty! show me you've got something! He lifted himself, dragged his knees under his chest. The sling of his rifle slid from his shoulder, the rifle's muzzle struck his right forearm. He pushed himself up until he knelt, lifted his face above the knee-high scrub and stared into the perfect white light that filled the sky and pounded the stony desert.

The desert and the sky were empty. Two voids, he thought, both full of heat and light.

I keeled over, he thought. Passed out. There was an aircraft, rotor or fixed wing. I couldn't make it out. It flew a straight, ascending course across south to north. Not looking this way. Bastards up in an air-conditioned bubble, chewing gum and thinking about vectors and navigation aids. Then I passed out. I wonder how long I was out. He squinted at the sky: ten, eleven in the morning, he guessed. He looked at his watch: 10:09. Mid-morning here in California. At Twentynine Palms. In the desert.

He moved his tongue in his filthy mouth. Got to get some water. He stood up, arms trembling, fingers shaking. Bad shape, he thought. I was unconscious. Heatstroke? Sunstroke? One of them, you get cold and clammy and pass out, the other you get hot and dry and pass out. I remember the shivers, a gush of chilly sweat, mist rising.

But no mist rises in the desert: there is no moisture in the desert.

He reached for the canteen attached to his equipment belt. The belt and harness were askew, the canteen behind his back, ammunition pouches over his gut and right hip. He pulled the harness straight, settled it, unhooked the canteen, moved it this way and that. The water sloshed and he thought, these are the last small waves anywhere in this waterless desert. Then he thought: why did I unhook the canteen from my belt instead of sliding it out of its cover? I'm losing it: that's why.

No drinking, now. A taste. Put another pebble in your mouth, take a single sip of water, hold it in your mouth as long as you can before you swallow. To wet your mouth, to permit the pebble to absorb water. He bent, picked a small smooth stone from the sand, brushed it as clean as he could against his trousers, placed it in his mouth beneath his tongue. He uncapped the canteen. Just a taste, now, he thought. His hand shook as he raised the canteen. When the mouth of the canteen was eight inches from his mouth he smelled the water. He placed the mouth of the canteen against his swollen, stinging lips, tilted the canteen and permitted a trickle of water to flow into his mouth. His hands trembled as he thought for an instant about tilting the canteen higher and gulping it all down.

But Sergeant Kline and Sergeant Quinlan were, he knew, standing in the scrub behind him, hands on their hips, gauging his performance and looking for signs of weakness.

He took the canteen down from his mouth, capped it, hooked it on his equipment belt.

All right, Sergeant Kline said. At least you're over that hump.

He turned. Sergeant Kline stood in the scrub. He wore red Bermuda shorts and a white tee shirt. And sandals. Standing beside Sergeant Kline, staring from beneath the brim of his flat-brimmed campaign hat, his drill sergeant's uniform immaculate, not a sweat- stain on him anywhere, Sergeant Quinlan nodded at him.

I wonder how the Drill Instructors did it. How did they keep up the appearance when we were dropping? And how did they go back to the office and make out reports for four hours while we were asleep?

Who knows? And right now: who cares? I don't have a lot of time right now to get all sentimental about Parris Island. Particularly since they spent all their time fucking with me. With us.

Got to get out of the sun, he thought. Get the light out of my eyes. I should have brought shades.

You should have brought a fucking limousine, Sergeant Kline told him. With a keg of cold lager in the trunk.

And a blonde for company, Sergeant Quinlan said.

Who the hell's inside this guy's head, Quinlan? You? Or me?

"Both of you," he said. "And you're fucking with me."

Fucking with you? Sergeant Quinlan said. We're getting you over the bumps here. That's what they pay us for.

You call that pay, Quinlan?

No. *They* call it pay.

"I've got to get the sun out of my face," he said. "If I don't . . ."

What the hell did you bring that shelterhalf for? To cuddle up to when you're jerking off?

"Right," he said. He worked the shelterhalf out of his belt, unfolded it. Crinkly rubberized cloth. Great: it's going to be real cool walking around underneath this. He unslung his rifle, worked the shelterhalf over his head, slung his rifle.

What the *fuck* are you doing? Sergeant Quinlan said.

"I've got it on my head," he explained.

I've got it on my head *Sergeant*, Sergeant Kline said. And who cares where you've got it? Take it off. Unsling your rifle. Unclip the sling from the swivel at the muzzle, thread the sling through the carrying handle, cinch it up, work your arm through the slack between the carrying handle and the butt, sling the rifle with the butt pointing at the deck, and then put the shelterhalf back over your head and the muzzle of the rifle, dumbfuck. It's awkward, but that way, the rifle's muzzle rides higher. It'll hold the shelterhalf above your head and you'll get some air circulating underneath. And let the shelterhalf hang loose over your face and shoulders: all you need to see while you're marching is the compass and the ground ten feet in front of you. That way, your eyes will be in the shade.

"Good point, Sergeant," he said.

Good point? What the hell is this, your fag debating society at college? 'Good point'. Stop fucking around and *do* it.

He slid the shelterhalf from his head, stuffed part of it into his belt. Then he unslung his rifle, unclipped the sling, threaded it through the carrying handle, clipped it, cinched the sling tight and worked his arm through the length of the sling between the carrying handle and the butt. He slung the rifle with the muzzle high above his shoulder and draped the shelterhalf over his head and the muzzle of the weapon. He peered through a narrow, descending tunnel of darkness at the white light that scorched the litter of brush and rocks. It helps. Not much, but it's better than nothing.

You *bet* it's better than nothing, Sergeant Quinlan said. It's a *lot* cooler under there. You understand me? Cooler.

A cool woods, he thought, damp and full of mist. A June morning. The sound of firing in the distance, men moving through shadow and shafts of sunlight.

Must have been an exercise somewhere, he thought. Back east somewhere. Or something.

And? Sergeant Kline said.

Yeah, Sergeant Quinlan said. What are you going to do next? Or do you want me to draw you a picture?

A picture would be nice, he thought. But he said, "Take a bearing with the compass, Sergeant."

This guy, Sergeant Quinlan told Sergeant Kline, is a fucking genius. Where the hell do we get these guys? In my day, we—"

He's doing all right, Sergeant Kline said. And he's not *completely* dumb.

Maybe not, Sergeant Quinlan said. He rubbed his cheek, shook his head and said, I don't know. What the hell, maybe he just *looks* dumb.

You remember the bearing? Sergeant Kline asked.

"One hundred thirty-five degrees, Sergeant."

Sergeant Quinlan said, I guess that's got to be it: he just *looks* dumb.

And the time? Sergeant Kline asked.

He looked at his watch. "Ten fifteen, Sergeant," he said, and as he said it he thought, four hours and more marching, part of the time out like a light. I can't have gone more than four, five miles. I wonder how long I was out?

Forget about that, Sergeant Kline said. It doesn't matter how far you've *come*. What matters is how far you've got to *go*.

"I can't know how far I've got to go, Sergeant Kline, if I don't know how far I've come."

Look around, Sergeant Quinlan said. What do you see?

He raised the tacky rubbery cloth so that he could see the horizon.

"The desert," he said.

*No* shit? Sergeant Quinlan said. What's the reciprocal of one hundred thirty-five degrees, numbnuts?

"That'd be, well . . . three hundred and fifteen?"

You tell me, Sergeant Quinlan said. You're the one with the compass.

"It'd be a hundred and eighty plus one thirty-five. Three fifteen."

So set yourself up facing one thirty-five and then do an about face and *take a look* back where you've come from, Sergeant Kline said.

He held the compass in his palm, turned himself until the needle lay above the arrow scored in the plastic base and he faced the bearing of one hundred thirty-five degrees. He turned about, raised the rubberized cloth from his face, folded it back onto the top of his head and the muzzle of his rifle, raised his face and squinted through the pure white light that filled the sky and the desert. Far in the distance through heat shimmering upward, a ridge rose from the gray and gold sand and dusty scrub.

I came from there, he thought.

"I see it," he said. "That's the ridge where I left the sign."

How far have you come?

"Not far enough," he told Sergeant Kline.

Not far enough? What the hell does that mean? You're not—as squid officers in the Navy say—quibbling with me, are you? How fucking far?

"Five miles?"

Did I ask you to ask me a question? Sergeant Quinlan said.

Remember what you were told about distances in the desert, Sergeant Kline said.

"They're deceptive," he said. "Distances are deceptive. Things seem farther away than they really are."

That's it. So how far away is the ridge?

"Couple of miles. Three and a half. Maybe four."

That's about it. In about four hours.

"Pretty slow."

Not bad for out here, though, Sergeant Kline said. You don't want to double-time it out here. You want to take it steady, one pace after the other, keep your respiration down, hold sweating to a minimum.

"Fuck a minimum," he said. "I'm dried out right now. I could drink a barrel of water and still be thirsty."

And I could do with a barrel of beer, Sergeant Quinlan said. So what? There's no water out here and there sure in hell isn't no beer.

Listen to me, Sergeant Kline said. You think you're more thirsty than you are. It's the discomfort in your mouth that makes you feel so thirsty. The tissue in the mouth is sensitive and it swells if it's not kept moist. That's why your tongue is swollen. Don't worry about it. That's an order, by the way: don't worry about it. You had an event: a touch of heat stroke. Now you're over it.

I still feel a little shaky, though.

Shaky? Sergeant Quinlan said. What's that mean, shaky?

You'll be all right, Sergeant Kline said. I've seen older guys than you come out into the field. Look at me, for example.

He looked at Sergeant Kline: spindly old man with knobby knees and sharp elbows, a faint pot belly, white hair combed straight back from a silver widow's peak, glittering glasses, gristle where he had once displayed muscle.

And I'm not talking about me, Sergeant Kline said. I'm talking about some general officers I've seen out in the field. Near fifty year old men humping it. I remember one general came out to Vietnam in 1967.

Name of Cunningham, call me Stewart, we're in the field, he said. Came out to do a report. Came up and went out with us. I didn't hardly credit it at the time. And I don't mean because he was Army. I mean: a fucking general?

A doggie? Sergeant Quinlan said.

Sergeant Kline tilted his face and said, You're not going to give me that stuff about the Army not being good enough, are you, Quinlan? You want to think before you let that kind of shit pour out of your mouth.

Well . . .

Come on, Quinlan. You know it's the man who counts. Some go. Others don't. Or won't. Or can't. But some go. A few—three in a division, three out of eighteen, twenty thousand men—will go against anything.

I guess you're right, Quinlan said. Though considering the fucking Army, it gives me a pain here and there to say it.

I agree: the Army could do better. Just like the Marine Corps ought to. But they do all right. So do we. On the other hand, like I said: in the end, it's the man who counts. Who gets up and goes. And this one here with the corner of his handkerchief in his mouth and the compass in his hand and the rubberized canvas over his head is one of the ones who gets up and goes. Look how far he's come already.

"Whatever you say, Sergeant Kline," he said.

That's right. Whatever I say. All right. You better get moving. The sun's up.

"I noticed that," he said. He turned about: one hundred eighty degrees. He checked the compass and looked once more along the bearing—one hundred thirty-five degrees—that led toward home. Or, at least, toward the Palms. The desert of sand and stone and scrub lay flat, uneven and immense before him. He raised his eyes. The horizon blinked, a flash of pure white light, warning him that he would have to endure.

I'm bigger, he thought. Or better be.

HE STUMBLED AWAY THROUGH the scrub, the shelterhalf tented over his head, boots shuffling in the dust and kicking stones. Behind him, Sergeant Kline and Sergeant Quinlan stood in the reddishgray desert chatting and handing one another sea stories as they watched him go.

Got to go on, he thought. But heat raged through his brain, his limbs trembled, and muscle and sinew ached as though he had marched a hundred miles in full field gear. A single drop of sweat stung his right eye. But the tag of cloth clenched in his teeth was as dry as his mouth: as dry as old bone.

Forget about the discomfort, he told himself. The nerves in your face and mouth are drying out, and that makes you feel as though you're in worse shape than you are.

Or so said Sergeant Kline, who has conducted enough trials in desert conditions to know.

Something small and quick skittered and fled from his boots, rushed this way and that beneath the knee-high canopy of dusty scrub bushes. Things live, he thought: even out here. Right now, being a lizard would be better. The lizard adapted itself to this environment long ago. You can adapt to anything, they said. To any environment. To battle. To existing in a protective suit and a gas mask. To fighting with bayonets and knives. To fighting to the death. To fighting on after everyone else is dead. To fighting on after they drop the fucking hydrogen bomb! some sergeant at Parris Island had screamed. You *can* survive, he had yelled. Whatever the conditions! Whatever the odds! Whatever they throw at you! Even the fucking *bomb*! *Every* Marine, he had cried in the whining cracker accent he'd learned somewhere between Ft. Smith, Arkansas and Tupelo, Mississippi, can survive the fucking *bomb*! *And* fight back! *And* kill the sonsofbitches!

What an asshole, someone in the second rank had muttered.

But maybe you can, he had thought then; and now he thought, maybe you *can* survive anything.

Except, he thought, this affliction of heat, exhaustion, thirst and decline. Maybe the odds against in this terrible place are too great. After all, it's not a race against radiation fleeing from a nuclear blast, or a terrible struggle against another terrified armed man. Here in the desert the struggle is written out in a single, stark equation that expresses the accelerating decline of a whole. I am a volume of water and I will be divided, and divided again, by time and heat. Anyone can compute the rate at which I am reduced: it is a simple matter of the reduction, by light and heat, of the water that is my self. And I cannot escape the day, the heat, the light: I am tied to this place and I am required to struggle against that which I must endure. Sergeant Kline and Sergeant Quinlan and the sun and this fucking desert tell me so.

They should have prepared a table, he thought. No. They *did* prepare a table. I saw it. They handed each of us a narrow pamphlet full of useless information, graphs and tables. I recall its advice. Stay in the shade and wait. Move at night, hole up in the day. Dig for water at the outsides of the bends in arroyos. Put out blue and orange panels, make a flare from a tin can and gasoline. A quart of water in the desert with the temperature above a hundred degrees will see you through one to three days if you move only at night and stay in the shade during the day. The table provided concise information about the interrelation of temperature, humidity, water and time. The implication of the table was precise: the higher the temperature and the lower the humidity and the less the amount of water, the less the time remaining until no one could go on. Absolute numbers, fudged a little here and there. Depending, the pamphlet's authors wrote, on the circumstances. Given the circumstances, a quart might not take you through three days, or two. Or even one.

But fuck the pamphlet's authors and the pamphlet's tables. And fuck the odds they give and fuck their advice. There is no shade in this desert. I cannot wait for night. There are no arroyos and no place to dig for water. I have no blue and orange panels, no tin can, no gasoline. I have a pint of water, no more. Whatever the temperature is, it feels like a hundred and twenty-eight degrees and more. And I am being reduced by the sun and the baking heat. And by my own effort: by each step I take, by each beat of my heart.

One thing about this, though. I guess they'll rewrite the orders that prescribe how road guides should be equipped and supplied. Maybe after this they'll be sure each of them has a barrel of water and a radio; and responsible officers and sergeants. And maybe they'll decide *not* to leave them waterless and alone out in the desert for no fucking reason. Maybe the Commandant will fix it.

But fuck that, fuck the future and fuck the Commandant. This is now: all that is for later. For now, I must do what I can; and I can do what I must.

Think about something else, he thought. Think about somewhere else: anywhere else.

Something about a woods, he thought: dripping foliage, soft damp ground, the fields bounded by woods. And gunfire rattling as dawn became morning became day, dew and rain on the leaves of the trees scored and notched by machinegun fire, mist rising, a June morning, shattered trees cut down, fallen leaves curling as they died in the rising warmth of morning, shadows running through the woods torn apart by rifle fire, machinegun fire, artillery fire. Through a field of wheat no higher than the calf strewn with the corpses of men killed; and then machinegun fire sweeping the field and men falling on either side of me; and as I ran on toward the woods beyond the field someone running beside me flinging his rifle down into the wheat, grabbing at his chest and falling on his back, his white face turning toward the sky.

If I remember right.

Another something skittered and fled beneath the scrub. Lizards, insects, rats. I wish I knew how they survive. In this place it is better to be a rat than a man.

He tripped on a rock buried in sand as slippery as mud. He caught himself, tripped again. Sweat gushed, poured down his burning back. The rubberized canvas draped over his head scraped the damp back of his neck. He shivered, and tremors ran along his arms. He looked down: his boots trudged through the sand, each pace no more than twelve inches. Burned red by the sun, the backs of his hands tingled. He peered along the tunnel of shade formed by the shelterhalf tented over his head. The sky tilted. A reddish mound of dirt and shattered rock five feet in front of him tilted, a hot wind blurred the dusty scrub, the stony mountains far in the distance leaned.

"Damn," he said as he tilted right. "Damn it all," he said as he fell.

His mouth was full of dust. Something small, swift and many- legged running across the sand rushed across the back of his right hand.

Down on my face again, he thought. Getting to be a bad habit. Wish it were cooler, greener. Wish this damned desert were somewhere else. Or I were somewhere else.

Stop wishing. The sun doesn't care what you wish, he told himself. Whatever I think, the sun will not fall faster: it will in its own time rise up the sky and sink down it; and if I lie here and pant and sweat my skin will blacken and crack and my tongue will swell until it fills my mouth and chokes me.

I'm bigger, he thought. Got to be. If I'm not bigger, I'm going to become nothing. All my water will evaporate. Ninety-six percent of me will be gone.

Get up, he told himself.

Sure. Get up and double-time it all the way back to the Palms.

Get the hell up.

I'd rather be back in that woods, in the mist. Even though I was fighting there. Where was I then? Where was that? And when? Something about the uniforms, the equipment. The rifle in my hands. Like a hunting rifle. Except for the bayonet.

Get up out of there.

If I can't go back to that woods, I'd just as soon go to the beach.

A thin giggle eased up his throat. Something skittered through the scrub. Something else rushed the other way, halted. But he could not see the quick creatures. Yet again, he thought: a gray haze rising in front of me, shapes moving through it.

The beach, he thought. Sure. Great. That's where I'd like to be. The Pacific. Blue water, surfboards, sand. And chicks. Lots of chicks. Too bad they all recognize the haircut. Still, the beach is better than this. If I can't have the cool foreign woods full of shadows and fury, I'll take the beach.

"SEE HOW IT LOOKS like a bird on its back?" Jack Cushman said. Jack Cushman was blond, tall, husky and handsome. His captain's bars glittered on his collars and he stood up straight: but with each starboard roll of the transport ploughing through the Pacific he leaned forward over the table on which the map lay, and when the transport rolled back to port he leaned toward the bulkhead behind him. "See the pier there? That's the bird's legs. The beach is to the right of the pier. Going inshore, that is. Red Two, they call it."

"Red Two," he said. "A bird's legs. I get the idea, Jack." He stared down at the map: another island. Which we will assault tomorrow morning—in ten hours. A piece of an atoll, a single island in an irregular circle of islands, coral lurking beneath the crystal water of the lagoon from which they would land. "I don't recall hearing its name."

"The operation? GALVANIC." Cushman smiled and nodded: he liked every code name he'd ever heard. For him, at least, every one of them seemed to contain some special, worthy meaning.

"I meant the name of the island, Jack."

"Betty O. At least I think it's pronounced Betty O. Some of them say 'Beh She O.' But whatever. Betty O's part of an atoll called Tarawa.

I never heard of it before. It used to be British. Now it's Japanese. It'll be American tomorrow about lunchtime. Why? Does it matter what it's called?"

"Nice to know where we're going."

"We came up from New Zealand and we're going to take this island, this Betty O, and the rest of the atoll, away from the Japs. What else do you need to know?"

"Are you going to give me that big Mac Marine grin, Jack?"

Cushman gave him his recruiting poster grin and said, "The Navy says it's going to pulverize the place." He leaned away from the table as the transport rolled to port and grinned again, displaying a lot of white teeth. Then he closed his mouth and looked eager. As though he's ready for anything.

Which Captain Cushman better be, he thought. But he said: "You know a lot of naval officers, Jack?"

"Sure. Sure I do. Lots of them."

"And you're *sure* they're going to pulverize the place."

"That's what they tell me."

"I've heard them tell me a lot of things, too. I remember them on the Canal. Or rather, I don't remember them on the Canal. They weren't around a lot. Not the aircraft carriers and not the warships, at least not often. And when they *were* around, the Japanese pretty much sank them."

"Look, *Lieut*enant," Cushman said as he stood up straight as he had learned to stand up straight when he was about to issue an order. But the transport rolled to starboard and Cushman leaned forward and the transport rolled farther to starboard and Cushman lurched forward and had to place his hands on the table to support himself.

"I know, Jack. I know what you're going to tell me about the Navy. I heard it before, at the briefing. Brimming confidence, assurances, warm words about gunfire support. I thought they were going to hand out written guarantees. I'm just telling you: they weren't around on the Canal. I don't recall a single carrier. Sure, they flew in aircraft, and the guys who flew them were great: but the admirals weren't around much. And even their air was an every now and then thing. On the other hand, I remember Marine Air. *And* the Army guys in their Bell P-39 Airacobras. They came, and they stayed, and they went up every time. Worthless aircraft, the P-39. No altitude. The engine behind the seat: I don't know why. I guess for balance, and to let them lay a cannon through the propeller boss. But worthless or not, they came right in every time, right down on the ground. Chewed up a lot of Japanese. And a lot of those P-39 pilots died flying around on the deck like that."

"You don't have confidence in the Navy." Cushman spoke as though he were a general in the Army and was trying to decide whether involvement with the Navy was risky—maybe too risky.

"In the Navy," he said, "too much depends on the guy in charge. And they worry about their ships: losing them, having them damaged, running them into things."

Captain and company commander, Cushman said, "Whereas here in the Marine Corps the guy in charge doesn't mean much. Is that it?"

"That's it," he said.

"You're not very enthusiastic about the chainofcommand," Captain Cushman said.

"I guess not, Jack. But that's the way it is. Fortunately we have a lot of sergeants and enlisted guys who will go on and fight them and kill them when the links in the chain of command snap. So we'll be all right. If we get enough support up front from the Navy's guns. And if the Japanese aren't too tough. Unfortunately, the Japanese are always tough. Every single time."

Cushman brushed aside the ships' naval rifles and the terrifying determination of the individual Japanese and said, "You don't think the planning means anything?"

"The planning, Jack, gets us through the gate, into the arena. Into the game. Then the whistle blows and it's up to the men."

"And the officers."

"I'm not so sure about the officers. Most of us, at your level and mine, get killed right at the front end, Jack. Then a lot of the sergeants get killed. Then the men have to do the job. That's the way the Marine Corps does it. You haven't noticed that?"

"No, I haven't."

"You weren't on the Ridge. On the Ridge, it pretty much ended up with Edson's sergeants, those of them who were still alive, trying to hold the line. They kept shouting, 'Raiders, Raiders, rally to me, rally to me,' while the perimeter contracted. I rallied to a nearby sergeant—Frank Masters. And I was his lieutenant, after all. Everyone just kept shouting something—anything. And shooting. And slashing away. Bayonets, knives, entrenching tools. I don't know where we'd be right now without the men."

"I heard about it. That's why you have your guys whetstoning their entrenching tools?"

"That's it. Look, Jack. I'm just telling you. Be ready. Plans are okay until the first shot is fired. After that, nothing works out like they say it will. Or almost nothing."

"Who's they?"

"They? You know: the ones who make the plans and give the lectures. Who think they've figured it out. Who plan the wars, design the battles, choose the weapons, make the confident announcements. But whatever they say, this island—this Betty O at Tarawa atoll—is going to be harder than anyone seems to think. Harder than the Canal for sure. There's near five thousand Japanese packed into this island, and twenty-six hundred of them are *rigosentai*—Imperial Marines—from the Sasebo 7th Special Naval Landing Force. Along with a lot of other Japanese naval personnel ready to fight to the death. *And* a thousand or so laborers from Korea, Japan and Okinawa."

"How do you know all this?"

"I read the briefing papers, Jack. I also asked around."

"Don't worry about the briefing papers," Cushman said. "And don't listen to rumors. And *don't* worry about the Japs on the island. The Navy's going to pound it to rubble. They're going to *sink* it. You'll see." Cushman stood up straight and raised his voice and spoke every word with care, as though he believed what he was saying.

"I hope you're right, Jack. But I don't think you are."

"If I'm not, why'd you come in here to talk about this? We were fully briefed. Fully. So all the lieutenants in the company know everything they need to know. You among them. And now you're back. Why?"

"I wanted to check a couple of details."

"What's that mean?"

"What have you heard that I haven't, Jack? Anything that wasn't in the briefing? From the Major and up? Anything iffy? Any questions? Doubts?"

"*Doubts*? Nothing. Not a single thing. I'm telling you: no doubts."

"What about the tides? I spoke with that British officer, Holland. Who lived on the atoll, on the next island down? Talked to him when we were training in New Zealand. He was worried about the tides. Not worried. He was adamant: said there won't be enough water to get the landing craft over the reef. The amtracs will make it, but not the LCVPs. And you know the amtracs: three, four miles an hour. If no one's shooting at them."

"The Navy's view is: he's wrong."

"He lived there for sixteen years, Jack. On the island next to Betio. And it was a British island. We didn't have anyone there doing hydrological studies."

"You mean, making measurements? The depth of the water? Tides? What difference does a few inches make?" Cushman asked, as though he really didn't know what difference a few inches made.

"You know how much water a Higgins boat draws, Jack. If there's not that much, and more, there will be trouble. Holland said something about a dodging tide this time of the month."

"You're spreading alarm and despondency," Cushman said, as though he had just remembered the phrase. "You don't want to make everybody nervous."

"You're not everybody, Jack, and I'm not spreading anything. I'm asking a question: have you heard anything else?"

"Nothing. Confidence reigns. We're going to walk in and shovel the dirt down on their corpses lying in the holes the Navy punches in the island."

"I hope you're right, Jack."

"I *am* right."

"All right, then," he said. But he knew Cushman didn't know what the hell. He didn't know anything about water, islands, or the Japanese. In particular, he knew nothing about the *rigosentai*. Who will fight to the death. Or kill themselves if they think they're going to be captured.

Ten hours later, crouched behind the wall of coconut logs at the top of the narrow beach, shoulders hunched beneath the drifting smoke, he listened for a break in the roar of weapons firing, ordnance exploding and heavy shells rumbling down the sky. But there was no pause: we're firing everything we've got, he thought. And the Japanese gunners are working hard inside their bunkers and blockhouses, their machinegun and smallarms and cannon fire ripping across the narrow margin of the island which I, and hundreds of others, have gained. And to which, he thought, those of us who have come this far cling for protection, hiding in the temporary safety of a seawall five coconut logs high.

He glanced over his shoulder: out into the bright lagoon beyond the reef and the end of the long pier that extended over the coral to the edge of the deep water. A destroyer was easing through the lagoon, firing all its guns at the island.

Beside him Martin lay in the sand shivering as though he were cold, coughing blood and staring at his gray hands pressed against the broad, leaky wound in his chest.

He had called for a corpsman. None had come. Can't hear, he thought: because of the tremendous noise. Can't see, he thought: because of the smoke drifting across the island that obscures the bright blue sky. Can't move: because they're wounded, or because they're tending other casualties lying along the beach among sprawled corpses, battered crates of supplies and amtracs halted at the water's edge by antitank fire. Or they're dead inside the amtracs struck by Japanese cannon fire as they tried to mount the seawall.

Discarded weapons littered the sand: one discarded weapon, he thought, for each man dead. And one for each man wounded. He glanced along the seawall: here and there a man sat with his back to the coconut logs, staring at the lagoon, transported by shock and horror from this terrible place to somewhere else, each of them waiting for fate to come and deal him life, or not.

And one discarded weapon, he thought, for each man who has broken. The dead, the wounded, and those who have snapped. A lot of men gone. A high rate of wastage.

He rolled over, leaned back against the seawall and looked out across the eight-hundred-yard-wide coral reef that lay between the beach and the channel in the lagoon. The long pier built by the company that bought and shipped the island's copra lay to his right. Men in the water beneath the pier slogged from one piling to the next, coming toward the beach. Away from the pier, up to their chests in the bluewhite water, other men were walking toward the island, plodding out one pace and the next as though they had had a long day and were tired and nearing home. But as they came on, the racket of weapons firing came out to meet them: Japanese bullets, mortar rounds and cannon shells cut at them and frothed the water around them.

One rifleman, his broad shoulders supporting his pack and rifle, his fists holding two boxes of machinegun ammunition he had tied to his harness with yellow rope, tried to run. The brown stock of his rifle stroked the water like a paddle with each slow plunging stride. He lunged forward through the water and the tremendous noise, lunged forward again, lunged into a hole in the coral reef. He bobbed up, shook his head. He looked surprised: as though he had been told a careful survey had found no holes in the reef. He flung up his hands: his rifle's sling was twisted about his right elbow. He paddled and slapped at the frothing water. But the sodden bulk of his pack and the compact mass of the ammunition boxes tied to his harness dragged him down. He beat the water with his arms, tried to swim, lunged upward: to thrust his panting mouth above the surface of the sea. Machinegun bullets whipped the water around him, split his face open, scattered blood across the water. As he sank, he held his clenched fists up against the sky.

At the edge of the reef a Higgins boat bobbed. He watched a naval officer in the boat reach over the side to a Marine crouched on the edge of the reef among other Marines. The water around the crouching Marines was tinged red. The wounded, he thought. Didn't even make it ashore. The naval officer slid his hands under the Marine's armpits and heaved him up out of the sea. He wrestled the Marine over the high steel side of the Higgins boat as though he were boating a big fish. As the naval officer dragged the last of the wounded man inboard, bullets struck the boat's side. The naval officer looked over the side of the Higgins boat, glanced at the silver furrows in the metal, shook his head at the burning island and displayed his profile to the Japanese. Then he reached down over the side to lift another Marine.

This naval officer, he thought, is going to become a movie star. If, that is, he lives through this day. And the rest of the war.

He turned toward a voice yelling in his left ear. Sergeant Masters knelt beside him, shouting through the huge crashing noise: "Gotta get out of here, Lieutenant. Goddamnit we *got* to get over this wall and do something. We can't just *lie* here, Lieutenant."

"I know, Frank," he shouted. "How many are left?" He glanced at Martin lying beside him. "Ready to go, I mean."

"Got twelve men of our own, and two or three from the next platoon to the right that got chewed up coming in. Everone of the fourteen or fifteen of them's to the right along this here wall of coconut trunks."

"A third of the platoon? That's all we've got?"

"And the two or three others from the next platoon in the line."

"Two or three. That's great. Great planning. And great naval gunfire. Just great. But all right: we go with what we've got. That's what they say, isn't it, Frank?"

"I don't know, Lieutenant," Sergeant Masters said. He grinned. "You know sergeants don't get too many of those kinds of lectures. We got work to do."

"Lucky you," he said. "Tell six of them to stay to the right. Move the others to my left. Start everyone throwing grenades at the bunkers out front." Machinegun fire ripped and gnawed at the shredded top of the seawall two feet above his head. "Make sure the men with automatic weapons are on the flanks. Got it, Frank? Six on the right, six on the left, the automatic weapons at the right and left ends of the line. Have the guys from the other platoon stay to the right. I'll go up and over from right here when we've got the Japanese keeping their heads down inside those bunkers. Make sure they lay down everything they've got, Frank. There are three bunkers right in front of us. Three I can see, that is. We know they've got more of them behind these three."

"I saw the three of them, Lieutenant," Sergeant Masters said.

He watched Masters lick his lips and thought: thinking about the bunkers. Low mounds blanketed with sand, a black, horizontal embrasure in the forward slope of each mound, the muzzle of a machinegun in each black slit flashing red and silver.

"Don't think about it, Frank," he said. "Tell them to throw grenades and then to start shooting at the slits. But tell Martinez and Stills to keep on throwing grenades. They're better throwing things than they are with rifles."

"Our ball players."

"That's it. They've got the arms." He raised his voice to be heard above the rising roar of weapons firing, men shouting, shells exploding. "When everyone's up and firing and Stills and Martinez are laying grenades in there, I'll take off."

Sergeant Masters looked at him, swallowed and nodded.

Sure, he thought: take off. Get up on your knees, breathe a couple of times, stand up, hoist yourself over this wall. And see what happens next. It *sounds* easy enough. Until you raise your head enough to see the top log of the seawall chewed down to soft, splintered yellowwhite pulp by Japanese machinegun fire. Until you see the muzzles of the machineguns in the bunkers flickering; and see the reinforced concrete structures clustered back from the beach behind the bunkers, more weapons firing from slits high in their walls.

Masters shook his head, grinned and said, "I thought the Navy was gonna take care of all this."

"So did I. But it seems they fucked up. So we're going to have to do it. If we want to get off this beach, that is. And we want to get off this beach. You know what staying on this beach is going to mean. Go on and tell them, Frank."

Masters said, "Okay, lemme go on then." He turned and crawled away, shoulder scraping the wall of coconut logs, left hand reaching to pull himself forward, the butt of the rifle in his right fist dragging in the sand. As he worked his way along the line of sprawled men huddled in the angle of the seawall and the sandy beach, he shouted at each of them. They nodded and glanced away from Masters: along the wall.

At me, he thought: at their officer. Their lieutenant, who gets to tell them what to do next, even if it's to stand up and fire two rounds and be killed by a lash of machinegun fire. Great, he thought as he watched Masters working toward the end of the line, passing the word about what was to happen next. As Masters spoke to Martinez, Martinez grinned and nodded, working his right arm as though he were standing on the mound, getting ready to pitch a no-hitter. Beyond Martinez, Crane glanced to his left along the wall, caught his lieutenant's eye, winked, grinned and shook his head as though he didn't think much of the lieutenant's plan but was willing to go along.

Crane scrabbled toward him, McPherson, Peters, Gudrow, Thomas, and Martinez coming on behind. As they crawled past him, each of them nodded. Thomas said, "Hey, Lieutenant. How's it going?"

"Seems like a walk in the park to me, Thomas. What do you think? What about you, Martinez?" he asked. "A walk in the park?"

"Haw," Thomas said as he crawled past, his weapon lying across his elbows. "A walk in the park. Pretty good, Lieutenant. Haw."

"Walk in the park?" Martinez said. "Choo crazy, Lieutenant?"

"I think everyone on this fucking island is crazy, Martinez. What do you think?"

"You bet, Lieutenant. Crazy." Martinez crawled on, a bag of grenades slung over his right shoulder dragging in the sand.

He shouted across Martinez's back at Thomas crawling away: "Fire into the slit in the lefthand bunker, Thomas. Whatever else, keep that machinegunner down."

"Slit in the lefthand bunker," Thomas shouted through the roar of machinegun fire whipping over the log wall two feet above his head, splintering it, flicking yellowwhite chunks of coconut log toward the smooth sliding edge of the sea. "Shoot right into it."

Crawling toward him through the noise, kneeing the sand, Sergeant Masters' hoarse voice shouted, "What the hell are you jawing about, Thomas? Get the hell along there. What the fuck you think is going on here, anyway?"

"On my way, Sergeant," Thomas shouted.

Sitting with his back against the logs, he stared out at the lagoon. The destroyer pounded one shell after another into the island. As he watched men shot down in the water through which they waded toward the beach, he shouted, "You remember the Canal, Frank? This is worse than that. Whatever plan they had last midnight is gone to hell now. Now it's us and them: there isn't anything else. I don't think we've got radio contact with the fleet, or even with that destroyer offshore. So it's us and them."

"The fucking Japanese," Masters said.

"Those are the ones."

"All right, then. We start working on them as soon as everybody's set."

"That's it. Everyone starts throwing. Like I said. And then Stills and Martinez keep on with the grenades while the rest of us start firing. I'll give the word when to go. We're going to have to leave Martin here. A corpsman will find him." He glanced at Martin lying beside him in the sand. Martin's torso and arms trembled. Blood from the terrible wound high in the man's chest stained his shirt to the belt. Not long, he thought. Minutes more. At most.

Sergeant Masters glanced at Martin, nodded, and said, "What do you mean, the word? What word?" Masters asked. "No one can hear anything with all this here noise."

For certain, he thought. The pall of smoke above the island reverberated with the explosion of heavy shells, vicious bursts of smallarms fire, the thump of detonating mortar rounds and the high rattling sweep of machineguns.

"Lieutenant?" Masters said.

"Tell them: when I go over the wall. That's the word. Tell them to keep an eye out for my move."

"One eye on the Nipponese, one eye on the Lieutenant? What you think we got here, Lieutenant, a bunch of iguanas can look two ways at once?"

"Frank, I tell you what. *You* watch me. And then you yell at them to come on. You've got enough voice for it."

"Think I'm loud, Lieutenant?"

"No," he said. "Not loud. Penetrating. I remember hearing you on the Ridge. Heard you along there calling, 'Rally to me, rally to me.'"

"I couldn't think what else to yell. And I'll tell you: I wanted company. With all those Nipponese coming up the slope? I would have been happy to see the Army right then."

"The *Army*?"

"Whoever. Boy Scouts. At a time like that? Old men with shotguns, even, Lieutenant. There was a time there that night, about ten minutes of it, I guess, when I didn't think any of us were going to come down off the Ridge. Come down off it alive, I mean. But we don't have the time to reminisce right now."

"You're right about that," he said. "Okay. Watch for me to stand up."

"I'm sure the fuck glad I'm no officer," Masters said.

"You'd make a fine officer, Frank. Better than I am. And you may be in command in a couple of minutes even if you don't want to be an officer. You know what to do."

"I do?" Masters grimaced and shook his head as though they were back in the company's office in New Zealand, chatting with the captain about an administrative glitch. Instead of crouching on this beach in the south central Pacific, getting ready to get up and go into the dark storm two feet above their heads.

"You do."

"Get up and go for them," Masters said.

"That's it," he said. "And the rest of it: do it smart."

"Unlike the plan that got us this far."

"That's it. I guess the admirals and generals are wondering what the hell happened. I'll bet they're looking over their briefing papers right now, trying to figure what went wrong. And I bet they don't know anything more than you or I."

"That's what I like about The Marine Corps," Masters said. "In the end, everyone's the same. It's only that . . ."

"What?" he asked.

"In the end, some are alive and others don't make it to the other end of the pipe."

"And the ones higher up the ladder have the least chance of dying," he said. "Right?"

"Right," Masters said.

"It's lucky you and I aren't carrying much rank, Frank."

"Lucky?"

"Sure. What would these young Marines never seen a shot fired in anger before today do without you and me here to show them how to do it?"

"Uh-huh," Masters said. "Sea stories. I think it's about time we cut the conversation and get started, Lieutenant. I don't want the men thinking too much, if you know what I mean."

"Okay, let's do it," he said as he picked a grenade from the sand. He glanced at Martin. Martin was dead. Blood was crusted on his mouth and throat and chest and puddled in his crotch. His hands still covered the wound that had killed him. Flies crawled across his hands, feasting on blood.

Masters looked at Martin, grimaced, hunched his shoulders and crawled away on his hands and knees, toward the right and then back again, to the left, shouting out orders as he went, his piercing voice carrying through the crashing noise of firing weapons and detonating explosives. As Masters shouted, men along the line lying in the sand turned, faced the wall of coconut logs, held their weapons closer, brushed sand from the breeches, lifted grenades, tugged at their harness. At the end of the line to his left, Thomas hefted his weapon, slid a magazine into the breech, slapped it home and nodded as though everything was going to be all right.

I sure hope so, he thought as he turned away from Martin's corpse, faced the seawall and knelt. A vicious burst of machinegun fire from beyond the seawall sawed at the top coconut log ten feet to his left.

As the gun traversed away, he thought: time to go.

He nodded at Frank Masters. Masters looked at him and shouted something he could not hear. The men all along the line hefted grenades.

He poked his head up above the splintered top log of the seawall. The muzzle of the machinegun in the bunker in front of him was angled to the left. He ducked down, pulled the pin from the grenade in his fist, shouted right and left along the line, opened his fist. The grenade's handle flicked away and the pin snapped down, igniting the fuse. He stood up, lobbed the grenade over the seawall at the bunker and ducked down. He picked up another grenade, armed it, stood and threw it at the bunker. As he picked up a third grenade and pulled the pin, he glanced right and left. Along the line of his reduced platoon the men were throwing. He watched as Frank Masters stood half-erect to throw. Thomas rested his automatic weapon on the seawall, aimed with care, fired a full magazine at the embrasure in the lefthand bunker and ducked as a machinegun fired at him, kicking up sand and chipping away at the top log of the seawall. As the machinegun traversed away, Thomas rose up, aimed and fired another magazine. Masters flung two grenades and began to fire his rifle.

He picked up his rifle, stood up into the smoke and noise, slid the rifle over the seawall, aimed at the black rectangular embrasure in the bunker in front of him, fired one aimed round after another. Not like the Canal, he thought. No room to maneuver here, no hills, no jungle. Here we are chest to chest with them. And soon we'll be among them.

He fired the last round in the clip, ducked down behind the wall and reloaded. Every man in his platoon was firing. He looked at Frank Masters. Masters nodded at him. He laid his rifle on the sand beyond the top of the seawall, hoisted himself up and slithered over the wall. Off the beach at last, he thought. A pace and I'm off the beach and on the island.

To his left, Thomas was firing methodical bursts at the embrasure of the bunker in front of him. Frank Masters was climbing the wall.

To his right four men—Heinrich, Morgan, Stills and Worley—were over the wall, shooting and throwing grenades at the firing slit in the bunker toward which he was crawling. He watched as Heinrich threw a grenade, fumbled a second one from his harness, threw it after the first. The second grenade exploded against the firing slit of the bunker. The machinegun in the bunker stopped firing. The muzzle of the weapon pointed up to the left.

Farther to the right, more men were coming over the wall, some of them firing and throwing while others crawled toward the bunker to the right.

He looked to his left. Frank Masters lay face down in the sand at the top of the seawall. The back of his shirt soaked with blood. Thomas, helmet tilted forward over his eyes, hoisted himself over the seawall and began shooting at the firing slit of the bunker on the left.

He crawled on through the smoke and noise, hands and knees working against the sand strewn with debris—chunks of concrete, chips of fibrous wood, a Marine boot with a jagged severed shin sticking from it, unidentifiable ripped and smashed bits of equipment. Fifty feet to the middle bunker, he thought. The barrel of the machinegun in the embrasure still pointed up to the left. A grenade thrown from behind him detonated against the firing slit. Keeping their heads down, he thought.

Might as well get this over with, he thought.

He dropped his rifle, unholstered his pistol, stood up into a crouch and ran forward, angling toward the right-hand slope of the bunker in front of him. The muzzle of the machinegun in the firing slit jerked down, shifted this way and that, steadied and swung toward him. He flung himself face down into a depression in the sand. The machinegun fired across his back. Behind him someone screamed. He looked over his shoulder: Stills was kicking at the sand, clutching his abdomen with both hands. Half of Stills's skull was gone, his gray brain exposed to the light. Worley knelt beside Stills, a cud of chewing tobacco in his left cheek, firing his rifle at the machinegun's flashing muzzle.

He watched as Worley fired a full eight-round clip, reloaded and began firing again.

The machinegun ceased firing. He jerked himself erect and ran forward toward the right-hand slope of the bunker. Got to be an entrance at the back, he thought. He flung himself down into the lee of the bunker and crawled forward. Someone inside the bunker was screaming. Someone else was shouting. In Japanese. Screaming shouting Japanese, he thought. Good. He crept along the curving slope of the bunker, looking for the entrance. A hatch of cross-braced planks concealed beneath the sand rose. A hand gripped the edge of the hatch. The rounded top of a helmet appeared and a man stepped up into the light and noise and smoke.

Naval uniform, he thought. Imperial Marine. *Rigosentai.*

He aimed the pistol and shot the Japanese in the face. The man spun away from the hatch, ducking as though he might escape what had come for him. He put his hands to his destroyed face, shrieked, and stumbled down the bunker's mild rear slope.

As he crawled forward to the edge of the hatch, he worked a grenade from his left trousers pocket. Before he could pull the pin from the neck of the grenade a second Japanese stepped up out of the hatch, his flopping right arm slick with blood. He shot the Japanese in the chest. The heavy round flung him rolling and flopping down the slope.

He stood up, yanked the cotter pin from the grenade, tossed the grenade into the bunker, kicked the hatch shut and ran and leapt away into a broad depression behind the bunker's entrance. The Japanese he had shot in the face sat nearby, screaming and screaming, hands hiding his shattered jaws and blinded eyes.

How the hell can this guy be alive? he wondered. I shot him in the *face.* He crawled across the sand, held the muzzle of the pistol two inches from the back of the man's right hand pressed over his face. As the grenade detonated inside the bunker, he fired through the Japanese's hand.

He squirmed in the sand, turning until he faced the rear of the bunker. The explosion of the grenade had blown the hatch open. Lying just below the low summit of the bunker, Thomas was firing his weapon, pounding rounds through the smoke and noise. He raised his head farther: Japanese were darting up out of the ground, sprinting from the rear of the bunker to his left. Thomas killed them one after the other as they ran. Lying beside Thomas, Martinez' arm flicked up, flung a grenade. He flung another and a third. All three fell in a neat series into a trench fifty feet behind the bunker at which Thomas was firing. An instant, and the first grenade exploded. Then the second, then the third. Screams rose with each eruption of smoke and sand.

A Marine on his hands and knees, a lighted cigar in his mouth, appeared beside Thomas and Martinez on top of the first bunker. He glanced at them as he scrambled past and flung himself down the slope, a heavy sack slapping and bouncing against his right hip. As he crawled forward, the cigar in his teeth see-sawed up and down. He shifted the cigar to the corner of his mouth and said, "Lieutenant? Corporal Mitchell. Got some TNT charges here I can make a dent in these bunkers with if you want."

"I want," he said. "How do you want to do it?"

"Nothing fancy. You cover me and I blow the sonsofbitches." He took the cigar out of his mouth and said, "Hate these damned cigars. Smoke's too heavy. But they're reliable when it comes to lighting fuse." He dug into the sack lying beside his right hip, drew out a rectangular solid of TNT blocks taped together. A trim fuse four inches long sprouted from the end of the block. "All set to go," Mitchell said. "Light her and let her rip. You want to start with this one here?"

"I killed the men in there." He nodded at the two Japanese lying dead in the sand.

"May be more than a couple in each of these here bunkers, Lieutenant. Best to be sure, don't you think? And I got eight of these here charges all primed and ready."

He thought about Japanese lurking in the dark inside the bunker, crafty and determined, waiting for the chance to shoot them in the back. Sure, he thought: of course some of them stayed behind. "You're the boss," he told Mitchell. "We'll take them in the order you want."

"You got it. Best get your guys down off there, though. These here charges make a hell of a bang and a hell of a bigger mess."

He waved at Thomas and Martinez. As he leapt down the slope, Martinez shouted at Thomas, "Choo see how I got those bastards in the trench, Tomas?" Rolling his eyes at Martinez's enthusiasm, Thomas grinned and shook his head as the two of them sprawled in the sand near Mitchell.

"This is Mitchell," he said. "He's going to blow these bunkers for us. We're going to cover him while he does it."

"Sounds good to me," Thomas said.

"Choo see me kill those bastards, Lieutenant?"

"I saw," he said. "You're doing good work. Keep that bag of grenades handy."

"Sergeant Masters was killed," Thomas said. "The sonsofbitches killed him."

"I saw," he said.

"And Stills," Thomas said. "They shot him in the head. Just after you went over the wall, Lieutenant. He raised up to throw and they shot him."

"I saw him," he said. "But let's forget about that for now. We've got work to do."

"I agree," Mitchell said. "Listen, Martinez. You toss a grenade in that entrance. Then you, Lieutenant, and you," he said to Thomas, "shoot into the entrance when Martinez here is out of the way. That'll keep them away from the hatch so's I can get close enough to shove this charge right up against them. All right?"

"I already tossed a grenade in there," he said.

"Nothing like doing the same job twice, Lieutenant," Mitchell said. "We can't know how many men they got lurking in any one of these here bunkers."

"Sounds good to me," Thomas said. "A grenade, then the charge. While we cover you."

"Sounds good to me, too," Martinez said. "These bastards killed Brown. I'm going to kill every one of them I see. Choo understand me?"

"We understand, Martinez," he said. "Mitchell, if it sounds all right to my guys here," he said, "it's fine by me."

"Okay, Lieutenant," Mitchell said. "Martinez. A grenade down the hatch there?"

"Sure thing," Martinez said. "Easy."

Martinez crawled up the slope toward the hatchway from which the two Japanese he had killed had stepped up out of the bunker into the roaring, smoky sun light. Ten feet from the open hatchway Martinez rolled onto his back and plucked a grenade from his bag. He juggled it, pulled the pin, opened his fingers and let the spoon flick away. He glanced over his shoulder up the slope and flicked the grenade backward over his head. The grenade fell through the hatchway.

Martinez grinned at them.

"The guy's got style," Mitchell said.

From inland a machinegun fired a single burst. The bullets pounded into Martinez's chest and gut, hammered his abdomen and thighs, severed the fine nerves that had controlled his easy compact movements. Martinez shivered and squirmed, his joints jerking and twisting without restraint.

The grenade Martinez had tossed into the bunker's entrance exploded and Mitchell said, "You guys fire at them shooting from behind. All I got is a pistol."

He turned, looked inland. The muzzle of the machinegun flashed at him through the smoke drifting across the island.

"See it, Thomas? In that blockhouse or headquarters or whatever it is? There in the second story? I gauge the range is two hundred feet." Thomas nodded and began to fire one aimed round after another at the muzzleflashes of the weapon in the second story of the concrete structure. The machinegun ceased firing and the weapon's muzzle jerked back from the embrasure.

"Good shooting, Thomas," he said. He rolled over and looked up the slope: at Martinez's broken body and at Mitchell, cigar in his teeth, taped block of explosives in his left hand, crouching as he ran upward. As he ran past Martinez's tattered bloody corpse, he took the cigar from his mouth, touched it to the tip of the fuse, hefted the block as the fuse sputtered and lobbed it into the bunker's entrance. Then he flung himself backward down the slope, off the bunker: away from what was coming.

Inside the bunker someone shrieked. Before he could stop shrieking, the charge detonated. The ground rumbled and shook. A moment, and the low conical summit of the bunker erupted. Lengths of coconut log heaved upward. He saw the silhouette of a Nambu machinegun and a hunk of a man's chest whirl up through the rising pall of sand and dust. Martinez, he thought. He looked. Martinez lay on the bunker's slope, the lower half of his corpse blanketed with sand.

"Got *those* sonsofbitches," Thomas said.

"That's it," he said.

Mitchell crawled toward them. His narrow sweaty face was speckled with sand. He grinned and said, "Almost as good as a seventy-five millimeter cannon round, they say. Makes a bang, don't it?"

"Good work," he said. "Which one do you want to do next?" he asked Mitchell.

"The one to the right as you face inland," Mitchell said, pointing at the bunker. "Then—depending on what happens—we'll go to that trench behind it and on toward that concrete building inland they were shooting at us from. You did good stopping that gun firing," he told Thomas.

"Thomas is an expert," he said.

"I'm thankful he is," Mitchell said.

"We'd better get out of here," he said.

"Sure thing, Lieutenant," Mitchell said.

"Here come the rest of them," Thomas said.

He looked: Heinrich, Morgan, Worley and three others—Peters, Gudrow and Cable—were approaching, crawling across the sand, skirting the bunker Mitchell had blown. Heinrich got up in a crouch and ran forward. A machinegun began to fire toward the seawall from the bunker Mitchell had pointed at. Morgan tossed a grenade and the machinegun stopped firing.

"I thought I killed them running out of that one?" Thomas said. "I thought Marty and I killed them all while they were trying to get out of there."

"Seems most of them leave in a rush," Mitchell said, "but a couple men stay behind."

"To fool us," Thomas said, as though he didn't like playing with cheaters. He faced inland, aimed his weapon and began to fire single shots at the two-story blockhouse.

"That's what they do," Mitchell said. "Doesn't matter. The orders were: deal with ever one these bunkers one after the other. Be *sure* they ain't no living Japanese left in any of them."

"Best orders I've heard all day," he said. As he spoke, the machinegun in the two-story building back from the beach began firing again. But they lay in low ground behind the blown bunker and the machinegun fire hammered over their heads, pounding bullets into Martinez's corpse lying on the slope of the bunker. Martinez jerked and shivered as though he were waking from a bad dream.

"We could use those grenades your guy Martinez has with him," Mitchell suggested as Heinrich crawled up to them.

"Right," he said. He squirmed about and propped himself up on his right elbow.

Heinrich glanced up at the bunker Mitchell's charge had torn apart. He saw Martinez's corpse, grimaced and said, "They got Marty."

"That's it," he said. "Where's the rest of them?"

"Five down, three of them killed. Stills and Willard and some guy from another platoon I don't know his name. Crane and McPherson are all torn up and I don't think McPherson's going to make it. The rest are coming on. There were some others from the platoon to our right but I don't know where they are."

He looked back at Morgan, Worley, Peters, Gudrow and Cable squirming forward across the sand as Thomas began to fire inland again.

"We could use those grenades," Mitchell said.

"I'll get them," he said.

Thomas turned toward him and said, "No, Lieutenant. I'll go." Thomas crouched. As though, he thought, he's thinking about running ten miles. But no one can run ten miles on this island: this island is not ten miles long.

He grabbed Thomas' arm and said, "No. You stay here. I need you to shoot at those bastards with the machinegun in the second story there. And the rest of you," he said. "Stay here and keep their heads down."

"Wait for the rest of them to come up before you go out there for those grenades, Lieutenant," Heinrich cautioned. "We're not going anywhere till they get here anyhow."

"No. I don't want them here. Wave them off. Have them head to the right along this low ground toward the next bunker," he said. "I don't want everybody all bunched up in one place. I don't like it crowded."

Mitchell grinned and said, "Make a hell of a mess all right if we got an artillery round in here."

"That's it," he said. As Heinrich began waving his arms and shouting into the noise, he crouched like a sprinter in the blocks. You better run like hell, he told himself. And don't forget to zigzag while you're doing it. He glanced at Thomas aiming at the concrete blockhouse from which the machinegun had fired and killed Martinez.

As Thomas began firing into the roaring crash of weapons hammering all across the island, he shoved himself up and ran forward, crouching and darting right and left as he slogged through the smoke. Bullets snapped about him, struck the sand in front of him, struck the sand to his left. Behind him, rifles joined Thomas' racketing automatic weapon. "I see the bastard," Heinrich shouted.

He ploughed on through the loose sand, climbing the rear slope of the bunker. Ahead, Martinez's corpse sprawled: his limbs had been broken and his guts had slid from his belly. Chewed up, he thought. That fucking machinegunner, playing with his corpse. The fucking Japanese and their fucking weird ways.

More bullets snapped in the air about his head, struck the ground all about him.

Or maybe not so weird, he thought: maybe he was finding the range. Maybe he saw Martinez take the grenade from his bag and knew someone would come out to get the bag. And so he used Martinez as an aiming stake: to be sure he would have the range if anyone showed himself.

As he slogged upward, he listened to Thomas and Heinrich firing. Then they found the range and the machinegun ceased firing.

Crouched, head bent, sweaty and gasping, he jogged the last few feet to Martinez's grotesque corpse. He reached for the bag of grenades caught beneath his riven torso. He jerked at the bag as though he feared Martinez might try to hold on to it. The bag slid from beneath the body as though Martinez had decided to give it up. The bag's strap was severed, the canvas of the heavy sack soaked with drying blood gritty with sand.

He held the bloody sack of grenades against his chest. The grenades inside the sack chocked one against another. He turned. A bullet struck the sand close by his left foot. He saw muzzleflashes in loopholes high in the concrete wall of the blockhouse. Thomas and Heinrich fired at the muzzleflashes and the volume of Japanese fire diminished. But it did not stop. Sonsofbitches, he thought as he began to slog down the slope. And leaving Martinez behind, he thought. Shit. We'll be back, Marty. Or someone will.

A whispering screech slid down the sky. Mortar, he thought. On the Canal, the sound of the propellant igniting in the tube had been distinct, the flight of the round a smooth falling murmur. Here there is no jungle and the sound is keener: but it's the same fucking weapon. He flung himself part way down the rear slope of the bunker. Mitchell knelt in the sand, watching him. Thomas and Heinrich were still firing at the two-story building. To the right, twenty feet away along the low ground Morgan, Worley, Peters, Gudrow and Cable crouched in the depression, taking cover from the Japanese fire.

The mortar shell struck Peters in the back. Blinding light and black smoke, brilliant fire. The explosion decapitated Peters, severed his arms, bisected him at the waist and scattered the pieces of him across the sand. Worley's legs were bent at awkward angles; his gut and groin were a ruck of torn, sodden red cloth and glistening lumps of things torn out of him.

Another whispering screech descended through the smoky sky. The second shell struck the sand between Morgan and Gudrow. They leaned from the roar of the detonating shell.

But no one, he thought, can lean that far. Morgan's bloodied face lay still against the sand, his arms caught beneath his quivering body. The blast had stripped Gudrow's shirt away. His pale skin was streaked with blood that pumped from wounds slashed in his heaving chest.

Cable sat up in the whirling smoke. Blood bright and slick filled the orbits of his eyes. Blinded, he thought. And more: a piece of the mortar round had torn a ragged hole in Cable's side. Cable raised his right hand to his face, leaned forward and fell onto the sand.

He hugged the earth as a third rustling screech fell down the noisy, smoky sky. As he glanced toward Heinrich, Thomas and Mitchell, he saw Mitchell fling his sack of taped and fused blocks of TNT away from him.

The mortar round—black, cylindrical and smooth: he saw it as it fell—hammered the sand beside Heinrich. The detonation heaved Heinrich upward, flung his rifle away and tore off his right arm. The blast rolled Thomas and Mitchell across the sand, ripped the weapon from Thomas' hand, shattered the stock and bent the barrel. Thomas hunched his shoulders as his dented helmet leapt from his head and bounced across the sand. Metal had pierced Thomas' skull: he raised his shivering, jerking hands and fell onto his face. His legs kicked and kicked again before he lay still.

Shirt and trousers burning, his body pierced by shell fragments, the punctures welling blood, Mitchell fell across Thomas' still back.

None of them made a sound, he thought as he got up and ran forward into the bitter smoke, clutching the bag of grenades Martinez had carried. None of them. He grabbed up Mitchell's sack of charges and ran on: toward the low place in the ground in which the rest of his men lay dead.

And now? he wondered as he lay panting ten feet from the ripped corpses of Peters, Morgan and the other three. Here I am with a bag of grenades and a sack of taped blocks of TNT and all my men are dead. What the hell now?

"Sir?"

A curious, concerned voice, he thought. Not used to speaking to officers. He looked back the way he had come, yanked his pistol from its holster and pointed it where he looked. Up on the slope of the bunker Mitchell had blown, climbing through the rubble of coconut logs and shattered equipment, skirting Martinez's corpse, a Marine was coming on through the drifting smoke. Can't be more than nineteen, twenty years old, he thought. Like most of the rest of them.

"Run, for God's sake!" he yelled up the slope. The boy started as though he had been caught doing something vile. Then he leapt past Martinez's corpse, ran zig-zagging down the slope jumping over coconut logs and debris. He slid the last ten feet through the sand as though he were stealing second base. His narrow face and thin neck were sunburned. Cool blue eyes examined the corpses strewn around him as though he had seen nothing this day that he had not seen before.

"Who are you?" He shoved the pistol into its holster.

"I was on the right, Lieutenant. I tried to help out with one of them wounded. I think his name was Stills. He was shot coming over the seawall. A head wound. He died pretty quickly."

"You're from the platoon to our right?"

"Yes."

"We're going to go on along this low ground," he told the boy. They were shouting at one another, voices raised to be heard. "You're going to cover me. Can you do that?"

"Sure."

"I'm going to blow that bunker," he said, pointing toward the low hump of sand piled over the rough structure of logs beneath. "Then we're going to move inland: to the trench behind the bunker. Take a look."

The boy popped his head up, jerked it down. "I see it."

"Martinez and Thomas killed most of them in the bunker and the trench. But we're going to make sure every damned one of them's dead. When we're finished with this bunker and the trench, we're going inland. See the blockhouse there, two hundred feet inland? Two stories, with a yellow stripe painted ten feet up near the corner?"

"With the palm tree leaning against it?"

"That's it. I'm going to blow that one too."

"Okay," he said.

"I want you to stay under cover, you understand me? I'll grenade the bunker and stuff one of these charges into it and you shoot at anything that moves. At anything trying to shoot me. Or you. Clear?"

"Clear, yes, sir."

"Don't call me sir."

"Okay," the boy said.

"Collect all the ammunition you can from these men killed here. We'll need it."

"Ammunition. Yes." The boy slung his rifle and crawled away among the corpses, tugged at their equipment belts, opened the ammunition pouches, stuffed clips into his pockets. He crawled back, rifle seesawing across his back. His pockets were stuffed with grenades and clips of ammunition and he carried a canteen in his right fist. The canteen's cover was unsnapped—and bloody.

"Thought we could use some water," the boy said. "I lost my canteen somewhere. This was Peters'. I took it from him."

"Good thought," he said. Thirsty, he thought. Gritty sand in my mouth, the taste of burned powder on my tongue. "You drink first."

The boy unscrewed the canteen's cap and said, "Here's to Peters. At least he carried a full canteen." He drank and passed the canteen over.

"What do you mean, 'at least'?" he asked. He raised the canteen and drank.

"Peters was a real bastard. Used to be a corporal in my platoon before he came over to you. Even for a corporal, though, he was a real bastard. Always on about something or other didn't make any difference. And mean, too: he liked to be mean."

"I didn't know," he said. But I should have, he thought.

"It doesn't matter now," the boy said.

"No, I guess it doesn't," he said. "Jesus, that water is warm."

The boy tilted his young face and grinned.

"Hang on to that canteen. We'll need it later." If, he thought, there is a later.

"Right," the boy said. As he snapped the canvas cover over the shoulders of the canteen and hooked it to his belt he grinned again.

"Something funny?" he asked.

"I was down on the beach back near the pier getting ammunition out of a stalled amtrac. The Colonel stopped me, asked me what was happening. Never spoke to the Colonel before. But I told him what I knew. Then he said, 'You look like you need a drink,' and handed me his canteen. I sure was thirsty. I took a big mouthful before I figured out it was liquor."

"When the Colonel says 'a drink', he means it."

"That's what I found out. Wish he'd told me, though. I don't drink liquor much."

"That's good," he said. "Stick to beer. Or water. Liquor's bad for the liver. And the brain." The boy looked at him as though he were insane to consider the future of his liver and brain. "I know," he told the boy. "We'll talk about it later. Right now, let's go on."

"You don't think we ought maybe to wait for some others?" the boy asked.

"Look around," he said. "There aren't any others." He himself did not look: he did not want to see Thomas, Martinez, Mitchell, Heinrich and the rest of them dead. He had seen them killed: that was enough.

The boy looked around. Then he nodded, as though he knew, now, that everyone else who had come over the seawall with him had gone on somewhere and left him behind. "Sure. I see. All of them killed. Or wounded, farther back. I sure hope Crane makes it. He seemed like a good guy. Shot in the legs. Right knee all messed up. But he's got a chance. He wasn't that bad. I put tourniquets on him and he was talking when I left him and came on."

"You did all right," he said. "You ready?" The boy nodded. "We'll crawl along this low place. See the bunker ahead there?"

"Yes." A smooth mound of sand—another smooth mound of sand—rose like an easy swell from the island's flat sand sea.

"We'll stop thirty feet this side of it. Near the palm tree that's been knocked over. See it?"

"Yes."

"To the left, inland from the bunker, is the trench: you saw it. I'll toss three or four grenades in there so any of them left in there will keep their heads down. Then I'll go on. You cover me. Shoot anything you see. I'll run to the front of the bunker: to where the firing slit is." At least it sounds easy, he thought. "That way, I'll be out of the line of fire from inland." Funny, he thought: they haven't fired at us from the blockhouse. Maybe they think the mortars got us all. "I'll shove in a charge and come back. Be sure you keep an eye on that building inland. A machinegun fired on us from there."

"Sounds all right to me," the boy said. He sounded cheerful: as though everything might work out okay now he was helping an officer win the war.

"You're all right?"

"Sir?"

"I said: don't call me sir. You're all right. Remember. Shoot them if you see them. Or if you can't see them, shoot at the muzzleflashes."

"Right. I've been doing that already. Haven't seen a live one of them yet. But I guess I killed some of them." He nodded as though he knew someone was keeping score for him.

"They're mostly under ground," he said. "That's the way they're doing it. Let's go." He slung Mitchell's sack over his shoulder, hefted Martinez's bag of grenades with his dirty, gritty left hand. His holstered pistol swung against his thigh as he crouched and started forward. Where else? he wondered. Can't go back. Forward's the only way left. Nothing else to do. And ahead? What waits for me? I know the answer to that: the rest of this island, and the five thousand Japanese defenders and a thousand unwilling—maybe—Korean laborers crammed into it. Tight fit: this island is five hundred yards wide and four thousand yards long, as the island bends from west to southeast. A hour's easy march. A half hour's mild jog. And here I am, alone with this child private, a bloody bag of clinking, shifting grenades clutched in one hand, a dirty sack of explosives slung over my shoulder.

And me with no cigar, he thought, recalling the long brown tube in Mitchell's grinning mouth.

"Hold up a moment," he said. "You have any cigarettes?"

"I don't smoke."

"Shit," he said.

"I can get one for you. I saw some on the sand over there." Before he could speak the boy turned and wriggled away, crawling with his rifle across his arms. As he was trained, he thought as he watched the boy slither among the slumped, hacked and quartered corpses. Medieval, he thought. Warfare at its most elemental, no art or science about it. As antique as the pike, the sword, the knife.

The boy crawled past Cable's slumped, stained corpse. Blood, he thought. And in a couple of hours, corruption. The boy halted, picked objects from the sand, turned and crawled back, two bright white and gold packs of Chesterfields in his right hand, a glint of silver in his left.

"I got a lighter, too, sir."

"Good going," he said.

"It was Peters', I think."

"I know," he said, taking the cigarettes and the lighter. He ran his thumb across the raised emblem: the eagle, globe and anchor. Peters had been proud of it: that he had the right to buy it, that it was his, that it identified him and gave him meaning.

He flicked the lighter open, flicked the wheel. A blueyellow flame leapt up. He closed the lighter, tore open a pack of Chesterfields, worked one out, stuck it in his mouth. He opened the lighter again, flicked the wheel, sucked smoke through the cigarette.

"You a smoker, sir?"

"Camels. I smoked them all on the beach. Right now what I need is burning punk, a cigar, anything to light fuse with."

"Oh," the boy said. "The explosives."

"That's it," he said.

He puffed at the cigarette. Funny, he thought. All this noise, all this firing. And there doesn't seem to be anyone anywhere except this kid and me shouting at one another and calling it talk. He grinned at the boy and said, "Come on."

He got up on his knees in the dirty sand littered with bits of palm leaf, empty cartridge casings, torn swatches of cloth, sludgy, drying spatters of blood. Bitter, dusty smoke drifted against his face. He coughed. The noise of weapons firing was tremendous: he wondered that he could speak at all and be understood.

A fresh sound distinguished itself from the ragged chattering of smallarms and machinegun and cannon fire: the roar of an aircraft engine slanting through the sky above him. He glanced up as the ungainly cruciform shape dove through the smoke. Ours, he thought. Bomb the little bastards, he thought. As though ordered, the aircraft released a bomb, pulled out of its dive and swept away. He lost sight of the bomb falling through the smoke, but he heard the distinctive rising whistle as it fell. The bomb struck two hundred yards inland. He glanced left: toward the two-story blockhouse from which the machinegunners had fired. Smoke, grit and dust leapt upward behind the concrete building. Noise rushed, concussion hammered.

Next to him, face down in the sand, the boy said, "Jeez."

"Let's go. While they've got their heads down."

"Yes, sir. We're going to grenade the trench?"

"No. Change of plan. You keep an eye on the trench. I'm going to do the bunker. And don't call me sir again," he said.

"Because the Japanese might hear you're an officer, sir?" the boy shouted through the irregular roar of weapons firing, shells exploding, charges detonating.

He shook his head, grinned, and jogged forward: toward the bunker, away from the low ground behind it where the dead Japanese Thomas had killed sprawled, limbs awry, holes in their uniforms, blood on their faces, flies swarming about their mouths and eyes.

A Japanese began to fire at him: sand kicked up to his left. He glanced toward the trench Martinez had grenaded. He could not hear the shots, but he saw the muzzle of the rifle and the helmeted head of the man shooting it and heard one bullet and then another and a third snap through the air near his waist, across his chest, above his head.

Crouching, he jogged on, his feet shoving at the loose littered sand as he changed course this way and that.

Behind him the boy fired his rifle, one shot and then another. Aiming the rifle, he thought. Good. A Japanese grenade cracked. The boy's rifle fired: three more shots. The Japanese rifleman did not return the fire and the boy stopped shooting. Good. The kid's making him stay down. Or he's killed the sonofabitch.

He began to pant as he slogged up the mound of piled loose sand that concealed the bunker beneath. In which, he thought, Japanese lurk and jabber and peer from the gloom into the bright smoky day. Bastards. Bastards aiming their machinegun from the black rectangle of the embrasure that faces the seawall. Ready to shoot anyone they see on the narrow beach clogged with wounded and dead men and damaged machinery. Ready to kill them slogging forward waist-and chest-deep in the sea, coming on across the coral. The Japanese machinegun began to fire and he thought: killing them now, or wounding them so that they will sink beneath the evil red flowers that conceal their drownings.

Murderous little bastards, he thought as he got down and began to crawl, dragging the sack of charges behind him, pulling the bag of grenades along with his left hand. He worked his way along the smooth, rounded slope of the bunker. You sonsofbitches, he thought: I'm going to kill every one of you.

He halted four feet from the muzzle of the machinegun—a Nambu—that twitched from left to right in the embrasure, twitched right to left, fired: a quick harsh hammering, flame flicking from the gun's muzzle.

He looked toward the beach. A man with one knee on the seawall, a rifle slung across his back, stared at him lying on the forward slope of the bunker, nodded as though they knew one another, clapped his hands against his chest and fell backward.

Inside the bunker a shouting voice jabbered Japanese. What a sound, he thought as he listened to the quacking rising yammer. What a people. Murderous and certain: them and their language both.

The damp butt of the Chesterfield in his mouth leached bitter juice into his mouth. The machinegun four feet in front of him fired again. He stared at the hammering Nambu's flashing muzzle as he felt with his right hand in Martinez's bloody crusted bag. He took out one grenade and then another. He jerked the pin from the first, heard the tinny sound as the spoon flicked away, wriggled two feet closer to the gun and shoved the grenade into the darkness beyond the embrasure. Even as he pulled the pin from the second grenade the muzzle of the machinegun jerked away from him and one of them inside the bunker jabbered more Japanese. Another screamed. He stuffed the second grenade into the gunslit and jerked his hand back, pressed it against his chest. The first grenade detonated: in the gloom inside the log bunker buried beneath the sand one of them screamed. The second grenade detonated and another of them shrieked.

Fuck you, he thought. Fuck you both.

He worked one of the charges from Mitchell's sack. He recalled Mitchell flinging the bag away from himself, trying for salvation. He held the charge up in front of his face. A rectangular solid of slabs of gritty gray material taped together. He touched the four-inch fuse to the tip of the smoldering cigarette in his dry mouth. I can't spit or swallow, he thought. How did the butt of this cigarette in my mouth get so wet? The fuse sputtered and hissed, flickered. He stared at the fire sparkling inside the fuse's fine woven cording, and thought: The force that through the green fuse. . . . Something I read. He coughed: his throat was full of smoke, dried spit, a taste of metal and dust. Ashes, he thought: the residue of all this effort, the end of trying.

The muzzle of the machinegun twitched. Another guy, he thought. Hand gripping the charge, he slid his bare arm across the sand and shoved the charge into the embrasure. As he withdrew his hand, the backs of his fingers touched the hot barrel of the machinegun and he felt the tremble of someone's flinching muscles through the metal. Fuck you, he thought.

He rolled and tumbled down the bunker's slope, Martinez's bag in his right hand, Mitchell's sack flopping about him, the grenades in the bag clacking against one another. Panting, coughing as though he were breathing the smoke of the explosion yet to come, he rolled onto the flat ground at the foot of the bunker. Behind him the boy yelled, "That's the way, sir!" The bunker in front of him heaved, subsided, heaved again: the tapering rounded summit of it blew out, flinging a whirl of sand, dust and black smoke inland. Coconut logs and a rifle's stock with the sling flapping tumbled end over end through the smoke. He looked toward the beach: a man, then another and a third and more of them were climbing the seawall, hoisting themselves up and over the topmost log, crouching and then coming forward.

Time to go on, he thought. Got more charges here. Mitchell and I each used one. That leaves six. With six of them I ought to be able to get at least six more bunkers. If things work out right.

From the scattered rubble at the smoking summit of the blown bunker a weapon fired. The bullet struck the sand in front of him, flicked grit against his face. He looked up into the smoke. A man wearing nothing but a loincloth stood among the snapped logs unearthed by the detonation of the charge. Blood glistened on his face and chest. He jerked at the rifle's bolt with his bloody right hand, the muscles in his naked arm bunching as he tried to yank the bolt back. A lucky Japanese, he thought: I wonder how he survived the blast. As he reached to the holster on his belt, he thought: a difficult pistol shot, perhaps an impossible pistol shot. But if he figures out how to make his rifle work, he's going to kill me.

From behind his back the boy shouted, "Hey, Lieutenant . . . ?"

A kid Marine, he thought. Asking questions and waiting while I'm out here with a clean sandy sack of explosive charges and a filthy bloody bag stuffed full of grenades. And a pistol, he thought. He fumbled at the holster that had worked from his right hip to the middle of his back while he stared up at the bloody Japanese jerking at the bolt of his rifle and hammering the receiver with his bloody fist.

The boy's rifle fired twice, a third time. Each bullet struck the Japanese in the chest. As they tore through his back, his blood sprinkled the sand and filthy broken logs.

The boy shoots a nice tight pattern, he thought as, at last, he hauled his pistol out of its holster and pointed it in the direction of the Japanese still standing up in the rubble of the bunker.

Three in the chest. Funny they didn't throw him back, lift him up, shove him away, toss him out of life and give him the glory he must have wanted. The rounds rising as they hammered through his chest and exited his back must have held him up.

The Japanese staggered forward a pace and wrenched his mouth open. A vomitus of white froth and blood lurched down his chin and chest and he collapsed into the rubble. All this way to come, he thought: from wherever he was born in Dai Nippon to this desolate place to be blown up and shot. To die with bloody foam erupting from his mouth.

He looked away from the dead Japanese and the torn up summit of the bunker: toward the sea.

Men were still hiking shoreward toward the burning island, struggling toward shore, the water about them whipped by machinegun fire and exploding mortar shells. Two men trudging side by side shrank away from one another. The one on the left slid below the surface as the one on the right leapt forward, fell, regained his feet, fell again. A third, eviscerated by a fragment of shell, flung his hands up in front of his face, jerked them down and beat at the water as he sank into the spreading stain that unfurled from the fearsome wound inflicted on him.

He looked for the men who had come over the seawall. They were gone: gone to ground, disappeared into the smoke and noise, headed another way.

"Sir?" the boy's voice shouted. He rolled over, looked at the boy crouched in the low ground thirty feet away. "Sir? Don't you think we ought to get out of here?"

"Coming," he shouted back. He got up on his knees. Something struck his left shoulder. A club, he thought. He twisted away from the savage blow, fell onto his side. Something else struck his chest, hammered into him, ripped out of his back. Blood filled his throat, smoke burned his eyes. His sweating face was pressed against the sand.

Damn, he thought. The shoulder. And the chest. He breathed, choked, spat blood into the sand; and even as he spat he felt more blood rising up his throat. He spat again, to save himself from choking.

Above him a rifle fired twice, paused, fired twice again. He saw the rifleman's right foot and left knee. He turned his head an inch, looked up at the boy kneeling and firing across him.

"Get down," he said. But the sound of his words was overwhelmed by the volume of blood rising up his throat.

The boy reloaded his rifle, bent down and said, "I killed him, sir. He poked his head up out of the trench and I shot him in the face."

Should have grenaded that trench, he thought. He moved his head and tried to speak: to encourage the young Marine, to tell him he had done well. But he could not get the words past the blood in his throat. He coughed and tried to raise his head.

"Lie still, sir," the boy said, lying down beside him. He was unwrapping a dressing, dirty fingertips holding the compress by the edges.

He's got to be kidding, he thought. A compress? I need an operating theater and a team of qualified surgeons to figure out how to fix me. To figure out if they can fix me.

The boy tore his shirt open, laid the compress on his chest and taped it down.

Something in his chest pumped where it should not have pumped; and with each pump pain seared him as though he had swallowed hot metal. He felt sick to his stomach and short of breath. As though I've breathed the fumes of a rare poison and then drunk it down. Chest, stomach, lungs: all gone.

He moved his right hand, felt along his side. His fingertips touched Martinez's bag wet and slick with blood. Or is it my fingers that are wet and slick with blood? Something exploded, flung sand and grit across him. Far enough away, though, he thought. I don't think I was hit again. Or maybe I'm in shock and cannot feel the infliction of another wound. Or maybe my hearing's gone, for I hear nothing but the rush of flowing water, the fall of surf. But there is no flowing water on this island, and the sea is calm today.

"You want me to take the grenades, sir?" the boy asked, his voice rising as though he too could hear the rushing.

He thought he nodded.

"And the charges, sir? The sack?"

Sack, he thought. Yes. Again he thought he nodded.

The boy's rifle lay in front of his face in the sand: in the bloody sand. Didn't notice the blood before, he thought. He examined the part of the rifle he could see: forepiece to triggerguard. Careful young man, he thought: put his rifle down with the receiver up, out of the sand. So it will not foul.

Hands touched his body, slid Mitchell's sack from his shoulders, worked Martinez's bag from beneath his body. Each touch of the boy's hands and each smooth, gentle tug of the sack's sling beneath his chest tormented him. He made a sound in his throat: a clotted whimper.

"I know, sir," the boy said. "I'm sorry." The boy put his cheek down against the sand. His eyes were close: young, full of concern and worry. The boy held Peters' lighter in his left hand.

A mouthful of blood slid onto his chin. He coughed and whispered, "Go on. Go on."

"I shouldn't leave you here, sir," the boy said.

I wonder why not? he thought. Nothing here. Dead Japanese, bunker blown apart, dead officer. Or dying, at least.

"Go on," he muttered. What else is there to do, after all? Set up camp and tell old stories?

"But, Lieutenant . . ."

"Go on," he whispered. "Order." The sky was darkening. More smoke, he thought. Saw the naval rifles' shells skipping across the island as we were coming in. Great planning. Like to talk to the gunnery officer. Like to give him a piece of my mind. But I have no time for that now. And no time to prepare for the journey I am beginning. Decent company on the voyage, though: Thomas, Heinrich, Frank Masters, the rest of them.

He closed his eyes.

"I'll come back," the boy said. "Either way, I'll come back for you."

He thought he nodded. He heard the boy heft the sack, the bag, heard him lift his rifle from the sand, heard his feet moving: away from the beach. Inland: toward the trench and the blockhouse beyond.

The sound of firing swept across the part of the island over which he had fought, swept on, as though the Japanese were concentrating on other targets farther down the shore. The racket of weapons firing and the concussion of explosives detonating diminished. Then the sound was muffled, and then it was inaudible, and for a moment he strained to hear.

THROUGH HIS SWOLLEN SLITTED eyelids, he saw the sun and thought, I am not killed. I live, and I am here: in the desert. And that desert island surrounded by the sea, the sky above it full of smoke and the sound of weapons firing and ordnance exploding? Gone, he thought.

He coughed. The sound creaked through the mucous clotted in his throat. Must have fallen again, he thought. And fallen unconscious. And while I was not here the sun rose higher up the sky and burned my burned back, burned my right cheek and temple and jaw, burned my scalp.

He got up on his hands and knees, raised his head and looked along the line of the march he knew he would have to follow. Anonymous, blank, each yard like the one before, and the one after, the desert stretched away, rising toward the southeastern horizon.

Time to go, he thought. Time to get up and go on. He stared ahead, gauging the huge distance to the horizon, measuring himself against the effort he would have to make.

First thing is to stand up. Second thing, check the compass. Third, a sip of water. If I still have water.

Water or not, get the hell up.

He got his feet beneath him and stood up; and as he stood, the cloth of his shirt and trousers dragged across his arms and back and across the backs of his legs. The touch of the cloth rasping across his burned skin was torment. He looked down, touched one shirt sleeve and then the other: his arms beneath the sleeves were encased in long, thick blisters bloated with liquid drawn from his flesh. Biggest damned blisters I've ever seen. Ever heard of. He moved his shoulders. The sun had fitted broader blisters to his back. The viscous fluid in them heaved each time he moved: each time he breathed.

At least I'm supplied with liquid now. He giggled, shook his head. A damp, smoking woods and a roaring beach, he thought. Two other places.

Go on, he thought. Getting late. It must be at least noon. He looked at his watch: the second hand was still, the hour and minute hands lay at 12:17. Busted, he thought. He looked up at the pale bluewhite sky. To the south, the sun rode through the sky. A little after noon, he thought.

Been at this six hours and more.

Bullshit. You passed out twice. Total time marching? Make it five hours. He glanced behind him, toward the low ridge from which he had begun this fearsome march. The air shimmered and slid, obscuring his view. A silver puddle lay on the desert floor at the foot of the ridge. Mirage, he thought. Forget it.

How far? he wondered. Squinting, he looked into the shimmer of light reflecting from the surface of the desert. Call it five, maybe six miles. Thirteen or fourteen more to go.

Better hurry. Something's coming after you. Better hurry before it catches up with you.

He held himself erect, shivering as though the season were winter and the sky were obscured by grey clouds laden with snow. The backs of his hands were glaucous twin blisters, the skin at the edges of the swollen sacks of liquid livid and painful.

Forget it, he thought. Nothing you can do about blisters. Think about one thing: going on.

He paced away through the scrub, one step, another, a third. Animals skittered away beneath the knee-high bushes. The surface of the desert was uneven and difficult: time and geology had scattered edged rocks across the sand and dust, laid broad clearings floored with stone here and there in the stunted brush.

All this, and my body aches as though I've been beaten and burned.

You have been burned, he thought. Temperature as high as a hundred fifteen or a hundred twenty degrees and no shade? Sure you've been burned.

Someone whispered, Go on. Go on. Order. He staggered forward through the brush.

He had walked on fifty paces before he realized he could not feel the weight of his rifle slung over his shoulder. He halted, turned.

Go back for it? he wondered. The desert's dry, brushy vegetation was monotonous and bland. No indication, he thought, where I was lying passed out dreaming I was on that burning island. I could follow my tracks back. But I can't see my tracks beneath the brush; and some of the ground was rock, I think.

To hell with it?

Better go back and get it, he thought. They'll be *pissed* if I leave my weapon out here. I can hear that fucking sergeant now, voice rising, spittle at the corners of his mouth, curses coming out of his throat as he bitches and huffs about a lost rifle and how he's going to have to fill in a lot of forms and write a lot of reports to explain why *one of his men* lost his rifle that he wasn't supposed to let go of right up to the moment he was killed.

He stumbled on the uneven ground, guessed where to go and waded step by step back through the scrub. The sunlight was to his right rear now. Dust rose from the stunted plants as he brushed against them. The dust filled his nose, coated the coagulated smear of spit inside his mouth. He glanced across the scrub, and in the sunlight falling on the dusty plants from behind him he saw a greener pathway through the leathery gray leaves. My track, he thought. I brushed the dust away as I came on. He lifted his face and squinted along the line of bushes from which his passage had dislodged the dust. The faint greener way through the scrub zig-zagged toward the horizon: toward the ridge from which he had taken his first compass bearing.

Not a straight course, he thought. I guess an admiral would get all scratchy and critical. But then everyone knows about squids: they go backward and hide behind clouds of ink.

Still, he thought. Better take note: walk three hundred paces, check the bearing and then look back to be sure I'm walking straight. Steer a straight course and you'll save some sweat. And time. Save, maybe, everything I've got.

He walked back along the path his march southeast had swept through the brush. Ahead, something glinted beneath the gray low bushes. He staggered on. His joints ached and his limbs were stiff. As though I have grown some new, less flexible skin, he thought. As though I am dressed in that new issue uniform of cloth impregnated with some special substance. A protectant, they called it: makes the cloth impervious to gas, radiation, biological agents. This here new type of uniform, they said, will protect you from all that shit.

But it was not the blisters he carried with him or his clothing that slowed him down and checked the movement of his limbs: he knew it. What's slowing me down, he thought, is dehydration. The heat is drawing water away from my muscles and joints into the blisters the sun has fitted to my limbs and back.

Water in the muscles and joints: the Doc said something about that. And about the muscles. The long muscles of the body slide and the joints swivel because they're immersed in their own private sea. Without water, your muscles are jerky and your joints are stone, the Doc said. What's jerky? Jerky's dried meat, son. It's good for nothing except eating. And it's not much good for that, either. Anyhow, you'll feel the lack of water: when the water goes, your muscles will begin to stiffen and your joints will creak and grind. Eventually your muscles will cramp and your joints will lock. In the end, neither your muscles nor your joints will be supple. And let me tell you: unsupple is bad when we're talking about muscle, and we're talking about muscle right here right now. So you have to drink a lot of water out there. Water's a lubricant. You understand me?

Mumbled acquiescence from nodding shaven heads. Gruff grunts from the noncommissioned officers in attendance: to indicate that they did not concede the Doc's point, for the Doc's knowledge and logic jabbed at the image of themselves they had been taught: the image of the individual rifleman marching through fire and demanding a half glass of beer on the far side of the conflagration.

But no one's that tough out here, he thought. Not anyone, Marine or no. Out here Mac Marine is as weak as the least civilian when the sun's up and the water's fifteen miles away.

He stumbled on toward his rifle glinting under the scrub, all his aching joints working, his limbs jerking as a puppet's jerk at the ends of the filaments that manipulate them and seem to give them life.

I was right to come back, he thought. The rifle may be salvation. And if there is to be no salvation, the rifle is a door that will let me out of the sun's white light and perfect heat into whatever comes next. A door I may choose to open, or not. Depending.

He bent to pick up the rifle and as he bent he saw, lying on the sand beside the rifle, the handkerchief he had worn as a headband and the shelterhalf he had draped over his head.

Forgot about those, he thought. Or perhaps I didn't forget? Perhaps dehydration inhibits the flow of thought as it inhibits the smooth swiveling of my joints.

He picked up the handkerchief, slid the knotted circle of cloth over his head, lifted his rifle and slung it muzzle up. The sling bit into the blisters on his right shoulder and back. He picked up the shelterhalf, shook the sand from it and arranged it over his head and the muzzle of the rifle.

My tent, he thought, looking out of the hot gloom under the shelterhalf at the light. Grit and dust sifted from the rubberized fabric into his eyes, his nose, his mouth. Great, he thought. Fall down, pass out, wake up. Twice it's happened: twice. I wonder what wakes me up and makes me get up and go on again?

The rifle's one way out, he thought. So is the compass, if I can hump myself far enough. He fished the compass from his breast pocket, held it in his hand, turned himself onto the bearing of one hundred thirty-five degrees and peered over his shoulder at the faint green trail through the dusty scrub. The trail wound away through the scrub on a bearing that was not the reciprocal of one thirty-five degrees.

I'm in trouble, he thought. I've been marching off course. He shivered as though a cold wind were sweeping across the desert. Got to do better, he thought. Got to stay on course: any course deviation will increase the length of the march. A big enough deviation and I will miss the Palms and end up nowhere when I can go no farther.

Keep thinking, he told himself. Think about what you're doing.

He faced the southeastern horizon, turned until he faced the bearing he would march. He looked at the compass again and set off along the bearing, marching up the huge barren slope of the desert that rose before him and led toward the blinding bluewhite sky.

Going to conquer this bastard, he thought. Got to. March. Stop thinking and march. A compass check, three hundred paces and a glance behind: to gauge the course I've marched through the scrub. Think of what you're doing. And think of anything but the heat and the blinding light. Think of Minnesota. Think of any season except the summer. Forget the burning island beyond a wall of coconut logs. Think of a damp foreign woods. Better still, he told himself as he put one foot in front of the other, the soles of his boots teetering on rocks strewn across the sand and dust, his puffy knees and trembling blistered thighs brushing through the scrub, think of something cold.

THE COLD THE NIGHT before had frozen the ruts that truck tires and tank tracks had cut into the narrow muddy road. Gray ice filled the ruts and the ditches at the verges. Beyond the ditches steep hills pitched upward. Like all the hills in Korea, he thought, they're treeless jumbles of rock and scrub encrusted with ice and frozen snow. The sky was lead tinged with yellow, and wind rushed against the crests of the hills, rasped against the frozen snow, swept crystals up into the dirty light.

More snow, he thought, listening to the engines of the vehicles that filled the road behind him and in front. More snow this afternoon or tonight.

As he marched on he paused now and then to examine the crests of the steep hills on either side of the road with care, and now and then he saw ragged batches of lumpy men slogging through the drifts high on the windy ridges. Chinese, he thought. Or North Koreans. He wondered how they endured and went on fighting in such conditions. Their creed, he guessed: the narrow discipline of their new religion. And commissars at hand to shoot them if they don't go on. He shook his head: he would never understand them. The cold was iron: the temperature had fallen since daylight, and now it was below zero. Marching on the hard, slippery rutted road was tiring. Marching through the deep snow up in the wind in the hills must be exhausting. Ten more degrees of cold, he thought, and the cold alone will kill them all and we can march down to Hungnam without opposition.

He paused at the edge of the road to look back. The company—what was left of it—was moving south along the sides of the road. They did not march: they shuffled. A few limped. But each man had his weapon. But however tired the last one of them is, he thought, they're ready: they know about the Chinese. *And* about the murderous North Koreans.

Between the files of men trucks labored south, the drivers changing gears with each rise and descent of the road. The trucks were laden with equipment, ammunition and the wounded.

He marched on. The ruts roughened and deepened as the road rose toward the next bend: a buttress of rock flecked with patches of dirty snow and glistening gray ice. A truck stood at the side of the road, its hood raised. A man was kneeling on the fender, leaning over the engine. He held his gloves in his grimacing mouth. His teeth were white against the scraggly black beard on his cheeks and chin, and now and then he nodded as though he were sure he had the problem figured out.

Two men with rifles stood in the road on either side of the engine compartment, their backs to the truck, watching the hillsides.

The bed of the truck was full of corpses stacked on one another like lengths of strange timber. Someone had drawn a tarpaulin over the highest layer of corpses and pulled it up so that it covered their faces. But the tarpaulin was not long enough, and layers of booted splayed feet stuck out from beneath the hem of the canvas.

"Trouble?" he asked the rifleman on the driver's side of the cab.

The rifleman looked out of the hood of his long overcoat, looked him over, glanced back down the road at the company coming on and pushed the hood back. He was pale and freckled and balding. "Yes," he said. As he spoke condensation flowed from his mouth like tobacco smoke. "Smith says it's the carburetor. Says he can fix it, though. I'm Franklin. Corporal Franklin."

"Better hurry," he said. A truck ground past, the driver staring straight ahead. Then the first of the company, the men spaced out on either side of the road, began to filter past. "There's armor a couple of miles back. And guns. They'll need the space to get by here."

"Right. Hurry. Uh . . . ?"

"Yeah?"

"You're an officer? I thought you were, but I didn't know. It's just that you're pretty young and all."

"First Lieutenant. The Captain was killed farther north. On the way down from the Reservoir."

"The fucking Chinese."

"That's it: the fucking Chinese. And the fucking North Koreans. But we've killed a lot of them." Another truck—this one with a crane mounted on the bed—eased past. Bandaged men up on the bed of the truck huddled against one another and against the mechanism of the crane as though it were a potbellied stove. Each of the wounded held a weapon. The driver shifted down and accelerated. His tires skittered and slid on the icy ridged surface.

He stepped back. Corporal Franklin stepped back too. The truck slid a foot closer to them and they stepped back again. Then the truck's cleated tires found enough purchase. The truck stopped sliding, straightened and went on up the road.

"Damn driver ought to know not to accelerate like that on a road icy as this," Corporal Franklin said. He spoke with authority, as though he had maneuvered trucks over roads like this for years.

Maybe he has, he thought. Maybe Corporal Franklin comes from east Tennessee, or east Kentucky, or any part of West Virginia, where the government's never done anything about the road system at all.

"Uh, Lieutenant?" Franklin sounded inquisitive.

"Yeah?"

"You sound pretty cheery about all this."

"We're getting there, Corporal. We've come most of the way. And up in these hills, they're freezing to death. You notice how cold it is down here?"

Corporal Franklin nodded as though the lieutenant had asked him a trick question. After all: they had all struggled through the cold for ten days, and the temperature had been no more than a few degrees above freezing one day in four. "Sure. Of course, Lieutenant."

"It's worse up there," he said. "More windy. And they have to maneuver through the snow. And they have a longer way to go, trying to get ahead of us, going up and down the hills. And we've got artillery, supplies, aircraft. I wouldn't like being in the Chinese army."

"I suppose so," Franklin said. "But if they cut this road, then . . ."

"We'll brush 'em aside," he said. "You're all right here? You'll get them back?" He jerked his head at the halted truck full of corpses.

"Get them back?" Franklin asked, as though he didn't quite understand. "Oh. You mean these guys in the truck. Get them back? Sure," Franklin said. "Every one of them is going home. I guarantee it."

"Good," he said. The middle of the company was passing him, slogging up the road. "Look, I've got to get on. You take it easy, Corporal."

"Here in fucking North Korea, Lieutenant?"

He grinned and said, "I should have said, take it easy if you can."

"All right, Lieutenant," Corporal Franklin said. "I can do that." He sounded enthusiastic about his prospects. As though it was all down hill to the sea and they could coast the distance if Smith couldn't fix the carburetor.

Which is almost the case, he thought as he turned away. A couple more passes, and then a tiring descent to Hungnam, that beauty spot on the hospitable shores of the Sea of Japan.

He strode up the left side of the road, passing one of his tired men and the next, making good enough time to catch up and pass a truck grinding forward. The truck rocked on the road and the canvas at the back swung aside and he saw a corpsman standing up, bracing himself with one gloved hand, his other hand raised to a bottle of fluid—plasma or whole blood, he guessed—hanging from one of the ribs bowed over the bed of the truck.

As he reached the head of the company, he saw Gunnery Sergeant

Phelps standing at the side of the road fifty feet ahead. A filthy, grubby Marine he didn't recognize stood beside Phelps, his back turned, the hood of his coat over his face. The coat was smeared with old mud. I bet I don't look as filthy as this guy. On the other hand, I don't look as good as I do wearing dress blues and waltzing a young lovely around. He noticed a Jeep loitering fifty feet beyond the Gunny and the hobo Marine; and then he noticed Gunny Phelps's posture: it was the posture of a tall, muscular gunnery sergeant attempting to look deferential in the presence of a senior officer.

Here we go, he thought. And as he came up, Gunny Phelps looked at him and rolled his eyes upward as though he were trying to see his eyebrows.

"Gunny?"

"Lieutenant, Major Carlson here's got a job for us."

"Major?" he asked. Carlson, he thought. Not in our battalion.

"Lieutenant. How are you? Pretty damned crummy up here, isn't it? But we're almost there. Couple of more rises and we're through the worst of it. Or so we're told by General Almond's people."

"The Army," he said.

Major Carlson grinned and said, "We have to have an Army, Lieutenant."

"For comparison purposes only, of course," Gunny Phelps said, his voice smooth and reasonable.

"Easy, Gunny," Major Carlson said. "Even out here, you don't know who's listening. And remember: we've got some Army people with us."

"Sure do, Major. And most of them are riding the trucks."

"They had a hard time," Major Carlson said. "Got cut off east of the Reservoir, got chopped up. And let me tell you, Gunny: I wish I were riding in a nice warm truck right now."

"Sure, Major," Gunny Phelps said. He looked up at the hills west of the road. "Sure you do."

"Anyhow, Lieutenant," Major Carlson said. "How's it going?"

"Fine, Major."

"No problems?"

"None at all."

"You're the luckiest guy out here, then. You even seem warm."

"I think I'm running a fever, Major. Which is a good thing right now."

The Major nodded. "Okay. As the Gunny said, I've got a job for you and your people. Sorry about that, but you're the available company.

Around the next bend—" he turned, pointed ahead a half mile to where the narrow rutted road disappeared around another buttress of rock— "the hills on the right are less steep. The next to last pass is beyond that. The hills beyond the bend ahead shelve down to the road. We're getting some fire from there. And it's building up. This is the only reasonably broad, reasonably sloped place from here on until we get through the pass. So the enemy wants it. They want to take the first crest above the road so they can put in enough men to cut the road. So you're to deploy your men on that first crest and keep whoever comes at you back until you're relieved. Got it?"

"Get up to the first crest and keep them away."

"Think you can handle it?"

"We can handle it, Major."

"Good. Your radios working all right? Mortars? Machineguns?"

"Everything is in good shape, Major."

"Good. I'm sending Corporal McKittrick with you. That's him at the Jeep." He looked. A man was hoisting a pack radio down from the Jeep. "He's your forward observer. I know: you should have a lieutenant. But there aren't any lieutenants available, and McKittrick knows everything there is to know about calling down fire. Eleventh Marines are setting up farther along. They'll be set in and ready by the time you get up there."

"Fine."

"You're sure you're all right?" the Major asked. "You say you've got a fever?"

"It's nothing, Major. Just a touch. I just feel warm, that's all."

"Company all right?"

"None better, Major."

"Good," Major Carlson said. "That's good. All right. I've got to go. You'll keep them back?"

He spoke as though he were asking a favor.

"Of course," he said.

"Good," Major Carlson said. "Good." He nodded and turned away. His shoulders were slumped, his head bent. A smear of dried blood dirtied the right sleeve of his soiled coat. He limped as he walked away.

"Nicked in the foot," Gunny Phelps muttered. "That'll be his sixth Heart."

"Six Purple Hearts?"

"Two on the Canal, one each at Peleliu and Okinawa, and one at

Inchon. And now one here. Somehow he seems to be in the wrong place at the wrong time."

"I never asked, Gunny. How many Hearts do you have?"

"Nine. I'm even worse than the Major about picking my spot."

"Nine? I want to hear about every one of them when we're leaving Hungnam harbor. But right now, pass the word, would you? About where we're going and what we're going to do. Have everybody get all the ammunition and grenades they can handle out of the trucks. And tell everyone to bring along all the machinegun ammunition and mortar rounds they can hump."

"You think we'll need all that?" Gunny Phelps asked, as though he thought his lieutenant wasn't considering the government's obligations to the taxpayer.

"There's no harm in being cautious," he said. "Everything they can hump. Got it?"

"Yes, Lieutenant."

"It won't be that far to carry it: it's just up to the first crest. We set in there and wait for them to come on."

"Okay, Lieutenant," Gunny Phelps said.

An hour later they were climbing the Major's 'less steep' terrain. The snow was knee-deep: crusted on top, packed powder beneath. The men were on line, spread across the slope, each of them struggling upward. Some hauled boxes of belted machinegun ammunition. Others humped backboards to which three mortar rounds were strapped. Still others carried machineguns, tripods, mortar tubes and baseplates. Exhausting, he thought. But there's less than a hundred yards to go to reach the first crest where Major Carlson wants us to set in. More high ground beyond that: but we're not here to take ground: we're here to kill as many Chinese and North Korean soldiers as we can. To hold the road open until we're relieved. It won't be that difficult: we'll set up and let them come on.

Panting, he bulled through the knee-deep snow, counting his paces. He had counted to thirty when the Chinese began to fire from the first crest. Bullets snapped through the dense cold air above his head. Firing high, he thought: at least that's something.

Going to have to push them off, he thought. No reason to hold up here and plan what to do next: there's no cover here, and there's only one plan, because there's only one way up there. And the platoon and squad leaders on the flanks know what to do as well as I do: build up fire as we climb up.

"Let's go," he shouted. He lifted his rifle and fired three shots at the crest a hundred yards away. Useless, he thought. Can't see anything. Beside him others fired their weapons and climbed on, paused, fired again and started climbing again.

He listened. The fire from the crest was sporadic, and he heard no hammering of machinegun fire. And no mortars, he thought. Yet.

"Come on," he shouted as he labored on, booted feet spiking through the brittle carapace of frozen snow. Right and left of him along the line rifles went on firing, and automatic weapons on the flanks of each platoon began to fire, tracer chasing knee-high across the rising ground. Panting, he shouted into the clatter, "There's no more than a few of them."

A bright voice called out, "You *sure* about that?"

Condensation puffed from his mouth as he yelled, "You better *hope* I am."

But he had guessed right: the solid sound of firing from the crest divided, separated into the crack of individual weapons firing, diminished to occasional single shots, halted.

Luck, he thought: just a few of them. Luck this time.

Now the line of his men crunched and slogged upward through the snow without pause, the men panting as they went up the last few yards to the crest.

In the snow just beyond the crest a Chinese soldier in a quilted jacket and pants and heavy felt boots with worn soles lay on his back. A bullet had torn his face away. Gunny Phelps shoved at the corpse with his right boot until it flopped over the crest and slid downhill.

Three hundred yards ahead, ten or twelve Chinese were darting from rock to rock, glancing back now and then as they climbed toward the next crest higher.

"You were right, Lieutenant," a voice at his elbow said. "About the number of them." He turned. Private Wilson grinned at him, held out a bloody leather hat with fur ear flaps. A star of bright red enamel was pinned into the fur of the folded up brim. "Here's a souvenir for you, Lieutenant."

He drew a deep breath. Icy air filled his lungs. "Wilson," he said, "don't you know better than to joke at a time like that? When we were coming up the slope and they were shooting at us?"

"Seemed like a good idea to me, Lieutenant. Relieve some the tension, like."

"What tension?" he asked. "I didn't notice any tension."

"Hah," Wilson said. "That's good, Lieutenant. You want this here communist star? It's a Chinese hood ornament. You could put it on the hood of your coupe back home."

"*Hood* ornament? Coupe back home? Are you all right, Wilson? Look, throw it away. I don't like booty. And you know what would happen if they found you with that on your person. So get rid of it."

Wilson dropped the hat onto the frozen snow, stomped his boot onto it, pounded it through the brittle, crusted surface into the packed snow beneath. "So much for the hat," he said. He glanced at the corpse Gunny Phelps had shoved down the slope. "And so much for the guy who wore it."

Along the line, Gunny Phelps was shouting right and left, "Get set in! Kick a hole in the snow! Then get the hell into the hole! Get set in! Hurry the hell up! You men think they aren't coming back here? Let me tell you: they're coming back!"

He looked up across the rocky ground in front of him and thought, sure they're coming back. For sure they are. And soon. That's what they do, the sonsofbitches: they come back.

"McKittrick," he called. McKittrick came forward, radio on his back, puffing and panting. "Call the guns. Have them register their fire right, left and center."

Still panting, sweat on his forehead, shards of ice glistening on the stubble of his beard, McKittrick nodded, knelt in the snow, unslung his pack radio and tugged a folded map from his overcoat pocket. He looked it over, flicked a switch, plucked the handset from the radio, and spoke strings of numbers to the man on the other end.

Behind him, far to the south along the road, he heard a faint thump. "Coming," McKittrick said.

"Right," he said. He raised his voice and shouted, "Everybody get down."

McKittrick raised an eyebrow and said, "Lieutenant, the Eleventh's pretty good, you know." He sounded as though he didn't *want* to criticize.

He stood with McKittrick while everyone else on the line flopped down in the snow. "Sure," he said. "Of course they're good. But what about the munitions workers? Short rounds, wrong fuses, all like that?"

"A fluke," McKittrick said, as a distant hissing in the sky rose to a shriek. "One chance in a million. And besides, these rounds are smoke."

The shell struck a boulder four hundred yards forward of their position. Clean white smoke rose into the sky.

"You seem to be right, McKittrick," he said. "Still . . ."

A second shriek filled the sky. The shell pounded the earth a hundred fifty yards to the left of the first. An instant and a third shell fell a hundred fifty yards to the right.

"Very neat," he said.

McKittrick nodded, but he did not speak. Too polite to tell me how good his gunners are.

"I hope the Chinese saw that," he said. "Maybe they'll decide not to try it."

"You think?" McKittrick said as though he could see the Chinese charging toward them.

No time to talk it over right now, he thought. Then, as though McKittrick had bidden them to show themselves, he saw men on the crest to his front.

"Get ready!" Gunny Phelps's big voice called.

The distant figures in bulky quilted jackets and quilted pants, fur hats on their heads, started forward. A bugle blew. I figure, someone had said, they blow those bugles to signal one another. Bullshit, someone else said: they're just crazy. That's why they blow those bugles.

More Chinese were coming over the crest above him: dozens, and then hundreds, a flood of quilted jackets and pumping legs struggling forward through the deep snow. The ones in front began to fire their weapons. Too far for anything but a lucky hit, he thought. From behind the Chinese pouring down from the high ground mortars fired: he heard the hollow detonations as the propellant in the butts of the shells ignited.

Down on one knee, McKittrick lifted the handset of his radio to his face and began talking.

For a moment he watched McKittrick examine his map and listened as he spoke to the guns. Then he glanced left and right as the Chinese mortar shells began to strike. The detonating rounds spewed snow, black smoke, dirt and chips of rock upward in front of the line. Short, he thought. But close. And next time they may be close enough.

The Chinese were coming: many, many of them forcing themselves forward, plodding through the deep snow on the slope. As they came on, they bunched up. As though they hope they can hide among one another, he thought.

The Chinese were slowing. They move, he thought, as though they think they have done enough. Or perhaps they're hesitant: as though they know this is the end.

Which it is, he thought as the Eleventh's guns fired far behind him and the shells approached, tearing at the sky.

"Keep it coming," McKittrick said into the mouthpiece. "We got a lot of the bastards right out front."

The shells began to explode among the slogging Chinese. A low moan—not fear, he thought, and not pain: despair—rose from them. Many fell. Some lay still. Others kicked and squirmed. Others tried to stand and could not.

The rest of them came on. The guns' first rounds had torn chunks from the flock, but most of them were still up, and accelerating: the snow at the foot of the slope ahead was less deep, the rocky ground beneath visible, the footing less arduous. No more than two, two hundred fifty yards away now.

To his left along the line, walking through the snow behind the men, Gunny Phelps called out, "Aim every shot. Kill them. Fire!" Men began to fire their rifles. Careful, distinct, considered shots.

Gunny Phelps shouted: "Machineguns! Mortars!" Phelps's voice carried: to both flanks, and to the mortars behind the line. And to any Chinese out front who knows English and who, therefore, now knows what's coming to him. "Fire!" Gunny Phelps shouted, and as he shouted the word he chopped his arm and fist down like an angry judge convinced he was doing justice. As Phelps's fist struck the bench, the machineguns began to fire. Tracer flicked across the rising snowy ground, hammered the crowding Chinese picking up speed now they were out of the last of the deeper snow. He turned his head and saw a mortarman drop a shell down his tube, heard the propellant ignite, listened to the thick sound of it rushing upward.

More Chinese mortar rounds struck the earth in front of him. The machineguns fired and fired, slashing holes in the packs of Chinese coming on, trying to hurry. To his left, a single mortar round struck among the men on line. Someone shrieked, coughed, choked on his coughing. Someone else screamed and went on screaming.

"Corpsman," Gunny Phelps shouted as he ran toward the screaming, shoving through the snow as through his were shoving through heavy surf. As he must have done, at Peleliu and Iwo Jima, to gain the beach.

Smoke drifted downhill from the screaming to his left. Two men, their clothing soaked with blood, lay on the snow. One was broken and silent, the other broken and grunting now he no longer had the breath to scream.

Gunny Phelps and a corpsman—Fletcher: he recognized the long thin frame, the quick bend of the back—leaned over the bloody grunting Marine.

He turned away and shouted "McKittrick," across the intense noise of rifle and machinegun fire. McKittrick looked at him, the telephone handset pressed to his face. "Tell them to shorten the range. Tell them to keep shortening it."

"That's what I'm doing, Lieutenant," McKittrick explained.

He nodded: it seemed McKittrick *was* as good a forward observer as any lieutenant.

He turned his face toward the Chinese. They were still coming on: through the shells that plummeted from the sky and exploded against the dirty ground, ploughing earth out of the snow; through the lash of machinegun and rifle fire killing them in batches, through the detonations of mortar shells that fell among them and heaved more of them away.

And here I stand, he thought: knee deep in freezing snow, dressed up like a potato in sweaters, shirts, socks, boots, a jacket and a long coat: watching the show.

He fitted the butt of his rifle to his bulky right shoulder. He fumbled at the safety. Stiff gloves, bitter cold: he could feel the frigid wood and metal of his rifle through his gloves' frozen fingers. The sling was stiff as tar in winter, the wood of the stock shrunken hard about the steel parts of the weapon. He fumbled the safety down and lined up the rear and forward sights on the center of the approaching crowd of Chinese. They were *near*, by God, some of them no more than seventy yards away. And still coming, still standing up slogging through the explosions of shells and the fire of rifles and machineguns. Afraid of something I cannot understand, he thought, more than they are afraid of death.

He aimed at a short Chinese with a wide flat face shoving his feet through the crusty snow, bucking and heaving side to side as he came on, a Russian submachinegun with a drum magazine swinging in his bare hands.

No gloves, he thought as he fired at the man. He missed, fired again, hit the Chinese high in the chest. The bullet halted him, jerked him upright. He held the Russian weapon in his right hand, pressed his left hand against the wound in his chest, glanced up as though to try to see who had shot him.

He shot the Chinese again, in the chest again. The Chinese dropped his weapon, stumbled backward, fell into the snow.

He shot another Chinese in the groin. The man's mouth jerked open as he fell.

In the groin, he thought. You're shooting up hill: aim higher. He aimed higher, shot a third Chinese in the stomach, shot him again in the chest.

"Mortars," a voice to his left said. He nodded: he could hear them coming, hissing through the frigid air. He drew breath and hunched his shoulders.

The mortar shells struck behind the long line of his men holding the crest above the road.

Next time they fire, he thought, they'll put them right among us. I should do something. But even as he thought it he knew there was nothing to do: the Chinese infantry were surging toward him, their dead and wounded strewn across the trampled snow behind them. Fifty yards away, he guessed. And *still* closing. Nowhere to go right now, and nothing to do except to shoot them.

He shot at a big man with a fur hat on his head. A red star was fixed in the center of the folded up brim. He missed, fired again, missed again. A hammering machinegun swivelling left to right across the slope broke the big man's stride, severed his left forearm and flung him into the snow.

Still, he thought: they're not stopping. They're coming here: right here.

He crouched, bit down on the fore and middle fingertips of his left glove, jerked his hand from the glove, fumbled a clip from the pocket of his coat, fitted the clip into the weapon. The bolt slammed forward. His glove hanging from his mouth, he aimed into the smoke full of bulky shapes rushing toward him.

"Fix bayonets!" Gunny Phelps shouted. "Fix bayonets!"

Bayonets, he thought. No one's fixed bayonets in this war yet. If Gunny Phelps thinks we're going to have to fight them with bayonets, we're in big trouble. Or, as Gunny Phelps would say, No, Lieutenant, *they're* in big trouble.

Obedient to Gunny Phelps's order, he jerked his bayonet from its scabbard on his webbing belt. The haft of the bayonet was fouled with snow and ice. He hammered it against the stock of his rifle. Snow and ice flicked away. He fitted the bayonet over the muzzle of his rifle, snapped the bayonet down, jerked at it to be certain it was locked in place. Then he took the glove out of his mouth and put it on.

"Get down," Gunny Phelps shouted.

He flung himself down as the Eleventh's artillery hammered the earth to his front. Dirt, grit, smoke and snow leapt upward. The explosions flung Chinese soldiers away, threw them down, hacked at them, quartered them. Lying in the snow beside him, McKittrick pressed his lips close to the mouthpiece of the handset and shouted, "Keep it coming. Keep it coming until I tell you."

As the Eleventh's shells swept the slope close in front of him, he heard the Chinese screaming. He saw an armless man thrown upward, his head accelerating toward the grey sky, his slower torso and broken flapping legs coming on behind. But still they came on. Thirty feet, he thought.

Three Chinese were running toward him through the smoke. One of them screamed and pointed at him: as though *I'm* responsible, he thought.

Someone along the line shot the screaming Chinese in the face. Someone else shot him twice more, in the chest and leg. A machinegun swept across the other two: he saw dust puff from their quilted jackets, saw them shiver as the machinegun rounds struck them, saw them fall.

All along the line the tempo of the weapons' fire rose. Frantic, he thought. He aimed and shot at shadows jerking in the drifting smoke. As he fired one round and the next he realized the Chinese were no longer coming forward. They were running right and left. And back. Looking for cover, he thought. Fleeing in terror.

Gunny Phelps's big voice called, "Keep firing! Shoot, damn it all! Kill them!"

Beside him McKittrick was speaking into the radio handset. Having a quiet conversation with the Eleventh. A technical talk: more numbers than words, the verbless sentences short and direct. He guessed what McKittrick was planning: raise the guns' fire to the next crest up the endless Korean hills. Plough the Chinese mortars and the Chinese mortarmen under, then rake the ground in front of the crest: to kill anyone else who thinks he's big enough to come down here; and to kill the few Chinese still able to retreat from our fire.

As he stood up, the Eleventh's guns thumped far behind his back. He coughed, breathed twice. The shells—a brew of high explosive and white phosphorus—arrived, striking the slope in front three hundred yards away. Not quite on the crest, he thought. But McKittrick's right: kill the rest of their infantry first, then the mortars and whoever else is up there on the crest above us.

High explosive killed many, many of the Chinese fleeing up the steepening slope. Some of them were torn apart, their pieces flung across the dirty snow. Others fell in mid-stride and lay still. White phosphorous brushed against others, set their clothes alight, bit into their flesh. Burning Chinese screamed and writhed in the snow as the phosphorus settled into their bones.

Two more ways to go, he thought. Dismemberment and burning. I wonder which is worse.

"Cease fire! Cease fire!" Gunny Phelps shouted as the Eleventh's guns fired again and their shells began to fall on the next crest higher. To kill the mortars, he thought.

"What the hell are you guys shooting at?" Gunny Phelps shouted "Cease fire! I said cease fire! Hanrahan, you fire that rifle again and I'm going to shove it bayonet and all down your greasy unwashed throat! You hear me?"

"I hear you, Gunny."

"But you don't *listen*, Hanrahan," Phelps's bass voice called across the slope. "You've got about as much sense as I thought you did, Hanrahan. And the rest of you," Phelps shouted, his voice rising through the frigid light wind. "I want some calm here. The sonsofbitches look like they're finished. But there are a hell of a lot of Chinese in Korea, and some of them might try it again. So check your weapons, *shut* the hell up, take a break, stay alert and wait for the word." He paused, considering his next opinion. "You did all right. Kept the bastards back and killed damn near all of them. Even you, Hanrahan: you did all right too. Though it gives me a pain in the ass to have to say it."

"Thanks a lot, Gunny," Hanrahan said.

"*Shut* the hell up, Hanrahan," Phelps said. "When I want your . . . Mortars!" he shouted.

More whispers sliding down the sky. Nothing, he thought as he glanced up at the sky. A couple of rounds. The last, mean, vindictive effort of a Chinese mortarman about to be torn to pieces by the Eleventh's shells.

He saw a flicker of black against the gray sky. Fire burst in front of him, a spray of icy water laced with chips of stone lashed his face. Something punched his gut, ripped through his bulky coat, through the sweaters and shirts beneath. A thick razor sliced his abdomen, slashed at his guts.

He lay on his back. The sky was darkening, the temperature dropping:

the snow in which he lay was colder, and he could feel it hardening as the temperature declined. Someone to his left shouted. He raised his head and peered over his chest: to assess the damage.

His heavy coat was stained red and as he looked the stain spread. From the ripped, tattered waist of his coat a mass of gray, ropey intestine speckled with blood protruded.

He let his head fall back onto the snow. Ah, me, he thought as he felt his heartbeat quicken. Pumping for all it's worth, he thought: pumping to keep the system going. Pumping blood out of me. Ah, well.

Fletcher—slim, lithe and quick—knelt in the snow beside him. He watched as Fletcher reached past the pistol in its holster on his webbing belt, grabbed his bag slung on its strap across his left shoulder and chest, jerked it around in front of him and opened it.

I know this bag, he thought. Fletcher's bag: stuffed with compresses, tape, hemostats, syringes and pills.

Fletcher's thin face was bony and freckled: but his cheeks bulged. Looks like a gerbil, he thought. Ought to tell him that. But he's not looking at me. Fletcher's long fingers ripped his ripped coat apart and lifted the ripped pieces of his sweaters and shirts aside.

"Get his left arm out, Gunny," Fletcher said. Young voice. A young man. Twenty, twenty-one years old, and going through this sort of thing.

He saw Gunny Phelps's profile, felt a knife slide blade up from his wrist to his elbow, cutting his left sleeve. Sleeves, that is. Like a bum, he thought as he heard cloth tear, I'm wearing all the clothes I own, and every garment is filthy. And now, bloody.

"Ready," Phelps said.

"Hold this," Fletcher said and he felt pressure against his abdomen. Trying to shove my guts back in, he thought. A first faint needling pain pricked at his groin and thighs, lanced upward into his guts. He grunted and felt his distant cold feet shove against the snow.

Fletcher glanced at him. Ice speckled the Corpsman's scruffy blond beard and the wind lifted his long hair from his forehead. He watched as Fletcher reached into his mouth with his thumb and forefinger and drew out a Syrette of morphine.

I forgot: the corpsmen carry the morphine in their mouths to keep it warm. So that it will flow when they require it to flow.

Fletcher looked him in the eyes and nodded. He felt Fletcher's left thumb press against the inside of his elbow. The metal tip of the Syrette trailed backward across the skin of his forearm, shoved forward, pierced his skin. Fletcher's left thumb pressed against the inside of his elbow stopped pressing and he felt the thick liquid drug flow into his forearm and, with each beat of his heart, felt it rise up his arm, threading into his neck and chest. Fletcher jerked the Syrette from his arm and said, "Let me have got the compress, Gunny."

A shifting of hands on his body. Gunny Phelps's hard, calloused right hand held his forearm still.

Phelps looked into his face and told him the first lie: "You're all right."

Then Gunny Phelps looked him in the face and told him the second lie: "Just lie there, Lieutenant, and we'll get you out of here in a couple of minutes. McKittrick's calling. And remember," the Gunny said, as though he knew his lieutenant had forgotten an important detail, "the road's only a couple of hundred yards downhill behind us. Nothing."

Trying to sell me something, he thought. An insurance policy, a washing machine. But not this time. I'm out of cash, out of time, out of this place.

Beyond Gunny Phelps's shoulder he saw McKittrick standing in the snow, talking into the radio's handset. What are the Eleventh's gunners going to do about this? he wondered. What can they do?

McKittrick nodded and said, "They're making the call right now, Gunny."

"Good work, McKittrick," Gunny Phelps said. "See?" Phelps asked him. "McKittrick's called the Eleventh and they'll call down the road to our guys and the surgeon will be there when you arrive."

"Not necessary," he whispered. "Wasted effort."

"Wasted effort? What the fuck does that mean? You're not hurt bad, Lieutenant. If you were hurt just a little less, hell, I'd make you walk down to the road. But since you're an officer we'll make an exception and carry you down."

"Gunny . . ."

Phelps looked him straight in the eyes and said, in the straightforward firm voice gunnery sergeants used when they told useful lies, "Lieutenant, I'm telling you I've seen guys hurt *lots* worse than this and they were up running around making trouble in a couple of months. It's just a slice across your gut. Don't worry about it."

"I'm inside me, Gunny," he whispered. "I know."

"You *don't* know. Fletcher knows. *You* don't know. Fletcher's the expert here. Aren't you, Fletcher?"

"That's it," Fletcher said, his hands moving inside the wound around the wound in his abdomen. "You take it easy, Lieutenant. Everything's going to be all right."

"Sure," he whispered. "Right."

But his feet and calves and knees were cold and the cold was creeping up his thighs. He was breathing faster. And each beat of his heart chased the one before.

"I'm telling you, Lieutenant," Gunny Phelps said.

"Listen to the Gunny," Fletcher said. He sounded cheerful, as though they were boarding ship for the long voyage home.

He struggled to breathe and whispered, "Don't kid me, Gunny."

"Look, Lieutenant," Gunny Phelps said. "You're hit bad. But I've seen worse and seen them survive. Isn't that right, Fletcher?"

"Gunny's right, Lieutenant," Fletcher said. But he could see something in Fletcher's eyes and in the cast of his face: the faintest evidence that Fletcher knew he could do no more. Still he was willing to perjure himself: "The Gunny's right for sure."

"Sure," he whispered. He could not say more: he could not catch his breath. As though I've been running. Running through this filthy country, running through deep snow. And getting nowhere: running toward yet another useless ridgeline, with another useless ridgeline beyond and another beyond that.

I wonder why we came here?

Whatever, we're leaving now. Down from the Reservoir, back from Yudam to Hagaru to Koto. A couple more passes and then it's downhill to Hungnam.

Not an easy trip, but then it doesn't matter: I won't be there to make it.

He thought of the stalled truck stuffed with the corpses of the dead. He moved his stiffening toes in his distant boots. Just another set of feet sticking out from under the canvas, he thought. Ah, me, he thought as he tried to focus on Gunny Phelps's set, sad face peering at him. Ah, well. To leave like this, after the battle is over. To die in Korea. What a place. What a people.

He wriggled his fingers. Gunny Phelps bent closer. The Gunny's got gray hair, he thought. An old man. With a big voice and the manner required for the work he does. And guts. Lots of guts.

He panted as though he had been thrown into icy water. And I have, he thought: I can feel it rising up my body. Feet solid insensitive blocks of frozen bone and flesh, legs hard with cold.

"Lieutenant?" Gunny Phelps said.

"Get me home, Gunny," he whispered. "Promise me."

"I promise," Gunny Phelps said. The Gunny's hand touched his shoulder. "Lie quiet. You'll be all right. Hang in there, Lieutenant."

"No," he whispered. "No time. For that. But. Promise me. That you'll get me home."

The wrinkles in Gunny Phelps's seamed old face drew together and his mouth twisted as though he had tasted something foul and bitter.

"Promise me," he whispered as he felt the cold rush from his guts upward into his chest.

"I promise," Phelps said, leaning over him. "I promise, Lieutenant," he said. He saw a glitter on the Gunny's eyelashes and thought, he ought to take care. In these temperatures, the liquid that lubricates the eye can freeze.

Then the cold slid up through his lungs and encased his heart and Gunny Phelps's face rose above him, rushing upward until he could no longer see Phelps's features; until he could see nothing but the cold gray sky darkening above him.

SOMETHING BLUNT AND HARD shoved against the back of his trembling right thigh. He jerked away from the shove, stumbled forward through the brush. The sole of his right boot caught against a jagged rock and as he stumbled again, crackling spiny scrub dragged at his trousers.

He lifted his burning hand into the darkness and pushed at the tented shelterhalf collapsed across his face. Light struck at his burning eyes, and the darkness—and the cold, and a seamed concerned face rising away from him—fled from his memory as the hard blunt thing shoved against the back of his leg again, and again.

Stumbling on through the scrub, he turned his face to the right, to try to identify the thing that jabbed at him. A quarter turn and he felt the puffy resistance of a leathery blister that the sun had drawn from the side of his neck. He turned his face to the left. The same resistance. He raised his hand, touched his neck, his throat. His throat was choked with dust. His neck was as thick as his skull. The blisters extended downward to his shoulders. He touched the blister on the left side of his neck, felt the liquid shift beneath the distended skin.

Ah, God, he thought: the sun has drawn all my moisture to my hard dry surface. More liquid sloshes in one of my blisters than in the canteen on my belt.

He stumbled on. Whatever it was that had shoved at him shoved at him again and he jerked away from it.

Easy, you dumb fuck, he told himself. Stop jerking and jumping and running.

He halted, gulped one long breath of air full of bitter burning dust.

The blunt hard thing that had shoved at the back of his right leg ceased shoving at him. He forced his face right against the resistance of the blister, looked down and back. The sling of the rifle had slipped from his shoulder. It hung from his crooked right elbow, the butt inches from the back of his leg.

You *recruit*. What the fuck is the matter with you? Jabbed by your own weapon and you jump up out of your skin?

You're losing it, he told himself. If you don't hang on to yourself, you're going to lose everything you've got.

Get yourself together. Or else.

Uneasy and reluctant, muscle and tendon slid beneath the blisters beneath his burning skin as he arranged his equipment. Settle the belt properly. Unthread the sling from the rifle's carrying handle. Lengthen the sling to give the blisters room—you're bigger now—and fit the rifle's sling over your right shoulder and under your left arm so the weapon will angle across your back, muzzle shoved up away from the shoulder. Shake the dust and sand from rubberized cloth of the shelterhalf so hot it is almost liquid. Settle it over the muzzle of the rifle and over your head and shoulders like the short shroud it may become.

In the scrub a rising dry rattle scratched a warning.

*Fuck*, he thought. Heat, exhaustion, thirst, blisters, fainted three four times, eyesight fading in and coming back. And now a *snake*?

A simple tactical problem, he thought. With a simple solution: unsling the rifle and blast the fucking thing.

No. That's dumb. There's no time to screw around with rattlesnakes. No time for anything except marching.

They should have remembered me. They shouldn't have left me out here.

That bastard sergeant with the dull eyes and the slow, angry manner. And the lieutenant, chewing gum and barking orders, every other word a curse: as though he thinks he going to be the next Marine Corps legend.

Got to get on. Can't be screwing around out here in the brush with snakes. He listened, heard the rattle warn him once again to go another way. He turned and walked straight away from the distinct rattling advice the snake was giving him. As he went he fumbled the compass out of his pocket.

Remember to put it away when you've taken the bearing. Remember to button the pocket.

Think. Keep thinking. Conserve the liquid left to you for your brain. Forget about the pain in your legs. Let your right lung stiffen like old paper, let your left lung become dusty leather. Let your muscles become dry strings, your bones sticks. But think. Without the governor the rest is useless jerking machinery that will, if it is not ordered, destroy itself.

From behind his back he heard a final dry rattle. A last warning that I should go.

He stared at the compass in his filthy hand, felt its ounce of weight sting his cracked palm.

Even the palms of my hands are burned red, he thought. What's next? What the hell's next?

That your palms turn black, he thought. That the sun boils the last bit of water inside you and you become jerky. That you falter and fall unconscious and pant until you die out here in the middle of nowhere.

Piss on that noise. I don't know about the rest of you—you, you fucking sergeant who failed, and you, you fucking lieutenant who set me down and forgot to come back; and you, you bastard captain, who should have ordered a roll-call; and the rest of you right up to the Commandant in his office—but I know about me: I'm going on, straight to the Palms.

No. Got to be fair about it. Gray wasn't part of this, and he wasn't here when this fuckup happened. He's in Washington, shifting bales of paper from one corner of his office to the other, dressed in utilities, sweat staining his armpits and crotch—tough work, heaving paper—and not knowing what's happening to me here, in this place, in this fucking desert I figure ten, twelve miles maybe from the Palms—if I'm estimating the distance travelled right.

Twelve miles from water. Maybe more. And if you don't make it? Then my paltry ocean will join a great sea.

He turned and looked behind him. The trail he had left through the dusty scrub before the snake warned him away from his course was straight enough. Not perfect, but good enough. He lined himself up on the bearing of the lighter green he had dragged through the bushes.

Facing the way I came, he thought. He about-turned. He looked at the compass lying on his stinging palm, watched the needle swing through small arcs and smaller arcs still.

The needle did not lie above the broad arrow scored in the base of the compass.

*Way* off course. Heading damned near east. I wonder how long I've been marching away from one thirty-five degrees?

You better get it together, he told himself as, watching the compass, he turned bit by bit until the needle lay above the arrow and he faced the bearing that he hoped would lead him home: one three five. He checked the compass one last time, slid it into his breast pocket, buttoned the pocket and looked straight ahead. A low, hundred-yard-wide hummock of sand a couple of miles to his front rose like a monster's back from the floor of the desert.

March there, he thought. Stay on course. And think. Plan. Act. And keep thinking. If you don't, you'll wander around out here until you drop.

No: you've already dropped a couple of times. Three times. Or four. Can't remember. Passed out, forced down by the hammering sun. And the next time you fall, you might not get up again.

And another thing: stop imagining you're somewhere else. A burning island, hills as cold as frozen iron and a damp June woods? Cut it out.

Maybe my mind is trying to desert. Maybe it knows what's happening to the machinery inside the hull and it's jumping ship, trying to get the hell out. Trying to save itself.

Bear down, he thought. March. He set off: toward the hummock of sand two miles, he guessed, ahead.

The night I left to join the Corps my uncle said: Whatever happens, hang in there. Stand up against it. You understand me? Whatever happens, you stand up against it.

I understand, I told my uncle then. And I thought I did. But neither he nor I could have imagined that I would have to hang in there in this place, on this day, and stand up against this day's blinding light and baking heat.

Still, he thought: what else can you do? Other than hang in here? Lie down here and wait to die? Shout at the day? Tell the heat to go?

The weight of the rifle eased against his back. Compact, comfortable in the hands, a full magazine shoved up into the breech.

Shoot yourself?

Shooting might be better than wandering until you die of thirst or your brains boil or you stumble one time too many and the insects, reptiles, rats and birds come to tidy up the mess you leave behind.

And without shooting? Life descending into rising heat, cells out of water dying one by one, the whole defeated inch by creeping inch.

Stand up against it, he thought. Hang in there. You never know what might happen next: never.

He marched on, his mind full of light. He thought of nothing except the steady fall of his boots against the sand. He raised the shelterhalf once and looked at the sun. It had moved across the sky a bit. Later—ten minutes? an hour?—he looked at the sun again and saw it had moved a bit more.

A faint buzzing whine rose to his front. Insect, he thought. The sound expanded, became mechanical. Helicopter, he thought. A bird come to get me.

He squinted, looking for the machine. Then he saw it: three-quarters of a mile away, just beyond the hummock toward which he was marching. The helicopter—painted sand and pale brown mottled with green—was flying a couple of hundred feet off the desert, easing through the sky south to north. He could not see the copilot behind the bulbous tinted canopy of the helicopter. But he could see a man standing in the helo's cabin, a visored flying helmet clamped over his skull, his flight suit fluttering in the wind, head turned down to the burning empty desert.

Speed no more than fifty, he thought as he watched the helicopter edging along. And they're not going anywhere particular. They're looking. Or at least they better be. They must be following the main track from the Palms.

I should have stayed on the track, he thought. I should have decided to go the longer distance, on the track, instead of cutting across the angle. If I had done that . . .

Can't retrieve that decision, he thought. Decisions made and implemented are gone. They cannot be taken back. So think: think what to do now.

Move, he thought. Make them see you. He raised both his burning hands, shoved the shelterhalf away from his face and blistered shoulders, flung it to the ground and semaphored his heavy encased arms above his head.

They won't see me, he thought. They can't. I am camouflaged. I am the color of dust. I am a gray, bulbous shape standing against a dust-gray background. Even the camouflage pattern of my dusty uniform was designed to make me invisible in this desert. Only the palms of my hands, the edges of my blisters and my stinging eyes are not gray: they are burning red.

The helicopter lolled on, cruising north. The man in the door of the helicopter turned his visored face this way and that. Looking for something, he thought. And not seeing. Eyes to see, and sees not.

Ah, God, he thought as the helicopter edged along its course, easing away. He lowered his painful, shaking arms. Didn't see me. Looking, sure. But not seeing.

The stock of his rifle shoved against his hip, reminding him of its potential.

Should have thought. Should have had my weapon ready when I identified the sound of the bird ticking through the sky.

He unslung the rifle. The sling rasped across his blistered shoulder and he grunted at the pain. He cocked it, lifted it in his awkward, heavy arms. The blisters on his back wobbled.

Gun the blind sonsofbitches down, he thought as he aimed the rifle. The helicopter slid and wavered, sliding into the haze of dust swept up by the wind sliding across the desert. Sure, he thought: gun them down at three-quarters of a mile. Even with a shoulder-launched antiaircraft missile you'd be lucky to hit anything.

Still: as they say, it's worth a shot. Maybe the guy in the door will see the muzzleflash. Pick it out of the blinding white light into which he stares.

He set the selector: single shots, he thought, are best in this type of tactical situation.

He aimed at the swinging distant shape, gripped the rifle's forepiece and pistolgrip, slid his finger over the trigger, drew breath, steadied the rifle and fired.

The crack of the rifle fled across the desert as the recoil buffeted his shoulder: a smooth minor shove. His blisters heaved. Something rustled in the scrub three paces away.

The helicopter swung and bobbled, coasting along its course northward.

Nothing, he thought. He aimed, fired the rifle again. Still the helicopter bobbled and flew forward as though it were on autopilot.

As though I'm firing blanks, he thought.

The sound of the helicopter's easy passage diminished. The distinctive sweeping throb and thump of the rotor blades stirring the hot air drifted away. Three instants and he could no longer hear the hiss of the turbine. An instant more and he could no longer see the helo: a faint shimmering disturbance low on the northern horizon marked the place of its disappearance.

As he put the rifle's safety on he smelled the bitter scent of burned powder. The memory of the rigorous geometry and careful drill of the rifle range flicked out of the white light that filled his mind. He glanced at the scrub at his feet. He could not see the brass casings of the two rounds he had fired. Screw them, he thought. What would I do with them if I found them? Carry them back and explain—*in detail*—the circumstances in which I expended—*without authorization*—two of the Marine Corps's valuable rounds of rifle ammunition? How I tried to shoot down a *Marine* helicopter?

A helicopter, he thought as he stared at the gray brush. They sent a single helicopter? No wonder they call us jarheads behind our backs.

No, they couldn't have been looking for me. If they were looking for me they would have sent out a squadron of aircraft, tens of vehicles, hundreds of men.

He slung the rifle across his back, bent, picked up the shelterhalf and arranged it over his head and the muzzle of the rifle.

Maybe. Or maybe they wouldn't send all that equipment out to find a single Lance Corporal stumbling through the desert. Maybe they think I've left for town. Or maybe no one's noticed I'm not around. Or maybe they just told one another: fuck it, he must be around somewhere.

No, he thought. The helicopter must have been going somewhere else. Who knows, down here at the level of Lance Corporal, what they choose to do? Or why they choose to do it?

I know one thing, though: whatever they think at Headquarters in Washington, D.C., they aren't supposed to leave me out here. I know that. And I know I'm going to march on through this hot nothing until I get back or it kills me: one of the two.

I knew you'd hang in there, a voice inside his skull whispered.

March: straight ahead. To that hummock of sand. And then go on beyond it.

He slid a foot through the rocks and sand. His puffy, blistered limbs trembled, and he thought: I must look like one of those divers in lead shoes and a rubber suit and a spherical brass helmet.

Except they walk in shadow and cold in the ocean. While I march across the desiccated bed of an ancient lake, the hammer of the sun above beating down the sky, each swinging blow striking at me. And no column of water lies above my skull; and soon none will lie beneath it.

He went on. His pace was solemn and his joints ached. Eyes slitted, staring out of the sloppy tunnel of rubberized cloth at the ground to his front, he felt the temperature rising. He marched on: a hundred paces, five hundred, eight hundred. At last, when the heat seemed to have risen another five degrees, he realized he was struggling and stumbling upward, boots slipping against a slope of loose sand. Done this before somewhere, he thought: on an island surrounded by blue salt water. Once he fell and felt the liquid in his bloated blisters lurch and pull at the livid, tender edges of each swollen tumulus. But he rose and struggled upward: up the smooth unstable slope. He grunted as though he had been beaten, panted as he forced himself up a final pace and stood upright on the summit of the mound that rose like a huge beast's back from the flat scrubby desert below. The sand on which he stood panting and shivering was gray and fine: almost dust. Ancient, he thought. Everything in this awful place is ancient. Reptiles and insects, fangs, exoskeletons, savage guts. And rats: uncomplicated fast mammals scurrying this way and that beneath the scrub, rushing to tear with strong jaws, to feed, to excrete.

From the low summit of the dune he stared ahead: toward the Palms. But he saw only the desert, and at the far edge of his vision a shimmer of haze in which things seemed to move and shift and begin to resolve themselves before they slid back into the haze and shimmered again.

God, he thought. I must have come farther. I must have. But I see nothing except the waste I have walked through all day.

He turned, examined the desert through which he had marched. In the shimmer of heat and light to the northwest he thought he saw the faint outline of the first ridge he had climbed that morning and from which he had begun his march through the desert.

A tremor ran up his spine and the liquid in the leathery blisters on his back heaved. The tremor rose higher: up the back of his skull and farther up, spreading across his scalp. Cool, greasy sweat slid from his forehead and stung his eyes. My ocean becomes smaller still, he thought. A chill ran down his chest, along his limbs. He trembled and recalled that these were the symptoms that had rendered him senseless and toppled him onto the sand before.

Awkward, clumsy, his cumbersome blistered limbs denying him balance and speed, he knelt in the sand and bent forward until he supported himself on his hands and knees. Not so far to fall, he thought as he felt the sling of his rifle slip from his shoulder. The forepiece hammered the blistered back of his right hand. Warm, viscous liquid spurted. But he had no time to examine this small disaster: he was falling toward the sand and as he let himself fall he heard the distant rising whine of the helicopter's turbine approaching. As he heard the paddling of the rotor blades whipping the hot, humid air, he fell the last inches into the darkness that washed over his brain and blinded him.

SWEAT SLICK AS GREASE sliding down his forehead, Private Thompson shouted "The medevac's here, Captain," through the hissing whine and slice of broad rotor blades descending.

Floating on the slow soft current of morphine they had given him, he stared at Thompson standing three feet away. Then he grinned at him. Dried blood dirtied Thompson's unwounded chin. Salt and liquid, he thought as he watched Thompson's sweat trickle through the crusted smear of someone else's blood.

"No kidding, Johnny?" he said. The medical evacuation helicopter swung and edged this way and that, fussed and bustled, descended through the last, difficult fifty feet of its approach toward the hard bed of the paddy strewn with the dead and the wounded and with exhausted thirsty men squatting on the hardpan, survivors waiting to escape from this useless terrible place.

No red cross decorated the helicopter's nose. Useless waste of paint, he thought: the bigger the red cross, the bigger the target. So we don't paint red crosses on our medevacs. That's one of our rules. On the other hand, the Army paints red crosses on theirs. Because they have their own rules. And their rules are different from our rules. Lots and lots of rules over here. One of the reasons we're not doing much: rules. Rules about this, rules about that. Where to shoot, where to bomb, where to urinate, where to go, where to die. Everything done by the numbers worked out in the new, logical, glinty-eyed, forward-looking, hair-combed-straight-back-from-the-forehead Pentagon. I wonder where General Shoup is today? Retired with his Medal, wondering what we're doing here, I suppose; and wondering, I hope, why the hell we're doing it at all.

Still, General Shoup can't help us now: we've been through the abattoir this morning, and now we're sorting out the carcasses of our killed and mending the hides of our wounded.

Long jaw stuck out, two inches of a fat cigar between his stained teeth, Thompson turned his head on his long sunburned neck and peered over his shoulder as the helicopter, turbine whistling and blades whapping, rotated on its axis, shifted its tail right and left, and landed.

Fussy, he thought. He's a fussy helicopter pilot.

"Uh, right, Captain," Thompson said. "I see what you mean. Me being this close to you and all. And the chopper landing right there fifty feet away."

"Good," he said. "That's good." He remembered Gunnery Sergeant Reichmann. He turned his face and looked at Reichmann standing four feet from him chewing tobacco and holding his rifle over his shoulder as though it were a hoe. "Millard," he said, "what's the count?"

Reichmann shifted his chaw to the trough between his teeth and left cheek and said, "Fourteen killed and twenty-six wounded. And you, Six. You make the count of wounded twenty-seven." Gunnery Sergeant Reichmann's voice was calm, plain and level. As though he's disinterested. As though he's talking about requisitioning boots or ammunition. But then he's been in eighteen years, he thought: he's older than anyone in the company, and he acts it. Acts as though he's seen it all before. And probably has, he thought. He was in Korea, after all.

"I'm not wounded, Millard."

"That's nonsense, Six. Your arm's torn up."

"I don't feel a thing."

"No kidding," Gunnery Sergeant Reichmann said, raising his voice to be heard above the whap and hiss of the helicopter. "You're full of dope, Six. You're working on your second Syrette. Or it's working on you. You must think Corpsman Robinson's running some kind of drugstore out here."

"It takes the edge off," he said. "And yeah, I think Levon's running some kind of drugstore out here. He's a Corpsman, isn't he? That's his job, isn't it? To give shots when and where they're needed?"

He did not look at his right arm. He had looked at it once as Robinson had fitted it into the compresses and taped the compresses to his arm and taped the elbow to his waist and his hand against his chest. He had seen bone thrust out of the wound, the ends of the bone shattered like a dried-out broken stick twisted apart. And he had seen severed muscle curled upon itself and white fat and burned black skin and vessels seeping blood. One look, he thought, is enough.

"Look, Captain," Gunnery Sergeant Reichmann began, as though he were trying to sell his officer something useless. "You ought to get on this chopper. We're fine. The North Vietnamese Army's taken off. As near as I can tell, at least. You ought to get that arm looked to."

"I swear to you, Millard: I'm all right."

"I thought officers didn't lie?"

"This officer certainly doesn't."

"That's bullshit and you and I know it, Six," Reichmann said. "A wound like that . . ."

"Forget it," he said. "As you said, this is finished. I think so too. As near as *I* can tell, at least. We're getting out of here *now*. I'll be on the next bird out. I promise you."

"All right," Reichmann said. "All right, Goddamnit, Six. If you want to play Marine hero company commander, then go the hell ahead."

"Pretty salty, Millard."

"Sorry," Reichmann said. "I just don't want to have to come to the hospital and talk over the pros and cons of you losing an arm and have to tell you how one arm is *of course* as good as two arms."

"I understand. And don't worry: I'm not going to lose an arm."

"What, you're a surgeon too, Six?" Reichmann shook his head and spat tobacco juice near his left foot, covered the gob of brown saliva with the sole of his boot and shook his head again. Beyond Reichmann men were humping in four-man groups toward the open door of the helicopter's cargo compartment, crouching as they went, tripping and panting, each group carrying a wounded man. The long broad blades of the machine whipped through a precise spinning blur above their heads.

"I knew I couldn't fool you, Millard." He smiled at Reichmann. Then he said, "What else is going on?"

"What else?" Reichmann said. "Look around, Six."

He looked around. Ahead, the helicopter squatted in the dried out paddy, blades clipping the muggy air, turbine whining, the pilot staring from behind the visor of his flying helmet through the canopy in front of him. Men were lifting one wounded man and then another into the helicopter.

And once it's loaded, he thought, the pilot will move his hands and feet and the chopper will leap from the ground and try to get the hell out of here in one piece. And then try to get the wounded to the surgeon before they bleed to death or die of shock.

He turned—with care, so that his arm did not jiggle and twist—and looked west, beyond the neat straight edge of the last of the stepped series of paddies: at the jungle. Dense, effulgent, displaying fourteen shades of green, the jungle smoldered: smoke rose from fires burning deep in the mysterious complication of vines, plants and trees. A light westerly wind eased a haze of smoke from the jungle across the dry paddy. Scorched leaves, burning cinders and soot soft as cotton fell like evil rain.

To his left the jungle flowed forward, a long, narrow tongue of dense foliage thrust between this paddy and the next one to the south.

The North Vietnamese had opened fire as Morgan's platoon went forward into the angle of the jungle to his front and the tongue of jungle to his left.

I should have argued with the colonel, he thought. The colonel said: go there. A terrain feature and a map reference lay beyond the tip of his blunt finger: an angle, jungle on two sides, open paddy on the third. Perfect place for an ambush. For an ambush thought through with care, planned for weeks, and executed with determination. The Vietnamese, he thought: crafty, opportunistic, thoughtful and hard-working. They consider for months: they think for years. They are patient. They dig and wait for the moment. And they are fanatic.

So we came here, and the North Vietnamese tripped the ambush, firing into Morgan's people from the jungle to Morgan's front and from the tongue of jungle on his left flank. Typical L-shaped setup. Them in the shade in the jungle, and us out here under the sun in the dry paddy, advancing toward our 'objective.' Toward, that is, another useless piece of real estate we would not have kept even if we had taken it.

"Air did a job on them," Reichmann said.

"That's it," he said. "I don't know where we'd be without air. And artillery."

"I know where we'd be," Reichmann said. "We'd be dead inside body bags, waiting for the trip home and not knowing we were waiting."

"I know what you mean. But they got it worse than we did."

"You think?" Reichmann asked. "You're pretty optimistic, Six. But I'm not so sure they were hurt that much. They never seem to be."

"The bombs? The artillery?"

"You know how they dig. They're regular engineers. They probably spent months preparing this ambush. They could be fifty feet underground right now, waiting for the smoke to clear."

"You're pretty pessimistic, Millard."

"I've just been around a lot," Reichmann said. "These guys plan ahead, Six. You know that. You've seen the bunkers, the tunnels. They may be little bastards but they're not messing around and they're not dumb."

"I know," he said. "I know that. But you know why we're here."

"Find them, fix them, fight them," Reichmann parroted, his voice rising. "You think I don't listen when the Army comes out with some neat slogan like that?"

"That's our mission, too."

"The mission's fucked up, Six. You know that. Far as I can see, all we're doing here is punching a lot of holes in the earth and making a lot of enemies. Move people out of their villages? Bomb them? Shoot them? What do we expect them to do, sit there and take it? Go where we tell them? Would you do what you were ordered if you were ordered like we order them?"

"I know," he said. "I know what you mean." The helicopter's blades accelerated, the whine of its turbine rose. He turned his head to watch as the machine leapt from the earth. No one fired at it from the burning jungle. "But whatever. This is finished," he said. "This part of it, I mean. Morgan's people got hit the worst."

"That's it. Chewed up, spat out. He had most of the killed, most of the wounded. Morgan himself was on the first medevac. It looks like he won't make it. Twice in the chest. And his right shoulder was messed up. And another thing, Six: you're the company commander. You're not supposed to go running up to help the lieutenants out. You're supposed to talk on the radio and listen and figure out what to do next."

"I talked on the radio," he said. "I called air. I called artillery. I just moved the command post forward, that's all. While I was talking on the radio. Morgan's that bad?"

"Bad enough so that this company's going to have to requisition another lieutenant. I'll call supply as soon as we get back."

"Here comes another bird," Thompson shouted.

He turned, bulky and awkward with his arm cinched up against his chest across his flak jacket. Funny how a thing like having your arm stuck to your body takes away balance, he thought. Makes me feel fat. But I'm all right: I feel no pain.

Inscrutable behind the tinted visor of his flying helmet, the helicopter pilot zigged and zagged his machine through the sky as he descended over the paddies, approaching from the right, flying across the green face of the jungle.

"What's he doing flying across our front?" Reichmann asked.

"Trying to confuse them, I guess."

"Nobody confuses these guys. This is their table. We just sit here and play for a while. Then we go home. Flying across our front is stupid. And it's dangerous."

"You've got a lot of confidence in the abilities of the North Vietnamese Army, Millard," he said.

A hundred feet to his left, thick purple smoke rose into the windless air. Near the smoke, a man with a radio strapped to his back nodded and nodded as he spoke into the handset. He recognized the man. Morgan's radioman. The front of his shirt was dark with sweat and smeared with blood.

Reichmann said, "You must be getting light-headed, Six. Like I said before: fourteen killed, twenty-six wounded, not including you. That's a pretty good indication of their ability."

"When are they lifting us out of here, Millard?" He watched men kneeling in the dry bottom of the paddy fifty feet from the rising column of smoke. Among the kneeling men Morgan's dead lay under shelterhalves drawn up over their faces. Their boots stuck out from beneath the shelterhalves. Seen that before, he thought. Somewhere else. Somewhere iron cold. He shook his head, he thought: fucking morphine ought to take me somewhere bright and gay.

"Six, you all right? You called for them to come get us and they said fifteen minutes. That was ten minutes ago. I want you on this medevac, all right? Let's go on over there now."

"I said I'm all right, Millard. And I know they said fifteen minutes. And I know they said that ten minutes ago. I was just wondering."

"Huh?" Reichmann said.

"All right. I was just making conversation, then."

"Huh?"

The medevac banked, veered to port. Toward the purple smoke. As it descended its shadow flicked across them. Then the fierce wind of the thumping rotor blades beat up dust and shards of desiccated vegetation from the hard surface of the dried out paddy and the bird passed over them.

"Where's my canteen?" he asked.

"Your canteen? Who cares?"

"I can't find it."

"That's all right, Six," Reichmann said. "Don't worry about it: you know Supply isn't going to ask you about how you lost your canteen. Not after what happened out here today."

"I just wondered," he said. "About the canteen, that is."

"I want you on this bird that's landing, Captain."

"I know," he said. "But I'm not that bad, Millard. You know that."

"Six?"

"Millard?"

"I'm going to shoot you and kill you if you don't get on that bird. Do you understand that?"

"Sure," he said. "Sure I understand that."

"Lieutenant Parlton can take over while you're in the rear getting a Band-Aid put on your arm."

"I thought you thought my arm was in bad shape."

"It is," Reichmann said. "They're going to put the Band-Aid on in San Diego when it's just about healed up six months from now. Look, Captain, do me a favor, okay?"

"Sure, Millard. Anything."

"*Get the fuck out of here and get on that helicopter.*"

"Pretty salty, Millard."

"You said that already."

"Said what?" He could not quite follow what Reichmann was telling him. Probably something to do with my arm, he thought. It didn't hurt; but it was awkward and it ached and the ache unfocused his thoughts.

"'Pretty salty, Millard.' You said that before."

"So?"

"So you only get to say 'salty' once a day. You may be in the Marine Corps, Six. But this is Vietnam. One 'salty' a day is all you get in this place."

"I think I understand that."

"If you don't," Reichmann said, "it's okay because you're going to have a lot of time to think about it. That's all I did when I was under the surgeon's hand in 1951. A through and through in the thigh. Nothing near as bad as your arm."

"You really think I should get on that chopper, don't you?

"Yes. I do."

"Well, all right, Millard. Anything to accommodate you."

"'Accommodate me?' What's that mean?"

"It means, I'll do whatever you say. But look, where's Lieutenant Parlton?"

"I'm right here," Parlton said.

He turned his head. Parlton stood three feet beyond his right shoulder. Square skull. Heavy beard, three days without a shave. Long eyelashes, short legs, a barrel chest, protuberant brown eyes glistening deep in the orbits of his skull beneath his bony brow, long hairy arms smeared with dirt, sweat glistening on the black hair on his wrists. A long, heavy jaw.

Gorilla, he thought. Then he thought: shouldn't think such a thing about one of my lieutenants.

He said: "Parlton, you take over here. I'm going to the rear for a little while. Do what Millard here tells you. Unless you think better. Then do that."

"Right, Six," Parlton said. A low, rumbling voice: as though he suspects I think he's hirsute, short in the legs and not very bright. "I can handle that. And I'll certainly consult with Gunny Reichmann here; and take his advice."

"Good," he said.

Reichmann nodded. But he looked as though he knew Lieutenant Parlton was going to need a lot of advice repeated over and over again. Or maybe not.

"I'm going, then," he said.

"Thompson," Reichmann said. "Take the Captain's gear and load it into the chopper. Be *sure* he gets on the chopper, Thompson. If he doesn't get on the chopper, you're responsible. You understand that?"

"Sure, Gunnery Sergeant," Thompson said. But he eyed his captain as though he wondered whether he could force against his will into a helicopter.

"Don't worry, Millard. I'm going. I'm not going to give Johnny any trouble."

"You better not, Six," Reichmann said. "Or he's in trouble. You with me, Thompson?"

"Yes, Gunnery Sergeant."

"Get the Captain out of here, Thompson. Now. And close your mouth, Thompson. Try to keep it closed. It's ugly when you hold it open like that."

"Right, Gunnery Sergeant," Thompson said. He closed his mouth, hefted his captain's pack and rifle and said, "This way, Captain," as though he thought his Captain might not have noticed the hissing, idling medevac helicopter squatting on the dry bed of the paddy. Thompson nodded at him, turned, and walked away.

"Take it easy, Millard."

"I'll see you in the States," Reichmann said.

"In the World, you mean."

"Fuck that jargon," Reichmann said. He moved his jaws, chewed, spat. "This is the world. Right here. And part of the world—the part that's all torn up, like you—is being loaded into that bird over there. Some of that part goes on this bird, and the rest of it goes on the next one and the next after that. The next part of the world—those who were killed—will go out on the next bird and the next after that."

"I understand," he said.

"You do? Yes, I suppose you do, Six." Reichmann spat again, nodded at his bandaged arm cinched against his chest, and said, "I guess you do. After all, you've paid a part of the price we're paying for this fucked-up mess they call a war."

"Okay, Millard. Take care," he said.

He turned away and followed Thompson across the cracked surface of the paddy. Like concrete, he thought. And four months ago, it was a regular lake with old men and women and children bending to shove the rice plants into the muck beneath the water.

As he walked toward the helicopter a Marine said, "You did all right, Six."

He looked at the man. The man's face was in shadow and the sun was behind him. He didn't recognize him.

He nodded and said, "Thanks." But he thought: all right? Many killed and many wounded and I did all right?

"Come on, Captain," Thompson called back to him. "They're going to want to get these guys out of here."

"Coming," he said. The colonel will say: these things happen. Those were my orders and you carried them out. It's too bad about the losses, but that's the way things go. We've had higher losses.

But he knew what the Lieutenants would say: this fucking war, and the fucking captain in command. Neither of them is worth shit. And that goes for everyone right up the line: to the fucking White House.

And I have no excuse. I should have done something else. I should have argued with the colonel, or refused the order, or done something different in the field.

But what else was there to do? he wondered. What else could I have done? Get out of the birds in the paddy, the colonel said, his blunt finger tracing the line of approach. Then go across the paddy, to right here: his fingertip tapped the map. If they're there, you'll flush them out. The colonel spoke of the enemy as though they were quail lurking in the stubble of the gray autumn fields of his native Virginia. He seemed to think they would flutter and fly up as we approached. But this isn't Virginia and they weren't quail and they didn't scatter. They were men, and they were armed with assault rifles, machineguns, rocket-propelled grenade launchers and mortars. They lay in the positions they had prepared with such care, levelling their rifles, readying their machineguns, aiming their rocket-propelled grenade launchers and crouching about their mortars. They waited for us to put our head in the sack just as the colonel told us to. And we did. I did.

No excuse, he thought. Whatever the colonel ordered, I have no excuse.

The bird's pilot throttled up and the machine's turbine hissed at him as the blades cut the air with the thick whipping sound of a heavy sword. The pilot turned his head and looked at him. The helicopter was light on its skids: it waited for him between the earth and the sky.

Thompson shouted, "We're there, Captain."

"No kidding?" he said, and thought: light-headed. Full of dope. Full of odd words. Screwy. But screwy is better than the pain that waits for me.

A clutch of Marines stood aside as Thompson helped him forward to the door. The helicopter's crewchief wore a bulbous flight helmet. The smoked visor tipped toward him as the crewchief reached down, took his rifle from Thompson and laid it between two wounded, leaned down again and took his pack, tilted it against the padded forward bulkhead of the compartment.

He placed a hand on the deck of the helicopter and said, "I can make it."

The crewchief gripped his left arm with a gloved hand and hauled while Thompson heaved from behind. He got a knee up inside the helicopter and pushed upward as the crewchief pulled him inside. As he settled against his pack, the crewchief shouted, his voice muffled by his helmet. The helicopter shivered, trembled and leapt into the air, tail rising, turbine hissing, rotor blades tilting forward. His stomach lurched. Shouting behind the visor that hid his face, the crewchief danced away, feet stepping from one narrow space between the litters to the next.

Can't understand him, he thought.

From the corner of his left eye he saw yellow fire trailing smoke rushing toward him from the jungle's green shadows. Weapon, he thought as he turned his face and watched it leaping toward him, wobbling as came on.

Projectile, he thought: rocket-propelled grenade. The warhead hammered the right side of the helicopter. The explosion shoved the bird to port. Blue sky filled the starboard doorway. He gripped a handhold in the deck with his good hand. Teetering on the coaming of the port door, the crewchief shouted, whirled his arms, lost his balance as the helicopter canted farther to port and fell from the hatch. Two wounded men lying on stretchers slid after him as the long trailing cord that connected the crewchief to the helicopter's intercom system whipped across the cabin and flicked away: toward the graybrown bottom of the paddy no more than sixty feet below.

Maybe they'll make it, he thought. He turned his head left and peered up into the pilot's compartment. The pilot's hands and feet shoved and jerked at the controls. The pilot's helmet was gone: so was most of his head. To the pilot's left, the copilot sat in his seat as though he knew he could relax since this difficult aerial moment was being handled by the aircraft commander.

He blinked. Something wrong with the copilot, he thought. Then he saw blood slide from beneath the rim of the copilot's flying helmet. He jerked his head right, saw the earth—hard, graybrown, its mud baked to concrete by the sun—rushing upward.

He jerked his head about to face the rear of the helicopter as the tip of one of the blades struck the iron ground. The machine bounced and levelled off: as though the pilot were still trying to make a controlled landing. Then the machine tilted to starboard and the rotors beat themselves to bits against the earth. The body of the helicopter struck the paddy. The complicated array of forces flung him upward through the hatch canted above him. His right leg dragged across a jagged piece of the crashing helicopter. He felt skin and flesh tear, muscle spring apart, bone break. The ground spun beneath him.

Moving fast, he thought. Flying.

His right shoulder struck the earth. He heard the solid bones in his shoulder crack, felt his collarbone splinter like a thin stick, gasped as the force that had flung him from the chopper hammered his face against the earth. More bones snapped. Then he saw the sky rushing above him, felt the abrasive surface of the paddy scouring the flesh from his back.

His skidding flailing body came to a halt. He screamed, breathed twice and screamed again. Someone in the distance shouted, "Jesus Christ. I *mean* Jesus Christ."

He thought about it: Christ, religion, order, tradition. All that.

Something exploded beyond his feet: the helicopter's fuel, he guessed: through the blood that veiled his eyes he could not tell.

Maybe another round fired by that guy with the rocket-propelled grenade launcher. He heard crackling flame and felt heat on the right side of his face. No. Must have been the fuel in the bird that exploded: why waste another valuable rocket-propelled grenade?

Someone gripped the collar of his flak jacket and dragged him away from the heat, dragging his bloody back across the concrete paddy. I am a sack of broken bones and bloody meat.

He screamed. The man pulling him said, "Take it easy, Six," and pulled him on across the rough ground. To his left and right, rifles were firing on full automatic. A machinegun began to fire: good weapon, he thought, though a little balky if not cleaned twice or more each day.

Broken jaw, he thought, broken nose, two jagged edges grating in my head: broken skull. Great. Just great.

He screamed, screamed again.

The man hauling him said, "Come on, Six."

Silhouetted against the flames rising from the helicopter, he saw a man running toward him, a bag bouncing on his hip. The man dragging him across the ground stopped hauling at him.

"Levon?" he croaked as the Corpsman knelt beside him.

"Right here, Captain. You take it easy. Everything's going to be all right. Going to give you a shot."

He turned his head, looked across the paddy. To Robinson's right, two riflemen knelt on the hard surface of the paddy, firing their rifles into the jungle. Beside them a third man crouched, firing one round after another from a grenade launcher.

"Another shot?" he mumbled. "Had two already."

Robinson did not seem to understand him. But he said, "Time for another shot, Six. Lie still now."

As he felt Robinson's fingers touch his bloody left arm, he saw Reichmann's face above him.

"Captain," Reichmann said. "Jesus Christ. What the fuck is this? I mean, this time you're for *sure* going to get on the next chopper out. Medevac or not."

"Not sure," he thought he mumbled, "about helicopters."

"What?" Reichmann asked him. "What did he say? What the hell's going on, Robinson?"

"The leg's not bad," Robinson said. "Sliced open, but no artery or large vessels have been cut. The leg's broken. Shoulder too, it looks like. And the other arm. But he wasn't burned. Lucky you got him away from the fire, Gunny. The rest of it can be fixed. It's nothing."

Nothing? he wondered. Okay, though. Robinson knows what he's doing.

"Right," Reichmann said, as though he agreed with Robinson's diagnosis. "You're going to be all right, Six. Robinson says so. Don't you, Robinson?"

"You got my word. What more do you want, Gunnery Sergeant?"

"Nothing, Robinson. For Christ's sake get to work, would you?"

"I'm working." His hands were full of bandages, his thumb stuck through the hole in the center of a tin wheel of tape.

"I'm all right," he mumbled.

Reichmann said: "I can't hear you, Six. But I'm telling you this: you're all right."

"Yes," he said, but the sound that came out of his broken mouth was "Yeth." Mouth full of blood, he thought. He tried to spit but his tongue wandered toward the inside of his cheek.

"See? You're all right. We're agreed."

"Not me," he mumbled.

"What'd he say?" Reichmann shouted. "Goddamnit, Robinson, what did he say?"

"Couldn't make it out. Gunnery Sergeant, put one hand here, the other here. Hold those bandages down hard. Press. Okay?"

"I got it," Reichmann said.

"This reminds me of something," he mumbled. His voice was caught: in a lacerated throat, behind a broken mouth, below a smashed nose, beneath his skull's grating plates. I'm in pieces, he thought. Slashed here, broken there.

About what I deserve: fourteen killed, twenty-six wounded? Less than I deserve. The colonel ought to be here with me, his bloody back against the concrete bed of this paddy. It was his hand on the handle, after all; his finger on the map.

"What's the word, Levon?" Reichmann asked. "Tell me, for Christ's sake."

"He's gonna make it, Gunnery Sergeant. Don't worry: I've got it covered."

"I love you, Robinson."

"Jesus Christ don't say that. That's bad luck, you saying a thing like that. You're the Gunnery Sergeant, and I don't want to hear nothing about how you got feelings. I been counting on you not having any feelings at all. You understand me?"

"Shut the hell up with that superstitious stuff, Robinson, and keep working," Reichmann said. "You and I are going to talk later."

"All right by me, Gunny."

"You bet your ass it's all right by you," Reichmann said.

"I . . . ," he said. But the sound that slid from his mouth was: 'ahhhh.'

"I know, Six," Reichmann said. "It hurts. But you're going to be all right. Robinson gave you another shot."

Something inside his chest shifted, squirmed between his lungs. He breathed, panted, gasped, trying to make room inside his chest for whatever it was that was expanding, pressing against his heart.

"What the fuck is going on, Robinson?" Reichmann said. "What's the matter?"

"Seems like . . ."

Pain leapt up his neck. His tongue was without feeling: thick, its movements sloppy, it slid this way and that in his mouth. Something going on here, he thought. What the hell am I . . . ? Where was it when I . . . ?

Something struck at him, probed at the meat inside his skull. Pain scattered through his brain. He gasped and spat blood.

"Something inside him, Gunny," Robinson said. "I don't know if . . ."

"Goddamnit, Robinson, you said he was going to make it. I mean Goddamnit, Robinson."

"It's internal," Robinson said. "I don't think . . ."

Both his hands pressed against the bloody bandages, Reichmann shouted, "Do something, Robinson. I mean, for God's sake come on, do something. Keep fucking trying, Robinson."

Millard Reichmann, he thought as the pain inside his skull darkened his sight. Reichmann, Millard: Gunnery Sergeant, USMC. My keeper and confidant. Kept me straight, kept me out of trouble. Right up to the moment that medevac chopper fell out of the sky. Was shot out of the sky by an implacable Vietnamese concealed in the jungle, a rocket-propelled grenade launcher on his shoulder.

Bad luck. A rearrangement of the pieces on the board, a change in the numbers, the odds shifting against.

"Fifteen now," he said. But the sounds that came out of his bloody mouth and broken jaw were twisted and blunt.

"What?" Reichmann asked. "What, Six? Tell me."

"Fif. Teen. Now."

Robinson said, "Gunny, he said, 'Fifteen now.'"

"Goddamnit no, Six," Reichmann shouted, pressing down on the bandages beneath his hands as though he could press the harm away. "Not fifteen. Not, Goddamnit."

He thought, It's okay, Millard. The press of Reichmann's hands eased.

Getting cooler: the sun must be going down. I recall snow and iron cold.

He tried to speak, choked on the blood in his throat. It doesn't matter any more, Millard. I'm fucked up. What good would I be damaged like this? Forget it, Gunnery Sergeant.

Jaws working, mouth moving, Gunny Reichmann shouted something else at him. But the riflemen began to fire into the jungle again as another helicopter approached from the east and he could not hear what Reichmann was shouting at him this time.

HE OPENED HIS SWOLLEN eyes. He saw nothing. Blind, he thought. He gasped, and heat and dust filled his lungs.

He moved his fingers: the puffy skin on the back of his left hand tingled and the liquid inside the blister shifted. The back of his right hand stung, and he recalled the rifle's forepiece striking him, the blister bursting, the viscous serum spurting.

He lay on his puffy back on a broad smooth stone. His spine and the bones of his neck ached. He turned his head: the collar of his shirt scraped his burning skin and he hissed at the pain. His swollen tongue filled his mouth. He tried to swallow. His throat was a dry shaft closed upon itself. His cracked lips stung. He touched them with the tip of the gritty swollen bulb of his tongue. The taste of salt, dust and dried blood sickened his guts.

He raised his puffy arms encased in blisters: his fingers touched the shelterhalf that shrouded his face. He pushed the shelterhalf away, held one arm across his eyes to defend himself from the blinding light. He rolled over, got up on his hands and knees and gagged, gagged again. He shuddered, recalled a trembling dog vomiting up shards of bone. He trembled and his guts heaved a clot of something bitter into the back of his mouth.

Ah, God, he thought. He shifted his swollen tongue in the dusty hole of his mouth, found a dry flat pebble beneath his tongue. He spat it onto the broad course of stone on which he crouched like any other animal.

Water? None left, he thought. Little enough to start with, and none left now. Drank it, sip by sip. Five, six miles ago. If I remember right.

He gagged, retched, tasted the clot of sludgy muck he had vomited up. Bitter as gall, dense as drying mud. He spat it onto the rock and thought, all messed up. No water, the sun still high in the sky. Hours until night.

Or maybe not, he thought. Maybe the night cometh right now.

Get up, he told himself. Get your feet under you. You're not an animal and you don't live on all fours. Get up.

He drew his knees beneath him, pushed with his hands, and knelt. The rifle's sling was tangled about his right arm. He lifted the sling onto his shoulder and thought, stand up. His thighs trembled and someone shouted, Give me ten more of those squat thrusts! So I can be sure you've got a pair!

Yes, Sergeant Quinlan. Ten more, to show you I've got a pair.

Shuddering, lifting the weight of the liquid in the blisters that had risen from his skin and distended his shirt and trousers, he stood. He swayed, looked for the horizon, found it: a long straight line above the heaped grayred sand and thwarted scrub. He forced himself to focus his eyes, to squint, to look. To think.

I was on a dune. I remember that. That is the last thing I remember.

He turned his head and looked about him. He could not see the dune. I must have moved while I was out. But I couldn't have been unconscious and marched at the same time, could I?

Forget it. No dune. And no anything else. No choppers. No sound except the rasp of the hot breeze sweeping fine, abrasive grit across the desert.

On the horizon a thin plume of dust rose into the pale blue sky. From the base of the plume, a flash of light blinked at him.

Incurious and disinterested, he waited for the light to blink again.

Someone out there. And some thing. A truck, a chopper skimming across the sparse foliage.

But they are not coming here. They are going another way. Like the aircraft and the chopper. And even if they fly right over me, or drive past a hundred yards away, they will not see me, for I am dust gray and dust red. I look like the desert I am becoming.

Perfect camouflage, he thought. The Department of Defense should send a team of camouflage experts out here right now, today, to assess this new concept in camouflage: gray and red dust. They could bring along a sergeant to shout about how valuable this innovation in the art of camouflage is to the field Marine. Powder it on your face! Sprinkle it on your hands! You'll be invisible! They can't shoot you if they can't see you! But *you* can shoot them!

The light blinked at him again. Flashing a message. All I need is a radio to tell them to come on with thirty gallons of water and a truck to take me back to the Palms. He stared at the horizon, waiting for another signal. But the light did not flash again.

Gone, he thought. As everyone in my head has said, you're going to have to work this one out by yourself. No buddy is on his way to help you. No corpsman is bringing you succor. No one in the platoon, the company or the battalion is looking for you. And sure not the battalion exec or the battalion commander.

This is as it has been since dawn, when that last truck screeched and rumbled away: you against the house. You will get out of here if you get yourself out of here. And if you fail, you will die in this desert.

Fuck them all, he thought. And fuck this desert. I'll make it: one step and then the next. I'll drink the viscous liquid in the blisters on my burning back. I'll march down the bearing and march up to the gate and tell the gateguard to get the hell out of my way and march to the barracks and drink a single glass of water and go talk to that fucking sergeant and his fucking lieutenant.

He staggered forward, one pace, another, croaking numbers as he went, counting his steps, his blistered lips seeping blood. He counted to one hundred twenty-seven before he thought: where are you going?

He stopped. He swayed as his blistered fingers unbuttoned the breast pocket of his shirt. As he picked the compass out a long blister on his forefinger tore. Oily silver liquid slid over the compass. He sucked his finger, licked up the salty flow, licked the compass clean. The sea, he thought. I taste the sea.

He looked at the compass. The capsule in which the needle had swung was smashed. The needle was bent and dismounted from the pin on which it had rested. He shook the compass, shook it again, heard the tiny sound of the needle tick against the casing of the compass. Finished. When I fell it must have smashed against a rock. Worthless.

He flicked the compass away into the scrub. Another useless encumbrance. An empty canteen. A broken compass. Fouled-up orders. Negligent officers, dull sergeants. Useless.

The butt of the rifle tapped his thigh. To remind me it is not useless. To remind me that its purpose is singular and that it will function in this environment. It and the lizard. And the snake. And the scorpion.

A way to slake my thirst without opening my mouth, he thought. A door out of the sunlight into the dark.

Take a look around, he thought. Figure out where you are. Something about the angle of the sun in the sky and the time of day.

He looked at his watch before he recalled it did not work. Now the crystal was shattered, the hands twisted and bent. Another casualty of one of the falls I took. Another useless particle of trash. He unstrapped it, flung it away.

The scrub and stones ripped my uniform, exhaustion shoved me down, broke my compass and shattered my watch that went bust hours ago. Soon I will have nothing left to help me in this struggle except blisters packed with sloshing liquid, desiccated flesh and dried tendon. And my rifle: its pieces will endure in this dry place forever. In a thousand years someone could dig it out of the sand, disassemble it, oil it, reassemble it and kill anyone he wants to with it.

Something skittered through the scrub. Clumsy, slow, the liquid in the blisters that had drained him dry heaving along his limbs and back as he moved, he unslung the rifle, raised the weapon, pointed it. A lizard preening on a rock ignored the weapon, stared at him with one eye, stared at the horizon with the other. A shadow flicked over him, another, a third. He looked up at the deathly sun, at the sky so pale it was more white than blue. Three black birds planed away. Filthy feathers, hooked beaks, beady hooded eyes. He knew them. He had seen them before. They gathered above the halt, the injured, and the reeking dead.

I'm carrion, he thought. Or soon will be.

Or so the birds think.

"Why don't you sling that weapon, get yourself set up and go on?"

He looked to his right, to his left. No one. He turned, hand clutching the pistol grip of the rifle, stared at the scrub. No one. Who the hell? he wondered.

You, he thought. That's who it is: you. You're talking to yourself. You're near the edge. Near, hell: you're *on* the edge. And stop complaining: pretty soon you'll want to join a group counselling session. Prattle, words, explanations. And caring. Useless.

Look at the sun. Look around. Figure. Think, for God's sake. If you can't figure it out, you'll go the wrong way. And remember: a single degree of deviation on a ten mile march will leave you hundreds of yards left or right of your destination.

He slung his rifle. He bent, picked up the dusty shelterhalf. His trembling hands tented it over his skull and the muzzle of his rifle.

He looked out from beneath the shelterhalf at the sun. Time? Make it three in the afternoon. Then the sun must lie in the southeastern quadrant of the sky: above the Palms. Or near enough.

March toward the sun, then.

Ponderous, he turned and looked behind him at the ground he had traversed: stark, stony, scattered with scrub. The color of the low mountains far to the northwest had altered. At dawn, they had been gray. Now the gray was tinged with red. The angle of the sun in the sky, he thought.

He turned, and as he peered forward across the desert he thought, You've come this far. You can go on.

And if I don't make it?

Then I will not need to eat again, or drink again. I will not need rest: I will not require a chair again, or a bed to sleep in, and I will not need to speak to anyone ever again. I will not spend another day at home, for I will not see another day.

Nothing, then. Nothing at all if I do not make it out of here. And if I do not prevail, what will I leave behind? Nothing except what they remember of me.

More than all else, be sure they remember that here, in this desert, you showed them how to die.

Be sure they remember that: be certain they know you died as you were brought up, as you were trained.

Sure, he thought. But how does a Marine die? And what evidence can I leave behind that will demonstrate what I was and that I died as I should?

Hang on to your weapon, he thought. And *don't* shoot yourself. If you die in this awful place, make it kill you: don't do the job for it. And keep going. Show them you tried. Show them you've got a pair.

That's it? he wondered. That's all there is? To show them you've got a pair?

That's it, he told himself. There isn't any more. In the end, that's all there is: to show them you went on. To prove to them that you continued, even when your mouth was full of stones and the last drop of water in your body had evaporated and you staggered as though your bones were cracked and your joints locked.

Don't think about it. You're not supposed to think. You're a Lance Corporal: you're supposed to march. That's what you're here for: to march, and to hang on to your weapon. The rest of it's for the Commandant and his subordinates. Who were supposed to know better.

He set off, stumbling through the waste, his trousers brushing the dusty scrub, one unsteady step following the next, his taut baked muscles and aching bones sluggish beneath the cumbersome blisters. So he proceeded, staggering toward the point on the horizon beneath the sun, marching toward the shade he knew lay somewhere beneath the light.

TEAR GAS DRIFTED THROUGH the shade beneath the poplars in the garden outside the tall windows of the embassy's library. Beyond the poplars against the south wall of the compound, the gas lay like thick mist. And beyond the wall, in the avenue, the mob chanted the same three words again and again.

"This here job is getting a little tough," Corporal Falk said. "What with the gas and all."

"We're all right," he said. "A few came over the wall but the gas drove them back out."

"What's that mean?" Corporal Call asked. "What they're chanting."

"Who the fuck cares?" Falk said. "But I'll tell you what it means, Call. Boiled down, it means fuck you, and fuck your country. That's what it means."

The guard commander, Gunnery Sergeant Simms, came into the library, looked them over, and said, "No shooting. If they start coming over the walls in number, there's to be no shooting unless they start shooting."

"No shooting?" Corporal Call asked. "What's that mean, Gunny?"

"Mean what it says, Call. No shooting first. You know the orders. We're here as embassy security. We're not here to start a war, or even a fight. If you want to fight, you should have stayed a field Marine and not joined the Marine Security Guard Battalion."

"What if they come in here armed and try something?" Corporal Allen asked, his voice rising with each word. "What if they start shooting inside the walls? What if they start killing the staff?"

"Then you can shoot. Unless you have the ambassador's orders to the contrary. Whatever he says, you do. But remember this: we don't start anything, Allen. You know that, and you better fix it in your mind. You start shooting without authorization and you can forget about them outside the walls and start worrying about me."

"Sure, Gunny," Allen said.

"I'm not debating you, Allen. I want to hear an 'I understand, Gunnery Sergeant.'"

"I understand, Gunnery Sergeant."

"That's better. Now just shut up, all of you, and do what you're told."

"Nobody's told us anything," Call said. "All I've heard is them out in the street chanting those three words."

Simms said: "You know what they're saying, Call. Or maybe you were asleep during the language lessons? And I'm about to tell you everything else you need to know right now, Call, if you'll shut up and listen. Any of you with loaded weapons, unload them. The word is, you can only load up again if shooting starts. And remember to be ready to disassemble them and hammer the pieces to junk if we're ordered to surrender. You got the hammer, Falk?"

"Sure I got the hammer, Gunny." He pulled a masonry hammer out of his belt and held it up in his right fist. "Hammer anything with this baby."

Simms said: "Keep it handy. If they start coming through the walls and the ambassador says give up, I don't want them taking these weapons in an operable condition. You can handle all this?" he asked them. "You can handle what's going on?"

"Sure we can handle it, Gunny," Call said. "What the hell? Sure we can."

"All right. Now, every one of you get out of here and get to your post. If you're driven out, come back here. You," he said, pointing at him. "You supposed to be in the vault. Get on in there."

"Right, Gunnery Sergeant," he said.

"Mr. Williams is in there burning stuff and wiping the computers and destroying the coding machines, just in case. Like you know, you supposed to guard him in there until he's finished. When it's done, you come out, like you know, and report to me back here—*with* Mr. Williams."

"Right, Gunnery Sergeant," he said. "I know the drill."

"I know you do. Now get on."

"Don't get caught inside there," Allen told him. "It's sealed up tight."

"No shit, Allen?" Gunnery Sergeant Simms said. "You an expert on sealed-up-tight vaults?"

"No, Gunnery Sergeant. I'm just telling him: don't get caught in there."

"Where you going, Gunny?" Call asked.

"Check out the rest of the guard. What else?"

"I still got some questions about when we can shoot."

"You know the standing orders, Allen," Gunnery Sergeant Simms said. "So just shut up and do what you're told. Do what you're *supposed* to do."

"Yes, Gunnery Sergeant."

"That's better. You," he said. "Come with me. I'm going past the vault."

"Right, Gunnery Sergeant."

As they went out of the room Allen began to work the slide of his riotgun. The shells leapt one after another from the weapon's breech onto the wide table in the center of the room. Call and Falk dropped the magazines from their rifles and slid them into pouches on their equipment belts.

Walking in step with him down the corridor, Gunnery Sergeant Simms said, "Soon as this is over I'm gonna get Call, Falk and Allen a transfer to a recon company, see how they like rapelling out of helicopters and humping through swamps and having mosquitoes eat their ass."

"Everyone's nervous, Gunnery Sergeant," he said.

"You don't seem nervous to me, Corporal," Simms said.

"It's a mob," he said. "Even if they come in here, they're not going to want to kill anyone. They want to be able to parade us in front of the embassy with our hands up. Like before."

"I hope you're right about that," Simms said. "Trouble is, you can't tell with a mob. Maybe this one will be different. Still, we got the ambassador's orders: no shooting unless they start. Or unless they try to get into the vault. So you got one more option than the rest of us to think about, Corporal. You get to shoot if they get in there before Mr. Williams is finished fucking up his machines and shredding his paper."

"I know," he said.

"That's why I chose you to be the one in the vault: because you know. You got the code for the keypad in your mind?"

"Sure, Gunnery Sergeant."

"That's good," Gunnery Sergeant Simms said, "seeing as you're the only one of us who knows it."

"I know," he said.

"Here we are," Simms said as they walked up to the door of the vault. Except for the keypad at chest height to the right of the frame, this door seemed no different from any other along the corridor. But he knew how different it was: the wood of the door was backed by steel, and the frame of the doorway and the walls, floor and ceiling of the room were steel overlaid with rebarred concrete. A complicated locking mechanism on the inside of the door, a miniature version of the lock on a bank vault's door, sealed the door into the frame. Williams had told him the door and the room would withstand any attempt at penetration.

Except gas, Williams had said, opening a box and showing him two gas masks. Gas will work its way through the ventilation system. And, Williams had said as he closed the box, a conflagration in the building would render it impossible for us to remain in the vault. If the building burns, the heat in here will become intense. But they won't do that, Williams had said, voice full of confidence. He had sounded as though he had consulted many mobs and had gotten assurances from them that fire was out of the question. They want what we have in here, he'd said. This is the communications center. Without the computers and coding machines and files in here, the embassy's relevant staff really doesn't know very much. In any case, Corporal, that's my worry. Yours is to be here if there's trouble. In case someone who isn't permitted gains entry during a crisis.

How? he had asked.

Who knows? Perhaps they'll be able to learn the keycode by threatening one of the relevant staff.

How long does it take to finish up with everything in here?

That's classified. But not long. Not an hour. I can't say more.

Right, he had said.

"Go on, now," Gunnery Sergeant Simms said. "Tap in those numbers and go on in there and help Mr. Williams out."

Simms walked away down the hall as he tapped in the numbers. The door's lock clicked. He swung it open. Williams stood in his shirtsleeves at the rear of the vault, feeding files one after another from a stack on a table to his left into the lips of the shredder to his right.

"How's it going, Mr. Williams?"

Sweat stained the armpits of Williams' shirt. "Seal the door and come over here, Corporal."

Williams isn't the most cheerful guy I've ever met, he thought as he turned to the door, shoved it closed and spun the locking handle. On the other hand, he's got more worries right now than anyone else here.

"You can put that shotgun down and feed these files into the shredder, Corporal. I have to get to work crunching the code machines and killing the hard disks in the computers. That's the order: destroy the code machines and low-level format the hard disks on the computer."

"'Crunching' them? What's that mean?"

"You'll see," Williams said. "Nifty little device that transmogrifies expensive electronic equipment into useless unrecognizable junk. Come on, feed these files in here."

"'Transmogrifies'?"

"Changes completely and forever." Williams gestured at his riotgun, gestured at the stack of files, the shredder. "Your shotgun and this device both transmogrify things. So, stow your shotgun and start feeding files into the shredder. You grind them up while I get to work on the machines."

He leaned the riotgun against a filing cabinet and walked to the shredder. The bin behind the shredder was full of minuscule bits of damp paper. "I thought these things slit paper into strips," he said.

"They used to," Williams said. He was down on his knees, dragging a bulky cardboard box from beneath a table shoved up against the end of the vault. "People glued the strips together and there we were: embarrassment and recrimination all round. Now the machine makes tiny dots of paper and sprays a chemical on the dots that renders these valuable files into a mush of pulp and ink."

He lifted a file from the stack on the table to the left of the shredder. A message printed in red letters warned him of the secrecy of the file's contents.

"Should I be doing this?" he asked.

"You have to. I've got to lobotomize these machines." He hefted the box, slid it onto the table, opened it, lifted out a heavy steel container with a long handle on the right side, dropped the cardboard box on the floor and shoved it under the table with his foot. "The cruncher," he said. "Sort of a trash compactor. And don't worry about the files, Corporal." Williams made the sign of the cross in the air in front of him. "Now you're blessed. Shred away. Hold it, though. Better rip the papers out from the back of the file and work forward. That way, you won't see what's written, and we can both swear later you saw nothing and know nothing. About what's in the files, I mean."

"Right," he said. He laid the file face down on the table, opened the back and tore out fifty or so sheets. "How much should I put in each time?"

"About that much," Williams said. "The machine can gulp sixty sheets at each go. I make it forty to be sure it doesn't jam, but it will take what you've got there. There's a sheet-feeder, but it's broken."

"Okay," he said. He fed the sheaf of papers in his hand into the lips of the shredder. The machine whirred, clicked and ground as it drew the papers inch by inch into itself. As tiny circular bits of paper fell into the bin behind the machine, he smelled stringent chemicals.

"You've got the idea," Williams said. "Keep feeding."

"No sweat," he said.

"I wouldn't say that," Williams said. "It's hot in here. But then, it's always hot in here."

He fed the contents of file after file into the shredder as he watched Williams disassemble coding devices and drop their complicated electronic guts into the steel container he had called a trash compactor. He closed the lid of the container. "Watch this," he said. He gripped the handle, leaned his weight on the lid of the steel container, pulled back on the handle. "It's geared," he explained as the contents of the container screeched.

"Geared?" he asked.

Williams let go of the handle and it eased back through an arc of a hundred thirty-some degrees.

"Take a look," Williams said as he opened the lid of the container. "Nothing secret here now. Be happy to have you take this junk away."

He stepped to the table, looked into the container. A compact mass of electronics a few inches wide crushed into itself lay on the gray steel floor of the container.

"Crushes it, see?" Williams said. "Grinds it into itself, anneals one piece into another. *No* one is going to untangle this. Particularly after

I crush it the other way." He reached into the container, turned the compacted mashed mass of esoteric electronic circuitry ninety degrees, closed the lid of the container, heaved on the handle a second time. Another screech. "That does the guts of the coding machines," he said. "Now for the computers' hard disks. You keep on feeding paper into the shredder, Corporal. A low-level format is going to take some minutes."

"How long all together?" He had noted two keyboards and two computer screens, one beside the other, at the right-rear of the vault.

"Ten minutes or so," Williams said. "Each of the two machines will run its own low-level format at the same time. Newer machines would do it faster. But these are entry-level computers, and the hard disks are large. I can't say how large. By which I don't mean I don't know. I mean I'm not supposed to say."

"Sure, Mr. Williams," he said. "Fine." He fed another sheaf of paper into the shredder. He felt dust on his fingers. Old paper, he thought. Old dust. Wonder why they keep all this stuff here at all. Who could care?

Williams leaned over the back of a chair, placed his hands on the keyboard and began to type. The computer screen replied with letters, numbers and a question mark. Williams tapped a single letter and hit the enter key. The screen began to count out one digit after another. Williams moved to the second keyboard, repeated the procedure, nodded as the second screen began to count out digits, stood up straight and said, "Let me help you with the last of those files, Corporal. By God, it's hot in here. Don't you think? I think it's hotter than it was."

He touched his forehead with dusty fingers, felt his fingertips slide through sweat smeared like grease on his skin.

"You're right," he said. "It's hot all right. Is it always this hot?"

"Not this hot," Williams said as he opened the last file and fed its contents into the shredder.

"Let me check," he said. But check what? he wondered, glancing at the utilitarian furniture, the machines, the steel walls. Check everything is the answer: to show how well-trained and efficient I am. To show that the every member of the Security Guard Detachment knows how to do more than sit at attention in the guard post at the gate and look sharp.

"I'm telling you," Williams said, his voice rising, "it's *hot* in here."

"Let me take a look," he said.

"Don't open the door," Williams yelped.

Near panic, he thought. Tight little room. A nervous, balding, reedy guy in a suit, waiting in his little room with his machines and files and secrets.

"I'm not going to open the door," he said. "What I meant was, let me check things out."

"There's nothing to check out," Williams said. Almost shouting, he thought. Next he'll be screaming. Sweat on his forehead, worry on his face. He's not cut out for any tension at all. He likes an orderly life. He wants to know where he's going.

"Give me a moment," he said.

"Hurry," Williams said, as though a moment might be too long. "Hurry!"

He walked to the vault's steel door, placed his hand flat against the steel. Warm. Almost hot.

"How thick is this door?" he asked.

"Four inches. It's special steel. It'll stop anything. An anti-tank rocket. Anything."

But not heat, he thought. Heat's how you make steel: melt different metals in precise proportions and you've got steel. Or so Jankowski had explained it in the barracks one night. A shit job, working steel, Jankowski said. Which is why, he said, I joined the Corps. Someone had said, you think the Corps is a cleaner, less demanding job than working steel?

"It's warm," he said.

"The door?" Williams screeched. "It can't be. We've only been in here twenty minutes or so."

"I know," he said.

"What could happen in twenty minutes?" Williams said.

He nodded as though he agreed nothing could happen in twenty minutes. But he knew the embassy was a wood and brick building thrown up during the First World War. Local material, local labor. A U.S. Government fire extinguisher on every landing, and two more in every corridor. Warnings printed in big block red letters about where to exit in the event of fire. They should have torn this dump down and built something else. But they didn't think to do it; or someone liked the antique lines of the chancery and objected to demolition; or no one cared.

Twenty minutes is plenty of time for a fire to take hold, he thought. In a place like this? Wood so dry the whole building is tinder. Hell, the whole city is tinder. A single earthquake in this, the capital city of this waterless, earthquake-prone mountainous country, and the last wooden structure in the last corner of town will burn to ash and the strongest stone and concrete structure will plunge into itself as it collapses. In the end, the whole city will be a heap of stinking dead trapped beneath the rubble. Including the embassy: this building.

And now there's the mob outside. Many footed, many mouthed. Each individual a part of the angry swelling mass pressing forward against the walls and gates. We had an unauthorized entry by a group of thirty or forty who poured over the wall. We drove them out with tear gas grenades lobbed among the trees in the embassy garden. But that might have made them more angry than they have been the last five hundred years. If possible.

And another thing: ten thousand of them could have come over the walls and we wouldn't have heard them in here. That's one thing about four inches of armored steel: it's tough to hear anything tapping on the other side of it, even heavy bullets.

"I smell something," Williams said. Tight voice right on the edge of breaking.

"So do I," he said. "Smoke. A faint scent of wood smoke. Nothing to worry about. It's not much. And if it gets worse, we've got the gas masks."

"I haven't tried one on. I don't know how to use it. I don't know anything about it except that there are instructions on a piece of paper in the box with them. Years ago I was shown how to use it. Years ago. I've forgotten."

"Don't worry about it," he said. "I know how to use them. There's nothing to it. You just put it on and breathe. Don't worry: I'll check you out. The gas mask is no problem."

"What about air?"

"Air?" he asked.

"There's a limited amount of air in here, Corporal. There's a duct through the wall and a set of filters in the duct. But if the electricity's out, the fan that pushes air in here won't work and the flow of air won't be enough. And if there's smoke outside . . ."

"We're going to be all right," he said, to stop Williams' worried chatter. "There'll be enough air." But he thought: there'd better be enough. Whoever the hell designed this vault better have thought about ventilation. "And remember: in a few minutes, we open the vault door and go out. Whoever's out there."

"You're right," Williams said, as though he hadn't thought about leaving the vault. "By Christ you're right."

"Let's cut the talk, though. All right, Mr. Williams? And let's get the gas masks out. I'll show you how to use one. Then we'll sit down and stay silent and wait for your computers to do whatever job they're doing to themselves."

"A low-level format. Destroys all the data on the disk."

"Low-level format. Great. Whatever, let's keep quiet now and breathe slow. Sit on the floor, why don't you. Take it easy. Where are the gas masks?"

As Williams sat down, he pointed at a wooden box beneath the table at the end of the vault. He walked to the end of the vault, dragged the box out, lifted it, set it on the table. The lid wasn't printed with the usual military explanation of the contents of the box. Each agency to its own, he thought. And Williams' agency probably doesn't want anyone to know what's in this box, or for that matter in any other box.

He opened the lid. Two gas masks stared up at him. The canisters jutting from the lower part of the masks were rubberized, the fine metal sieves at the base of each canister black. Standard military issue, he thought. Nothing new here.

He handed Williams one of the masks and said, "You ever skin-dive?"

"Never," Williams said, as though skin diving were another risk he had avoided.

"No problem. We're not skin-diving here anyhow. Just put the mask over your face and pull the straps around the back of your head. See the tabs on the straps? When you've got the mask over your head and the straps behind, pull the tabs until the mask is seated firmly—just firmly, not tight—on your face. Usually the first thing you'd do when you've got it seated on your face is breathe out everything in your lungs to clear the mask. But that's when you're worried about gas: you breathe out to get any gas that's inside the mask out of it. Here we're only going to have to worry about smoke. *Maybe* worry about smoke. So don't worry about clearing the mask. Try it."

Williams put the mask to his face.

"Take your glasses off first," he said. "The earpieces will interfere with the seal."

"I won't be able to see very well."

"There's not a lot to see in here, Mr. Williams."

Williams nodded, held the mask between his thighs, took off his glasses, folded the earpieces and placed the glasses in a case he took from the breast pocket of his shirt. He put the case back in the breast pocket of his shirt. Then he lifted the mask to his face, scrabbled the straps across the back of his head and pulled at the tabs. He turned his head this way and that, the canister beneath jutting out like the snout of some fearsome animal.

"All right?" he asked.

"Seems to be," Williams' muffled voice said. "Good God, how do you fight in one of these? If you have to?"

"I don't know. You just do it, I suppose. I've never had to worry about it."

"Until now."

He shook his head. "We're not doing any fighting today. Those are the standing orders. No fighting, unless they shoot first. And I haven't heard any shots."

"What if they shoot, though? When we come out?"

"I've got my riotgun and sidearm. Don't worry about it. I doubt there's going to be any trouble. If there's a fire outside, that's trouble enough."

"There's a fire outside," Williams said. "I can't smell it now. But I smelled it before I put on this mask."

"You're probably right. Look, take the mask off. And let's cut the conversation. Okay?"

Williams nodded, tugged the mask from his face and held it in his lap. Its snout and triangular plastic eyepieces stared up at Williams' blank, peering face.

He looked away from Williams, watched the two computers counting out numbers. I wonder how high they have to count before this is over?

"What about the phone?" he asked.

"The phone?" Williams looked at him.

"Right," he said, and thought: what else, semaphore flags?

"I don't know if it works."

"We might as well try it," he said. "Why don't you make the call?"

"Who should I call?" Williams asked.

He looked at Williams and thought, what's that word, 'obtuse'? "The guard post," he said. "Or the ambassador's office. Or your people's office."

"What do you mean, 'your people'?" Williams asked. He raised his face and looked down his nose as though he had been asked a question about a secret matter so delicate and controversial no one knew anything about it.

"You know," he said. "The people you work with." He sniffed. "Why don't you give them a ring, then? I think the smoke's rising a little higher."

"I could do that," Williams said. "Give them a ring. Or the guard post. Or even the ambassador's office." But he seemed hesitant about calling the ambassador's office: as though he knew the ambassador had better things to do than chat with the guy who ran the code room.

"Give them a ring," he said. "Any one of them. And if they don't answer, try the next."

"Right," Williams said. He got his feet under him and stood up. Mr. Williams, he thought: long, pale, angular, stringy. And nervous. Williams fumbled open a steel box fixed to the wall, jerked out a telephone handset and pushed buttons on a keypad inside the box. "Hello?" he said. "This is . . ." He stopped talking and pressed the receiver against his ear. His voice rising, Williams said, "What do you—? Who do you think you're—?" He jerked the handset away from his face, slammed it into its cradle. The handset fell out of the metal box, swung on its springy cord. Williams reeled in the cord, gripped the handset and hung it up in the box. "They're there," he said.

"Who?"

"The locals. The mob. The hostage-takers."

"Where?" he asked. "Who did you call?"

"My people. They're *in* there. In *our* offices."

"Call the ambassador's office."

"I don't think I should . . ."

"Would you like me to call?" he asked.

"Call the guard post," Williams said.

"If they're in your people's offices, they're *way* past the guard post." He wondered how Gunnery Sergeant Simms was making out. Don't worry, he thought. Simms knows how to handle himself. If anyone knows how to handle himself in a situation like this, Simms does.

"Call them anyhow," Williams said.

"Sure." He got up, stepped to the box on the wall, took out the handset, dialled the guard post.

Someone fumbled the handset at the other end from its cradle and shrieked into the mouthpiece, "You *die*, American. Die. You hear? We will burn your bones. You *die*."

"Could you repeat that?" he said.

"What? What you say?" the voice on the other end said. Thick accent, a weak hold on English grammar, bitter thoughts, bitter jealousy tearing at his gut. And fifty thousand more like him chanting three words in five syllables out in the desolate, stony, dust-gray street.

"Would you be kind enough to repeat that?" he said. "I didn't quite understand what you said."

"I say you *die*, you filthy American come to our country."

"You can have it, Ali. I've had enough of your filthy country to last me a lifetime. Happy to leave it to you."

"You, you!" the voice shrieked. "You die. You burn in hell like your father."

"I'll see you there," he said. He hung up.

"Who was that?" Williams asked.

"One of them." He walked to the riotgun, picked it up, took shells from his pocket, loaded the weapon and leaned it back against the filing cabinet.

"This country," Williams said, his voice rising again. "Ignorance, poverty, religion, anger. What a brew."

"I could do with a brew right now," he said. "And a quiet place to drink it. Out in the garden, say."

"Hah," Williams said. "Hah, hah."

Supposed to be laughter, he thought. "You think the ambassador would mind me drinking a beer in the garden?"

"Mind? He minds your presence in the Embassy. And mine. He doesn't believe in the Marines, or in intelligence. Which is understandable, if you've met him."

"Once. He seemed all right."

"Narrowminded. Doesn't read much. Certainly doesn't know much about history: not about the history of this place—you can't call it a country—or our own history."

"And he doesn't like the Corps?"

"I once mentioned I'd been in Korea with the Marines. He sniffed."

"You were a Marine?"

"A lot of people were Marines in Korea, Corporal. And in World War Two. I was a Sergeant in Able Two-Five. In communications. All I can say about Korea is: thank God for General O. P. Smith. He saved every one of them on the retreat from the Reservoir. And I was one of them he saved."

"You were at the Reservoir?"

"I was shot in the thigh north of Yudam. That's northwest of the Reservoir. I was evacuated by truck to Hagaru and they flew me out. That was before the retreat began. And it *was* a retreat. Whatever Marine public relations said at the time."

"What was it like?"

"Like? You mean, Korea? The fighting? Filthy. Disgusting. Cold. Brutal. It was shit, Corporal. If you hope anything, hope you don't ever have to do it yourself."

"That bad?" he asked.

"Worse. Worse than that bad. You notice how your sergeants don't talk about it?"

"I never thought about it. But you're right. They don't."

"They didn't when I was in, either: talk about it. And a lot of them had been in World War II. They didn't talk about it because there's nothing to say about it that's worth a Goddamn. It's shit. Like *this*." Williams gestured around the utilitarian room. "Tension, sweat, waiting, threats. The prospect of violence. The possibility of a filthy demeaning death. Except now we get it by remote control."

"Through the phone," he said.

"Right. How hot is the door?" Williams asked.

He stood, stepped, placed his hand against the steel above the locking wheel. He jerked his hand away.

Williams said, "Maybe we should call Hamid whoever he is down at the guard post and tell him to come up and piss on the door."

"That'd be defacing government property," he said. "Too bad the door's steel. If it were wood, I could shoot through the door into him while he's pissing."

Williams guffawed, gripped his gas mask with long bony white fingers and said, "Now *that* would be a filthy demeaning death."

"Anyone who urinates on a door in the Embassy of the United States *deserves* a filthy demeaning death."

"So what do we do now?" Williams asked. He sounded less nervous. Even optimistic: as though he had discovered another door that led out of the vault.

"Can't go out," he said. "The door's hot. The corridor must be on fire. We'll have to stay here until it cools down."

"That could be hours."

"Right."

"We don't have hours," Williams said. "Not with the smoke seeping in here. And don't forget: the building is brick, beam and board. And the wood's old. Built eighty years ago. Diplomats like tradition. Even if it's stupid and dangerous. The point is: if the building burns enough, the floor will give way. You know what that means."

"All right. We stay here until your machines are finished. Then we open the door, however hot it is, and leave. Whatever's outside."

"That's about the only option we've got," Williams said.

One of the computers beeped at them.

"Finished," Williams said. "Look, Corporal. When we go out, I'd like to have your sidearm in hand. If it's all right with you and the regulations and the standing orders."

"It's not," he said. "But given the situation . . ." He unholstered the semi-automatic pistol, held it by the barrel, handed it over. "You know how to use one of those." It wasn't a question.

Williams snapped the automatic's safety off, eased the slide back half inch and peered into the pistol's breech.

"Round in the chamber," he told Williams.

"Always best to see for yourself." He let the slide ease forward and put the weapon's safety up. "You have another magazine?"

"Three," he said.

"Loaded for bear," Williams said.

He handed Williams the magazines. Williams put them in the left-hand pocket of his trousers.

"We're not supposed to shoot," he said, "unless we're shot at."

"Let me give you a piece of advice from the Korean War, Corporal. Shoot first, explain it to the General—or in this case the ambassador—later. You see anything out there at all that isn't American and is carrying a weapon, shoot and shoot to kill and be sure you kill. Got it?"

"I got it."

"You agree?"

"I agree, Mr. Williams. Better to make them take the chance."

"And to hell, just this one time, with the Foreign Relations Of The United States Of America. Understand me?"

"I understand," he said. "I think we'd better put on the masks." A haze of smoke filled the vault, and the bitter stench of it filled his nose and mouth and touched the back of his throat.

Williams nodded. He put the pistol in his belt, picked up the gas mask, fitted his face into it, worked the straps over the back of his head, settled the mask and goggled at him from behind the clear plastic eyepieces.

He took the other mask from the box, put it on and nodded at Williams. As he did so the second computer beeped. Williams showed him his fist, the thumb jutting straight up. The tiny underlines on the computers' screens blinked and blinked. The computers did not seem to mind the smoke. Or the heat.

But they will, he thought, his right hand flat on the floor feeling the rising heat of the fire burning beneath the vault.

Williams placed his hand on the floor, lifted it and stared at him through the faint haze of smoke thickening between them.

He nodded at Williams, stood up and said, "We've got to get out of here. Now."

Williams' muffled voice said, "I see what you mean. But the building must be burning outside the door."

"We can't stay here."

"Can't stay here, can't go out. Jesus, I . . ." Williams paused, nodded and nodded, the triangular eyepieces of the gas mask glinting.

"Once a Marine, always a Marine," he said.

"That's what they say. But I'm not too sure about that anymore."

"You'll make it. We'll both make it. We open the door and run out through the flames, if there are flames."

"There'll be flames."

"I hope you're wrong. But whatever, we run out. We go left, away from the center of the building. I'll go first. You follow me. If there's fire, keep running. Whatever happens, keep running."

"Christ. Fire and guys chanting outside the walls, spittle in their beards, sweat on their foreheads. And turbans. I wonder what our interest in this shit country was?"

"*Our* interest is to get out of here. Nothing more."

"Right," Williams said.

Sweat slid down his chest and the bitter taste of wood smoke cut at the back of his throat. He took his riotgun from where it leaned against the filing cabinet. The weapon's barrel was warm: as were the ribbed cylindrical handle of the slide and the stock.

He put his hand on the locking wheel of the vault door. The wheel was warm, but not as hot as the door. He jerked the wheel to the left. It did not spin, as it had when he closed it. It moved, but it was reluctant. Good we're leaving, he thought. A few minutes more and it might not turn at all.

He thought of being trapped inside the vault as the temperature rose and the smoke thickened and the building crumbled. He turned the wheel to the stop. He jerked at the heavy door. The door screeched as it shifted an inch. He heaved with his left hand, heaved again, a third time. The door screeched again and gave up another of its four thick inches.

"Give you a hand," Williams said. The long fingers of his bony left hand gripped the wheel. "Together now," he said. "One, two, *three*."

They pulled together, hauling at the swollen door stuck in its swollen frame.

The door gave: a peep of sound. Sweat slid down his forehead inside the gas mask. Drive you crazy to spend more than ten minutes in one of these masks, he thought.

As they hauled it open another inch, the door gave up an extended, vibrant shriek.

One inch to go, he thought as he set himself to drag and jerk at the thick sticking door.

"Hold it," Williams said.

"One more and we're there," he said.

"Wait. I'll heave. You stand back and be ready. We don't know who's out there."

"There's that," he panted. "There's that."

He stepped back three paces, raised the riotgun, pointed it left of the vault's door. Round chambered? he asked himself. On safe?

No. Safety off, no round in the chamber.

He worked the riotgun's slide, jacked a shell into the chamber.

"Ready?" Williams asked. He nodded. Williams gripped the door's locking wheel with both hands. The semi-automatic pistol hung by its triggerguard from the little finger of Williams' right hand.

Neat trick, he thought: long weapon empty, no time to reload, the pistol's right there, a grip of the fist away. Seven more heavy shots in a tight place. Worth knowing.

"Ready," he said.

"One, two," Williams said, and shouted, "Three!" as he heaved all the weight in his thin frame backward, dragging at the steel vault door with both bony hands.

The door squeaked in its frame and he saw the first crack of light layered with smoke in the corridor. But he did not see fire. Thank Christ.

"Once more!" Williams shouted through the rubber and plastic snout of his gas mask.

"Easy, now," he said. "I see smoke but no fire. Someone might be out there. So take it easy when you yank on it again."

Williams nodded, set himself and pulled. The door jerked once. Then it swung open an easy ten inches before Williams halted its swing.

He poked his head out of the vault, looked right and left. "No one," he said. Roiling smoke rippled through the ten inch crack between the jamb and the four-inch-thick edge of the door. "We're in luck."

"We don't have time for anything else," Williams said.

Like a fucking submarine, he thought. Water tight doors, smoke tight doors, caution, procedures, squids in little round white hats everywhere. An indoor life: I'd hate it.

He listened, heard the hiss of burning wood, the rush of a hot wind through the corridor outside the vault. He saw bright sunlight beyond the shifting smoke. Odd, he thought: this is a windowless corridor folded inside the embassy's windowed outer offices, and thus sunlight is impossible.

"Now?" Williams asked.

"Open her up," he said.

"Wait," Williams said. "Toss a gas grenade before we go out. Let's use what we've got."

"Good thought." He shoved the riotgun under his right arm, unclipped a cylindrical tear gas grenade from the webbing strip sewn to his flak jacket. He held the grenade in his right fist, shook it: the ring jiggled and clicked against the tin casing.

Williams nodded at him. Then he swung the heavy door open.

Bitter gray smoke—he could smell it through the mask's filter—poured into the vault and obscured the bright light he had seen. Williams halted the swing of the armored door just before it pounded back against the steel wall of the vault. Williams stood back from the door, the pig's snout of his gas mask and the muzzle of the semiautomatic pistol in his right hand pointed at the doorway.

The riotgun wedged between his right biceps and the rack of his ribs, he jerked the pin out of the grenade with his left forefinger, held the grenade tight in his fist. Williams nodded at him. He took the riotgun in his left hand, stepped to the door, flung the tear gas grenade left along the corridor.

The doors of the offices along the opposite side of the corridor were smoking. Fire burning behind them, he thought.

But I thought I saw bright sunlight.

The tear gas grenade popped, hissed. All right, he thought: the gas will hold them back. If there are any of them there.

He put the butt of the riotgun to his shoulder, pointing the muzzle as though he were aiming at the middle of a man ten feet away. Facing left, he stepped into the hall.

Through the swirl of filthy rushing smoke and whipping sparks and the pure white billowing discharge of the gas grenade, he saw a man in a gas mask standing at the end of the corridor, a weapon held up across his chest. As though to show he has a weapon. As he would were he eleven bring a new toy home from the market to show his family.

He stared through the triangles of the plastic eyepieces of the gas mask at the proud man standing in the smoke. The weapon was the standard Russian assault rifle.

Hamid himself, he thought. And then he thought: you should aim the weapon, Hamid: that's what it's for.

He fired the riotgun straight down the narrow corridor at the man's gut. The explosion of the round and the skittering rip of the double-O buck packed more smoke and a big buffeting clap of noise into the hallway.

The man with the assault rifle thumped against the smoking right-hand wall, dropped his weapon and slid to the smoldering floor.

He worked the riotgun's slide. The smoking shell casing leapt from the weapon, clattered against the wall, bounced on the floor. Another shadow rose inside the smoke: a smaller shadow, with another assault rifle in its hands, the stock held tight against the right hip.

As I would have told Hamid if I'd had the time, you should aim it if you're going to use it. As Sergeant Hanscomb used to shout: fuck gangster movies! *Aim* the fucking thing! Shoot it like a rifle! Use the sights!

He fired the riotgun a second time. Better than a rifle, he thought: *much* better in the narrow solid geometry of this corridor full of smoke and shadows.

The ball bearings in the riotgun's shell hammered the second one of them in the chest. The man flung the assault rifle away and danced and leapt backward, falling into the smoke.

As he worked the riotgun's slide, Williams shouted, "Good shooting!" through the muffling rubber and plastic of his mask. He glanced to his right: Williams was pointing the pistol down the corridor, elbow bent an inch to receive the recoil, fearsome masked face tilted toward his right shoulder.

All right Mr. Williams, he thought. Maybe it is true when they say once a Marine.

He felt heat rising from the scorched floor through the soles of his boots and thought, damn near burning.

Another of them appeared in the smoke. Hamid's other younger brother, he thought. He fired a third round from the riotgun. The gray smoke about the shape flashed red. The buck bounced the man against the sooty wall, flung him onto the floor. The man drew his knees upward, crossed his arms over his narrow chest. The tips of his thin white fingers plucked at his collarbones.

A small people, he thought: I'm five ten and I tower over them in the streets; but still they stare and glower at me to show me their anger and frustration.

"Another!" Williams' stifled voice shouted inside his mask. Williams fired the pistol twice at a shadow lunging through the smoke. A weapon in its right fist—not a firearm, he thought—the shadow whirled away into the side corridor that led to Administration: a tidy clutch of offices that dealt out small sums to the embassy's gardeners, monitored the frequency of oil changes in the vehicles in the motor pool and tended the inventory in the commissary.

He glanced back: twenty feet beyond the door of the vault, roaring flame leapt from an office door. It flowed up the wall and a length of the ceiling collapsed. Plaster dust, charred lath and burning hunks of antique molding fell onto the smoking floor. No going back, he thought. Should have built this place out of stone and concrete.

He looked forward. Williams was a pace ahead of him. "Stay back," he ordered Williams. "I'm wearing a flak jacket. In case anything happens."

"You mean, in case anything *more* happens," Mr. Williams shouted through the gray smoke that raced between them.

He nodded his black rubber and plastic snout. The thick, bitter stench of smoke filled the mask, filled his throat. He gasped as fire touched his scalp, raised his left hand to slap the searing ember away. As he raised his hand another shadow rose from the smoke at the end of the corridor. Another short one, he thought. The shadow was aiming an assault rifle at his gut.

Better miss.

The shadow's weapon fired, the muzzle rising as each round kicked the barrel upward. This one, he thought, doesn't know how to handle his weapon either.

Something pounded the breast of his flak jacket, hammered the breath out of him, spun him to his left. He fired the riotgun as he hit the wall.

The assault rifle stopped firing. Except for the rising wind full of smoke, the corridor was silent. Panting to catch his breath, he thought: hope I got him.

Beside him, Williams fired the automatic twice. Huge noise. He smelled bitter black wood smoke stinking of burned gunpowder. Mask doesn't seem to work. He looked down through the eyepieces: the front of his flak jacket was shredded. Chips of ceramic spilled from the rents. But no blood, he thought. Gasping, he turned his head, saw Williams advancing along the corridor toward the man who had fired the assault rifle. The man was hauling at the vicious curve of the weapon's magazine, and he thought, little bastard doesn't know how to release the magazine.

His masked face black and bulbous, long right arm extended, the pistol in his fist, Williams darted through the smoke, springing down the corridor. He thrust the muzzle of the automatic pistol at the face of the man jerking and tugging and fumbling at the weapon's magazine, shoved the muzzle of the pistol against the man's skull and shot him: once in the skull and a second time, as the man fell backward, in the throat.

Another haze of red tinged the swirling smoke. He pushed himself away from the wall. His left arm and the left side of his chest were numb. As though I've been hit with a bat. Better numb than the other thing, he thought. He forced his left hand to his face, touched the mask, opened and closed his fingers. Hand works all right. But the arm's unwieldy.

Williams came out of the smoke, sparks swirling about his head. His white shirt and tie and trousers were flecked with blood, as though the man he had killed had touched him a thousand times with bloody fingertips. Williams stared at him and said, "You all right?"

"All right. Left arm's numb, but all right. There's blood all down your front."

"Not mine. It was his. A kid. A kid with an assault rifle. We've got to get out of here."

"A kid?" No wonder he couldn't hold the weapon's muzzle still when he fired. No wonder he did not know how to release the magazine.

"Kid or not," Williams said, "he had a weapon. I shot him twice. In the head. In the throat. You all right? Look, we've got to hustle." Williams brushed sparks from his thin hair with a stained, sticky hand.

"My chest hurts. And my left arm's stiff."

Williams looked at the shredded cloth of the flak jacket. "There's no blood. But you took a thump from the round that hit you."

"I'll be okay," he said. "It's nothing." But his left arm hurt and when he moved it it was stiff. And getting stiffer. The air he breathed was bitter. More smoke getting through the gas mask's filter, he thought.

Williams gripped his right arm, hauled him into the smoke, guided him down the corridor and over one sprawled corpse and another. He stepped on a loose, unidentifiable part of one of them.

I killed three, he thought. He glanced down, saw the distorted skull of the boy Williams had killed. Half his head gone, hot ash and cinders sifting onto the exposed topography of his brain, his throat a mess of blood and bits of stuff.

Four killed, he thought as Williams dragged him past the boy's corpse. And there's a fifth one. I fired at a fifth. He ducked away. Into the Admin corridor. Neat offices, tidy bureaucrats, a calculator on each desk, a coaster under every coffee cup, no dust anywhere.

He raised his head and looked forward through the thickening smoke. Can't see more than ten feet. Williams led him onward, away from the fire roaring in the corridor behind them. He listened to the hissing, humming fire, thought of the computers melting in the vault.

As Williams dragged him onward, he thought, pretty good for a thin old guy.

Ten feet away, to the right, he saw the entrance to the Admin corridor and he thought, the fifth one. He fled right. Into Admin's domain.

"Wait a minute," he murmured.

"Get on," Williams' muffled voice shouted inside his gas mask.

"Wait," he panted. He choked on the bitter, stifling air that seeped into the gas mask. "There was. . ." he said, but heat and grit filled his throat and stung his eyes and a cough interrupted his words.

Williams hauled at him. The turn into the Admin corridor was three paces away. Williams forced him on a pace more. He dug his elbow into Williams' ribs, shoved him back against the smoking lefthand wall of the corridor. Thin old guy, he thought. Too bad to push him. Williams' thin, angry voice shouted, "What are you . . . ?"

He raised the riotgun in his right hand and pointed the wavering muzzle at the turn into the Admin corridor. Obscure, he thought: now it's filled up with choking smoke, the light in the windowless corridor is dim.

He tried to raise his left arm to steady the riotgun and to jack a shell into its chamber. His arm hung at his side. Nothing. Fucking thing won't work. Just when I *need* an arm, he thought. As he stepped the next to last step toward the turn to the right, he looked down at his left hand. He closed it into a fist. Hand works fine. But I can't raise the arm.

From the corner of his right eye, he saw a shape in the Admin corridor rushing out of the smoke toward him. He turned his face toward whoever it was who was coming at him out of the gloom.

Slim, a narrow hawkish nose, long black swinging hair. Oval weeping red eyes and a handsome face full of anger and fear. He glimpsed gold earrings under the long hair and thought: A girl? A girl: bluejeans, a white tee shirt and a bandanna handkerchief around her neck. And clutched in both her hands, a knife. Long straight silver blade, he noted. Not a spot of grit or a smudge of soot on it.

Behind him Williams shouted something.

He pointed the empty riotgun at her. But one-handed he could not hold it steady. Empty anyway, he thought. He drew the weapon back. Club her. Beat her in the face.

She ducked beneath his awkward swing as she leapt from the Admin corridor.

Shoulders turned half-left, he felt the first bite of the knife against his side above his right hip. Wasp, he thought: stung me just beneath the skirt of the flak jacket. She dug the knife in, sawing it back and forth, cutting flesh. He shouted and choked, dropped the riotgun. His right elbow struck her in the face, bounced her away. But she hung on to the haft of the knife, and he felt her working it into him, shoving and sawing at the complex of organs below his ribs. He shouted again, struck at her again, screamed at the wriggling streak of pain that rushed through him. He felt his elbow crack against her skull beneath her swirling black hair. Still she shoved and heaved at the handle of the knife, working the blade farther into him. He felt sick to his guts: as though he were going to vomit. He struck her again, his elbow pounding her cheek. She shrieked as though he had wounded her and as she shrieked she fell away from him, both hands gripping the handle of the knife, wrenching it and turning it inside him, yanking at it.

He screamed again as he felt the knife slide out of him, long blade slick with his blood yanking at his viscera, ripping his guts and slicing into the bone of his hip as it withdrew. The girl sprawled on the smoldering floor. She shrieked and flung herself about. Feels the heat, he thought, but doesn't seem to be able to get up. She threw the knife away, down the hallway, and as vomit and blood welled up his throat and filled his mouth, he saw a line of brown, simmering points of blood on the scorched wall to his left. My blood, he thought as he felt his knees give way. My blood this time.

In the instant his knees and hands touched the floor, he jerked his hands from the smoldering wood. He knelt, buttocks against the backs of his thighs, strands of glutinous blood hanging from his mouth. The smoking floor scorched the cloth of his trousers and seared his knees.

I would scream, he thought. If my blood did not fill my mouth, I would scream.

He turned his head toward the girl who had done her best to gut him. She flailed about on the floor. Then she lay still. Then she looked at him and shrieked. As though I am a monster.

Fire beneath the curve of my ribs, he thought. And blood gushing from beneath the skirt of my flak jacket. And flowing out of my mouth.

He glanced down through the eyepieces of the gas mask, raised his trembling right arm, turned his head to examine the wound torn in his side.

She stabbed me as she would stab an animal she feared. She wanted to butcher me.

He bent his head toward his right armpit. As though I am trying to tuck my head beneath my shoulder, he thought. To hide. To not see.

Pouring out of me, he thought as he looked at his brilliant blood sliding down his hip. Staining my trousers. Gushing out of me, ticking and hissing as it drips to the floor near on fire.

A shadow stepped from behind him: Mr. Williams. Stringy old guy. Done pretty well so far, though.

Williams stepped forward and bent over the shrieking girl lying on the burning floor. He pointed the pistol at her face, nodded his black-masked head at her and shot her in the forehead. Blood, brain and bone burst from the back of her skull. Williams stood over her as he might stand over a wounded animal. Her legs trembled and jerked, her hands flopped and beat against the floor. Williams pointed the pistol and shot her in the chest. Then he shot her again in the same place.

Some Mr. Williams, he thought as smoke drifted across the girl's still corpse.

Williams turned toward him, and as he turned the light ahead and in the Admin corridor to his right brightened as smoke rushed toward him.

Wind, he thought. Something behind me is pulling wind through this corridor and the Admin corridor, dragging the smoke away.

The fire behind me, he thought. Must have opened a hole somewhere, got a draft moving.

The smoke thinned. Williams tore his gas mask from his face, flung it away into the howling fire down the corridor: toward the vault. He shoved the pistol into his belt. Then he bent and shouted, "We're going to be all right."

He gagged on the blood rising up his throat one pumping gout after another. He sneezed: blood sprayed from his cold nose, spattered the inside of his gas mask, slid like syrup across his cold cheeks. He saw Williams' strained white face pointed at him and he heard Williams' voice shout, "I'm going to get you up now."

He gasped as Williams grabbed his flak jacket and lifted him to his stumbling feet. He coughed, tried to speak, but no sound escaped his mouth stuffed with drooling blood.

Williams' left arm slid around his back, held him erect. He tried to walk, but he could not move his legs. Step by step, Williams shifted him down the corridor. Sack of grain, he thought. Sack of slaughtered oozing meat.

"Easy," Williams grunted. "We're all right now," Williams shouted. "The smoke's clearing. It's not far. We're getting out. And Lance Corporal: thanks for pushing me back."

He opened his mouth to tell Williams there was no need to thank him and that he was wrong about the smoke clearing. But he could not speak: blood gobbled from his mouth. He turned his head, looked at Williams through the blood smeared on the insides of the lenses of his gas mask. Pain rushed through his guts. An old Marine, he thought as he stared at Williams puffing and humping and hauling him along. Old and stringy. But tough.

Williams halted, held him erect. He saw Williams' bloody right hand reach toward his face, felt it grip his gas mask and drag it from his head.

He coughed, choked, coughed, spat blood down his chest as Williams started maneuvering him down the corridor again.

Williams panted and shouted, "You're going to be all right. We're getting out. We put those sonsofbitches down and we're getting out now. You hear me?"

He nodded. I cannot speak, he thought. Dumb bleeding animal: I cannot speak.

As Williams humped his weight and hauled him forward, he leaned his head on Williams' shoulder. The blood pouring from my mouth stains the shoulder of his white shirt, he thought. And the blood pumping from the wound hacked in my side stains the belly of his shirt and his trousers.

But Williams hauled him on. Another, he thought, might have left me and gone for help. Not Mr. Williams. Carrying me with him. Doesn't care about blood, smoke, fire creeping up behind. And sure doesn't care about the locals. But then he's been here before: he knows all about it.

Williams dragged him from one corridor to the next, out of the old wooden building that had served embassy administrators since before President Wilson lay half-paralyzed in The White House. Panting, near winded, Williams lugged him into the adjacent block: new offices, spacious rooms, narrow corridors, muted lighting, carpeted floors, large elegant views from the offices of the dusty garden and the dun city beyond the wall of the embassy compound.

All the doors along the corridor were closed. A distant voice called out in English from beyond the next turn in the corridor and the next.

"We're all right here," Williams told him. "I'm going to put you down. But I'm not leaving you."

Williams eased him to the floor. He grunted and hissed as his body flexed against the wound torn in his side. His legs trembled as Williams laid him out on the carpet and bent to peer into his face. "All right?"

He coughed, spat blood onto his chin and throat, nodded and gurgled, "Okay."

"Let me take a look at you." He felt Williams' hands lift his right shoulder and push at his right buttock. Turning me onto my side, he thought. His right arm and hand flopped onto the carpet in front of him. The carpet beneath his palm and fingertips was damp. He looked at his hand lying on the carpet: his fingers were bloody and he could not move them. Gore, he thought: a word I have not used. He shivered, his hips trembling as pain flickered through his gut.

"Lie still," Williams said, panting out the words as he eased him onto his back and lifted his forearms and hands and crossed them on his gut. He shivered, squirmed away from the rat gnawing the bone of his hip. "Lie still, I said." Sounds like the Sergeant he was, he thought. "And don't worry," Williams said. "You're going to be all right. Hang in there, Corporal. You hear me?" He coughed and moved his head.

He saw Williams raise his narrow head into the roiling smoke, saw his grimy gray throat turning, heard him shout "Anyone! Help!" With all this smoke, I wonder he can find the breath to shout. His left hand slid from his gut, flopped onto the carpet. The carpet was sticky, his hand cool. He closed his eyes. He felt sick to his stomach. He opened his eyes.

Williams was staring down at him, looking and looking. He watched Williams turn his face away and heard him shout, "Corpsman! Corpsman!" And then all he heard was the rush of air along the corridor and all he saw was the thickening gray smoke that blocked the light.

A SPASM CREPT UP his left arm, knotted the tendons in his shoulder and flexed the long muscle to the left of his spine. He wriggled away from the savage, unremitting cramp. Pain became agony and he opened his mouth to scream. His mouth and throat were as dry and hot as the dust and stones on which he lay. He croaked, extended his trembling left hand and arm; and as he reached, the torment subsided.

He opened his eyes. The prehistoric detail of the desert had vanished. He stared at his hand extended in front of him, but he saw nothing except the brilliant light of the sun.

I'm blind, he thought. He blinked his eyelids and stared at the brilliance, the pace of the arrhythmic contractions of his heart accelerating.

A gauzy gray image stirred in the brilliance, became a faint, spiky shape. He worked his fingers among the dusty stones and pulled himself forward. The ragged spiky shape developed in the light, became substantial: a bush, he thought. Just a bush. As he stared at it a long rush of hot wind swept across him: he saw the bush quiver, heard its branches click and rattle against one another. He closed his eyes as the wind beat up dust and grit. As the wind rushed away across the desert, he opened his eyes and saw the bush swaying among a thousand identical bushes. In the middle distance the ground rose. He turned his head and looked behind himself, saw the distant mountains far beyond the haze of heat and dust.

Not blind, he thought. He examined the puffy, blistered back of his grimy left hand. Stinging red flesh edged the blisters. I must have passed out. Passed out again, that is. For the fifth or sixth time. I wonder what it is that brings me back each time.

Got to take hold. Got to get up and go on. If you lie here the blisters will draw the last moisture from your body and you'll die. And you're more than halfway there.

Sure, he thought: but where is there? Twentynine Palms? Or the other place?

"What do you care?" Sergeant Kline said. He looked up, saw Kline's old feet and veined ankles. Kline wore sandals, grey slacks, a blue and orange rugby shirt and a white baseball cap. "Didn't I tell you you don't need to worry about that? All you have to do is get up and march. You know what they say in the Foreign Legion, don't you?"

"Foreign Legion?" he croaked.

"The *French* Foreign Legion. They say: 'March or die.'"

"Maybe it should be, 'March and die.'"

"They say that too. When they're feeling sorry for themselves. Or if they've got *le cafard*. You're not feeling sorry for yourself, are you?"

"I don't know. I can't remember. I must have the other thing. The . . . ?"

"*Cafard*. How many times do I have repeat myself? *Le cafard*. Got it?"

"What's 'cafard' mean?"

"It means 'cockroach'. To have the cockroach, in the French Foreign Legion, means to be depressed."

"That's what I've got," he muttered. "I'm depressed."

"That's all right," Sergeant Kline said. "So long as you don't start feeling sorry for yourself."

"There's a difference?"

"Of course there's a difference. What, are you screwing with me? Get the hell up out of there and get going."

"I don't think I can make it," he said.

"Think? I told you about thinking, didn't I? You don't seem to remember a hell of a lot."

He nodded, trying to remember what Sergeant Kline had said about thinking. He couldn't remember. He tried to remember something else. Anything else: the taste of water, his room at home, the words of a song he had heard, how to estimate windage. He could not remember: not any of it. It all lay somewhere behind the light that filled his skull and seared his flesh.

"It doesn't matter," Kline said. "You don't have to remember any of that. The only thing you have to remember is how to put one foot in front of the other. You think you can remember that?"

"Yes, Sergeant," he said.

"Okay. All right. Then get up and start marching. Now. You hear me?"

"Yes, Sergeant," he whispered. "I hear. I hear you."

"And don't think about them that left you out there by the road. Don't worry about them. You know the Commandant? No? I know him, and

I'll tell you this: when he hears about this, he's going to jump up and down on them until he breaks every bone they've got."

"Great. But that's not going to get me out of here, is it?"

"Of course not," Sergeant Kline said. "You're going to get yourself out of here. You've come fifteen miles, I make it. Four more to go. You can do four miles, can't you?"

"Sure," he said. "Sure I can."

"Then get up."

"Right," he said. He slid his filthy hands beneath his chest and pushed. His unlubricated joints cracked and his long, dry bones creaked. He panted as though he had been running: his breath was as hot as the burning air. He drew his swollen tongue into his mouth and clenched his jaws. The burning, blistered skin of his forehead, cheeks and chin tightened across the bones of his face. He pushed, panting through his clenched teeth and nose packed with dust. He pushed again. More, he told himself. More. And harder.

He heaved his chest up, drew his right knee beneath himself, knelt, breathed twice and stood up. As he stood he thought, I've done this before, and more than once: heaved myself up, gotten my knees under me, stood up. Done it so many times my knees are burning.

"All right," Sergeant Kline said. "Now sling your weapon, tent that shelterhalf over your head and go. I want to see you marching."

He slung his rifle and draped the shelterhalf over his head and said, "Yes, Sergeant."

"I'll wait here. Go straight on southeast: toward the sun. You understand me?"

"I understand, Sergeant."

"And don't worry about it."

"Worry? Worry about what?"

"That's what I mean. Now get on out of here."

"Right, Sergeant."

He turned southeast, peered from the cowl of the shelterhalf, the weight of his rifle dragging at the puffy blister his shoulder had become. He stared at the sun, then bent his head and began to walk.

"March, damn it!" Sergeant Kline shouted. "Don't drag your feet like that. You think I'm going to resole those boots for you every third day? Pick 'em up."

"Yes, Sergeant," he mumbled. He swung his head and looked out the short tunnel of hot darkness at Sergeant Kline. Sergeant Kline stood with his hands on his hips. He was wearing brown and white golf shoes, knee-high argyle socks, knickers, a V-necked grey sweater and a short-sleeved white shirt.

"Well?" Sergeant Kline said. "What are you waiting for? Go on."

He faced the sun. He took one shaky step and then another. His ankles wobbled in his boots. The long surfaces of his legs and arms burned. But his guts were clammy and he felt sick to his stomach. As though I'm going to vomit, he thought. But I have nothing to vomit: no half-digested food, no liquid, nothing.

He dismissed the queasiness in his guts, ignored the hurt and pain he suffered, ceased thinking of the damage the miles behind had done him: he went on, slogging through the soft dust, teetering on stones, slipping on gravel.

Not that far to go, he thought. Sergeant Kline said that. And you can hang in there. Whatever it is, you can stand up against it.

But when he raised his head and peered ahead, he saw nothing but the desert and the mountains far to the southeast. Rock, dust, creosote bushes, withered patches of grass and stunted scrub extended to the horizon. And with each step I take, he thought, the horizon recedes a step.

Still. What else can I do?

Lie down and die, he thought. Why go on? I move through this desolation, but however far I go I do not arrive. Why do it? I could lie down here—against that slope of gravel and dust, or in the spindly shade of that fragile bush—and wait for whatever comes next.

You know what comes next, though, he thought. Nothing comes next: blinding white fading to grey fading to black. The end: that's what comes next.

And if I lie down and wait for it they'll know when they find me that I wasn't marching. They'll figure the distance and figure what I might have done. And they'll know I halted and waited for it.

And Sergeant Kline in his slacks or shorts or bathing suit or whatever the hell he'll be wearing: he will know I gave up. Him and Sergeant Quinlan and whoever else is out here will know.

Go on, he told himself. Go the hell on.

And remember: there's no one out here. No one. The lizards, the snakes, the insects and the desert: that's all that's out here. You're hallucinating, like the Doc said you would. If you think Sergeant Kline is out here, you're an out-of-your-skull basket case. It's the heat, and the sun, and thirst that makes Kline appear. But he *isn't* there when you think he is. Remember that: Sergeant Kline is retired. He's not out here in this desert: he's *not* walking around out here in knickers.

Or maybe, he thought, I'm not crazy and Sergeant Kline *is* out here. He and Quinlan both: the two of them. Marching around, looking sharp, passing out orders and shouting advice. Maybe this is some sort of test, part of an exercise. Maybe they're waiting right over the next low rise in the desert, taking notes and looking through fieldglasses and bringing up the Palms on the radio to tell them how I'm doing out here in the sun.

No, he thought. That's crazy: Quinlan and Kline aren't out here, and suspecting this is some kind of test is nuts. Don't kid yourself: this isn't that. This isn't anything like that. This is exactly what it is: they forgot to pick me up. And it looks like they didn't bother to figure out who got on the trucks and who didn't. They didn't have a formation. They didn't call the roll. And so they don't know where I am. They think I'm somewhere, but they don't know where. So forget about Kline and Quinlan and training exercises. Think about what you're doing. Tell yourself it isn't that bad out here. Believe that if you make it another twenty thousand paces you'll be somewhere. Think about something useful: about moving your feet one after the other across this shit desert. And don't get excited. Don't be nervous. That's what they told you: when you're out in the wilderness alone with no water left and no one knows where you are, don't get excited. Think, they tell you: think about what *you* can do to improve your situation. Build an igloo, for example. Make a lean-to out of available materials. Stay out of the sun. Put out markers so that air rescue will be able to find you expeditiously. In snow, be sure the markers are orange. In the desert, be sure the markers are at the opposite side of the color wheel from the color of the desert itself. For example, if the desert is white, or gray, put out black markers. If you have no issue markers, use stones: black stones on a white background, white stones on a black background, red stones on a green background. You get the picture. But be sure the stones are large enough to be seen from a chopper at a thousand feet. Be certain to give that chopper crew the best chance to find you.

Advice, he thought. Useless third-rate advice from guys who write pamphlets. They drive out into the desert supplied with water, tentage, air-conditioners, sun block, radios, trucks, air support, medical personnel, artillery, tracked vehicles—whatever anyone needs out in the desert, the guys who write the pamphlets have it. So they can go out in what they call 'controlled' conditions and come back and write a pamphlet. And some *other* guy comes in and says, Want a beer? And the guy who's writing the pamphlet says, No thanks, I couldn't drink a beer right now: I just drank fourteen gallons of water. You know: that stuff that comes in plastic bottles from somewhere in France? A beer right now might make me bloat up. But drop by later when I've finished my draft of this pamphlet on survival in desert conditions and we'll break open a bottle of scotch.

The sonsofbitches, he thought. Every last one of them. sergeant so-and-so and his nervous, cursing, know-it-all lieutenant and the captain dozing somewhere. And up the line, the major glancing over a map and the colonel thinking about the big picture. The sonsofbitches. Like that captain back at Lejeune who gave the lecture about the traditions of the Corps. He got up and told the company how no one is left behind—not ever. Alive or dead, not a single man is left behind. That's a sacred promise.

Let me tell you something you sonofabitch if you can hear me from where you're sitting in your office: you left *me* behind. Every one of you left *me* behind.

"So what?" Sergeant Kline said.

Stumbling on, he swung his head left and peered out into the light. Sergeant Kline was walking beside him. He wore a blue blazer with gold buttons, a button-down white shirt and a striped tie. Plus clean white flannels and polished black Oxfords. "You *believed* that bullshit meant they're great guys all the time?" Sergeant Kline said. "Sure, they bring them back: the living, the wounded, and a pile of corpses. That doesn't mean some of them aren't useless as shit. Take my advice: when you get back and get a little more rank, *you* choose your officers and the guys you're going to be with. *Don't* let them choose you. And let me tell you: right now you're pissed off, and I understand that. In addition, it's good: it's better to be pissed off than depressed. Being pissed off makes the adrenaline flow."

"I don't think I have any of that left," he mumbled.

"Don't tell me what you do and don't have left. I *know* what you have and don't have, and you've got plenty of adrenaline left. Plenty. Take my word. And let me tell you: not every officer's a shitbird. Take my word on that. There are a lot of them who are smart, capable and conscientious. For example, take a look at the Commandant. I served with him. You won't find a better officer anywhere."

"Particularly not out here right now today," he said.

"What do you expect? That he should come over in a chopper with a case of cold beer and pick you up? He's responsible for everything, not just one man. Though I'll tell you this: he *believes* he's responsible for you personally and he's going to be pissed off when he hears about this. Like I said before—you remember?—he's going to jump up and down on the people who fucked up in your case. He's been through a lot of hard things, seen a lot of shit. But no one's ever said he didn't look out for his men. Something like this? You stand three blocks away from his office in Washington when he's told about this and you're going to hear every single word he shouts."

"Wish I could be there to hear it. Better, I wish I could be there to not hear it."

"You mean, when you get back all right, he won't notice what happened here? Let me tell you, the sound level might be one decibel lower, but you'll still hear every word three blocks away. He doesn't *like* stuff like this. He's got a rule about stupid things that jerk people around and fuck them over. The rule is: whoever does it is going to be in trouble up to his eyebrows. And no one is even going to *try* to talk him out of doing what he thinks is right. Sure, there'll be all kinds of lawyers in pressed uniforms swirling around with papers in their hands and words pouring out of their mouths. But he doesn't like a lot of quibbling. Hell, I once saw him eat a broiled lawyer in full uniform for breakfast—and *like* it. But all that's for later. Right now, you're on your own and it's up to you to go on. You understand me?"

"And when I can't go on anymore?"

"Don't think about that. Think about something else. Think about shade."

"Shade," he whispered. An angular wall of black shade slid across the brilliant white light that filled his mind. "Sure," he said. "Shade. Why not. As dark as possible. Sure: ink black shade."

THE MAJOR SAID: "GET one of your lieutenants, get him a truck, a driver, a sergeant and four men and tell them to find Washburn and his men. And the truck they were in." An Army colonel stood at the major's elbow. He was old for a colonel: more than fifty.

"Better if Gunnery Sergeant Higgins and I handle this ourselves, sir," he said. He nodded at Gunny Higgins standing beside him. Higgins' face was without expression. Higgins knew as well as he did that the lieutenants were good men and diligent officers. But this was something new. Something not in the manuals. Something unusual had happened to Washburn and his men. Something that had not happened in the weeks they had been in this terrible place of poverty and death. Looking for Washburn and his people was a chance that had to be taken, because something bad had happened in the jumbled city: he knew it.

"You don't have confidence your officers can carry out this mission?" the major said. The Army colonel grimaced. Then he looked around the tent, glanced down at the slatted floor and grimaced again.

"I have complete confidence in every one of them, sir," he told the major. "It's just that this might need a little more experience than they've had."

The major nodded. "All right. I don't have time to debate personnel issues with you. If you want to go, go. But find this truck. And when you find it, I want to talk to Sergeant Washburn personally. To find out what the hell he thinks he's been doing."

"Seven of us," he said. "What about support, sir?"

"Support?" the major said, as though he didn't understand the word. The colonel shook his head.

"What if something goes wrong, sir? Who's backing us up?"

"Nothing's going to go wrong, Captain. You think there's going to be trouble? Let me tell you something: I've examined all the reports from Defense Intelligence, Naval Intelligence and Central Intelligence. Plus the satellite take, and everything any of them's got in the way of electronic intelligence. Nothing's going on. You've been here three months, so you know this country is a mess of tribes fighting one another. They're not interested in us. All they're interested in is that we leave so that they can get back to doing what they do best: killing one another and starving their people."

"I agree," he said. "On the other hand, Major, I suspect the best way for them to hand us our hat and point us to the door is to do a number on eight or ten of us. They may be a bunch of guys in gowns and turbans, but some of them have been overseas. They read Italian, and French, and some of them know pretty good English. So they know that any losses they inflict on us will encourage us to leave."

"We've thought about that, Captain. We've thought over every single angle and the decision is—and will remain—that the appropriate way to find this missing truck and the men in it is to send a small group in another truck. Besides, you'll have a radio. If there's trouble, call. We'll decide what to do next."

He glanced at Gunny Higgins' expressionless face and said, "I don't have the authority to call direct for what I need, sir?" The Army colonel bent over the map on the table. The major looked at the colonel. He saw the colonel shake his head and he thought, no kidding, colonel: you're not going to be there in the truck with us, going downtown.

"Need?" the major said. "What do you mean, Captain? Need what?"

"If we find ourselves in trouble, Major, do I have authority to call in gunships?"

The Army colonel stood up straight and raised his eyebrows. The major said, "No. Absolutely not. Any use of that sort of weapon system has to be discussed by the various commands and agreed."

"And there's no artillery. Except for the five-inch rifle on the frigate offshore."

"You know why there's no artillery here, Captain. And you know the five-inch gun on that frigate isn't available. You know that because you know the rules on using artillery in an urban environment," the major said.

"They say it's too, ah, destructive," he said.

"Precisely. We're not here to blow the place up, Captain."

"Okay, Major," he said. "What about the mortars, then? They can reach almost anywhere in the city. Do I have authority to call on them if I need them?"

"We're not fighting a war here, Captain. We and the troops from the other cooperating nations are here to assist these people to get some order back into their lives so they can move forward. That's the mission."

The Army colonel nodded as though he had drafted the mission-purpose paragraph in the operational plan.

"All right," he said. "If there's trouble, I call in and a decision is taken."

"That's the procedure, Captain," the major said. "Now, look at the map." The major's finger followed a pencilled line on the map laid out on the rickety table between them. The line began where they stood: at the airport at the southwestern edge of the city. The line ran east into the city, turned left into the main north-south avenue eight hundred meters back from the sea, turned right at the intersection of the main north-south avenue and a smaller east-west avenue. From there the line led to the port. "That's the route Washburn and his men took. The thinking is that they broke down somewhere along the way. You're to follow their route, find them, and retrieve them and the truck they were in." The major handed him the map.

Gunnery Sergeant Higgins said: "They didn't have a radio, sir?"

The major glanced at Higgins, frowned, and said, "Of course they had a radio, Gunnery Sergeant. It must have gone on the blink. They didn't call in."

"So the thinking is," he said, "that their truck broke down and then their radio went bust?"

"That's it, Captain. Why? Are you implying something else happened?"

"It seems a little strange both the radio and the truck would go bust at the same time." The Army colonel raised his eyebrows.

"The equipment's had a lot of hard usage, Captain. You know that. There isn't any of it that doesn't need maintenance. And a lot of it is going to need major maintenance."

"All right," he said. "We'll find them, Major. If they're anywhere along that route."

"They will be," the major said. "Absolutely. I can't think of any reason why they would have deviated from their assigned route."

"Yes, sir," he said. "All right, we'll go, then." He saluted. Higgins saluted. The major and the colonel returned their salutes.

They left the tent. A hundred meters from the tent, he said, "What do you think, Gunny?"

"Straight up, Captain?"

"Sure."

"It's bullshit. My nose tells me something's happened to Washburn and his people. And I don't mean the truck broke down and then the radio went bust and nobody came by and they couldn't find a taxi. If you'll pardon me, Major Maintenance back there in his tent with his papers and maps and satellite take doesn't have much of a feel for what might be happening to Washburn right now."

"He knows the intelligence, though. And how to talk to our allies."

"Allies?" Higgins said. "The only ones I'd call allies are those guys in the French Foreign Legion. You see how they do their patrols? They don't go out for coffee without two trucks and a jeep. A heavy machinegun on the jeep, *two more* heavy machineguns in each truck. And ten men and a sergeant in each truck, a driver, an officer and a machinegunner in the jeep. And they load up before they leave the airport. They carry enough stuff to handle anything they come across—or anything that comes across them. Grenades, rockets, demolition charges. I asked one of their officers—a captain—why they carried the demolition charges. The guy spoke reasonable English. He said: 'Gunnery Sergeant'—he even knew my rank, Captain—'such charges are very useful if one is confronted by a sniper in a building. If you blow the building down, the sniper will stop shooting. Do you not agree, Gunnery Sergeant?' I agreed. Sure I agreed. Then I said, 'What about civilians who might be in the building along with the sniper, Captain?' He raised an eyebrow and said, 'Ah, civilians. Were a civilian killed, I would say, '*Quel dommage*!' As you would say, 'What a pity!' And if I had the time, I would also say, '*Très triste*.' As you would say, 'Very sad.' Would it not be so, Gunnery Sergeant? Were a civilian killed?' No one messes with them, Captain. You've noticed that? No one in this country even thinks about shooting at them. Maybe they've heard about them. Or maybe they've heard about their orders."

"I know," he said. "They nod at the rules we follow. Then they tell their men to do whatever is necessary to deal with whatever happens."

"There it is," Higgins said.

"Get the truck, Gunny. Get four men. Be sure one of them is a machinegunner."

"I can handle the machinegun, Captain."

"Okay. More: load everyone up with grenades. A few smoke, and a lot of frags. Be sure we've got all the machinegun ammunition we might need. Have everybody carrying, say, sixteen magazines for his rifle."

"Twenty is better, Captain."

"Twenty, then."

"MacKinnon is going to wonder, me asking for all this stuff."

"Tell him I ordered it up. Tell him the sun's got to me. Tell him I'm the cautious type."

"I'll get it, Captain. MacKinnon and I go back. He knows if I say I want it, I may need it."

An hour later, two hundred meters south of the intersection of the north-south avenue with the narrower east-west one, he glanced at the map in his lap and raised his left hand. Thomas let the truck roll to a stop. Thomas held the clutch to the floor, his right foot on the accelerator, his right hand on the gearshift lever, the lever in first.

He looked right: down an alley one vehicle wide that ran between two-and-three story buildings. The sun was in the southeast and the alley was filled with shade as dark as the alien people who called this heaped slum home. At the end of the alley he saw a narrow slice of sea: flat, smooth as oil, the sea lay like dark blue metal beneath the pale blue sky. He looked ahead: the broad, six lane divided avenue laid out in better times and driven through the warren of the city's jumbled buildings ran straight toward the northern horizon. The avenue was littered with bits of stone, brick and concrete. Years before, the median strip had been planted with saplings. Every sapling had been cut down. For fuel, he thought. Nothing to burn here except dung, the occasional tree and a one-liter tin of kerosene every three months.

A third of the avenue, to the right, lay in black shade. The rest of the avenue lay beneath the brilliant light of the equatorial sun. Shops lined both sides of the avenue on the ground floors of nondescript two- and three-story buildings. The shops were closed, metal shutters rolled down over their fronts. Sand had drifted up against the bottoms of the shutters. The windows on the upper floors of the buildings were without glass.

Sure, he thought. They've been shooting at one another for ten years and more. I bet there isn't a single unbroken pane of glass anywhere in the city. Or, he thought as he glanced at the uniform dun color of the buildings, a gallon of whitewash on offer anywhere in the country.

And here we are: seven guys in a truck on the major's and, more to the point, the colonel's orders. Travelling through the ruins, looking for another truck that didn't arrive or report in by radio. Which should have arrived or reported back three hours ago. A lost truck and four lost men: Sergeant Washburn and Jones, Marchetti and Carson. They came this way: and so we came this way, too: me and Gunny Higgins, the driver, and four men.

The avenue ahead was deserted. He could not see a single human being. He said: "What do you think, Gunny?"

Higgins leaned from the bed of the truck into the roofless cab. "I don't like it, Captain. No locals? Something's going on for sure."

He nodded. Every day for three months the avenue had been choked with people crowding the sidewalks, walking in the roadway, hawking odd foods and used clothing and bits of metal from carts, wheelbarrows and their hands, chattering their swift, spiky, guttural language at one another. The crowds were dangerous: who could know whether someone standing behind twenty women carrying woven reed baskets might be about to level a weapon? When they drove this avenue yesterday, and twelve weeks ago, they travelled at forty miles an hour, people scattering like chickens as the driver weaved from one side of way to the other. But the long empty avenue and the tattered silent buildings were, he knew, more dangerous than any busy street.

No one. He looked far down the avenue: no one at all. Not in the sunlight on the left, not in the black shade to the right. He glanced right again, down the dark, narrow alley toward the sea. The graceful, stately bow of a frigate eased into view. Making way, he thought. Easing along. As he watched, the frigate's gun turret appeared, the long thin barrel of the five-inch gun trained forward. A cruise, he thought. Loll around, maintain the machinery, eat, sleep, bounce off the bulkheads.

"You're right, Gunny. No people. We must be getting close. How're your guys doing back there?"

"We're close to the equator, Captain. No one likes the sun in this place. Or the heat."

"'Captain'? We're in the field, Gunny. Call me by my first name."

"We only do that in a war, Captain. And then only when there's shooting. This isn't a war."

"It isn't?"

"They told us that when we got here, Captain. This is not a war, they said. They gave us a pamphlet to read. The pamphlet said: this is not a war."

"They did? A pamphlet? Oh, yeah, sure," he said. "Now I remember: that stuff about peacekeeping. I remember that now. It's strange though, Gunny: I don't see any peace around here. All I see is buildings pockmarked by gunfire. And no glass in the window frames. And no people. And every day I saw thousands of locals every mile and heard shooting three blocks away. And now I hear nothing and see no one."

"I saw one of them, Captain," Simmons called from the back of the truck. "He just ran across the alley to the right. He had something in his hand. Not a rifle or a pistol. But it was metal. Longer than a knife. A machete, maybe."

He turned his head, looked past Higgins standing up close behind him at the front of the bed of the truck. Simmons, Parnell, Jenkins and Hamilton sat on the truck's bed: the knee-high metal sides of the truck wouldn't stop a rifle bullet, but they might slow it down. On the other hand, he thought, a local with a weapon wouldn't have to worry about anything stopping his fire if he shot from behind: the tailgate is down, to permit Gunny Higgins' machinegun a field of fire to the rear.

Simmons and Parnell faced right, Jenkins and Hamilton left. Simmons and Parnell had their weapons up. Simmons said, "There goes another one. He was carrying a weapon, Captain. Looked like an assault rifle."

Higgins said: "I don't like this, Captain. Sitting here? We ought to be moving."

"I agree," he said. "Thomas, get us rolling. Turn right at the east-west avenue. You know it?"

"Sure, Captain," Thomas said. "Come this way every couple of days. Back and forth. From the airport to the harbor. And back."

"Good. Everybody look down the alleys as we pass. Gunny, you watch behind." Thomas accelerated the engine and engaged the clutch. The truck rolled forward, gained speed.

Higgins said: "There's another one of them: he just ran across the avenue three hundred meters back. He was carrying one of those old French or Italian rifles they think are big time. I'll tell you, Captain: if I see one more guy carrying a weapon, you and me will be on a first name basis. Peacekeeping mission or not."

"I saw one," Hamilton called out from the back. "Down the alley we just passed. No weapon. Barefoot. Wearing that long dirty white gown thing they wear. And that cloth they wind around their heads."

"Rag," Parnell said. "As in raghead."

He turned in his seat, braced himself against the swing and sway of the truck and looked at Parnell. A smart, capable man who was aware of what he was doing and what was going on around him. But as yet without much judgment. Which was the way: Parnell hadn't had enough experience or made enough mistakes to have learned good judgment. "Parnell?" he said. "That's as may be: that they're ragheads. But don't forget that any one of them may be a good enough marksman to do a number on any one us. And if he's got his friends with him, a number on all of us. Whatever he wears on his head. Whether he's barefoot or not."

"I understand, Captain," Parnell said. His knee was braced against the truck's side. The hot wind lifted his hair. He grinned. "I know that, Captain."

"I'm not breaking your bones, Parnell. I'm just thinking out loud. You know what I mean?"

"Be careful is what you mean, Captain."

"That's it," he said. "And that goes for the rest of you. We're here looking for that truck and the guys who were in it. You know as much about it as I do. Four guys in a truck. A sergeant—Sergeant Washburn—and three others. They went out, but they didn't arrive. And they didn't come back. We're driving their route. We're here to find them. As I told you before we left the airport: keep watch. Something's going on. You agree, Gunny?"

"I can smell it, Captain," Higgins said. "And I'll tell you: what I smell is shit."

"I might agree with you, Gunny. Except for the Major's assessment of the available intelligence. You recall he said the intelligence indicates nothing's going on?"

"You want to know what I think about his—the—intelligence, Captain?"

"Gunny, you know I can't sit here and listen to you heap all kinds of stuff on the heads of our seniors and betters."

"Sure, Captain," Higgins said. "But what about that Army general who's been lurking around lately? The one in the colonel's uniform who's in Special Studies or Special Operations or Special Forces or Special Services or whatever the fuck they call themselves these days? Is he one of our seniors and betters? You know, the one who was there nodding and grimacing while the Major was telling us how routine this ride was going to be?"

"Colonel's uniform? You mean that guy who was in the tent with us and with the Major? He's a general?"

"That's the one. Guy in the Army told me about him. I said, who's he? Nodding at this new colonel I hadn't seen around anywhere before. And the guy says, 'Who, General WhatsHisFuck? Whoa, it'll be my ass if you mention he's a general. He's here in*cog*nito.'"

"The regulations still say he's one of our seniors, Gunny."

"You know what I think about that, Captain," Higgins said. "Any general shows up in a colonel's uniform, he's got a yellow stripe right down his back. And his head, as those guys who fly airplanes say, is up and locked. You think one of our generals would dude himself up in some colonel's uniform? I mean, what the fuck is a general good for except showing himself—*as a general*—to his troops?"

"I might agree with you, Gunny," he said, "But . . ."

"I just saw three of them," Jenkins said. "They ran across that alley we just passed. They were two hundred meters in from the avenue. And they had weapons. Automatic weapons."

"That makes seven we've seen," Higgins said.

"Okay, people. Everybody chamber a round and put your weapons on safe. Gunny, get on the machinegun. But no shooting unless someone shoots at us."

"Or you give the order, Captain?" Parnell said.

He turned and looked into the bed of the truck, watched as the four riflemen cocked their weapons and Higgins charged the machinegun pointing straight back from the bed of the truck. "That's it," he said. "Or I give the order."

Thomas swung the truck to the right: into the avenue that led east, toward the port.

"There's five or six of them," Thomas said. He turned, faced forward. "Just standing there," Thomas said. "Off to the right, in the shadow, two hundred meters on. I don't see any weapons."

"Let's hope they're just curious," he said.

"You said it, Captain."

"Hold it!" Simmons called out. "The truck's in that alley we just passed."

Thomas braked the truck even as he said, "Thomas, stop and back it up."

As he brought the truck to a halt, Thomas put the gearshift into reverse and backed it up. "Simmons," he called, "say when."

"*When*," Simmons said. "There it is, ten meters in there, in the shadow."

He looked into the gloom, saw the rear of the truck. It filled the narrow alley side to side. But he did not see Washburn, or Jones, or Marchetti, or Carson.

"No one," Gunnery Sergeant Higgins said. He sounded grim, as though he knew exactly what had happened to Washburn and his men.

"Gunny," Jenkins said. "There are eight of them coming down the avenue from behind us: from the west. I don't see any weapons. But none of them are women. Or kids. And more are coming out of the alleys behind them."

"And to the east," Thomas said. "Four more of them. One woman, three teenagers, coming up from the port."

"Over here," Parnell said, "'teenager' means all grown up. And armed."

"Gunny," he said. "Get on the horn, bring up the Major. Tell him we've found the truck. Tell him there's no sign of Washburn or his men."

"Captain?" Thomas said.

"What's the word, Thomas?"

"Captain, there's something there, see along the avenue there, fifty feet on? In the shade to the right? Looks like something's tied up and hanging to the grate rolled down over the front of that shop."

He looked. A bulk of something in the black shade. A weight, a bundle of something forked bound to the grate. He couldn't make it out.

"We'd better go over there, Captain," Gunny Higgins said.

He turned and looked into the bed of the truck. Higgins was standing up, the radio handset in his right hand, looking along the avenue at whatever it was tied to the grating. "Gunny?"

"One of ours, Captain. He's strung upside down, legs splayed and tied to the grate. I can't see the ball and anchor upside down on his chest. But I recognize the uniform."

"Gunny?" he said. He turned and stared at the forked bundle but he could not see what Gunnery Sergeant Higgins saw. "I see it. But I can't make it out."

"We better go over there," Higgins said.

"Thomas, drive the truck up on the sidewalk so it blocks the alley. Leave some space—ten twelve feet, say—between the side of the truck and the entrance to the alley. So we can move around."

"Right, Captain," Thomas said.

On this equatorial day, Thomas' face was white: as though he had been living in Antarctica six months, eating penguins and blubber, waiting for the sun to reappear in the sky.

"Take it easy, Thomas," he said. "Everything's going to work out all right."

"You sure, Captain?"

"Yeah, I'm sure. Certain. Gunny's on the radio and we've got enough stuff here to shoot every last one of them if anything happens. And they're not doing anything right now: no more than fifteen, twenty of them standing around. And they're all two hundred meters away. But keep your weapon handy. Show it to them. Show them you know what to do with it. All right?"

As he spoke, Thomas' face began to return from Antarctica. By the time he had finished speaking Thomas looked like his same old blond, ruddy self. Words, he thought. Behind him Gunny Higgins was speaking on the radio. More words, he thought. I'd rather have a battalion of artillery at the other end of the horn than Major Maintenance and an Army general wearing a colonel's insignia.

Thomas shook his head, drove the truck forward, reversed ten feet and parked it across the mouth of the alley. "Leave the engine running, Captain?"

"You bet," he said. He got out of the truck as Thomas got down from the driver's seat and jogged to the tailgate.

He said, "All right, everybody. Get your stuff together and get out of the truck. Two of you—Parnell, Simmons—get up against the wall on either side of the alley. Keep watch. Jenkins, Hamilton, Thomas. Get everything out of the truck into the alley. And keep looking. You never know."

"Captain?" Higgins said as Parnell, Simmons and Hamilton jumped down from the truck. "The Major says they'll think over what to do next."

"Great," he said. Then he raised his voice and said: "Everybody? Keep watching. Like I said: you never know."

"That's for fucking sure," Higgins said as he jumped down from the truck. "You people listen to the Captain."

He said: "Hold it. Change of plan. Any of you qualify high on the machinegun?"

"Captain?" Hamilton said, "You're looking for me."

"Gunny, hand Hamilton the machinegun. Take his rifle. And let me say this a third time even though I know none of you need to hear it: every one of you keep watch. Across the avenue. And up: look *up*. If there's someone interested in us, they won't come down the street walking. They'll be in the windows and on the roofs across the way and above us. Hamilton, you come with Gunny and me."

"Right," Hamilton said.

He said: "If there's a need, Gunny Higgins or I will be your assistant gunner, Hamilton. We both served as A-gunners at Peking during the Boxer Rebellion."

"Captain?" Hamilton said.

"Just fooling around. Gunny, get a box of ammunition out of the truck. The rest of you take everything else—the ammunition, the grenades, the radio and your gear—and get it into the alley."

"Captain, we ought to think about getting out of here pretty soon," Parnell called from behind the truck.

"Parnell, I'd agree with you if we hadn't found anyone. Who needs a beat-up truck? But we've found someone. He's one of ours. And we're not leaving until we've got him with us."

"I didn't mean that, Captain," Parnell said. "I mean this bunch coming down the avenue."

He looked back. A loose group of them, fifty or more, were walking in the avenue as though they were heading for the port. He looked them over. Men and boys. A few women, no girls. And no old people. And no weapons visible. But the men all wore the long gray gown every adult male wore, and a few of them had their hands behind their skirts. Weapons, he thought. "Looks like some of them have weapons. You know the drill: if they're a hundred meters away and coming on, fire over their heads. If they keep coming, shoot at them and kill them. If they're not moving and anyone among them shoots at us, open fire on the shooter."

"You got it, Captain," Parnell said.

Higgins lifted the machinegun down from the bed of the truck, handed it to Hamilton, took Hamilton's rifle. A long glittering belt of ammunition swung like a snake's skin from the machinegun's breech. Higgins slung the rifle, lifted a box of ammunition down from the truck and jogged forward. Simmons and Parnell stood right and left of the mouth of the alley with their rifles up, each of them examining the windows in the upper stories of the buildings across the way and the thickening groups of locals gathering up the avenue and down it. At the back of the truck Jenkins was handing gear, ammunition, a box of grenades and the radio down to Thomas standing at the lowered tailgate.

"Let's go get him down, Gunny," he said. He set off toward the man hung upside down from the grating.

Higgins said, "Thomas, when you've got everything into the alley, stay on the radio, shout out if you hear anything. And call them if anything happens."

"Right, Gunnery Sergeant," Thomas said.

Lugging the ammunition box, Higgins caught up with him. He glanced over his shoulder. Ten paces back, Hamilton was hurrying to catch up, and as he strode out of the lee of the truck, he pointed the muzzle of the machinegun down the avenue: toward the gathering crowd.

He halted eight paces from the upside down man. Beside him, Higgins set the ammunition box down on the gritty sidewalk. Hamilton came up behind them. Hamilton sighed and said, "Jesus they tied him up like a hog, gutted him, and hacked off his manhood."

The man was hung from his ankles roped to the highest twisted strand of the steel lattice drawn down across the front of the abandoned shop. They had gutted him—opened him up from the groin to the breastbone with a single ripping slash of an edged weapon. His intestines hung down over his chest and battered, swollen face. They had cut his pants away, castrated him, and chopped his penis off. His upended thighs and crotch were a dense clot of coagulated blood that had rushed from the long gashes they had slashed in the soft flesh of his thighs and in his groin.

Just as Hamilton said, he thought. But Hamilton was wrong about the order of this Marine's calvary: the fucking sonsofbitches mutilated him first. Then the fucking sonsofbitches gutted him.

A distinct, methodical hum rose from the crotch and looping ropey black mass of the corpse's intestines. Higgins handed him his rifle and stepped forward, unsheathing his knife. The black mass of flies whirled away from the corpse, their even hum rising to an intense drone as Hamilton shouted, "Jesus Christ I gone kill every one these motherfuckers. Every motherfucking one of them I find. That I *see*."

"Easy, Hamilton," he said. He glanced back at the truck: Simmons and Parnell were standing guard on either side of the mouth of the alley, Simmons looking up the avenue, Parnell down it, both of them scanning the roofs, the vacant shopfronts, the empty windows of the buildings across the way—and the gathering crowds approaching from both directions. Rifles slung, Thomas and Jenkins were humping the last of the ordnance into the alley.

As he reached up to cut the rope knotted around the corpse's left ankle, Higgins said, "What are we doing here, Captain? More to the point, what's this poor guy doing here butchered like this?"

"I don't know, Gunny. You heard the Major. They ordered us out and here we are, seven guys—eight guys—and two trucks. Is it Washburn?"

"No aircover, no artillery, no one to back us up. Nothing but chat on the radio. They talk and call it support. And no, it's not Washburn. At least I don't think it is. I don't see any rank. Though it's hard to tell with his guts in his face and the blood clotted on his arms like that."

Higgins gripped the corpse's booted left foot and cut the single length of rope that bound the corpse's swollen ankles against the highest course of the metal lattice. His left hand holding the corpse's ankle against the steel lattice, Higgins slid the knife into its scabbard and maneuvered the awkward forked shape of the body to the sidewalk. He stood up, stepped back from the stench and the swirling flies and said, "I agree with Hamilton, Captain: I want to kill every one of these sonsofbitches I see."

"So do I, Gunny. But you know we can't do that. That's not what we're here for."

"What *are* we here for, Captain? No, screw it, we can talk about that later. Right now we better hurry. See them gathering down the avenue?"

He looked. The crowd was thickening. The newcomers were men, a few women and many male teenagers. The men were dressed in the long gray gowns they wore—*gallabahs*, they called them: no, *gallabiyahs*. The crowd shuffled and reformed as it eased toward them. He stared at one of the woman. She was dressed in brilliant primary colors. He recalled the stories he had heard of the predilection of the women who lived in this awful place for castration of dead or—still better—live enemies.

Like the Shawnee, he thought. *Just* like the Shawnee.

"Let's get him back to the truck, Gunny."

"I'll take his shoulders," Higgins said. "It'll be okay: he's stiffened up a little. Not much, but a little."

He stepped forward, bent, gripped the corpse behind the knees as Higgins grimaced, squatted, got his hands beneath the corpse's shoulders. He nodded and he and Higgins lifted the riven corpse and began to crab along the sidewalk toward the truck. Ten feet behind them, the ammunition box swinging from his left hand as he backed step by step, Hamilton swung the muzzle of the machinegun across the front of the crowd coming up the avenue. He heard Hamilton whispering furious imprecations at the crowd and said, "Hamilton?"

"Captain?"

"Easy."

"Right, Captain. All right. For right now, easy."

He shuffled on, watching Higgins: he did not glance down at the gutted Marine.

Disturbed by their lurching passage, the flies swarmed and buzzed, flicked at their lips, their eyes, their ears. He clamped his mouth shut, closed his eyes to slits, shook his head once and again, and again. The flies were unimpressed: they flicked and darted at his face and arms and hands, seeking sweat—and more, if they could find it. But his sweat was not good enough for the flies: they swarmed on the corpse's exposed guts, burrowing and working their iridescent wings. A cloying stench of rotting meat, dead blood and excrement filled his nostrils. A clot of stink thickened at the back of his throat.

He looked up: Higgins' throat was working, and Higgins was looking at him.

He said, "I think . . ."

Higgins shook his head and said, "Swallow it, Captain. There's nothing else to do. Just swallow it."

He swallowed the mass of sour saliva, turned his head, looked over his shoulder. Down the avenue a tall turbaned man flourished a sword—a *sword*, for God's sake—raised his voice and began to chant. The crowd behind the swordsman was expanding, armed men sifting through the dense mass: he saw the stocks of rifles, the flash of edged weapons, the flared mouth of a rocket-propelled grenade launcher.

"Gunny . . ."

"I see them," Higgins said. "We're almost there." They shuffled sideways into the shelter of the truck. The truck's working engine pumped acrid exhaust into the hot air. Then the engine screeched. Something screwed up in the mechanics somewhere, he thought.

As they lugged the corpse past him, Parnell coughed and looked away. He and Higgins went on, crabbing down the length of the truck. As they turned the corner at the rear of the truck, Simmons whispered, "Oh, Christ."

He swallowed and said: "Easy, Simmons. Gunny, let's get him up." Higgins nodded. They heaved the corpse up, set it on the lip of the truck's bed and stepped back.

For an instant, he and Higgins stared at one another. Then Higgins said, "I'll cover him." As he climbed up into the bed of the truck the stock of his rifle knocked against steel. Higgins stepped past the riven, stinking corpse, picked up a folded bundle of canvas, unfolded it and spread it over the dead Marine.

"He'll be all right now," Higgins said. He jumped down from the truck, looked up and down the avenue at the crowds advancing. "We better get ready, Captain. It's going to happen right here right now."

"You got it," he said.

From the alley Thomas called, "Captain, I called them about the crowds thickening up every second and coming closer like they are."

"And?"

"They said: 'Wait.'"

"Great news," Higgins said. "What now, Captain? They're blocking the road in both directions."

He looked along the length of the truck. Hamilton was prone on the sidewalk beside the truck's right front tire. He had opened the box of ammunition and hooked up the belt in the gun to the belt folded into the box.

He raised his voice and called out, "All right, everybody. At a hundred meters, fire over their heads."

From the front of the truck, Hamilton looked over his shoulder and said, "And if the motherfuckers keep on coming?"

"Kill the ones with weapons," he said. "If the rest of them keep on coming after that, kill them all." He walked into the alley. "Thomas, bring the Major up," he said. "I want to talk to him."

Thomas spoke into the radio's handset, listened, spoke again, handed the handset to him. He raised it to his face and heard the major speaking to someone—the colonel: ". . . *old* him specifically to find the truck and the men in it. *Nothing* more." Funny the major is holding the microphone open, he thought. Guess he doesn't want to hear what I have to say. And doesn't mind me hearing him talk with the colonel.

He heard two clicks from the major's end. He keyed the handset and said, "Major, we have a situation here."

"Wait," the major said. He waited, listened to fuzzy mumbles. More talk, he thought. More words. Then the major said: "What the hell's going on, Captain?"

"We found the truck and one of the four men. We've got a threatening crowd gathering in the avenue."

"I know that. The private told me that. Where are the other three men?"

"We haven't found them, Major. The one we found is dead."

"Dead. Yes, yes, I know that. Wait." He listened while the major spoke to the Army colonel general again. He could not hear what they were saying: more muzz-muzzing. Then the major said: "Captain. Bring the KIA, both trucks and your men back here at once."

"What?" he said.

"You heard me: bring the KIA, both trucks and your men back here at once."

"What about the other three men, Major?" he asked.

"They're just going to have to take their chances for now. We don't want a confrontation at this time. Just—leave."

"Leave?"

"You heard me, Captain. Leave."

He glanced out of the alley right and left: more locals coming out of alleys up and down the avenue had increased the bulk of the two milling crowds. The tall local in the turban chanting to the mass down the avenue flourished his sword. "I don't know if that's going to be possible unless we start shooting, Major. As Private Thomas told you: we've got a situation here, and we may have to open fire."

"Negative," the major said. "Negative. There's to be no shooting."

"I meant over their heads, Major. To see if they'll back off."

"No," the major said. "Negative. You're not to fire, Captain. You understand me? Not a round."

"They've got weapons, Major. I see a guy with a sword. A couple with assault rifles. And more with pistols and those antique rifles they have. One of them has a rocket-propelled grenade launcher."

"They know what you've got in the way of weapons, Captain. They won't take a chance on attacking you."

"Major, I don't think I'm getting through to you. I don't think we're going to get out of here unless we fight our way out. And I'm not sure we'll be able to do that. Furthermore, I don't want to leave the three guys we haven't found who were in Sergeant Washburn's truck."

"Which one is the KIA?"

"What?"

"You haven't examined his tags? Come on, Captain, get with it."

"You're right about that, Major. I haven't examined his tags. I'd rather leave that to a corpsman. Or the surgeon."

"We don't understand."

'We'? he thought, and as he thought it he heard someone clear his throat: the general in the colonel's uniform, listening on another handset.

"Major, these motherless sonsofbitches hung this guy up by his ankles from one of those gratings they roll down over the shopfronts. Then they castrated him and cut off his penis. Then, after a time, they gutted him. His guts and stomach are all over his chest and face. I will not try to find his tags right now. Besides, Major, who he is is meaningless. The important thing is he's one of four. The other three are still missing. You sent us down here to find a truck and four men. We found the truck and one man. The mission's not finished. Wait," he said, and held the mouthpiece of the handset against his thigh. "Gunny. The Major says we're to return immediately."

"Without finding the three guys who are missing?"

"That's what he said. He also said: no shooting."

"If you want my advice, Captain, I'll tell you this: right now I'm beginning to think we're going to have to shoot a lot of these people if we want to get out of here. As for leaving without the other three who were in the truck, the proper procedure is for the Major to send a couple of platoons down here right now to help us search until we find them. Alive, if we can. Dead, if we can't. But find them."

"I agree." He lifted the handset from his thigh and said, "Major, an alternate course of action would be for you to send two platoons down here to help us look for the three missing guys. And to provide us with the support we're going to need."

A thread of whispering at the other end. Then the major said, "Negative,

Captain. Absolutely not. That would just stir things up. My orders are unchanged: load up and return here immediately."

From the corner of his eye he saw the crowd down the avenue pick up the pace, the mass of them breaking into a jog, coming straight toward the truck. The crowd was silent: not a sound came from any of them. Except from the guy with the sword: he chanted and sang as he jogged in the middle of the first rank, the sword in his black hand glittering as he swung it through the sunlight above his head.

Okay, buddy, he thought. Whatever you want.

He turned and looked up the avenue, and in the instant he looked, the crowd that had thickened and eddied there lunged toward him. On orders, he thought: coming for me and Higgins; and our men. The pace of the crowd was quick and steady. At the streaming dark edges of the mass, some of the teenagers were running. A steady humming murmur rose from them: because, he thought, they don't have a guy with a sword and a turban chanting and calling them forward.

Trouble, he thought. Big trouble. Into the mouthpiece of the handset he said, "We've got trouble, Major. They're coming straight for us, jogging, some of them running, from both directions five hundred meters east of the intersection of the north-south and east-west avenues. I estimate their numbers to be six to eight hundred up the avenue and the same down it. I need support right now. Everything you've got."

"You've screwed up, Captain," the major shouted. "Screwed up for sure. Goddamnit if you'd *listened* when I told you to get out of there everything would have been all right."

"Whatever," he said. "Right now I need muscle. A couple of gunships would be best. The mortars are my second choice. Third is a couple of platoons out here right now. But I don't think there's time to get them here."

"No," the major shouted. "I told you: no, absolutely not. No shooting, I told you. Get out of there. You are not to fire."

"That's going to be out of my hands in about fifteen seconds," he told the major. He took his mouth away from the handpiece and called out, "At a hundred meters, fire over their heads."

From the handset the major's small voice shouted, "No . . . I . . . now . . . order."

What a turkey, he thought. He tossed the handset to Thomas. "Get rid of them, Thomas. Give him an Air Force over and out for me. Then get ready."

Thomas put the handset to his ear, jerked it away, stared at it and said, "Lot of shouting, Captain. Can't make it out. And I can't talk to him. Major won't let me: he's holding the transmit button down." He grimaced. Then he said, "All right," and keyed the handset. Thomas held the mouthpiece to his lips, the earpiece pressed against his shoulder. He raised his voice and said, "Can't hear anything, Captain. Must be the atmospherics." Then he said, "Good-bye," and tossed the handset away as he rose, his rifle in both hands.

"We're going to fight them, Captain?"

"Fire over their heads first. Then we'll see what they do next. You, Parnell, and Simmons are to stay at the rear of the truck. Gunny Higgins, Hamilton and I will be at the front."

"Right, Captain. Rear of the truck."

"Jenkins, stay in the alley. Keep watch above you. And keep an eye on the truck down the alley. Shoot anyone with a weapon you see on the roofs or coming up the alley. Got it?"

"Got it, Captain. Keep watch all around. If they're armed, shoot them when they show themselves."

"Good man," he said. He turned, looked up the avenue and down it. The two thick crowds of jogging men and boys and a few women were each a precise hundred and thirty meters away. He raised his voice, looked right and left and called, "Get ready. On my order, fire one full magazine over their heads. Hamilton, you fire three two-second bursts. And remember, everybody: over their heads. Is that clear?"

None of them turned his face toward him as they called out, "Yes, Captain." They were aiming their weapons at the deliberate, orderly dark masses coming forward. He glanced up the avenue and down it toward the sea: the two approaching halves of the horde surged forward, sprinting. He thought: they're a hundred and twenty meters left and right of the spot on which I stand.

But they're not a horde, he thought. And not a mob. They're ordered, they believe, they have a cause, and they are trained to obey. A memory of something he had read ticked in the back of his mind. Something about the horns, the chest, the loins. A quotation: "Kill the wizards!" and then a fearsome description of warriors with broad-bladed stabbing spears rushing forward, gripping their enemies, dragging them to a hillside, impaling them on pointed wooden stakes and battering their skulls with knobkerries. Old times, he thought. Last century: some time, some where.

He put the memory aside and glanced left and right again. As he looked the two crowds accelerated. A buzzing hum rose from the two rushing masses. He watched the tall black in the turban in the center of the front rank of the mass coming up the avenue. The man raised his face to the sky, swung his sword and shouted into the drone rising from those he led. His followers answered his shout with a chant they cried out as they ran forward.

He aimed his rifle above the head of the swordsman and shouted, "Fire!" into the hot dark shade. Before the last of the word was out of his mouth he took up the last pressure on the trigger and fired the rifle, letting the weapon's muzzle ride upward with each light recoil. From behind him he heard the racket of three rifles firing. In front of him Hamilton, prone on the gritty sidewalk, fired the machinegun while Gunny Higgins, kneeling to Hamilton's left, fired single shots.

The chanting crowd in front of him wavered, slowed to a confused whirl of darting teenagers, ducking women, shrinking men. He dropped the empty magazine from his rifle and inserted a fresh one. He glanced behind at Simmons lying, Parnell kneeling to Simmons' left and Thomas standing behind them at the rear of the truck, each of them firing single shots. The disciplined crowd that had come down the avenue slowed. Individuals retreated into the mass, flinching from the ripping mechanical threat of the rifle fire cracking above their heads. And flinching from the threat of worse, he thought. And of worse still.

The firing ceased. He opened his mouth to order them to reload. As he did so he saw a magazine drop from Thomas' rifle and Parnell's, a third from Simmons'. He faced forward, saw Higgins slide a fresh magazine up into his rifle. Higgins said, "How's it going, Hamilton?"

"Smooth as silk, Gunnery Sergeant," Hamilton said. "I tell you, though: who needs an assistant gunner in a place like this here? No need for an A-gunner to spot anything with them out in the open like they are. We gone kill every one of them if they come on like that again. What the hell they doing, Gunny, coming on like that?"

That's it, he thought: a good, reasonable question. Why are they out in the street? He turned, ran to the mouth of the alley. Jenkins stood with his back to the near wall, his rifle aimed at the edge of the roof of the building across the alley. "Jenkins?" he said.

"They're up there, Captain. Two of them. I saw them look over the edge. And there's some others down the alley beyond the truck. I looked under the truck, saw their feet and ankles twenty, thirty meters away."

The horns, he thought. And ahead of us, the chest. And behind the chest, the loins. No question about that. The crowds in the street are for show: they are the chest. They present themselves so that we will confront them while their buddies slide around and get behind us. And above us, he thought as he looked up at the edge of the roof of the building across the alley. These are the horns.

A narrow black face peered over the edge of the roof. The man pointed with a long, thin black arm and finger: first at Jenkins and then at him aiming their rifles at his face. Then the local grinned and jerked his arm and head back.

He lifted the muzzle of his rifle two inches, drew breath and aimed at the bright blue sky above the edge of the roof where he judged the man's head would reappear. Beside him Jenkins aimed his weapon, but to the left, farther down the alley. Smart guy, he thought. He took up pressure on the rifle's trigger, breathed twice to slow the hammering of his heart. Three heartbeats, and he saw the bulbous tip of a rocket-propelled grenade fitted into its launcher ease forward over the edge of the roof. He fired a single round at the warhead. The weapon jerked back. Jenkins did not fire. Smart guy, he thought.

In the avenue the murmuring of the two crowds rose to a single crashing chant and he heard Higgins shout, "Captain. Here they come."

"Jenkins," he said. "Kill every one of them who shows himself, armed or not. Hold them off until Gunny or I get back here."

"Kill them," Jenkins said. "Hold this position."

"Good man. What's your first name, Jenkins?"

"Allan."

"Don't hesitate, Allan." He tapped the box of grenades with his foot. "Use these. Toss them over the truck down the alley. Get up against a wall or take cover under the truck and shoot anyone who shows himself on the rooftops. Shoot anything that moves. And if it falls down, shoot it again: to be sure it doesn't move again. You understand me?"

"Kill every one of them who shows himself."

"That's it," he said. He turned and ran out of the alley, the soles of his boots scrabbling on grit, broken stone and shattered glass ground to glittering powder. Beyond the truck the mass stepped forward, shouting their chant again and again. They flourished broad-bladed spears and jabbed rifles at the sky, waved revolvers, semi-automatic pistols and assault rifles.

Assault rifles, he thought: ferocious, reliable weapons, exported by every country to every other country. Including the US of A. Where everyone who wants one thinks he needs one.

As he came up behind Higgins, the Gunnery Sergeant raised his voice to be heard above the shouting mass: "They're inside eighty meters and they're coming on, Captain."

He raised his rifle and aimed at the crowd, looking for the tall turbaned black with the sword who had led half the mass up the avenue from the port. The swordsman was gone. He aimed at a skinny guy who held an assault rifle above his head and jammed its muzzle again and again at the sky. The guy's head was shaven, his teeth were rotten and he wore a scraggly beard.

"Fire," he shouted, and as the last of the word came out of his mouth he shot the shaven-headed rotten-toothed scraggly-bearded guy dancing with his assault rifle. An intense rush of dark aortic blood spurted from his throat as the guy leapt backward, attempting escape from the wound that had killed him. The thick rope of blood dispersed into droplets that settled on the adjacent portion of the crowd. A teenager in a green tee-shirt holding a revolver wiped blood from his face with his left hand. He shot the teenager through the head. Behind him Simmons, Parnell and Thomas began to fire their rifles into the crowd from the rear of the truck. At his feet, the mechanical pounding of Hamilton's machinegun ripped the air apart. Higgins fired single aimed shots, the muzzle of his rifle shifting inch by inch from left to right across the front of the crowd. Killing the ones with weapons, he thought. Higgins, he thought. His name will be cut in granite somewhere.

From the alley he heard Jenkins fire his rifle on full automatic, heard the flat detonation of a grenade. Someone in the alley screamed words in the spiky, guttural local language. Good, he thought. Then Jenkins' weapon stopped firing.

He drew breath, heard another grenade detonate in the alley. Jenkins' rifle began to fire again. He exhaled.

In front of him, the crowd wavered, fell back, the even repetition of its determined chant dissolving into random shouts, screams leaping up throats, a shriek here and a shriek there: the last in this life.

"Gunny," he shouted above the tremendous noise of Hamilton's machinegun firing. "Get into the alley. They're coming at us from behind. Jenkins needs help."

As Higgins rose, he reached to his right hip pocket, drew out a black revolver with a two-inch barrel, proffered it and said, "You might need this, Captain."

He took the revolver thrust at him and said, "I'm shocked, Gunny. A private weapon? I mean, *you* know the regulations."

"Every single line," Higgins said. "Every dirty word. Keep it handy, Captain. We may need the firepower. It's a five-round .44. And right now? Fuck the regulations."

He hefted the blunt black revolver. ".44? I'm loaded for bear, then. What about you?"

"I'm a Gunnery Sergeant, Captain. I've got another one in a holster under my flak jacket."

He grinned at Higgins, shook his head, shoved the .44 into his belt beneath the skirt of his flack jacket and said, "What else do you have in a holster on your belt, Gunny? Napalm bomb? Fifth of Scotch? A battery from the Eleventh Marines?"

Higgins grinned at him, and said, "Wish I did, Captain. Particularly the scotch. But I'd settle for the artillery." He turned, bent forward and jogged to the mouth of the alley. He halted, jerked his head forward to peer into the gloom, jerked it back. He fitted the butt and stock of the rifle to his shoulder and cheek, eased forward with the muzzle of the rifle raised eighty degrees and as he stood out from the corner began to fire: at the edge of the roof across the alley. For a moment he watched as Higgins advanced, stepping with care through the litter beneath his feet, firing one round and then another, aiming here and there as though he were shooting birds.

As he turned back toward the mass of groaning shouting humming locals sixty meters away, a clear rising voice called out from among them. Those armed with projectile weapons began to shoot. Those with edged weapons slashed them at the air and rushed forward. Dressed in long gowns, ragged shorts or tee-shirts, they came on without hesitation into the ripping crack of grenades exploding, rushing toward the grinding machinegun fire, fleeing toward the spaced shots of the rifles.

They believe, he thought. Why else would they run with such determination out of life?

At his feet, Hamilton fired the machinegun with care: a three-second burst, a pause, a two second burst. With each burst, many fell, more shrieked and dodged. But those Hamilton had not killed or wounded came on: hundreds of them, and hundreds more behind, humming and chanting.

Some, he thought as he aimed at a stocky black in khaki shorts flourishing a long, broadbladed knife, would call them fanatics. I call them determined and courageous. Even though they are unprofessional. Even though their fire is spotty and unaimed.

He shot the stocky black through the forehead, shifted the rifle's muzzle right, aimed at a boy pointing a revolver and shot him in the chest, shifted the rifle's muzzle left, aimed at a woman holding a handgrenade, shot her in the face, shifted the rifle's muzzle right and aimed at a guy with a turban and a sword. He examined the man's face and thought, not my guy. Then he shot the man in the gut, shot him again in the throat.

Where are the better soldiers? he wondered. Where are the men who have handled weapons for years and who created the hell that is this city and the barren waste that surrounds it?

Behind us, he thought. And while we may prevail over the mass before us, we may not defeat those dashing through narrow alleys and climbing to the roofs of the buildings. And we may not even see those who control this operation from somewhere behind the chanting crowd, safe beyond the border of the beaten zone.

These to the front are for show, he thought as he aimed at and shot a man flourishing a machete, another with a broad-bladed spear, a third with an old revolver. Their purpose is to fix us in place, to force us to face front. These are the chest, he thought as he shot another clutching an old rifle by the forepiece. And the horns? They reach forward on either side and meet behind us. And somewhere beyond the massive dark chest to our front are the loins. Those who think, consider and order: those who planned and who now direct the execution of their plan.

In the alley, the racket of firing rifles and exploding grenades expanded, became frantic.

He looked toward the rear of the truck. Thomas was emptying a bag of grenades onto the sidewalk. Simmons was shoving another magazine up into his weapon. Parnell was firing one shot after another, aiming here and there, picking his targets. He waited until Parnell fired the last round in the magazine of his rifle and Simmons had his rifle up and was firing before he shouted, "Parnell!" Parnell jerked his head around and looked at him. "Get into the alley with Gunny and Jenkins and help out."

"Got it," Parnell shouted. He reloaded, picked four grenades one after the other from the pavement, shoved them into the broad pockets on his thighs and walked without haste toward the entrance of the alley. At the corner, Parnell eased his face forward, peered into the darker gloom inside the alley and jerked his head back. Then he raised his rifle and walked into the darkness.

He heard Parnell call, “Gunny!” Then he heard the distinctive, fizzing wobbly rush of a rocket-propelled grenade launched from somewhere down the alley. He shouted, “Cover,” flung himself to the pavement and rolled into the angle of the sidewalk and the building front behind him. He grunted as pebbles cut his knees, ground glass sliced the backs of his hands, grit scored his chin and cheek.

In the instant he dropped his rifle and pressed his hands over his ears, the rocket-propelled grenade exploded. The immense, ripping rush of sound shoved a wall of heat shot with smoke, grit and dust out of the alley. A ragged, ripped bundle no larger than a full pack leapt out of the smoke, thumped against the truck’s chassis and fell to the pavement between the truck and the sidewalk.

Parnell, he thought. Or Gunny Higgins. Or Jenkins. One of them. For it’s certain none of these motherless, murderous sonsofbitches wears a uniform shirt.

He stared at the horrifying thing: by length, the upper half of Parnell. By weight, two thirds of him. The remains of his face were fearsome: the explosion had ripped away Parnell’s reasonable good looks and exposed the bones beneath. His left arm was missing, torn from the shoulder. But the fingers of his right hand lay white and intact on the gray pavement that glistened as though someone had sprayed it with watery red ink.

Not a lot of blood, he thought. Out here in the shade, that is. The greater volume is in the gloom inside the alley. For in the instant the round struck Parnell, his blood rushed downward under pressure, pumped from the mush of splintered bone, tendon, vessel, artery, gut and bowel the explosion left behind when it chopped away his legs, the lower half of his hips and his groin. And his left arm.

Poor guy, he thought as he gripped his rifle and scrambled to his feet. He glanced down, saw the cuff and sleeve of his shirt were stained pale pink. From the roof beyond the swirling smoke and dust inside the alley an automatic weapon hammered, ceased fire as Higgins’ rifle and Jenkins’ began to fire.

He turned toward Hamilton lying behind the machinegun at the right front of the truck. The back of Hamilton’s flak jacket was pale pink. A thicker, more vivid red stained the back of his neck beneath the rim of his helmet.

Your weapon, he thought. Make sure it’s operable. He raised the rifle, fired over Hamilton’s back at the dense crowd, fired again, switched the selector to full automatic and emptied the remainder of the rounds in the magazine into the shouting dancing crowd. Celebrating, he thought: shouting with determination and joy. But the rifle works. As he shoved a fresh magazine into the rifle, he realized the truck's engine had stopped. He glanced at the hood, saw a long rent in the metal. Sure, he thought. That's what rocket-propelled grenades are good for: destroying soft vehicles.

He glanced at Hamilton, realized he was not firing the machinegun. "Hamilton," he shouted. "Keep that gun working."

Hamilton lay across the stock of the machinegun as though he were taking a break.

Bent at the waist, he rushed across the five paces that separated him from Hamilton. He gripped the back of Hamilton's flak jacket, dragged him from the machinegun and rolled him over. Blood slid from a single hole punched in Hamilton's left temple. More blood leaked from his nostrils and streamed from the corners of his mouth clamped shut. Gone, he thought. Killed by some sonofabitch who knows how to use a rifle. He laid his weapon on the pavement, lay down behind the machinegun, fitted the butt of the stock to his shoulder, aimed at the chanting crowd and pulled the trigger.

Nothing. He yanked the cocking handle. Nothing. He yanked at it again. Jammed, he thought. Out of service. This machinegun needs Major Maintenance. That useless bastard. I wonder what he's doing right now. Talking? Looking over a map? Drinking coffee with the camouflaged Army general?

He shoved the machinegun aside, picked up his rifle and scrabbled backward. As he did so a round hammered the machinegun's stock. The machinegun jerked, tilted, and fell on its side.

Guy can shoot, he thought. From the rear of the truck Thomas shouted, "He's on the roof of the building right across the way."

He edged to the front of the truck. A man crouched behind the parapet on the roof of the building across the avenue. The man was working the bolt of a rifle, the long barrel pointed at the sky. The stock and forepiece of the rifle were wood and a telescopic sight was fitted to the top of the receiver. Not a military weapon, he thought: a hunting rifle.

He stepped out from the protection of the truck, aimed at the rifleman. From the corner of his eye he saw a tall thin black in the front rank of the crowd point a pistol at him, and thought: Fifty meters? Too far, buddy. The rifleman's head and shoulders shifted as he closed the bolt and fitted the weapon to his shoulder. The man was bareheaded and wore a khaki bush jacket; or maybe, he thought, antique colonial battledress collected from his former European rulers. Who cares? As the man laid his cheek against the stock, he fired. A pink halo leapt from the man's head. The man dropped his rifle from the roof and fell back behind the parapet. A fragment of the crowd swirled about the weapon. An arm rose above the mass, the hand gripping the hunting rifle. Hope it blows up in your face, he thought.

He swung the rifle's muzzle down and left. He aimed at the tall thin black stepping forward firing his pistol and shot him in the chest. As the man fell, a spasmodic jerk of his right arm flung the pistol away. The crowd contracted, hands reaching up to catch the weapon. Hungry for weapons, he thought. Can't get enough of them.

In the alley behind him Jenkins' rifle and Higgins' were firing. And other weapons: bolt action rifles, a couple of pistols, an assault weapon on full automatic.

He looked toward the rear of the truck: Thomas was firing and firing into the crowd, jamming one magazine and the next up into his weapon. As he watched, Thomas fired the last round in the magazine in his rifle. Thomas ducked down, squatted. He laid his rifle on the sidewalk, picked up a grenade, yanked the pin from it and flung it toward the crowd as though he were throwing a baseball. Before it exploded he had lobbed another over the truck and was lifting a third from the pavement.

Six feet to Thomas' left, Simmons lay on the sidewalk, his arms beneath his back, his chest a sticky ruck of splintered bone and brilliant blood, flies swirling about his face and nestling into the wound that had killed him.

Three gone, he thought: Parnell, Hamilton and Simmons. Gone.

Thomas glanced his way as he picked another grenade from the sidewalk. Thomas nodded at him, pulled the pin from the grenade and threw it into the crowd, reached, took another grenade from the grit and dust.

A length of shadow thin as a stick appeared on the pavement to his left. He turned and looked up: a grinning man with a thin black face was leaning out over the edge of the roof, aiming a black semi-automatic pistol at him. The grinning man nodded at him and fired the pistol: the round struck the pavement beside his right boot. He flung his rifle up and shot the thin black man in the chest and throat. As the rifle's rounds flung the black's corpse backward onto the roof, he dropped the pistol. The pistol clattered to the sidewalk two paces away. He stepped and picked it up. The grips were sticky with blood. He identified it: nine millimeter, our standard sidearm. One of ours, he thought. He turned and tossed it into the cab of the truck.

From the rear of the truck, Thomas shouted, "They're taking off, Captain. Take a look at the sonsofbitches run."

He turned and looked. The fearsome mass was dissolving into darting groups fleeing up the avenue and down it, knots of sprinting blacks disappearing into alleys across the avenue littered with their killed and wounded countrymen. And countrywomen. Grown men, teenaged boys, women. But no teenaged girls, he thought: must be some local custom. Here and there, a maimed man dragged himself among the dead. A woman whose right forearm had been amputated by gunfire or grenade screamed and screamed as she stared at the wound that would kill her.

"They're taking off!" Thomas shouted.

Except, he thought, listening to the hammer of weapons in the alley, for the ones trying to kill Higgins and Jenkins: except for the horns. And the loins. He scanned the rooftops along the avenue, right and left across the way and above his head. Then he darted across the mouth of the alley. As he stopped beside Thomas, the crash of gunfire in the alley mounted.

Thomas said: "Why are they . . . ? Hey, I hear a helo."

He listened. Above the racket of weapons firing in the alley he heard it too: the whopping of helicopter blades, the whine of the bird's turbine. "Easy, Thomas," he said. "Eyeball the rooftops and the windows. Both sides of the avenue. They're on the rooftops above us and across the way."

"It's coming from the south," Thomas told him. "It's flying up the big avenue."

"Coming the same way we did," he said as the helicopter's sound intensified. He recognized the sound, identified the type of helicopter that was approaching.

Not going to be good enough, he thought as Thomas pointed up the avenue and shouted, "There it is."

Swinging through ninety degrees, turning toward them, the bird was flying two hundred meters up: too high to do any good, too low to avoid small-arms fire.

In the alley behind him, the firing diminished, ceased: as though Higgins and Jenkins and those shooting at them had heard the helicopter too. Maybe, he thought, the locals shooting in the alley are taking off.

But I doubt it.

"Aw, Jesus, Captain," Thomas said. "It's not a gunship. It's one of those fucking . . ."

"I see it," he said as he stared at the bulbous teardrop canopy balanced at the front of the long thin boom.

What the *fuck* did they send a reconnaissance helo for? No room for anyone but the pilot and an observer? More talk, more indecision, more caution. What we need is a company of men, or a gunship. Or a battalion of artillery and a guy at the other end of the pipe who knows what he's doing and will do it when I tell him to do it. What we need is anything except someone who has come to see and to report back.

The helicopter halted and hovered five hundred meters away: above the intersection of the north-south and east-west avenues. The bulbous canopy turned right and left as though the pilot couldn't decide which way to go. Then the bird's nose tipped forward, the boom rose and the helicopter flew forward, the pilot staring straight ahead, the guy in the other seat looking through fieldglasses.

Thomas spat and said, "At least it got the crowd out of here." He stepped out from behind the rear of the truck into the street, raising his rifle in both hands above his head and pumping it up and down.

A hundred meters up the avenue he saw movement on the roofs of one building and the one next to it and the third one on. "Thomas," he said as he reached to grab him, "get back here."

From the roofs on both sides of the avenue weapons rattled. Tracer rose toward the chopper. He realized this was the first time today he had seen tracer. Not stupid, he thought. Organized and thoughtful: why use tracer on anything except an aerial target? Locals in rags and dirty tee-shirts. Barefoot, without insignia or supply, never seen a computer or an aerial photograph, armed with whatever they can scrounge. But they know what to do with what they've got. And they ought to: they've been at this for decades.

The chopper leapt straight up, rotated one hundred and eighty degrees and fled back toward the intersection of the avenues. And as it fled and his left hand touched Thomas' shoulder, Thomas threw his rifle down on the street, stepped back, tripped and began to fall. He gripped Thomas' flak jacket to steady him. But Thomas was tall and heavy and he could not hold him. Staggering backward into the shelter of the truck, Thomas hissed. He looked at Thomas' face: Thomas' eyes were rolled up into his head, blood slid from his mouth yanked open as though he were screaming, and more blood—a thin sticky strand of red bright against the unrelieved dun color of the buildings along the avenue, of the city and of the country of which the city was the capital—ran from an entry wound above Thomas' left eyebrow.

Thomas pitched backward onto the sidewalk. Blood filled his mouth and overflowed onto his dirty throat. His legs trembled and he drew his knees up. He coughed a single gout of blood onto the filthy litter of shell-casings, bits of concrete and grit on the sidewalk. He straightened his legs and lifted his right hand. He closed his fingers into a fist. Then his fingers opened and his hand fell, palm upward, onto the sidewalk.

From the alley, Gunny Higgins or Jenkins shouted, "Captain, Captain." He looked at the roofs across the avenue: no one. Not a single man anywhere. But they're there.

He put two fingers to Thomas' bloody throat. Nothing. Gone. A fly ticked against the back of his hand. He glanced at Simmons lying face up on the pavement five feet away. An iridescent mass of flies clustered in the savage wound torn in Simmons' chest. Cleaning up, he thought. Working hard.

"Captain," the voice called from the alley.

"Coming," he shouted. He stood. He glanced once more at Thomas lying at his feet, once more at Simmons. He dropped the magazine from his rifle, inserted in a full one. Then he stepped around Thomas' body, walked to the entrance of the alley and looked into the gloom.

Gunny Higgins stood against the far wall of the alley, ten feet into the hot black shade. He held his rifle in his right hand, the muzzle pointed at the sky two stories up. His left arm hung at his side: glistening blood dripped from his left hand. His right pantleg was charred black.

"Gunny?" He walked into the alley, stood with his back to the wall across from Higgins.

"I got winged in the forearm," Higgins hissed. "A little trouble moving the left hand."

"Jenkins?"

"Killed. They rolled a grenade under the truck. The blast took him in the face. The bird?"

"Observation. A pilot and a guy with fieldglasses."

Higgins shook his head. "Great. What do you think, Captain?"

"I think they better get a platoon of men here in the next five minutes."

Higgins nodded. "These guys up on the roof and in the alley beyond Washburn's truck are going to try again now the chopper's gone."

"The radio?"

"Bust."

"Great," he said. "Still, at least they know we're here."

"That's a lot of help." Higgins spat at the filthy ground to his left. "Captain? What do you want to do?"

"Keep on. We're doing all right. We've killed a lot of them. And we can kill a lot more of them."

"I've got six full mags left. Ten grenades. You?"

"Ten magazines," he said. He tapped the cargo pocket on his thigh. "Two grenades."

"I got more grenades here in the box. Thomas? Simmons and Hamilton?"

"Gone."

"Five KIA," Higgins said. "Not counting the guy in the truck they gutted. That leaves you and me, Captain. The machinegun's out of service?"

"That's it. It needs Major Maintenance."

Higgins shook his head and winced. Then he grinned and said, "You got a good attitude, Captain. For what it's worth, I know the men in the company appreciate it. How do you want to do this?"

"We'd better stay in this alley. They've got snipers on the buildings across the way. You stay over there, I'll stay here. We'll each cover the opposite roof."

Higgins said: "I've been shooting them like snipe." He shook blood from his wrist and said, "You'd think they could have sent a gunship and a helo with a squad of men. Or just a squad of men in a truck."

"I agree."

"But they didn't."

"That's it," he said. "Nothing to do except shoot every sonofabitch who shows his face in this alley."

Higgins grinned. More blood dripped from his left hand. "I agree with that, Captain. Nothing else to do. And I've been here before. Up in the Arizona in I Corps. Same thing. They were Asians in a jungle. These are Africans in a city. Same thing every time. Except, in the jungle, we had artillery and air on tap."

Down the alley in the gloom beyond Sergeant Washburn's truck voices whispered, feet stepped, steel clicked against stone.

"They're coming," Higgins said.

"Gunnery Sergeant, shoot every other one of them," he ordered. "I'll do the other half."

Higgins grinned at him and said, "You want some grenades, Captain?"

"Call me by my first name," he said.

"This isn't a war, Captain. I told you that."

"No?"

"No. This is a stack of shit higher than a man can shovel."

"That's a hygienic problem, Gunny. We'll get Major Maintenance to deal with it. Hygienic problems are his department."

"Grenade, Captain?" Higgins said.

"Sure," he said as he looked at Higgins and thought, none better.

Higgins bent, laid his rifle on the ground, reached into the box with his good hand and tossed a grenade across the alley. He caught it, yanked the pin from its collar, flung it over the truck wedged in the alley, yanked the pin from the second grenade Higgins tossed him, flung it at the explosion of the first.

Left arm hanging at his side, Higgins picked up his rifle with his good right hand and stood up straight. He raised the rifle's muzzle and fired a burst.

Above him, someone on the roof screamed, screamed again. Someone else fired one round and then another at Higgins. The second round hit Higgins' left shoulder, shoved him against the wall. His wounded left arm, wounded a second time, fluttered and jerked. Higgins groaned and sighed. Then he shouted through his clenched teeth and slid down the wall.

The shoulder? he thought. He could have shot Gunny in the face. Why the shoulder?

He looked up to his right, saw a rifle thrust over the edge of the roof above Washburn's truck. The rifleman was aiming at Higgins across the alley. A round dark face lay against the rifle's stock. He raised his rifle, stepped away from the wall, aimed at the round dark face. The man on the roof jerked his face from the rifle's stock and stared at him. He shot the man in the face. As the round flung him backward, he dropped his rifle. The rifle clattered on the ground.

Beyond Washburn's truck someone shouted.

He ran across the alley, took a grenade from the box, pulled the pin and lobbed it over Washburn's truck. Another shout. The grenade exploded. A scream.

"Gunny?" he said. "You all right?"

"Shoulder," Higgins said. "Sonofabitch." He grunted and shoved himself back against the wall.

"Give me a couple of seconds and I'll give you a shot."

"No time for that," Higgins hissed. "Just keep shooting, Captain. I don't think I'm up to a hell of a lot right now."

"Right," he said. He stood to Higgins' right, his back against the wall. More shuffling and whispering beyond Washburn's truck. He glanced right, examined the roofs of the buildings across the avenue. He saw no one: not a single one of them. And he heard nothing except the moans and screams of the wounded and the dying.

But they're there, he thought. Waiting for us to come out. Waiting for the chance.

"Gunny, you got a smoke grenade?"

Higgins panted, hissed and said, "Purple." He reached into the cargo pocket on his right thigh, handed the grenade up to him. He pulled the pin and tossed it out of the mouth of the alley, under the truck. Dense purple smoke spurted from the grenade skittering across the concrete and billowed upward from beneath the truck, rising straight up into the windless sky.

"They're out there somewhere," Higgins grunted.

"Ours or theirs?" he said.

"Theirs. Ours are drinking coffee and looking at aerial photographs." Higgins shivered and said, "I hear more of them coming. On the roof."

He heard it too: guttural consonants and spiky ones, a shouted order, the chink of metal against metal. He raised the rifle, aimed at the sky above the edge of the roof across the alley; and as he did so the heads and shoulders of four men with assault rifles appeared, each of them taking aim.

He shot the one on the right in the chest, shot the next one to the left in the face, shifted the rifle's muzzle left: toward the third. As he sighted on the man's face, he heard the familiar fizzing launch and accelerating rush of a rocket-propelled grenade fired from far down the alley. The third and fourth riflemen on the roof leapt backward.

Getting away from the blast that's coming, he thought as he sat down beside Higgins.

Bad aim, he thought as he watched the wobbling rocket-propelled grenade arc toward the rear of the Washburn's truck. He laid his rifle on the ground to his right and raised his hands to his face. Higgins rolled toward him, flopped his bad left arm across his officer's waist, raised himself on his good right arm.

"Gunny . . . ?" he said. But the ripping crack of the explosion of the rocket-propelled grenade interrupted him. He bent his face to his raised knees and thought, Higgins rolled against me and raised himself up to shield me from the blast. I wonder why? Then he thought, they're not shooting from the roof: they should be shooting from the roof.

Higgins coughed, gasped and rolled away from him. He raised his face and reached for his rifle. The rifle was gone: the explosion had plucked it from the ground and flung it away into the last of the purple smoke rising about the truck at the entrance to the alley. He looked for the box of grenades, saw it beneath the truck beyond his rifle. No weapon, he thought. He scrambled to his feet, looked up through the whirling smoke and dust. A rifleman on the rooftop forty meters down the alley fired at him. The bullet hammered him above the right knee, flung him back against the wall. Higgins rolled toward him, reached up, steadied him as he slid to the ground. He dragged himself upright, gasping and shaking, and shoved his back against the wall. He clamped his mouth shut. His jaws trembled. He opened his mouth and screamed at his jerking leg as he stared at the flow of blood wetting the cloth of his trousers.

"Easy," Higgins grunted. "It's not pumping. Can you move the leg?"

"No."

"Try to move the leg, Captain."

He stared at his leg. Nothing. "It's broken. I can feel bone grating. What about you, Gunny?"

Higgins shoved himself upright with his right arm and hand, sat with his back to the wall. "Bunch of stuff peppered me in the back of the legs. Another bunch in the arm again. I can't move my legs. Or my left arm. How come they're not shooting at us?"

"I don't know," he said.

But he knew: they want us, for a time at least, alive.

Higgins reached across himself and picked up his rifle. Holding it in his right hand, he pointed the muzzle at a rising giggle beyond the rear of Washburn's truck. He pulled the trigger. The rifle did not fire. "Jesus," Higgins said. "Take a look at it, Captain."

He took the rifle from Higgins, tried to release the magazine. The magazine did not drop. He tried to cock it. The mechanism was jammed. He yanked at it, yanked at it again. Nothing. "It's bust, Gunny." He laid the useless weapon beside him.

Higgins picked up his left wrist and laid his left forearm on his lap. "Christ," he said. "Oh, Jesus." He breathed, breathed again, and said, "All right. Better now. I've got my sidearm and the .44, Captain. The last magazine is in the pistol. What have you got?"

He felt for his sidearm: the holster was gone, torn from his webbing. "Sidearm's missing. The explosion blew the box of grenades and my rifle under our truck. I've got a couple of grenades in the cargo pocket on my right thigh. And the revolver you gave me," he said. "That's it."

Higgins said: "Two dozen rounds, maybe. A couple of grenades. Not much to fight the fucking world with." He turned his head, nodded at Washburn's truck. "They're coming. You better handle the pistol." Higgins worked the semi-automatic pistol from its holster, handed it over, drew the .44 revolver from beneath the skirt of his flak jacket. "You want to grenade them?"

He looked Higgins in the face and said, "I guess I'll hang on to the grenades for now. Gunny, I'm sorry about this."

"This is what we do, Captain. This is what we are."

A thin black man in khaki shorts and a bloodstained white shirt stepped from behind the far side of Washburn's truck jammed in the alley. He was unarmed. He raised both hands above his head, gesturing that they should surrender.

"Fuck you," Higgins said. He raised the stubby black revolver in his wavering right hand and fired two shots. The man in the bloodstained shirt jumped back. "Missed. They want us to surrender," Higgins said. "The sonsofbitches."

"I don't think so," he said. "You agree?"

"You bet I agree."

On the roof beyond Washburn's truck a man stood up and waved a sword. He examined the man's face and thought, not my guy. He raised Higgins' sidearm, fired three rounds at the swordsman. But his leg jerked and his arm wavered as he fired. The swordsman ducked away. "We better let them come closer, Gunny."

"You got it," Higgins said as the same man appeared on the roof, waved his sword and danced and sang.

A skinny teenager stepped out from behind the rear of the truck and levelled an old rifle. He raised the pistol and fired three rounds. The teenager grinned and leapt back. Laughter rose from behind the truck.

"Celebrating," Higgins said. "The sonsofbitches." He drew breath and shouted, "Come on, you sonsofbitches."

He heard a sound to his right: at the mouth of the alley. He turned his head: a man was aiming an assault rifle at him. He pointed the pistol. Pain made his leg and hips and hand tremble. He fired two rounds as the man ducked out of sight. Another appeared on the roof across from him, aiming an antique military rifle. He fired the pistol twice. The man jumped back and he thought, they show themselves, I shoot and they duck back. They know a pistol's near useless at these ranges. And no good at all when the hand of the guy holding the pistol is shaking. When the guy holding the pistol is grinding his teeth to stop himself screaming with pain.

Higgins fired at a man who stuck his head around the rear of Washburn's truck.

Another one of them leaned out over the edge of the roof and grinned at him. He fired the pistol at him, but the man did not jump back: he leaned out farther and his grin widened. He shot at the man again, missed again, glanced at the pistol in his hand: the slide was locked back. Empty, he thought. He tossed the pistol aside and drew the .44 caliber pistol Higgins had given him from his belt. Five rounds, he thought. And two grenades.

A man with a revolver in his fist stepped out from behind the truck, came forward two paces. Higgins fired the revolver at the man. The man grinned at Higgins but he did not jump out of view. Higgins fired at him again. The man turned away and walked back behind the truck.

"I'm dry," Higgins said. He flung the pistol at the back of the truck. It fell in the middle of the alley.

A tall man in a turban appeared at the mouth of the alley, a sword in his right hand.

My guy, he thought: the one who sang and chanted as he led the crowd that came up the avenue. One of their leaders. He aimed the revolver at him as a long tremor in his leg and hip thrust agony up into his groin and gut. His hand shook and as another vicious tremor rose through him, he fired the revolver, fired it again. The man stood at the mouth of the alley grinning and swinging the sword. He fired at him a third time, a fourth. The swordsman laughed. He looked over his shoulder and spoke to someone out of sight beyond the alley's mouth.

More of them, he thought: more of the sonsofbitches waiting outside the alley.

The swordsman stepped forward a pace.

He drew breath and aimed the revolver at the center of the man's chest. Ignore the pain, he thought. Ignore the tremors springing through you. He exhaled and pulled the trigger. The crack of the revolver filled the alley. The swordsman weaved and danced, swinging his weapon in front of him.

Missed, he thought. He flung the revolver at the swordsman. The swordsman caught it with his left hand, glanced at it, laughed, tossed it over his shoulder and paced forward until he stood above him and Gunny Higgins.

"You sonofabitch," Higgins said. The swordsman nodded and smiled as though he and Higgins had known one another for years.

Behind the swordsman another man appeared in the mouth of the alley. He too wore a turban and a long gown. But instead of a weapon he carried a coil of thick rope in each hand. He grinned as he stepped forward a pace. Four more of them stepped into the alley and stood with their backs to the opposite wall. Each of them wore a turban and a long gown. The loins, he thought. Those who plan. Those who decide. Those who order.

At the entrance to the alley men without turbans wearing shorts and trousers and tee shirts appeared, grinning and hauling on ropes. He knew what they wanted him to see: the savaged remains of the three missing men who been in Washburn's truck. Then they dragged them into the alley: three dusty bundles, ankles roped together, the features of each face raised to the sky ground to the bone. The first's right arm was missing. Gunfire had ripped away the top of the second's skull. Something—a burst from an automatic weapon, the explosion of a grenade—had torn a ragged hole in the third man's chest. You sonsofbitches, he thought as he looked at the grinning faces of the young men hauling on the ropes.

This shit place, he thought. He put his left hand on the filthy ground and pushed himself up against the wall, worked his right hand into the cargo pocket on his jerking, trembling thigh. Beside him Higgins spat blood onto his lap, nodded at the swordsman standing over him and hissed, "Fuck you. And fuck every one of them with you."

The one with the sword grinned and giggled, spoke to the one with the coil of rope, raised the sword above his right shoulder and looked down at Higgins. The graceful curve of polished steel gleamed. Even here, he thought: even in this alley full of black shade.

Higgins raised his right arm, grabbed at the man's gown. The swordsman grinned. He gripped the hilt of the sword with both hands. Then he swung it through a precise descending arc.

The blade severed Higgins' right hand, his wrist and four inches of his forearm. Trailing strings of blood, it fell among the debris of shell casings, concrete chips, trash, filth and grit that littered the alley.

Higgins shouted. Then he screamed. His useless left arm flopped and shook as he tried to raise it. Higgins gritted his teeth, lifted the stump of his forearm spurting a thick pumping stream of blood and swung it as though it were an edged weapon. Blood spattered across the swordsman's long gray gown.

The tall thin black stepped back a pace, nodded at Higgins, raised the sword glistening with blood up and back behind his right shoulder.

Higgins spat blood at the swordsman, spat again. The swordsman spoke to the man holding the coil of rope. Then he nodded at Higgins and swung the sword. Higgins jerked his head and shoulders back against the stone wall behind his back. The tip of the sword flicked across his throat below his jaw. Blood leapt from the severed artery in his neck. Without a sound Higgins rolled away onto his side and lay still.

He slid his forefinger into the ring of one of the grenades in his pocket: to the first knuckle.

All we've got left, he thought.

The tall thin black stood above him, his sword raised in both bony fists. He nodded at Higgins' corpse and said, "*Kan huwa rajul. Wa inta*?"

He did not understand the tall black's words, but he knew what he meant. He worked his forefinger to the second knuckle through the ring of the grenade and said, "You bet, you sonofabitch."

The tall thin black raised the point of his sword another foot toward the blue sky above the alley and the brilliant sun above the sky. His shrouded left biceps hid his broad grinning mouth.

He looked up at the swordsman's solemn muddy eyes. He nodded at him, and thought: I'm far from home. He saw the swordsman's hands tighten on the iron hilt. As the long curve of steel glistening with Higgins' blood flashed down through the gloom he yanked the pin from the grenade.

HE TURNED HIS BLISTERED face as though he were blind: to his left toward the light, ahead toward the light, to his right toward the light. Wherever he looked, the light was as hard and sharp as chipped white stone, and each time he closed his swollen lids, grit rasped across the delicate, desiccated surfaces of his eyes.

His mouth was a dry clenched hole packed with dust. The swollen bulb of his tongue braced his jaws open, the broad wedge of the tip protruding between his teeth. His throat burned beneath his burning jaws.

Each breath shifted the viscous fluid within his blisters and each movement of the serum jerked skin from the flesh at the periphery of each blister.

The sun has flayed me.

He listened to the light wind rustle through the bushes and tried to think where he had come from, where he must go, how he would go there.

Wincing, a faint keening rising up his throat, he lifted his heavy right arm, touched the rubberized shelter half riding on his neck. At dawn it had crackled when he had unfolded it. Now it was as slick and smooth as oil and it lay like burning slag against his flesh.

And now? he wondered.

He tried to think, but only shreds of ideas came to him and the meaning of the simplest words shimmered and vanished into the light.

He centered his thoughts. And now? He stared at marks cut in the slab of stone on which he stood. He tilted his head forward, examined the marks. But heat encased his brain and filled it with a blank white glare.

Think, he told himself.

A word rushed out of the brilliant light inside his mind: hoofprints. These are the impressions of the hoofs of a four-footed animal that came this way when this stone was damp earth. Ancient, he thought: a last reminder, cut in the rising course of stone on which I stand, of an extinct species.

I can think no more, he thought.

"Think no more?" Sergeant Quinlan said. "What the fuck does that mean, think no more?"

He could not speak. He turned his head right, left, right, looking for Sergeant Quinlan. The sluggish movement of his head reminded him of a heavy quadruped looking side-to-side, staring and staring without comprehension.

Sergeant Quinlan's voice rose, hectoring and angry: "Can't talk, hey? Thirsty, are you? Think you need a drink? Don't think you can make it? *Fuck* that. You're going on, you got me? You're *not* going to stand here and stare at the sun and think about hoofprints in the stone. Forget about hoofprints. Think about marching."

He swung his head. His face burned and blazing white light struck at him.

"Move!" Sergeant Quinlan yelled. "I don't care what you don't think you can do! I don't care whether you're thirsty or whether you hurt! I don't give a damn! I want you to *move*."

He shuffled his right foot across the ancient rock beneath the sole of his boot.

"That's a start!" Sergeant Quinlan yelled. "You're moving! Another! And fifty more!"

What mark will I leave here? he wondered. To show I passed this way?

As though he were feeling his way through the dark, he drew his left foot forward. Waves undulated through the oily salt liquid packed in the blisters that enveloped his limbs, his back, his throat. Agony, he thought: another word I remember.

"Another!" Sergeant Quinlan shouted. "Come on, another!"

He dragged his right leg forward, the sole of the boot scraping the rock.

Sergeant Quinlan's shouting voice receded. I am moving, he thought: away from him. Or he is moving away from me. Or something else.

I cannot see, he thought. I cannot hear. I cannot go on.

From a great distance Sergeant Quinlan shouted, "I'm telling you you *can* go on!"

Sergeant Quinlan shouted something else, but he could not understand the words. The sunlight that had blinded him tilted and his forehead struck the hard edge of a cloven hoofprint impressed in rock.

A CRUISE, HE THOUGHT as he stepped down past the walls of sandbags into the bunker. That's what they called it: a Goddamned cruise. Big grins all around: a cruise east through the Med, with orders from Stuttgart and The White House about peacekeeping; with lectures about civil affairs, the indigenous populace, local customs, local politics.

And while we did the hard work of preparation and deployment and carried out the uneasy approach to this hostile shore, the plump faces of the prominent peered from television screens, reasoned discourse pouring out of their lying mouths as they spoke of American intentions, American will and American commitment.

And right after was landed, the hangers-on showed up. Reporters. Congressmen. CIA types. Memo writers from the Department of State and the Department of Defense. They all came—right after we had put in troops enough to ensure their safety.

And every one of them wore a bush jacket, even though none of them's spent an hour in the bush. But if they're not in the U.S.A. and the sun is shining, they wear bush jackets. They go overseas, and all of a sudden they're dressed up like big game hunters in Africa, even though none of them knows one end of a rifle from the other.

I don't get it. Must be some kind of uniform they wear. That they think is just as good as a real uniform.

And when they all flocked ashore *right* after we got here, each of them—each politician, intelligence type, military bureaucrat, correspondent and TV reporter—preened in his bush jacket. And every one of them was eager to listen for a minute, speak for an hour and get the hell back aboard ship before nightfall.

As someone said, they're all tourists, and I'd guess every one of them could clean both his ears at once with one long swab.

And pretty soon now, in hours if they can make the connections or their private jets are handy or they can order up free transport from the Pentagon, they'll be here again: for the *big* story, for the tragedy, for the details, for the "lessons" to be learned from this latest fuck-up. For the story they've waited for and helped create.

He looked at the roof of the bunker: corrugated iron overlaid with sandbags supported by bowed timbers six feet apart that creaked when the wind blew. Tinny, he thought. Wouldn't stop an artillery shell, might not stop a mortar round. Not dug deep enough, not enough timber supports, not enough engineers on the ground to do the job right.

He glanced at the cases of ammunition, ordnance and racked weapons that filled the bunker. The light from the ramp that led from down into the bunker was bright. *Too* bright, he thought: blinding white. The ramp should have been built with an offset, to protect the bunker's contents from blast and the odd lucky shot.

Fortunately, he thought, we were lucky: the locals didn't care about destroying this matériel. They knew Uncle wouldn't care about the metal bits and pieces; but they were sure Uncle would become cautious if his Marines were hammered. So they destroyed us and left the equipment whole.

All here, he thought as he looked at the munitions: stacked, laid out, racked, arrayed. Waiting for someone to come down here and carry it all out into the light and put it to good use.

What a waste, he thought. No real perimeter, not enough wire strung, not enough mines laid down. Backs to the sea, a warren of local housing across the road and the guards on the gate threatening the street that led to the highway with unloaded weapons. And the men flaked out in racks in a high-rise. In a fucking high-rise.

We ought not be here, Major, Gunny Stone said. A building, Major? None of these guys should be in this building. I mean, Major, just one artillery shell could . . .

And I said: I know, Gunny. I know.

And now? Now Gunny Stone lies with his men under the broken concrete and snapped re-bars: bones crushed, chest collapsed, stinking like any other corpse. I wonder what he thought at the last? If he had time to think anything at all?

I know the answer to that. If he had the time, he thought, you *sons*of-bitches. And he wasn't thinking about the indigenous populace. He was thinking about us. About me and everyone else up the line from him.

Dumped down here at the edge of the slums of this God-forsaken city at the eastern end of the Mediterranean. Running five man patrols through the narrow, slimy streets stinking of excrement and urine. Staring locals in the doorways of hovels beside the way, filthy children in the dust. Call that a patrol, do we, Major? Gunnery Sergeant Morgan asked him. Ought to be birds overhead, artillerymen with the lanyards in their hands, a platoon of men out there on every trip. And *no* one walking alone down one of those shit-stinking alleys they call a sidestreet.

I know, Gunny. I know.

And now Gunnery Sergeant Morgan is closer to death than he was at Khe Sanh. A leg chopped off by a sharp, slicing fragment of concrete slab, a corpsman—Fletcher—crouched above him in the rubble, a bloody hemostat in his bloody hand, the angled silver jaws of the instrument darting at the jerking spurting artery while Morgan gritted his teeth and cursed and cursed.

And I know who he was cursing. Not the ragheads. Us. Me.

And our local allies? An army as able as a crowd of opera singers to defend themselves, let alone assault an enemy. Lots of fast moves with their hands and hips, lots of standing around and drinking tea and yammering at one another and not doing much the fuck else. And up in the hills: twenty-nine varieties of venomous sonsofbitches: Syrians, Druze, Sunnis, Shi'a, Communists, Fascists, whatever you want. And the Israelis driving their tanks up this way, into our area, to show us what big balls they have. And the intelligence services of two great powers and eight lesser ones trading information, fucking one another, playing musical chairs and making hundreds of faulty estimates and thousands of idiot predictions. But none of them predicted this.

We should have done what we were supposed to do. We should have put the men in two-man holes. We should have done a lot of other things, too: but we should have done that at least. We should have been what we were supposed to be. But the fat, thoughtless, clueless talking faces on the tube said: you're peacekeepers. No loaded weapons, no secure perimeter defense, no threatening actions. We want, one of them said, a collegial atmosphere. Think of yourselves as campus cops.

And the fat-faced bastard wore a uniform when he said it. The sonofabitch.

He lifted the weapon he wanted from its place at the end of the rack of rifles. Flash-suppressor at the end of the long heavy barrel, telescopic sights, a magazine of rounds heavy enough to travel the distance to the target and not tumble. And to do the job when they arrive. The metal of the sniper's rifle was matte black, the stock and forepiece dull black plastic.

He held the rifle under his right arm, removed the magazine and held it in his left hand. The metal-jacketed tips of the shells glinted. Well kept, he thought: clean and bright. Just what I want. What I need.

Fucking bastard, he thought. Killing them like sheep in their racks, collapsing the shit building on top of them. And grinning, the shocked gate-guard shouted at me. Grinned, Major. He grinned as he drove the truck through the useless gate and under the building.

And blew the charge that blew the explosives and the cylinders of propane gas. And blew the building down, killing near every one of them inside and maiming the ones not killed.

And now?

And now we'll have an investigation. Admirals and generals. Politicians in smooth suits. Lawyers. Close-mouthed staff writing successive drafts of the committee's report. Cautionary words, elegant conclusions absolving every last fucking guy from private up of any responsibility whatever. Absolving me along with the rest.

When the fact is: more than one someone ought to be shot for this. Or at least court-martialed. Myself, for example. But no one will be disciplined. A few comments in the files, a couple of oblique remarks, this officer and that passed over. Me for sure, he thought: Major's as high as I'm going.

He hefted the sniper's rifle, fitted the magazine beneath the breech, shoved it home. Heavier than the standard infantry rifle. About the right weight for hunting big game. But that was natural: the sniper's rifle was a hunter's weapon.

Clean, purposeful, direct: that's what this weapon is. Whereas I am filthy: concrete dust pounded into my dungarees, the back of my left hand ripped open when the concrete shattered, the right leg of my trousers torn from knee to cuff, hair full of grit, the sweat on my chest mixed with concrete dust ground from the wreck of the building by the blast and the slabs snapping as they fell.

I was lucky: to have been awake and walking what we called the perimeter and knew was not. A hundred yards from the building in which they died, and the blast knocked me flat on my ass.

A guy in a truck, the gate-guard said. One guy, one truck. And a couple of hundred and maybe more found dead so far. How many dead did we suffer to assault and take Tarawa? And kill every one of the sonsofbitches? And *win*? Nine hundred and some. Heavy losses. But we sent a message to *Dai Nippon*: that they would not win another battle. That we would prevail. And they didn't. And we did.

And here? Here, someone sent us the message. I wonder if we understand what we've been told. I doubt it. I doubt the wheels and the cogs and the gears even realize a message has been delivered.

He gripped the sniper's rifle in his hands and thought, time to go. I wish I had a battalion and a position to assault, enough ordnance to level Denver and orders to kill anyone with a weapon in his grubby hand. But I don't. All I have is this sniper's rifle. But it will be big enough. Even without a spotter, or thirty-six riflemen, or three companies, or three battalions or the Navy or the Army or the Air Force, this one magazine and this elegant rifle will be big enough.

He heard a scrunch of boots behind him on the ramp of sand that led down into the bunker. He turned, the rifle in his hands. He watched as booted feet, filthy trousers, grimy hands, the hem and breast of a flak-jacket spattered with rusty bloodstains and the man's head descended into the bunker. But he was looking into the brilliant light that poured down the ramp and he could not identify the Marine who had come down into this cheesy sandbagged pit they called "the armory bunker": the man's face was a black oval cut out of the bright glare behind him.

"Who is it?" he asked.

"I thought I saw you come in here, Major."

"Crane? Is that you?"

"Yes, Major," Crane said as he came forward, moving out of the yellowwhite light flooding down the ramp into the bunker. Rivulets of sweat ran through the dust that coated Crane's face.

"You can go on, if you want, Sergeant. I'm just checking some things here." He watched Crane look at him: the Sergeant's intelligent eyes measured him, glanced at the rifle he held. Crane's high forehead tilted forward. Confirming his suspicions about my intentions.

"No kidding, Major?" Sergeant Crane said. "I thought you were down here because this was where the help was needed."

"Take it easy, Sergeant." He could think of nothing else to say, and he knew Crane would brush aside his feeble suggestion. Crane had served and served, in peace and in Vietnam, and he was intelligent: smarter than most officers. Smarter, he knew, than a sergeant needed to be. Or, maybe, ought to be.

"Right now, Major? You want me to take five? While they're trying to get them out from under that concrete layer-cake Ali cooked up with his exploding truck? Still, whatever you want: you've got the rank. And the rifle, of course. Though I'd guess you don't need a weapon. What you need right now is about six twenty-ton cranes, three field hospitals, three hundred gallons of whole blood and a flock of chaplains. I figure we'll get the chaplains at least, don't you? That's the way we are now: words, feelings, ideas, advisers spiritual and advisers tactical and advisers psychological. In case one flock of advisers doesn't work out, we've got another flock of them handy. But a weapon? I don't think there's an officer ashore in the eastern Med who needs any kind of a weapon right now. Particularly a sniper's rifle, Major."

"Go on back to whatever you were doing, Sergeant."

"I was digging them out, Major. Lifting chunks of dusty, bloody concrete. I looked down in a hole and saw Kalinski's face. He was dead. Know how I knew he was dead? Simple: he'd been chopped in half just below the breastbone. A movement of the slabs as the building collapsed, I suppose. The chance of things. Something cut the lower two thirds of him away from the top third of him. Right through the lower ribs, through the stomach, through the spine. We're going to have a hell of a time fitting Kalinski back together, Major. For that matter, we're going to have a hell of a time fitting a couple hundred and more of them back together. Anyhow, I looked at Kalinski's face—he had blood packed in his nostrils and gore stuffed in his mouth, but he looked peaceful enough—and then I glanced over my shoulder and saw you coming in here fast. Wondered if I could help you out here in the armory. So I took a break."

"That's not what I meant," he said.

"I know what you meant, Major," Crane said. "You want me to go away so you can sneak out of here with that fancy rifle and do whatever it is that you think you ought to do. Shoot someone. Kill some ragheads: Ali Whoever and his cousin Hamid Whogots."

"Get out of here, Sergeant."

"What are you, Major? Thirty, thirty-two? I'm forty. I've put in twenty-two, Major. But I'll tell you: I would have come in here to see what you were doing if I were no more than a year into my first enlistment. So tell me: what the fuck do you think you're doing?"

"You've got a foul mouth on you, Sergeant. You know that?"

Crane said: "That's good, Major. 'Foul mouth.' 'On you.' Two hundred plus chopped to bits, and you're worried about deportment. But all right, I'll rephrase it: what are you doing in here?"

"That's none of your business. Now get out of here and go back to what you were doing."

"You want to kill someone, don't you? Doesn't matter who, so long as he's one of these bearded peasants they have over here. You think that'll clear things up, do you?"

"Get out of here, Crane."

"You know I'm responsible for the contents of this bunker, Major. No one takes anything out of here unless they sign and I sign. And you haven't signed and I won't."

"What the hell are you talking about?"

"Talking about? I'm talking about you taking that rifle out of here without lawful authority, Major. If you want, I can give you a lot of manuals to read about lawful authority and who has it and how it's transferred to someone else. But what it boils down to is: I'm the guy whose signature's required on the paper if you want that rifle. And I won't sign. So, as we used to say, there it is."

"We'll talk about signatures later," he said.

"No we won't, Major. You have to sign a form when you check the weapon out. A printed multi-part form. Tough thing is, I don't have any forms right now: they're in the office and the office is buried under all that rubble that used to be a building. I'm stumped: I don't know what to do in a situation where there aren't any forms. So you'll have to wait while I thumb through the regulations, Major. Of course, we'll be going ashore in the States by the time I figure it out, but there it is. Tell me why you want to kill someone, Major."

"Get the hell out of here, Crane."

"Officers aren't supposed to curse, Major. That's the duty of noncommissioned officers. Although I've heard a lot of officers reeling out longer strings of curses than any sergeant. Tell me, would it be good enough if you just shot *at* someone? And missed?"

"Let's get something straight, Crane," he said. "You're a sergeant. I'm an officer. I gave you an order: to return to whatever you were doing. I'm giving you that order one last time. If you don't obey it, I'm going to charge you and see that you're . . ."

"Shooting someone without lawful authority is murder, Major. You know that. And that's what you want to do: shoot someone without lawful authority."

"They killed my men," he said. Pain pierced his skull: as though he had opened his eyes and stared at the sun. "Your men, Crane. Your friends and mine. That's authority enough."

"I know who got killed," Crane said. "That doesn't change the rules."

"Get out of here, Crane."

"I'll get out of here if you put that rifle down and come with me. You're not authorized to be in here picking over the weapons and deciding what you want to do next. Not you, not the Colonel, not the Commandant himself."

"Goddamnit, Crane, they're firing at the people working on the rubble trying to get the men out."

"That's dying down. And besides, we've got men on perimeter defense dealing with it."

"You call that a perimeter defense, Crane?"

"Why not? That's what you called it four weeks ago, and five days ago and yesterday. I heard you say it: you called it a perimeter defense. If you didn't think it was good enough, you should have done something about it, Major."

"We were ordered not to," he said.

"They ordered you to be stupid, Major?"

"You'd better watch your mouth, Crane. You're going to be in trouble if you keep on this way."

"No I'm not, Major. But if you don't rack that weapon, you're going to regret it."

"You'd report me?"

"I will if I have to. But that isn't what I mean."

"So what are you going to do, Crane? Wrestle me for it?"

"No. You're going to regret it because you know using that rifle is an excuse."

"You call this an excuse?" he asked, holding up the long-barrelled sniper's rifle. "This isn't an excuse. This is reality. And I'm going to show those sonsofbitches some reality. Right now."

"We're not about that, Major. That's not what we're for."

"Because it's against orders, Sergeant? Is that it?"

"Orders? Orders have nothing to do with it, Major. What you want to do is murder. We don't do that. And it's not just that we're not supposed to do it: it's that we don't do it."

"I guess there's a difference in there somewhere, Sergeant. But I don't think I can see it right now. I mean, I feel for you, Sergeant. But right now I can't reach you."

"You can't?" Sergeant Crane said.

"No, I can't," he said as Crane eased toward him.

"That's tough," Sergeant Crane said.

Crane grinned at him, shoved him in the chest, plucked the sniper's rifle from his hands and tossed it away onto the dusty floor of the bunker. Then Crane grabbed him and spun him around, snatched his wrists and shoved them up his back between his shoulder blades. "We don't do that kind of stuff, Major. You got me?"

Bent at the waist to ease the pain in his arms and shoulders, he said, "No. You've got me."

"That's funny," Sergeant Crane said, shoving his wrists an inch higher. "Another like that, Major, and I'll break your arms and you'll have to tell them you fell down in a ditch backwards."

"That's enough, Sergeant."

"You're sure about that, Major? Right now I can only think of one way to keep you from picking up that sniper's rifle again. That's to break one of your arms. On the other hand you could agree to leave quietly. But then you might think about walking out of here now and coming back later. So maybe I ought to break one of your arms. That way, you'd get to go home. And we wouldn't have to deal with you again."

"Goddamnit, Sergeant. Let me go."

"You're not anywhere near where you ought to be if you want to give orders, Major."

"You let me go. They killed my men."

"You said that. And I can smell their guts right now, Major. But you're a Marine, Major. Or at least you say you are, and you wear the uniform and an officer's insignia and tell others what to do. But you seem to forget what we are."

"What's that? Goddamn you Sergeant you better let go of me."

"We're not what you want to do. We don't fight private wars." Crane twisted his wrists and shoved them higher. The bones in his joints creaked and pain flashed through his skull. "Goddamnit," he hissed. "You let go of me. Now."

"Major, I could let you go out and shoot Ali. And while you're out there shooting him, I'd have to go report this to someone in authority and they'd toss you into the Red Line Brig for twenty-five years. If they still call it the Red Line Brig, which in the modern, computerized, jogging-shoe shod, cerebral, thin, aerobic and caring Marine Corps, they don't."

"They killed my men, Crane. You bastard they killed them like sheep. They slaughtered them in their beds. Your men."

"Let me tell you something, Major. Muhammad or Hamid or whatever his name was who drove that truck didn't kill them. It was your obligation to keep your men safe: they told you that when you first came in. So you should have used your judgment and ordered the men into two-man holes. You should have told the guard on the gate to keep his weapon loaded and to fire at and kill anyone who tried to get past him without authorization. But I guess you figured if you did that they'd have said it was a 'provocative act' and put a mark on your paper and told one another you weren't judicious enough to fleet up to general."

"Those were the orders, Goddamnit. Now you let go of me or *you'll* be in the brig."

"The way I see it, I ought to be talking to the Colonel about you coming in here trying to take that rifle. But he's on his way offshore, seeing as how he got blown up too. Major, get a grip on yourself. You can't get back what you lost by shooting a couple of guys named Mostafa and Boutros out beyond the fence. Maybe that would make some boot lieutenant feel like he's got big balls, but you and I know Ali and Hamid aren't responsible for what happened."

Panting in Crane's grip, he said, "We were mistaken."

"Mistaken. That's the scope of your obligation, Major? To avoid mistakes? Next," Sergeant Crane said, "you're going to tell me no one's without sin. Then you're going to tell me the men were as responsible as the officers. Then you're going to tell me the men were responsible and the officers weren't. Get away from me, you useless sonofabitch."

Crane let go of his arms and shoved him away, pushing him down. As he fell on the sand and dirt floor of the bunker his head struck the corner of an ammunition box. Pain lanced through his skull and the bright yellow light at the entrance to the bunker flashed crimson. Crane snatched up the rifle with the scope and the big magazine and the special stock and the flash suppressor, tossed it from hand to hand and looked him in the eye. Then Crane gripped the rifle by the barrel behind the flash suppressor, swung it as he turned toward the ramp and let go of it. The fancy rifle flicked end over end up the ramp through the sunlight. "Let the sonsofbitches have it, Major. They need it. We don't. Jump jets, aircraft carriers, specialized assault ships, helicopters. Let me tell you something, Major. We don't need any of that shit. We've done it before, and done it better, without satellites, computers, staff colleges, and horseshit. Because you know, Major: in the end, you have to go out and do what you're supposed to do. And nothing else. But if you want to, go find that weapon and do whatever you please. But whatever you do with it, it's not going to make you an officer who used his head and did what he should have done. Your guys are butchered meat. You should have thought that might happen, Major, before you went along with what they told you to do. So remember this: however much you try to explain it to yourself and one another, none of you did what you should have done. Your people are dead. No matter how many Lebanese you shoot, you're not going to get them back, and you're not going to get the stain out."

He shoved himself up and staggered away from Crane. Through the blinding light that blurred his vision and beyond which Crane stood with his fists on his hips, he shouted, "Goddamn you, Crane. I don't know what you're talking about. But understand this: you're going to pay for this. For shoving me."

"What's the matter, Major? Not big enough without your fancy rifle?"

"You hurt me," he said, and as he spoke he swayed and the bunker tilted. "You'd better not touch me again."

"Don't worry about that," Crane said. "I don't want to put my hands on you again ever."

"You know, Crane. . ." he said. But the bunker tilted to the right, and farther to the right and he realized his feet did not quite touch the floor. As he fell Crane grabbed him and held him upright and he thought, a decent man, a good sergeant. And right about all this. He tried to tell Crane he understood; but the light through which he looked at Crane's frowning concerned face became blood red and then purple and then black and he could no longer remember what he had wanted to say.

HE RAISED HIS HEAD, shifted his swollen tongue in his mouth and spat a stone into the ancient hoofmark impressed in the rock close by his mouth. He squirmed as he stretched his trembling arms in front of him. The backs of his shaking hands were black and his wrists were reddish gray. He turned his hands over. His palms stung, but they were no longer red: they were as pale as old paper. The Marine Corps, he thought, has remade me in its image; for the Marine Corps left me out here to burn, and I have become red, and black, and pale gray.

He recalled the old saying: I like the fucking Marine Corps, and the Marine Corps likes fucking me. It looks like it's true, for it's certain I like the Marine Corps. And it's certain the Marine Corps likes fucking me. That fucking lieutenant, for example. And the company commander: what a fuck. And the sergeants and the battalion commander and his boss, the fucking regimental commander. And you, General Gray, where the hell were you? You were supposed to be watching out to be sure this kind of thing didn't happen. Where were you when this exercise that has killed me was planned and all your officers told one another they knew their jobs in the sawmill?

"I know," the General said. The brim of his hat set square on his gray head was a crust of gold. A bulky man of medium height, with a bluff manner and a broad chest, his face was seamed and reddened by the sun. But his dress uniform was immaculate, and the rows of decorations laid one atop the next ran upward toward his shoulder.

And he isn't sweating: not even here, in the Mojave, more miles than I can march from the nearest water source at the Palms.

"I should have seen to it that this didn't happen," the General said. "I wasn't doing enough. But I will do more. I promise you that. This won't happen again."

That's going to help me out? That you're going to be sure this doesn't happen again?

"No. I know it won't help you. You'll have to do what's required here. I'm sorry, but there's nothing more. You'll have to get yourself out of it. I'm sorry."

I didn't think generals were sorry about anything.

"You don't know a lot about generals. If they've got any brains—and yes, I know the joke: you have to kill a lot of generals to get a pound of brains—they regret everything they do. Win or lose, they regret. Either way, they lose too many not to regret."

Okay, he said. All right. If there's nothing you can do, I'll work this out for myself.

The General nodded at him: as though he expected him to get up and march to the Palms and then do another twenty-five miles and *then* fight them dug in at the other end, grinning at him as he staggered forward, a huge blister with a sere man inside trying to figure how to operate his rifle with fingers blistered fat as sausages.

The General stepped back: a single step. As he did his uniform glittered and shone. He stood stock still and saluted.

He coughed. A little liquid moistened his throat and he whispered, "I can't raise my arm."

"I'm saluting you. I don't expect you to return it. Not here. Not now. And rightly not."

"Get the hell up out of there," a strong voice bawled. "What the hell you doing lying down there when the General's talking to you?"

He croaked out the single straightforward serviceable lie he had learned so long ago: "I'm not doing anything down here anywhere, Sergeant." He looked up: the General was gone. Blues, brass, piping, stars, manner, position, name in the papers: gone in a puff. He looked at the burning, dusty stone on which he lay as though someone had thrown him down unconscious and left him. He turned his face and looked along his right flank. His blisters bulged inside his filthy uniform. He could not see his boots, and he thought, they must be twisted behind me. His feet had roasted all day inside his boots like dry twigs held close to fire. Yet his feet hurt no more. He dragged his heavy, roasted arms across the stone in front of him, laid his hands palms down beside his shoulders. He shoved. Gimme fifty. And if you can't gimme fifty, gimme one.

But he could not lift the weight of his dried bone and stringy muscle. He could not shift his rusty gristle and the bladders of liquid fitted to his limbs and torso. He stopped pushing against the stone and stretched his arms that burned no longer into the sunlight he could see no more.

I'm blind, he thought. I cannot see my puffy arms. I cannot see my blackened blistered fingers. He turned his face, but he could not see the brush, the jumbled broken reach of the desert, the distant mountains. He looked up. But he could not see the hard blue sky he knew surrounded the sun he could not see.

But I feel its light, he thought, and as he thought it a blur of bushes appeared beyond the stone on which he lay and he saw the light had waned.

I see again, he thought. It is afternoon. And night is coming.

"Fuck afternoon," the strong voice bawled. "And fuck night too. Lying down there when the General's talking to you? What the hell's that mean? What the hell's going on here? Who the hell are you? Who the hell do you think you are?"

"I don't . . ." he said. But he could not say more. His cracked lips leaked salt liquid: blood. He licked his lips and swallowed. Grit mixed with blood lay like clay in his throat. My arms beneath my shirt are graysilver tubes, he thought: they encase the last of the liquid I carry with me.

Pain returned: the joints in his legs and hips burned, and the bloated flesh beneath his hair burned. Something in his chest knotted and one tremor and then another surged through the viscous serum packed in the blisters bound about him.

I cannot think. I cannot decide. I know nothing except that I am here, alone and, now and then, blind in this terrible place.

"I said get the fuck up out of there," the bawling voice shouted across the space between them. He raised his head, turned his face toward the bawling voice. Back where I began, he thought as he looked at the Drill Instructor: campaign hat, creased starched uniform, tie, glossy shoes. And the bawling mouth jerked open, each gritty word torn one coarse syllable at a time up the thick, working throat and spat across the space between the bawling mouth and me lying on this burning stone marked long ago by another animal that passed this way.

The Drill Instructor's voice yelled and yelled, but he could not hear the words. Loud, ignorant, meaningless speech, he thought. Pouring out of this clean, uniformed, starched fuck standing up above me.

I don't like anyone standing over me.

Where's my weapon? he wondered. A single magazine—a single round—will shut this bastard up forever.

He dragged his right hand across the stone, feeling for what he could not quite see. My sight, he thought: now I see and now I don't.

A fresh voice, muffled as though it were shielded from the dust by thick cloth, slid into the space between him lying down on his stone and the sergeant's bawling voice pouring one demand after another down onto him: "Why don't you shut your mouth, Sergeant?" the voice said.

"Who the hell are you, telling me to shut my mouth?" the bawling voice yelled.

"John Basilone. I was a Sergeant. Then they promoted me to Gunnery Sergeant. And I'm telling you it's time for you to shut your mouth and go."

"This man's going to get the hell up, Gunny, or I'm going to know the reason why. And he's going to tell me what he's going to do next. You understand me, Gunny? Standing on his feet at attention. And he's going to explain himself. Not you."

"No," Basilone said as though he were speaking out of a mouth stuffed with sand. "It's time for you to go."

"Who are you to tell me to go, Gunny? And what the hell are you doing in that outdated gear out here in a training area? This is a restricted area. You know that? Say, you're not from the Palms anyway, are you? I mean, look here, Gunny . . ."

"I told you twice: leave. I'm not going to tell you a third time."

"Leave?"

He listened to them chew it over. He stared at the white light and the thin, spiky bushes while he listened to the hot wind blowing across the broad flat stone on which he lay, waiting for them to get on with it and decide.

"Okay," the Sergeant whispered. "I see: you showed me. All right." He coughed, choked on something he was about to say, and said. "All right, then. I thought I might do more. But all right, Gunny. It's John? Manila John, right? I remember you."

"That's it. And thanks," Basilone said. "I'll see you sometime."

"I know. I'll see you then. And I understand," the voice said: smooth, quiet, a bit embarrassed, as though this Drill Instructor had been brought up by decent parents and they had expected him to be mannerly, calm, quiet and decent. And not to bawl at people. "But I'm sorry about it," the voice said.

"I know," Basilone said. "So am I. But there it is."

"I'll be seeing you then," the voice said. "At the time."

"That's it," Basilone said.

Booted feet paced away, scrunching sand, kicking stones, the cloth of the trousers rustling through the stunted scrub.

"You're all right," Basilone's muffled voice said. "You can get up now."

"Up?" he whispered. His fingertips worked against the stone. He tried to look at Basilone, but white light slashed at his eyes like a polished sword and all he could see was a faint shape standing between him and the sun.

"Sure," Basilone said. "Up. We've got to go on a little more and then we'll be there."

The fingers of his right hand traced the edges of the hoofprint fixed in the stone. "How far?" he asked, even though he knew a single pace would be too far.

"Don't worry," Basilone said. "You can make it."

"I agree, John," a second voice said. "Sure he can make it."

He looked. Another wavering gray shape stood between him and the sun lying halfway down the sky.

"How's it going, John?" Basilone said. "I didn't know you'd be out here today."

He looked up at them. Two Johns. Basilone, and the other one. He grunted an interrogatory.

Basilone nodded at him lying on the wide flat stone and said, "This guy? John H. Pruitt. Fayetteville, Arkansas. 78th Company. October 3, 1918."

"1918?" he whispered.

"1918," Basilone said. "October 3. Just before the end of the war. That's the First World War."

"I know about the First World War," he whispered. "We learned about it. Names. Places. All that. History. The History, they called it."

"Sure," Pruitt said. "The History. The Corps is big on history. This thing, that, the other one. And it's gone on since 1918, I'm told."

"Gone on?" he asked.

"The History. More wars, more fighting. You know: The History."

"1918?" he asked. He could not remember what the numbers meant.

"Sure. 1918," Pruitt said. "You know: the Great War. The war to end all wars. All that."

"I read about it in school. The French. The Germans. The British. President Wilson."

"That's it," Pruitt said. "I was there. Take a look at me."

He raised his head from the burning stone. Pruitt wore tan ankle boots, puttees, brown green trousers and a brown tunic buttoned with five buttons, the highest at the base of his throat. A heavy bandolier slung over his left shoulder hung across his chest. Webbing suspended from his shoulders carried the weight of the cartridge belt that encircled his waist. Ten pouches on the belt, each pouch closed with a snap stamped with the eagle, globe, and anchor. A rectangular cloth pouch was fixed in the second buttonhole of his tunic and a first-aid pouch hung from the cartridge belt in front of his left hip. Behind the first aid pouch, a trench knife in its scabbard was hooked to the cartridge belt. Pruitt held a rifle in his right hand, a bayonet fixed to the muzzle. The rifle's bolt was open, the breech empty.

Antique, he thought. A young Marine in a clean, pressed antique uniform. Without a helmet. Carrying an old bolt action rifle. With the bolt drawn open.

"What's in that pouch on your chest?" he asked.

"It's what you'd call a flashlight. In the Great War, it was called a Liberty Light. I lost it when I lost my helmet."

"One of those old flat helmets?"

"That's it."

"How'd you lose your helmet?" he asked. "And your flashlight?"

"I don't remember. There was a lot going on at the time," Pruitt said. "And nobody asked about it afterwards." He grinned. Basilone nodded, shook his head as though he knew all about the anguish equipment lost in battle caused quartermasters.

"Who are you guys?" he croaked.

"Who are we?" Pruitt asked. "You don't know John Basilone here?"

"I don't think so," he said. Yet he knew the name was somewhere in his memory.

"Manila John Basilone? You don't know about Manila John?"

He looked at Basilone. Wide angular face, dark curly hair. "I think . . ." he said. But he could not remember.

"Take another look at him," Pruitt said.

He looked again. Basilone wore the plain trousers and shirt he had seen in black and white photographs taken in the Pacific on islands with alien names: Guadalcanal, Tarawa, Peleliu, Iwo Jima, Okinawa. He carried a rifle in his left hand. A small pack rode high on his back. On his right hip was a holstered semi-automatic pistol.

"Come on," Pruitt said. "Sure you recall Manila John. I mean, what are they teaching you these days?"

To be polite, he said, "I think I recall." But he could not remember. Something was there, a single fact hidden beneath the rubble his memory had become. But he could not reach it.

"Let me tell you about it," Pruitt said.

"There's no need," Basilone said.

"Sure there's a need," Pruitt said. "This guy ought to remember things like that."

"He's had a long day."

"Which," Pruitt reminded Basilone, "is almost over."

His dusty fingers slid against the smooth stone. "Tell me," he said.

"John was on Iwo Jima. A mortar round landed between his feet."

He looked at Basilone. A little dated in uniform and weapons, but all of a piece: a whole man.

Basilone winked at him, and in the single instant Basilone's eye was closed he saw Basilone flung down on the sand, his legs chopped away, his spine snapped and his ribcage shattered, his guts thrown out of him as though his back had exploded forward through him, his left hand fingerless, his face burned black, the char that had been his eyes smeared with brilliant blood. The riven legless corpse raised its right hand and he saw Basilone standing beyond the edge of the wide stone on which he lay, the rifle in his left hand as it had been before, his trousers neat as they had been before, his wide handsome face nodding at him as it had nodded before.

"God," he said. "I thought I saw . . ."

"You did," Pruitt said. "Manila John's pretty dramatic. A lot more dramatic than I am, say."

"You?"

Pruitt nodded at him and said, "Uh-huh," and as he watched Pruitt nod his head again he saw that Pruitt's tunic was ripped from his back and chest. A puncture wound in his left shoulder beneath the collar bone leaked blood. His pale skin was stained black and red with blood. The flat bone of his sternum, snapped into ragged irregular plates, was exposed to the light. From the terrible wound, more blood flowed.

Pruitt nodded at him a second time and he saw Pruitt standing with Basilone beyond the edge of the stone. Pruitt's antique uniform was whole and clean again, his gear fitted about him in proper order, his rifle in his hand, the bayonet clean, the bolt open.

"Shell fire," Basilone said. "October 3, 1918. Five weeks before the end of the First World War. Pruitt attacked two German machineguns, killed the gunners and captured forty Germans in a dugout. He did all that, and more. Then he was wounded by shellfire. Later, he died of his wounds."

"That's it," Pruitt said. "Of course, it wasn't much compared to what Manila John did on the Canal."

"Guadalcanal," he said. "I've heard of Guadalcanal."

"Sure you have," Pruitt said. "Manila John was a machinegunner. He pretty much stopped the Japanese east of the Lunga River all by himself. They made six attacks. He cut them down every time. Got to be so many dead Japanese out in front of his machinegun he had to have men go out between attacks to shift the corpses: so he would have a field of fire. When they ran low on ammunition, John went back, got more ammunition and lugged it back up to his gun and started firing again. He killed them until they stopped coming."

"Why do you call him Manila John?" he asked.

"I served a hitch in the Army before the war," Basilone said. "I spent a year in Manila. When I joined the Corps they tagged me with that nickname: Manila John. And Pruitt: don't tell me what you did wasn't much compared to what I did. You know that's not true."

"I'm not sure you're right about that, John," Pruitt said. "But we'll call me saying it good manners, all right?"

"I don't understand," he said.

"What don't you understand?"

"Who you are. What's happening. What's going on."

Hallucinating, he thought. The Doc said something about hallucinations. Heat, he said, does funny things to you. Dehydration does funnier things still.

"We told you who we were," Pruitt said. "What's happening is you need some help here. What's going on is we're here to help you out. I mean, why else would we be here?"

"But you said you were killed. In the first war. And the second."

"That's right," Basilone said.

"But I . . ."

"Don't worry about it," Pruitt said. "I was a little surprised about it, too, the first time I found out about it. But that's the way it is, and you get used to it."

"I see you guys found someone," a new voice said.

"Yeah, what is this?" a fourth voice said. "What's this guy doing lying down there like that tangled up in his webbing with the sling of his rifle wound around his elbow?"

"Charles, you come to help out?" Pruitt asked.

"You know the answer to that," Charles said. "This guy all tangled up in his gear is going to be coming with us."

He looked up at the two new arrivals and thought, getting up a crowd: right out here in the fucking desert. At least they're standing between me and the sun. I wonder if any of these guys has a full canteen and isn't thirsty.

"This one here," Manila John said, "is Charles G. Abrell. He was in Korea. After my time, of course, but he's told us about it. June 10, 1951: Charles was wounded three times on Hill 1316—that was on the rim of a valley in Korea they called 'The Punchbowl'. Wounded three times as he was, Charles went on and attacked a bunker with a handgrenade. The grenade killed the gun crew inside the bunker. It also killed Charles. Charles was nineteen."

"That's what happened," Abrell said. "And I was there, so I ought to know." Abrell glanced at the fourth man standing beside him, turned his face back and nodded at him lying down on his stone; and as Abrell nodded, he saw that the legs of Abrell's trousers were soaked with blood. His muddy boots glistened slick and red, his shirt was torn away, and his left shoulder was ripped open. A bullet had pierced his right side above the hip: the insignificant, graypurple crater of the wound leaked fluid and blood. Abrell nodded at him again and the gruesome display of his mortal wounds dissolved.

"I don't get this," he told Abrell. "I don't understand it."

"Sure you do, man," the fourth voice said.

"This," Manila John said, "is James Anderson, Jr. He's from Compton, California. February 8, 1967. A Vietnamese threw a grenade at him and his buddies. He covered the grenade with his body. So he's with us now."

He looked up at Anderson: skinny, lithe, long muscles laid over long bones. Anderson tilted his head to the right and he saw Anderson's savaged groin and abdomen. Blood pumped as Anderson doubled over himself, his shattered hands shoved against the terrible wound that had killed him. Anderson tilted his head left, drew himself up, slung his rifle over his shoulder, pushed his helmet back from his forehead and smiled at him. His fearsome wounds were healed. Anderson said, "Why don't you get up out of there? I mean, you can't go on lying on that rock."

"I can't get up." He shivered. How can I be cold? he wondered.

"Can't?" Anderson asked. "Sure you can."

"I agree," Abrell said. "I mean, what the hell?

"It's not that far," Manila John said, as though he knew he could climb up off the stone and go any distance at all.

"John's right," Pruitt said. "It's not that far. It's just up ahead."

"I can't," he said. "Go on, I mean."

"Sure you can get up," Abrell said. "I mean, what the hell?"

"I need water."

"There's a pool up ahead," Anderson said.

"We keep on saying the same thing again and again, guys," Abrell said. "Look, guy, you've got to get up. Know why? Because we've got to get back, and we're not leaving unless you come with us."

"Great," he said.

"What's that mean?" Pruitt asked. "'Great?' What's he mean, 'great?'"

"Language has changed some since your time, John," Anderson told him. "Like the weapons. When he said 'great,' he meant 'not great.'"

"He did?" Abrell said. "He meant that? Why didn't he just come out and say it wasn't great?"

"I'll explain it to you later," Anderson said. "When this guy gets up and comes on."

"I can't make it," he said. He couldn't move any part of him except his bleeding lips, the tip of his tongue, and his fingertips working in the hoofprints that the sun had rendered out of mud so long ago.

"He says he can't make it," Pruitt told Basilone.

"I heard. But don't worry about it," Manila John said. "He can make it. I know it."

"How can you be sure, man?" Anderson asked.

"'Man?' What do you mean, 'man?'" Pruitt asked.

"It's an expression," Abrell said.

"What is this, some seminar about the history of the English language in America?" Anderson said. "What we got here is a problem. This guy got to get up. And do it by himself."

"Get your knees under you," Pruitt told him. "At least you can do that."

"I'd like to," he said. "But I don't think I can. Look, why don't you guys go on? Leave me here and I'll come on after you."

"What the hell does that mean?" Abrell asked.

"What you mean, we go on and you come on after?" Anderson said.

"Go on?" Pruitt said. "Without you?"

"Easy, guys," Manila John said. "After all, he's been out here all day and he's probably forgotten some things."

"*Some* things?" Anderson said.

"If I said something," he said, "that I shouldn't have, I'm sorry. But I can't go. So you ought to go on without me."

"You know we can't do that," Pruitt said.

"Why not?" he asked. "It doesn't matter whether you go or not. Not to me, at least."

"To us," Manila John said, "it matters."

"Why?" he panted, his tongue working in the filthy hole of his mouth.

"Why?" Pruitt asked. "Let me tell you why. I'll give you a formal report. I was killed in France. North of the Marne. When the war was almost over. The night before I was killed, it rained and at dawn I saw dripping foliage, felt soft damp leaf and damp earth beneath my feet. We attacked from a wet field through a neat woods into the next field. The fields were orderly, rectangular, precise. Weeds grew where wheat had grown every other year. The Germans fired out of the woods beyond the second field. As we went through the woods, machinegun fire scored the trees and whipped the mist that filled my last morning. Their artillery was vicious: it shattered trees or cut them down and filled the air with splinters and bitter smoke. The leaves of the branches cut from the trees curled upon themselves as they died. Fires burned in the woods and the racket of artillery shells exploding and weapons firing filled the morning. We sweated and stank as we ran east into the Germans' fire. I ran and ran: east, toward the rising sun, into the field beyond the woods. Beside me Nelson dropped his rifle into the weeds and fell. His face slid against the damp crushed weeds and the muddy ground. He tore at his chest with his bloody hands as he lay on the earth, shivered and turned his face to the sky. Owens was killed too, his throat and face shot away. And Thompson, shot through the stomach with the same burst of machinegun fire. I ran on: all about me bullets snapped. And all about me more men fell, shivered, kicked the ground and lay as still as the earth itself. The Germans were firing everything they had: pistols, rifles, machineguns, mortars, artillery. I ran through the field of pale green calf-high weeds bent eastward before the chilly autumn breeze. The dead sprawled in the weeds and I guessed that in seconds the Germans would kill me too. But I did not care: I remembered them killing Nelson, Owens and Thompson. And others: many others. I was almost across the field when a bullet struck my left shoulder. I ran on into the woods from which the Germans were firing. My shoulder was numb, and blood streamed down my arm and dripped from my elbow. I shot three Germans firing a machinegun. I killed two infantrymen. I shot one of them. I killed the other with the bayonet socketed over and locked to the muzzle of my rifle. A third German shot at me and I shot him in the face with the last round in my rifle. I could not reload the rifle: I had no time. I slung the rifle and threw two grenades at another machinegun and killed two of the three men manning it and wounded the third. He screamed like a wounded animal. His guts had spilled out of him and he plunged his hands into them as though he thought he could stuff them back inside himself. Then he stopped screaming and fell back against the muddy dirt wall of the pit in which his machinegun had been sited. Beyond his corpse along the trench that led out of the machinegun pit was the sunken door of a dugout. I slid into the muddy trench and lay beside the dugout's entrance. I called down into the darkness and German soldiers, forty of them, came up out of it one after the other gabbling at one another. I marched them out of the woods and as we passed through the field west of the woods I saw dead and wounded Marines lying in the weeds, their faces bloody, shot through the legs, shot through the chests, shot through the heads. I marched the Germans through the woods at the western edge of the field and handed them over. Then I went back through the woods and into the field of dead and wounded lying in the weeds. German artillery shells began to fall in the field, stirring the ground, killing the wounded, savaging the dead. One shell fell ten feet from me. Jagged metal cut at me, hammered my chest, tore it open. I lay in the field until the German artillery stopped firing and corpsmen came out and found me. They checked the men lying all about me: to see if any of them still lived. But I was the only one they found who was not dead. I lay on the stretcher in my own blood and as they carried me out of the field I looked at the dead I was leaving behind and regretted I could not bring them with me and regretted I could not stay with them. That's why it matters to me that you come with us."

Lying on a bloody stretcher looking at the dead, he thought. And regretting. And looking at me here on this stone, and refusing to leave, so that he will not regret again.

"That's right," Anderson said. "It's a sad choice: leaving, or letting others leave. I remember thinking that as I saw the grenade skitter and hop among us and I just, well, dove on it. Someone standing with me said, 'I . . .' Another shouted, 'Down!' No one else spoke. But I heard the hiss and sputter of the grenade's fuse and I felt it hard and smooth against my gut. I scrabbled for it with my hands, tried to grab it. Then it detonated and I was lifted and slammed down. I felt cold. I felt hands on me and someone said, 'Ah, Jim, for Christ's sake.' I was glad they lived. I knew they would remember me. But I was sad I had to leave them behind. Then I felt nothing. Now I'm here. And I ain't leaving you behind. You got that?"

Basilone said: "You understand now? I knew I had been blinded and my body torn apart by the mortar round that killed me. But all I felt was loss and sadness that I had to leave them to finish the battle. Then I felt nothing, heard nothing, thought nothing. And now I'm here, too. In the desert. Near the Palms."

"Near the Palms?" he asked. "How near the Palms?"

"No more than two miles away," Anderson said. "Can you make it that far?"

Two miles, he thought: might as well be Australia. "No," he said. "Not fifty feet. Not five feet. I can't stand. I can't move."

"If you can't make it to the Palms," Pruitt said, "you're coming with us."

"I can't make it to the Palms," he said. "And I can't go with you, either. I thought I said I can't get up?"

"And I thought we said we're not leaving you," Abrell said. "It's like Manila John and Pruitt and Anderson here said: if we left you, we would remember it. And we don't want to remember it. So you have to get up and come with us."

"That's it," Anderson said. "You got to come on, man."

"Just get up," Sergeant Kline said, as though getting up were the easiest thing. He raised his head and looked: Kline stood with the four of them. He was clothed in his dress uniform. Every button shone. "I guarantee you," Sergeant Kline said. "It's not far. But you already know that."

"I do?"

"You do. A couple of paces. By the way, you know about these guys?"

"They told me," he said. "They showed me."

"No, I don't mean that. Don't you remember each of them got The Medal?"

"Big deal," Pruitt said.

"I didn't get it," Abrell said. "Some officer awarded it to me, I guess. I didn't know a thing about it until Jim Anderson here mentioned it. Just like Pruitt here. He didn't know he'd gotten it until Manila John recalled he'd been given it and told him about it."

"Only Manila John knew he won it," Sergeant Kline said. "He got his on Guadalcanal. But Abrell had to tell him he'd won the Navy Cross on Iwo Jima."

"I don't think," he said, "they're going to give me any medals."

"So?" Basilone said. "I know plenty of guys got nothing who should have, and a few who did who shouldn't have. But you won't find those few around here: they don't come around much."

"What did they give you, Sergeant Kline?"

"Me? Oh, the usuals for long service and being there when the shooting happened. But nothing special."

"Still," Pruitt said, "Kline's one of us."

"I don't understand," he said.

"Sure you do," Kline said. "I died six months ago. Of a heart attack, if you can believe it."

The four men clustered around Kline grinned and shook their heads as though Sergeant Kline had been caught unawares.

"I was caught unawares," Kline said. "The sonofabitch came at me from behind while I wasn't looking out. Him and his three buddies: time, age and disease. I fought them off for a while: in the ambulance, on a gurney at the hospital, in the cardiac care unit. But the four of them together were too much for me. So here I am. But that's the way it happens. No one believes they're going to die. But every one of them dies: every one of us. You can read about it anywhere. No one talks about it. But you can read about it anywhere you want."

"I know," he said. He raised his face. Beyond the five of them standing at the edge of the stone to which he clung he saw a German officer in an antique, spiked helmet shouting orders at two Japanese soldiers manning a machinegun on a bi-pod. To his left four Chinese in quilted winter coats and fur hats jogged along a trench crusted with snow. He looked to his right: in a clearing in dense jungle four Vietnamese dressed in baggy black pantaloons and loose black shirts, each of them holding an assault rifle, hissed at a fifth loading a rocket-propelled grenade launcher.

And where is my enemy? he wondered. He raised his face to the sun. There, he thought, staring at the yellow disk low above the horizon: there is my enemy.

"There it is," Sergeant Kline said.

"Time to go," Manila John said.

"I agree," Pruitt said. "Let's get on out of here."

"You can do it, buddy," Abrell told him.

"Listen to Abrell, man," Anderson said.

He shoved with his filthy palms, fingertips working in the hoofprints cut so long ago in mud that had become stone. The blisters on his arms bulged. He raised his panting chest. The blisters on his back wobbled and swayed.

"You're getting there," Manila John said.

"I knew he could do it," Sergeant Kline said.

He shoved again, felt a blister on his neck burst, turned his head to lick the flowing salty serum from his shoulder as he forced himself upward. Crouched on all fours, panting, fingertips gripping the worn edges of the hoofprints imprinted in the stone by time and the sun, he felt the blisters that contained the last of him heave with each small motion of his body.

"All right," Abrell said.

"You're half way there," Pruitt said. "More than half way there."

He worked his abraded, bloody knees forward across the rock, gasped as the long smooth blisters on his thighs tore, felt the warm syrupy liquid within drench his trousers. He drew his right booted foot forward. It scraped across the stone. Crouched like a sprinter in the blocks, he pushed down against the stone, wobbled upward, drew his left foot forward as he rose and stood, swaying, squinting at the five shapes wavering in the light.

"Outstanding," Anderson said.

"You did it," Kline said.

"Now you're getting there," Pruitt said.

"And this guy said he couldn't get up," Abrell said.

"Easy, everybody," Manila John Basilone said. "Let him get a hold on himself. Then we can go."

"I'm up," he muttered. The five shapes in front of him wavered as though the light desert wind were passing through them. "I'm up. I'm all right," he said. He thought about what he had said and laughed: a hoarse quick cough in his throat packed with hot grit and burning dust. He eased a single cautious step forward toward the five indistinct shapes of Pruitt, Basilone, Abrell, Anderson and Kline standing beyond the border of the stone.

"How far?" he asked.

"Not far," one of them whispered.

He slid his other foot forward, feeling with the sole of his boot. As though, he thought, it is night. As though I am blind.

And I am blind, he thought. Or half-blind, at least. All I see is white light, the faint, distant yellow disk of the sun, and five gray shapes that recede a pace with each short shuffle forward I take.

"This way," one of them murmured. The shapes were moving ahead of him, walking through the scrub, leading the way.

"Coming," he croaked. He heaved himself forward another step: to the edge of the flat, ancient stone on which they had found him. Toward the sun: toward my enemy.

"This way," one of them called back to him. "We've got a table waiting." A table? he wondered. He thought the voice was Manila John's, but he was not sure: it might have been Anderson's, or Abrell's, or Pruitt's. He knew it was not Sergeant Kline's voice. He would have recognized Sergeant Kline's gruff voice anywhere: even in this awful place.

As he stepped from the stone into the desert the viscous liquid in the blisters on his back sloshed. The blisters tore and the liquid slid smooth and thick as oil down his back. He fumbled his right hand behind him, slid his hand through the liquid, lapped it from his palm, smeared it over his face and forehead.

With my enemy near at hand, a glittering silver sword in his silver hand.

Ahead of him one of them called out—encouragement, an order, something—and he stepped out, picking up the pace, staring at them going on before. They seemed to glide through the stunted brush, to float across the sharp rocks and the uneven reddishgray desert.

Freed from the blisters that had entangled and hampered his legs and back, he strode after them, panting and trying to swallow something that filled his throat: something rough that muscled his heart and lungs aside.

I'm all right, he told himself.

The brush all about him was greener, as though its roots had found water.

I'm all right now.

Something struck at him, pounded at his chest, shoved against his lungs, wriggled toward his heart.

Got to keep up, he thought. But another blow hammered his chest. He tried to march. He could not. He tried to breathe, but his breath had thickened in his throat and he tasted blood.

"Don't worry about it," Abrell said. "You're doing all right." Abrell slid an arm about his waist and helped him forward. He heard water gurgle from a canteen. Must be Abrell's, he thought: mine is full of dust.

"No," Basilone said. "It's yours."

"Gimme his weapon," Anderson said.

He felt Anderson's hand slide the sling from his shoulder, felt crusted coagulated serum and a flap of dead skin raked from his burning back.

Yet I feel no pain.

"Lemme get a hold on part of him," Pruitt said. A second strong arm slid across his lower back.

"He's not that heavy," Abrell said.

"Still, I got part of him," Pruitt said.

"You guys need any help?" Basilone asked.

"Sure, John," Pruitt said. "Why don't you carry me while I'm carrying this part of this guy here?"

Basilone said: "Talk to me later, John, when I've had the time to figure out what that means."

"You all right now?" Sergeant Kline asked him. Dress uniform, polished shoes: the full regalia.

He nodded, gasped as his chest heaved and his lungs squirmed away from whatever it was that was clawing its way toward his heart.

"You're all right now," Sergeant Kline informed him.

Maybe, he thought. But whatever it was that clawed inside his panting chest clawed closer his heart.

So I go on, he thought as they shepherded him through the scrub, his boots dragging in the sand as they carried him up the desert, marching with him toward the sun.

IN MEMORY
OF
JASON J. ROTHER
August 30, 1988 ∞

ON THE EVENING OF August 30, 1988, during a training exercise conducted in the roughly one thousand square miles of the Mojave Desert that constitute Twentynine Palms Marine Corps Base, Lance Corporal Jason J. Rother got down from a truck far out in the desert and stood his post, alone, as a road guide.

When the road guides were picked up five hours later, Lance Corporal Rother was left behind.

His absence was not noted for forty hours.

Investigators later estimated that the temperature in the Mojave Desert on August 31, 1988 reached 107°, and that the humidity was nil.

Lance Corporal Rother was not equipped or supplied to survive in such conditions, and he could not have expected that he would be able to reach safety before the negligence of those responsible for him killed him.

Lance Corporal Rother ignored the terrible odds against him: he set off, marching toward home.

The last of three extensive searches found Lance Corporal Rother's skeletal remains on December 4, 1988. Dehydration is thought to have killed Lance Corporal Rother on August 31, 1988.

In January and February 1989, newspapers reported the investigation into the abandonment of Lance Corporal Rother and described the ensuing courts-martial of his superiors. Of those prosecutions little now remains except old paper, forgotten argument and ruined careers. Indeed, only a few words reported during the investigation and the subsequent prosecutions still ring like iron beaten against stone. Those few words were written by the then Commandant of the United States Marine Corps, General Alfred M. Gray. Addressing his officers and noncommissioned officers—and more generally anyone in authority over others—General Gray wrote: "The American people . . . will not—nor should they—accept our maiming and killing their sons and daughters. . . . Neither will I."

Newspaper reports stated that Lance Corporal Rother died after marching seventeen of the nineteen miles that lay between his post and safety. This is factual, but the verb "die" is inaccurate. Lance Corporal

Rother did not die: he fought against the terrible circumstances he faced until those circumstances killed him. So he displayed those characteristics that the author, who has never served in the military, senses are the finest that any Marine—or anyone at all—can display when faced with fearsome adversity.

It would be fitting were the location of Lance Corporal Rother's abandonment marked with a warning to those responsible for others. General Gray's words, quoted above, would constitute a suitable inscription. So would that sentence known to every Roman soldier: "What is permitted to others is not permitted to you."

To demonstrate what character can accomplish, it would also be fitting were a monument describing Lance Corporal Rother's march erected at the place where his remains were found.

That no such warning and no such monument are likely to be erected is part of the price we pay to rent the place in which we live.

This novel is not about Lance Corporal Jason J. Rother: the author knows nothing about him except the few details that appeared in the newspapers. Nor is this novel about the conduct of Lance Corporal Rother's officers and noncommissioned officers.

It is, however, true that the fortitude and courage with which Lance Corporal Rother confronted his ordeal and faced his death encouraged the author to imagine, and to write.